C00 44810385

EDINB   D0238568

CATHERINE LIM
Miss Seetoh in the World

WITHDRAWN

Marshall Cavendish
Editions

© 2011 Catherine Lim

Cover art by Opal Works Co. Limited

Published by Marshall Cavendish Editions
An imprint of Marshall Cavendish International
1 New Industrial Road, Singapore 536196

All rights reserved

No part of this publication may be reproduced, stored in a retrieval system or transmitted, in any form or by any means, electronic, mechanical, photocopying, recording or otherwise, without the prior permission of the copyright owner. Request for permission should be addressed to the Publisher, Marshall Cavendish International (Asia) Private Limited, 1 New Industrial Road, Singapore 536196. Tel: (65) 6213 9300, Fax: (65) 6285 4871. E-mail: genref@sg.marshallcavendish.com. Website: www.marshallcavendish.com/genref

All characters appearing in this work are fictitious. Any resemblance to real persons, living or dead, is purely coincidental.

The publisher makes no representation or warranties with respect to the contents of this book, and specifically disclaims any implied warranties or merchantability or fitness for any particular purpose, and shall in no events be liable for any loss of profit or any other commercial damage, including but not limited to special, incidental, consequential, or other damages.

Other Marshall Cavendish Offices:
Marshall Cavendish International. PO Box 65829 London EC1P 1NY, UK • Marshall Cavendish Corporation. 99 White Plains Road, Tarrytown NY 10591-9001, USA • Marshall Cavendish International (Thailand) Co Ltd. 253 Asoke, 12th Flr, Sukhumvit 21 Road, Klongtoey Nua, Wattana, Bangkok 10110, Thailand • Marshall Cavendish (Malaysia) Sdn Bhd, Times Subang, Lot 46, Subang Hi-Tech Industrial Park, Batu Tiga, 40000 Shah Alam, Selangor Darul Ehsan, Malaysia.

Marshall Cavendish is a trademark of Times Publishing Limited

National Library Board Singapore Cataloguing in Publication Data
Lim, Catherine
  Miss Seetoh in the World. – Singapore : Marshall Cavendish Editions, 2010.
  p. cm.
  ISBN-13 : 978-981-4328-36-4

  Singaporean fiction (English). I. Title.

PR9570.S53.L477
S823 — dc22   OCN670151473

Printed by KWF Printing Pte Ltd.

EDINBURGH LIBRARIES	
C0044810385	
Bertrams	25/01/2012
	£8.99
NT	

One

In April 1993, barely a month after her husband's death, Miss Maria Seetoh reverted to her maiden name. It was surely a slight to the sanctity of the married state, endorsed both by her church in a major sacrament, and by her society in a major economic policy by which only married women qualified for government-subsidised housing. Moreover, it spoilt the good name of the quietly, properly mourning widow.

Miss Seetoh made her students use the desired name when they stood up to greet her as she entered the classroom each morning. It had to be a carefully considered, systematic re-training of forty young voices to make the switch from the old address, after such long habituation, but she succeeded in a week. If a few forgot, the rest would giggle and watch for her reaction, a full-blown ritual of pure entertainment. She would instantly, in frowning protest, step out of the classroom, wait outside for a few seconds, and then re-enter to face, with calm severity, the forty boys and girls still standing at their desks. Magisterially erect, she would wait for the little ripples of giggling whispers to subside into one hushed enveloping silence, and then, as the last act of the elaborate ritual, cup a listening hand to her right ear, now fully turned towards them, for the corrected greeting. It always came in a perfectly synchronised roar of 'GOOD MORNING, MISS SEETOH!', upon which the sternness vanished, and with a broad smile and theatrical bow she acknowledged their success, and the students – oh, how she loved them! – broke out in loud applause and laughter.

Many years later, long after Miss Seetoh had left St Peter's Secondary School, one of her students who became a well-known Singapore artist held an exhibition which included a portrait of a young woman leaning against the wall, her arms folded across her chest, her face lit up by a smile that was the total glowing configuration of skin, mouth, teeth, eyes, eyebrows. Miss Seetoh's smile was ever unique. The nostalgia of memory had perfectly reproduced her trademark turned-up shirt collar and slightly rolled-up shirt sleeves which together with her ponytail gave an impression of perky confidence that some of her female students tried to copy. Less imitable was that dazzling smile, also the tiny bird-like waist discernible in the portrait.

The principal of St Peter's Secondary School liked to speak of its portals of learning and tolerated their occasional battering by the seismic eruptions from Class 4C on the third floor. The effect on school morale, though, had to be carefully monitored and assessed, for the walls separating the classrooms were thin, and already some students were asking their teachers why only Miss Seetoh's students were having all the fun. In the staff common room one floor below where the teachers went between lessons to mark students' homework or sip coffee, some would ignore the ruckus, and a few silently roll their eyes upwards at the antics of St Peter's maverick English language and English literature teacher. Collectively, they were dull, dowdy and dour, beside the effervescent Miss Seetoh.

'Come and look,' said Mrs Neo one morning. She was the longest serving teacher in the school, with thirty-four years' service, just one short of earning the Golden Merit Medal from the Ministry of Education, and she courageously defended her traditional teaching methods against the newfangled methodologies that the younger inspectors at the Ministry were sometimes emboldened to pass on to teachers in their training workshops. It was said that after each workshop, she made a show of throwing away the folders of teaching guides and notes, being completely secure, as the rest of her colleagues were not, in her white-haired seniority and status as the widow of one of Singapore's most revered wartime heroes during the Japanese Occupation. His heroic underground activities and eventual execution by the Japanese merited some paragraphs in the history textbooks used in the schools.

Mrs Neo was just now standing at a window in the staffroom that looked out on the school grounds. Two colleagues joined her, and all smiled to see the strange scene in the distance. Under a large shady tree, earnestly watched by Miss Seetoh and a group of students, two boys, dressed in oddments of clothing meant to pass off as ancient Roman garb, were engaged in a fearful struggle that ended with one falling to the ground with a roar of 'Et tu Brute!' and the other triumphantly standing over him with a dagger realistically smeared with red ink. A third student, in a borrowed sarong worn toga-style, stepped out for a full oration over the corpse of the murdered Caesar before it suddenly sprang up from the grass, in an unscripted frenzy of crotch-pulling, screaming 'Red ants!', and then all was pandemonium.

The creative eccentricity of Miss Seetoh's teaching methods could be copied, but not of her married life which had ended as sensationally as it had begun, creating little private stirrings of gossip that were not allowed to disturb the smooth surface of life at St Peter's.

Once the principal came to investigate, probably sent by the surly discipline master who did not want to confront Miss Seetoh himself – Miss Seetoh of the refined manners and classy way of speaking that exposed the fumbling inadequacies of the adversary.

'What was that noise?' the principal asked, and Miss Seetoh said, her eyes sparkling, 'The noise of being happy, sir.'

Her new bright world would exclude the judgemental and censorious, the dull and the lackluster, and would be confined to her students, fresh-faced, eager-eyed, pure-minded, in their ridiculous uniforms matched precisely to the pristine sky blue and white colours of the Virgin Mary as she stood in her shrine in the school grounds.

For the few laggards who forgot the new address for their teacher, there was a penalty: each had to pay a fine of fifty cents, which Miss Seetoh promised to double or triple, for the amount to snowball into a grand prize that would go to the student who had made the greatest improvement in English grammar by the end of the year, just before the exams.

'There you are,' whispered Miss Teresa Pang to the colleague sitting beside her at the staff common room table.

She was the other English language teacher, secretly seething from the invidious comparisons, even if implied only, with Maria Seetoh. A school day was too long to sustain the appearance of cool, unconcerned professionalism, which consequently broke into little sharp comments to whoever was around to listen: 'Breaking another school regulation with all those money transactions going on in class! Doing it with *impunity*, in her high class English.'

The famous carrots and sticks used everywhere in the society, from the government downwards, to get people to behave – Miss Seetoh used both with equal ferocity, the school being society's microcosm. She was in a witch-hunt, she told her students, to drag out and destroy every one of their grammatical mistakes. 'Of course,' she said, 'it's important for you to secure good grades in the O Level exams. But it's important for me to do something when I see you mangle and murder the language of Shakespeare and Milton and Jane Austen!' Miss Seetoh knew all the plays of Shakespeare.

A poster hung on the classroom wall, done by the same artistic student whose interest then was only in cartoon caricatures, showing Miss Seetoh in black witch garb riding on a broomstick, carrying someone behind her, a man recognisable by his pronounced forehead dome, beard and ruffled Elizabethan neck collar as the revered Bard, cheering her on as she used another broomstick to put to flight a giant octopus with a dozen waving tentacles. Each deadly tentacle carried a sentence that carried a common grammatical mistake, coloured bright green, to suggest a venomous snake. The double deadliness, explained the artist, was to reflect the seriousness of the problem, for according to Miss Seetoh, a composition with just three major grammatical errors would instantly earn a poor grade from the examiners in the Cambridge Examinations Syndicate.

One error which most certainly originated in the schools, had, in the most alarming way, become ingrained in the speech of a whole society – 'I ever went to a circus when I was a child' – resisting the remedial efforts of at least two generations of English language teachers.

Another was one that Miss Seetoh had picked up from an entry for a national essay competition of which she was one of the judges – 'Mr TPK our great Prime Minister with vision and high endeavour have given prosperity to Singapore.'

Indeed, the largest number of errors she had picked up from classroom compositions had to do with the Prime Minister. Either the deep awe inspired by his name led students to borrow the laudatory phrases regularly used in the local newspapers and string them together in complex, formal sentences, only to flounder in a mess of grammatical, lexical and stylistic contortions. Or there were simply too many students choosing to pay tribute to the Prime Minister whenever a composition title allowed them to do so.

'Why don't you write about what you know best,' said Miss Seetoh. 'It's perfectly okay to write about your funny grandfather, you know. Or your aunt who goes to the temple to get lucky lottery numbers. Swee Hua, you told us about your Ah Kor who went to a cemetery to get help from your grandma's ghost, and won two thousand dollars? Or your awful neighbour who keeps you awake all night because she plays mah-jong non-stop. Jun Ling, has your family solved the problem yet? But no more leaving dog shit in the shoes outside her flat, do you hear?' The student, during the weekly forty-minute session called 'Improve your English through fun story-telling' had described the operation in the grossest of gratuitous details until stopped by Miss Seetoh.

Her students tittered. They had no inhibitions about sharing the comic indignities of their lowly lives in the large, sprawling housing estates, during the creative writing sharing sessions. To bring these, however, into the austerely formal world of the G.C.E. O Level examinations was a different matter, and so, despite Miss Seetoh's advice, they chose to play safe and write about safe, adult-approved topics in the composition paper, the safest, presumably, being responsible citizenship under a responsible leadership. One student had written about Mrs Neo's hero husband by simply lifting the paragraphs from the history book. Miss Seetoh made him cry by telling him that dishonesty was a hundred times worse than a hundred bad grammar mistakes, and then made him rewrite each plagiarised paragraph in his own words. On the school bulletin board were pinned up the regular newspaper reports of official speeches extolling hard work, discipline, tolerance, the community spirit. School mottoes and slogans on every wall screamed back their support. There was a rule for her weekly composition writing lesson: nobody was to use any expression taken from *The National Times* or *The Singapore Tribune*.

In her creative writing class, Miss Seetoh had a large waste-basket into which she dropped each pathetic echo of the language of cheap romances and TV soaps, filling it with rosebud lips, starry eyes, honey kisses, tender embraces.

' 'A shiver ran down my spine'? Yuks!' She instantly consigned it to the waiting receptacle of shame. 'Rashid, you had written 'I was really scared. Worse than when I saw Grandfather's *hantu*',' she continued, reading from a script. 'Why on earth did you cancel it and replace it with that atrocity?' She had a rule in her creative writing class: everybody was to describe his or her feelings from the heart and the guts, never from imitation.

The clear favourite with Miss Seetoh, among the identified twelve horrors on the poster, had elicited a deliciously wicked chuckle. It was a spelling rather than a grammatical error, and it bore the full force of the punitive broomstick – 'We can be proud that our Singapore is now an effluent society.' The class had laughed at previous misspelling howlers that Miss Seetoh liked to draw to their attention and challenge them to depict cartoon-style. The classroom walls were decorated with drawings cheerfully showing students being 'canned' by the discipline master if they came late to school, the giant tin cans, into which the screaming culprits were dropped, actually bearing familiar local sardine or luncheon pork labels; and of hunters firing 'shorts' into the air, the shorts, emanating from huge gun barrels, being the recognisably navy blue ones used for the Physical Education lessons.

The principal, on his regular rounds of the classroom, sometimes stopped by to look at the pictures and ask Miss Seetoh about them. Dressed in impeccable white, his hands clasped behind his back, a puzzled frown on his grave face as his head twisted this way and that to follow the wild cartoon swirls of the artist's crayons or marker pens, asking the same earnest questions as he did at educational seminars, he was himself a humorous sight, and the subject of a student cartoon drawing that had to stay out of sight. A member of that brave band of ageing, conservative community leaders who tried to adapt to the changing times by occasionally wearing a bright floral shirt and clapping to the impossibly loud music at a student party, he was happiest when in his habitual white and doing his rounds of the school.

The students had stared blankly at the 'effluent society' sentence on the chalkboard, and Miss Seetoh had said, 'Go look in your dictionary. Make that one more word for your vocabulary list.' She loved the witch-and-Shakespeare poster so much she removed it from the classroom wall after a while to take home and put up in her apartment.

The penalty money went into a round tin box that stood on Miss Seetoh's table, prettily decorated by a student named Maggie. It was Maggie, a bright, bold, fun-loving girl who had

had the idea to circle the tin box with a broad band of white paper that carried the message, in bright colours: 'Mrs Tan is no more. Long live Miss Seetoh!'

It was shocking – a secret joy suddenly revealed to the world with the public aplomb of a portentous royal announcement. Miss Seetoh stared, feeling a hot flush spread on her neck and cheeks. A picture of composure, she was now all cringing embarrassment in the bright glare of an exposed truth that was both frightening for its guilt and exhilarating for its promise. Between the two appellations of society's recognition of a woman's status, scrolled her private story of breathless escape. It was surely the work of a single moment of inspired genius for Maggie who made the most deplorable grammar mistakes in speech and writing, even for the Special Needs class of overaged students held back for two years for extra coaching to prepare them for the O Level exams. Strictly, Maggie did not qualify to be in the creative writing class, but had begged so hard that Miss Seetoh made an exception for her. Her short stories, always in bad English, swung between the mawkishly sentimental and the crudely earthy, both held up as samples of bad writing, with the name of the author erased. 'I don't mind,' said Maggie airily. 'You can use my name. My stories, they all true, I tell you!'

The girl was holding up the box with both hands and turning it round very slowly before Miss Seetoh's eyes, so that she could read, as a continuous statement, the words on the encircling band. They danced before her eyes, like a flock of released butterflies. Maggie was grinning and watching her with keen interest.

It was one thing to reclaim a maiden name upon widowhood, and quite another to flaunt it in concrete, documented proof. The society, taking its cue from the government, could be unforgiving towards single women boldly disavowing the sanctity of marriage. Renegades were safe if they kept quiet, never if they openly challenged authority. 'Do you like it, Miss Seetoh?' said Maggie. 'Yes, I do.' It was only partly a lie. She wished Maggie had not done anything like that. But she was impressed by its brilliant audacity. If she had wished to celebrate her new status, she could not have expressed it better. Out of the mouths of babes. Or rather, of worldly-wise teenage girls like Maggie, teetering on the brink of womanhood, sensing its perils, ready to test its intoxicating power.

The principal had, shortly after, called her into his office. 'I understand,' he said in his always polite and guarded manner, 'that you would like to be called by your name before your marriage. But have you made it official? Because, if not, your name will continue to be 'Mrs Bernard Tan Boon Siong' in the school records.'

'Oh, that's okay,' said Miss Seetoh. 'I only meant for my students to greet me by my old name. Makes me feel more comfortable.'

The principal had given her a quick quizzical look, but said no more on the matter. He assiduously ignored the rumours that sometimes came to his ears about this teacher, his favourite because almost single-handedly she guaranteed the school's consistently high national ranking in the English language examination results every year. From a humiliating position of twenty-nine out of forty before Miss Seetoh arrived, it had leapt to number ten, then number five. The school had actually been singled out for honourable mention in one of the Education Minister's speeches. A good speaker of the English language was not necessarily its best teacher. Miss Seetoh was both, and best of all, she showed a creative flair for speech writing, which, the principal noted with quiet satisfaction, she very generously used to help him craft or fine-tune the many speeches he had to make at principals' seminars, especially those where senior representatives from the Ministry of Education were present.

'Then I and the rest of the staff will continue to address you as Mrs Tan.'

Two

Long live Miss Maria Seetoh Wei Cheng!

Never again would she abandon that designation for the prized honorific that women were supposed to seek before they hit thirty, spurred on by society's grim reminders of that relentless biological clock. Anxious mothers, her own mother being a typical example, reminded their daughters, ambitious for university degrees, not to forget the most important one of all – the MRS. Indeed, the whole society seemed to be in thrall of some imperative to get its many single women married, mothered and launched on the road of respectable womanhood.

It was a movement called 'Family Values' spearheaded by the Ministry of Social Development which had marshaled its substantial resources of money and talent to set up an organisation with the sole purpose of helping women find true fulfilment. It was remarkable that her mother who had to endure the feckless ways of a husband for years was always saying to her, 'If you don't get married, who will take care of you when I'm gone?' Her father had suddenly disappeared from their lives when she was a little girl, fleeing from debtors to Thailand where purportedly he had been living with his Thai mistress since.

The great TPK himself had appeared on TV several times to urge women to cooperate in the national exercise. It did not matter that the reason he gave for its purpose did not match that of the 'Family Values' campaign. He left it to the junior ministers to use the soft approach to deal with a delicate subject, so as not to offend an increasingly well-educated electorate, while he and his senior ministers went all the way of the brutal truth, as they spoke to the people on TV, through the newspapers, in face-to-face encounters in the walkabouts through the sprawling housing estates.

The economy, he warned, was in serious danger. If the birth rate continued to decline, there would be massive labour shortages in the future. Incapable of the language of sentiment used in the campaign posters everywhere showing happy pictures of smiling families, though himself a happily married man with an adoring, adored wife and two bright daughters, he concentrated on the hard statistics of the tiny island-state's struggle to survive in a relentlessly competitive world. 'Make no mistake,' he said sternly. 'We will be in deep trouble if we do nothing now.'

Thirty years ago, he had warned of an opposite but no less dangerous demographic trend – Singapore women were having too many babies, and creating a crisis of overpopulation. The Singapore General Maternity Hospital, to the society's shame, had one of the highest birth rates in the world. These overproductive women were straining national resources and therefore had to be stopped. TPK, looking his sternest on TV, his hair back then still a deep gleaming black, the admonishing forefinger and thrusting jaw already the trademarks of his bellicose style, had threatened a slew of penalties for recalcitrant women who dared to have more than the permitted two children. At the same time, he offered an incentive: the woman who could produce a sterilisation certificate from a government hospital after two children was entitled to enrol her children in Singapore's choicest schools.

The man had struck the tenderest of parental chords. For there was but a small number of these elite schools, and parents would kill to get their sons and daughters into them. It was rumoured that the policy, which soon provoked cynical coverage in some international newspapers, would be tweaked to target a special group of women – the uneducated group from the lower socio-economic strata who married early and produced broods.

The angry protest of V.K. Pandy, the leader of the sole opposition party in Parliament, back then a young aspirant for political life, was almost incoherent in its mix of thunderous denunciations and obscure references to Darwin, eugenics and totalitarianism, and went unreported.

'Mrs Tan, I thought I had sent round a circular that classroom discussion topics should not include politics.' The principal had called her into his office. Even among the forty adoring students in her class, there must have been a spy or two.

'We were not discussing politics, sir. V.K. Pandy's name had just come up only very incidentally.'

The principal winced visibly.

The opposition leader, always untidy-looking with his bristling eyebrows, overgrown beard and glittering close-set eyes that gave him a simian aspect, always loud, cantankerous, unreasonable in his demands for this or that government policy to be subjected to public debate, had become a national embarrassment, a blot on the society's pristine face.

Years ago, the newspapers ran a lengthy report on his attempt to go by foot all the way to the United Nations headquarters to present his anti-sterilisation plea on behalf of Singapore's women, highlighting its abrupt end when he developed stomach cramps in Malaysia, twenty-one miles into the heroic walk, and had to accept a car ride back home. The debacle prompted a derisory editorial captioned, 'Pandy, You're No Gandhi,' and for a while the taunt, repeated for its serendipitous pun, was bandied around at cocktail parties and coffee shop gatherings. His few sympathisers marveled at the tenacity of his political aspirations against such overwhelming odds; both sympathy and admiration were necessarily muted. The schools, by tacit agreement, had banned all mention of him in classroom discussions and debates. He could sometimes be seen, in busy shopping centres, waving pamphlets, a lone figure in the centre of a large empty space invariably carved out for him by the crowds, hurrying past, always looking the other way.

The student editor of the school magazine had inadvertently included, in a commemorative anniversary issue, a photograph showing visitors to St Peter's School Fun Fair, in which the opposition member could be distinctly seen in the background, waving cheerfully. The oversight was discovered by the magazine's teacher advisor who rushed to inform the principal who at once picked up the phone to stop the printer. But it was too late and he had to make the decision, a painfully expensive one, of having all eight hundred copies of the magazine destroyed and new ones printed, minus, of course, the offending photograph. The teacher advisor and the student editor were forgiven their carelessness, but never again would they be entrusted with any important assignment.

'Mrs Tan,' said the principal who hated having to call teachers into his office to admonish them on this or that, 'you were seen yesterday afternoon talking to the opposition

member in Middleton Square, just outside Shelford Building.'
The school had spies everywhere.

'Yes, I was,' said Miss Seetoh, 'but it was on my own time,'
adding, 'and I wasn't in school uniform.'

Her husband had dropped her at a dispensary in Shelford
Building to collect some medicine for her mother's asthma;
during the fifteen minutes of waiting for him to pick her up,
she had seen the opposition member in his lonely precinct
in the shopping mall, waving his pamphlets at the streams of
shoppers assiduously avoiding him. As she watched him, she
instinctively joined forces with them by stepping behind the
dispensary door, a safe peeping presence only.

Then something very like shame swept over her,
corresponding precisely with the moment that she saw a
small child in a Superman suit break away from his mother
to stand and stare in fascination at V.K. Pandy, saw the man's
frowning face break into smiles, and the mother rushing up
to pull the child away. The small rebel, despite the scolding,
turned round several times to look at V.K. Pandy who was
still grinning and waving. The shame flared, then settled into
daring resolution. She strode out of the dispensary, walked
straight into the space, a scrupulously cordoned-off infected
zone in a clean city, and stretched out a hand to greet its sole
occupant, 'Hello, Mr Pandy.'

It didn't matter what he or she said after that; she had
done the defiant deed for the day, so that when her husband
returned to pick her up at the dispensary, the assertive glow
on her neck and cheeks saved the rest of her demeanour from
the usual docility. Exuding a radiant confidence before her
principal, her colleagues and her students, she shrank in timid
deference before her husband. Glowing in the queendom of her

classroom, she crawled back each day into the oppression of the marital sanctuary.

'Look at that idiot,' he said with a smile, pointing to the man now squatting on the ground, his tie askew, his pamphlets still in a large stack beside him, staring absently into the distance, 'thinking he can bring down the government. Did you see that?' he continued with a spiteful chuckle, as the man took a small bottle out of his pocket, looked around furtively, drank from it and wiped his beard with his hand. 'A drunk as well.'

Bernard Tan Boon Siong had written a number of scathing letters to *The Singapore Tribune* about the obstreperous opposition member, which he always passed to his boss for approval and endorsement. She had actually offered to help him craft some of the letters, after he told her that the boss, the formidable Dr Phang with his two PhDs, the first from Oxford University, the second from Harvard, someone clearly being marked out by the government for a life in politics, was a stickler for perfect grammar and appropriate style. He had once invited Dr Phang and some office friends home for dinner, an expensively catered affair that had her nervous mother on tenterhooks all evening repeatedly inspecting each tray and pot of food as it was brought in by the caterers.

The disobedient act of her adventure in Middleton Square had given rise to a confusion of many feelings: surprise at her own audacity, fear of recrimination from her husband, dislike of his boss, guilt towards V.K. Pandy for her hypocrisy. For she had played the part of the loyal government supporter, delving into her rich repertoire of derogatory terms to spice the venom of her husband's letter to the newspaper. He had smiled in approval and later told her the boss had thought it an excellent letter.

It was an act of unkindness to V.K. Pandy for which she was prepared to pay the price of more secret ventures into that banned space, perhaps even with the offer of a hamburger and a can of cold beer for his lunch. The confusion of feelings was soon no more than a whirligig of emotions easily tamed into a single, very pleasurable sensation, as she thought in tremulous excitement, my God, what if he finds out. V.K. Pandy's pamphlet was safely tucked between the pages of her teacher's record book which was placed, in a continuing show of defiance, side by side with his briefcase on the sitting room table.

The act of rebellion had brought back the memory of a girlhood incident very similar in its triumphant reclaim of self-regard. She was eight years old, a bright, alert pupil who enjoyed the English language lessons, in particular, the dictation lesson during which the pupils were required to transcribe each sentence of a short story, as it was slowly read out, phrase by phrase, by the English language teacher, Sister St Agatha. The story was usually taken from a small collection of readers which, from a very young age, she had read voraciously and knew by heart.

Sister gave the students a few minutes to get acquainted with the more difficult words in the story before the dictation lesson began. Proudly dispensing with the assistance, she wrote down in her copy book the entire story, perfectly registered in her memory, in a fraction of the dictation lesson time. So when Sister began the exercise, it was a simple matter of pretending to write, by letting her pencil tip float lightly over each phrase in her copy book. Sister's sharp eyes caught the pretence; her nostrils flared with the angry triumph of catching a cheat red-handed. She pulled the culprit up from her seat, pinned the evidence of the dishonesty to her blouse and made her stand in front of the class all morning. It all happened so quickly that she was unable to explain the truth to Sister, and in any case, probably could not have done so in her confusion. Burning with shame, she wished that she would die that instant.

In the next dictation lesson, Sister was astonished to see her furiously writing down in her copy book the entire three paragraphs of the designated story, even before the dictation lesson had begun. Then she got up with her book, laid it on Sister's table without a word, and returned to her desk glowing with restored self-esteem.

'Mrs Tan, you know that even outside the school premises, staff and students are supposed to behave with decorum.' Miss Seetoh's large innocent eyes widened in surprise.

'I was behaving with perfect decorum, sir, since we were in an open, public place. Mr V.K. Pandy was explaining something in his pamphlet. It had to do with the sterilisation policy, sir.'

The principal muttered, 'That was so long ago,' his acute discomfort betrayed by a facial tic and a tightening of the hands clasped behind his back. He sometimes wondered if Miss Seetoh, of the refreshingly open countenance and helpful writing skills, was secretly mocking him.

The government organisation, tasked with helping single women find husbands and unburdened by any memory of that awful time of draconian population controls three decades ago, went all the way of friendly cajolery, and would probably have no objection to extending its help to widows still capable of bearing children. Miss Seetoh, aged thirty-nine, happy once more, thought, never again. The government organisation's request for help, very discreetly worded, went out to the schools which were known to have large numbers of single women on their staff. The principal of St Peter's responded to the request by passing on the official letter to the unmarried women teachers, together with his own personal encouragement, also delicately worded, about the Christian ideal of motherhood and the importance of cooperation to solve a problem highlighted by the Prime Minister himself.

There was a form to be filled by the single women to indicate their interest or otherwise in participating in a variety of social events, such as tea dances and computer games, being organised for them to meet eligible single men. Here was another reason for poor plain Miss Teresa Pang, never courted in her life, to be unfavourably compared, in whispered comments, to the pretty widow, Miss Seetoh. An unkind joke went round, in the form of a riddle, purportedly started by a waggish young trainee teacher: what is the only thing, desired by Singapore men that Miss Pang has which Miss Seetoh doesn't? Answer: her virginity.

Miss Seetoh had put a large tick in the 'Not Interested' box on the form, and then, as an afterthought, had added, 'But thank you for the kind consideration.'

Three

The celebration of her new status would have to remain private in an atmosphere charged with matrimony's sanctity, so she quickly peeled the proclamatory label from the tin box, taking care not to dislodge the absurd little pink rosettes that Maggie had sprinkled all around it. She rolled up the band of paper and put it inside her handbag.

'Thank you, Maggie,' she said. 'As I've told you, I like it very much but it had best stay out of sight!'

That was invitation enough for the girl, ever inquisitive and talkative, to engage in conversation clearly intended to draw out information on the carefully guarded private life of the fascinating Miss Seetoh. If her favourite teacher remained unyielding, she simply changed the topic to other teachers' private lives. Mrs Naidu, the geography teacher, had again been taken ill in class, sitting down heavily in the midst of a lesson and furiously rubbing Tiger Balm on her forehead and chest. In such moments of distress, her carefully coiled hair uncoiled into a mess of waving strands around her face, giving her the appearance of a grieving Medusa, frightening the students. Everyone knew that the cause of her endless headaches, stomach cramps and mouth ulcers was her husband.

Miss Monteiro, the physical education teacher, spoke openly about her German boyfriend: once she took medical leave for two days, and somebody saw her on the resort island of Sentosa with him. She kept a photo of him in her wallet, shirtless on a beach, his wind-blown, sun-drenched blondness instantly placing him among the advertising world's golden boys, and passed it round among her colleagues and students. One of her students, the scary Jaswant Singh, sixteen years-old, hairy, deep-voiced, a muscular six-footer towering over his classmates, had tried to date her once.

Maggie had developed the knack of catching hold of teachers while they were walking along the corridors, down the stairs or across the yard to the school canteen, and in the few available minutes, mixing innocuous student inquiries with a load of trivia and gossip, watching their reaction, storing up for future use whatever they said in response, no matter how brief or brusque. Some teachers chose to simply ignore her and turn away. In class, they chose to ignore her hand raised eagerly to answer every question of which she had not the faintest idea. The overaged student had surely overstayed her welcome in the school. They were reproachful of the young sports coach who was nicknamed Singapore's Tony Curtis, for his being unable to turn away from the persistent Maggie; someone had seen him once give her a ride on his motorcycle.

Her net of influence, cast out to reach the largest possible number of St Peter's Secondary School inhabitants, included the humble workers, such as the gardener, the cleaning woman and the noodles seller at the school canteen, for these too could be sources of useful information or pleasurable gossip, and occasionally the opportunity for the commendable practice of Christian charity. Maggie once initiated a class donation for the school gardener when his wife fell ill and had to be hospitalised for a month.

'*Aiyoh*, so pitiful!' exclaimed the girl, in an easy swing from biting criticism to genuine concern and back. 'The man so useless, spending money on drink, and the wife sick all the time, and five children to take care.'

Miss Seetoh wondered how much Maggie had pieced together a picture of her marriage from clues inadvertently dropped during her talks and discussions in the creative writing lessons. The girl had eyes and ears that claimed the entire school as their territory, roaming it relentlessly, like a tiny, agile, quick-witted predator that knew when to pounce, and when to sit on its haunches and beg. She reminded Miss Seetoh of the lowly eunuchs and maids of old in the ancestral country, who glided noiselessly through the large imperial courtyards and chambers, sniffing out or initiating intrigues, rising to important positions through sheer cunning.

Maggie knew which teacher was gay, which boy-girl pair was having sex. She dragged into the respectable orderliness of the school the private chaos of young lives: Bin Choo was always sleepy in class because she helped at her mother's noodles stall every evening till past midnight; Gary copied others' homework; Bina sometimes slipped into the classroom during recess and stole things; Hock Soon knew how to avoid paying bus fare on his way to school every morning by choosing only very crowded buses; Ah Leng belonged to a secret society and had a dragon tattoo on his right shoulder; it was the quiet Ravi who was responsible for the shocking incident, still unsolved by the discipline master, of the pubic hairs slipped between the pages of a library book.

Maggie said, 'Miss Seetoh, you know what? Everyone, they talk, talk about why you have drop the Mrs.'

The girl was intensely disliked and distrusted by the majority of the staff and students. Miss Seetoh held in check her own deep aversion in the face of so much trust and adulation by a student completely isolated in a school of teeming hundreds. It was most embarrassing that the girl had actually taken the trouble to find out her birthdate and present her with a large chocolate birthday cake, probably bought at great expense, lavishly inscribed: 'For Miss S, the best understanding teacher in the world.' 'Please,' said Miss Seetoh awkwardly, opening her purse, but Maggie clamped it shut again, 'No, Miss Seetoh. You are special. I'll do anything for you!'

At the wake of her husband, only a month before, she was startled to see the girl, dressed in full mourning black, present herself among the visitors and proffer the traditional gift of condolence money. 'Oh no, Maggie, you mustn't,' she had insisted, and this time had succeeded in pressing the sealed white envelope back into the girl's hand. How on earth had she got the money? There were rumours about her mother working as a lounge waitress in one of the city's seediest districts.

'I know they all talk, talk about me, but Miss Seetoh, it's not true! One day I tell you everything, because I trust you.' She could already be telling her stories in the submissions in the creative writing class.

'Maggie,' Miss Seetoh had said, trying not to sound too shocked, 'don't get carried away by your imagination. For the next assignment, don't write about sex. Or rape.'

To reject the already much rejected girl would be to bring upon herself lifelong remorse. As a child in primary school, she had one day pushed to the ground a classmate, a scrawny, scanty-haired little girl with a perpetual trickle down her nose, who followed her everywhere, and carried the guilt right up to secondary school.

Every teacher was relieved at the thought that Maggie, who resolutely kept her strange family background impenetrable to the good work of the school's corps of hard-working counsellors, would be gone once she finished the O Level exams and be fully absorbed into her dark world, dominated, it was rumoured, by a hard-drinking, abusive father who lived on the earnings of her lounge waitress mother. The complaints of some of the teachers, brought into the office of the principal, ended there, absorbed into the school's benign mission of educating the young and preparing them for a useful role in society. The noble goal was announced in a motto in giant white letters above the school entrance.

The formidable Mrs Neo had said to the principal as she barged into his office and he stood up to greet her, 'For the good name of the school, that girl should be expelled!'

The principal had replied calmly, 'I'll see what can be done,' meaning nothing would be done.

He already had a fearful picture of Maggie Sim taking her story to the newspapers, of the burst of publicity in the Chinese media ever hungry for sensational news, of the annoyance of the Ministry of Education at having to respond with a public investigation. A freakish presence in a noble institution of learning, the girl would be allowed to stay till she left of her own accord.

Once or twice, the principal called Maggie into his office for a mild reprimand. 'You were rude to Miss Pang, and again to Mrs Doraisamy.'

Genteel man that he was, he left it to the lady teachers to deal with the surreptitious make-up, the vulgarisation of the school uniform by an undone shirt button here, a lifting of the skirt hem there. There was something that he had heard from one of the teachers which had deeply disturbed him: Maggie had once gone for an abortion.

'Do you know anything about it?' he had asked Miss Seetoh, possibly the girl's only confidante.

'No,' said Miss Seetoh who did not want to know, and the matter was never referred to again.

She suddenly had an image of the girl in a secret visit to one of the government hospitals where abortions were performed with utmost discretion and minimum fuss, so that the misguided teenager could get up, go home, and be in school the next day. She remembered Maggie once or twice excusing herself from class to go to the sick bay because of stomach pains from her very heavy periods, conspicuously taking out of her schoolbag a large wad of sanitary towels.

Her world at St Peter's Secondary School was a truly happy one, and Maggie was part of it. If she wrote a novel one day, the teenager, astonishingly shrewd in the ways of the world, might even be the female protagonist. Her imagination, ever active and on the alert to store potentially useful material for that dreamt-of novel, was already storing images of the girl, her large pretty eyes, her expertly plucked eyebrows, her impossibly large breasts, all in keeping with the hard opportunism of a Singapore-bred Lolita.

When I was her age, Miss Seetoh thought with some wonder, I knew nothing about the birds and the bees. Her mother kept her in a protective capsule, still plaiting her hair every morning well into her teens and watching her recite her night prayers kneeling beside the bed they shared. Even then she was already responding to the cry for freedom deep inside that had begun with the smallest of wishes – 'when I have a bed of my own' – for her mother slept badly and kept her awake with much tossing, moaning and teeth-grinding. Over the years, as she grew into adulthood, the wish was systematically enlarged, from bed to room to house, and became the final longing born out of despair – 'when I have a life of my own.' She had panicked at the sight of her first menstruation, her mother explained that it wasn't any injury, that it was natural and God-given, bought her the proper towels and took her to church for a special blessing.

'Miss Seetoh, that poor Mr Chin, his heart broke when you got married, now he can try again!' Maggie giggled and furtively looked around to make sure the maths teacher, hopelessly hanging around Miss Seetoh for years, tongue-tied and fumbling in her presence, his comically bulging goldfish eyes and stutter a perfect target of student impersonation, was not within hearing distance. 'I want to tell him, 'Hey, Mr Chin, give up! Where you got hope? You cannot pronounce English words properly. Suppose you say, 'Oh, Miss Seetoh, I lub you so velly much!', she will surely faint!' '

The girl was a slick clown with a ready stock of jokes that could be manipulated to fit the occasion, the special target being the Chinese-educated speakers of English struggling with the intricacies of a foreign tongue. Storing up yet another comical episode for later sharing with friends, Miss Seetoh managed to suppress a laugh and say severely, 'Maggie, how many times have I told you to speak in correct English?'

Maggie persisted and this time her eyes sparkled with the sheer piquancy of the new information, 'Miss Seetoh, you know or not, even Brother Philip, he come to our class, pretend to ask about this or that, but really it's all excuse to talk to you.

We all notice! Miss Teresa Pang, she jealous as hell, because Brother Philip so tall and handsome with his *ang moh* brown curly hair and blue eyes! Like the *Magnum* TV hero. She so ugly with her Bugs Bunny teeth, no man will look at her and you so pretty, with no make-up even, they all want you. Miss Seetoh, you interested or not, my uncle he got many rich businessman friends, can introduce –'

The girl was impossible, overstepping her limits. She could be dangerous.

Miss Seetoh looked closely at her and said in as severe a tone as she could muster, 'Maggie, you're wearing eyeliner again. You know make-up is against school rules. I've told you that before.'

The girl said airily, '*Aiyah*! Only a little bit. See, you never notice before. How come Sebastian Ong can come to class with powder on his face? That's more worse!' She saw Miss Seetoh's eyes settle on the loosened button of the school white shirt, that allowed a peep at a lacy bra if she turned in a certain way, and quickly did it up. 'Alright,' she said resignedly and adjusted the waistband of the school skirt to let the hem drop to the obligatory three inches below the knee. 'Alright,' she said again, and removed the rhinestone clip partly covered by a large swatch of hair.

'What's that?' said Miss Seetoh, sniffing. 'Maggie, you know you're not supposed to wear perfume to school!' There was a list of regulatory don'ts for the girl students, pinned up in every classroom, that would not have been necessary but for one Maggie Sim Peck Ngoh.

While the girl was petulant and defiant with the other teachers, she good-naturedly obeyed Miss Seetoh, upon whom had duly fallen the responsibility of holding her in check.

The girl was to be feared, for her relentless probing of secrets as she chattered endlessly, ignoring Miss Seetoh's diversionary strategy of scolding her for her bad English and her make-up. Miss Seetoh, who adroitly broke school regulations. was now using them, like a cane, to manage a difficult student. She even echoed the language of the regulations. She did not at all enjoy that role.

Four

Maria Seetoh went straight into her room, locked it, took out the celebratory circle of paper from her handbag and once more stared at it. She saw the story of her life in a full-length novel, reduced to a one-page synopsis, reduced finally to this amazing nine-word distillation that left none of the drama out.

It was a three-part drama: her determined singlehood, followed suddenly by a marriage that the school knew about only when she returned from her honeymoon after the long December vacation, followed by widowhood, only three years later, that appeared blithe enough to invite the 'Merry Widow' label to be attached to it. Each part had its share of unsavoury speculations. Was she a lesbian? She seemed to be very close to two other conspicuously single women, a Miss Meeta Nair and a Miss Winnie Poon, both from the Palm Secondary Girls' School that was rumoured to have a disproportionate number of teachers and students so inclined. When the news of her sudden marriage spread, starting from the school office where the clerk was the first to note the official change in name, the staffroom was caught in the grip of intense conjecturing for weeks, even distracting the mild and pious Sister Elizabeth from her preparation of lesson notes. Nobody dared to ask, because nobody dared invade Maria Seetoh's lofty solitude, even as she moved in smiling amiability among the scores of students and teachers at St Peter's.

Had she found her husband through the services of the government matchmaking organisation that she had so disdained? Or was she already – ? The young male science teacher with the impish smile and crewcut who enjoyed entertaining the lady teachers, said, 'Let's see, she got married in the month of –' and did an elaborate crude finger count.

Soon there was another matter for speculative wonderment. Was Mrs Tan happy? A sullen-faced husband dropped her every morning at the school gate on his way to work, and she got out of the car, equally grim-looking. The first year of marriage should still be sunny honeymoon, and here were Mrs Tan and her husband, dark-faced and brooding, in their first month, clearly avoiding having to look at each other. The newly wed Mrs Jasmine Auyang and her husband exchanged effusive kisses at the gate each morning, oblivious to student stares and giggles. How could things have gone so wrong so early for a couple so obviously well-matched, he a senior civil servant, she a respected teacher, both practising Catholics, both good-looking?

Mrs Tan, without the familiar bright smile of Miss Seetoh, was almost unrecognisable. Then as soon as she stepped into her classroom and started the day's lessons, the smile was magically restored. If there were teachers who dragged themselves to school every morning, like poor Mrs Naidu of the endless headaches and Tiger Balm, Mrs Bernard Tan positively danced into it, like fluttering butterfly out of confining cocoon. What did it say of her married life that she escaped it every morning with such undisguised joy?

The most avid whispers were reserved for the widow's immediate dispensation with every sign of mourning and bereavement.

'What bereavement?' said Miss Teresa Pang, whose close observation of her rival's strange behaviour was being well rewarded. 'A red blouse. Screaming chilli-red. And yesterday a bright pink one that I've never seen before. A whole new wardrobe. A subtle re-arrangement of that ponytail. And the wedding ring gone from her finger from the first day. Advertising her new status, or what?'

Mrs Khaw, the domestic science teacher, whispered back, 'She was seen being dropped at Robinson's by a guy in a Mercedes, only a week after the funeral.'

Mrs Khaw, like many married women, lived in mortal fear of her husband falling victim to the special predatory skills of newly divorced or widowed women, and was herself the target of much racy gossip: she employed only certifiably ugly or virtuous maids, and even then, made sure that her husband, of the incessant roving eye and hand, was never alone with them in the house. When he was abroad on business, she called him at his hotel room during those hours she knew him to be out to test his fidelity. For a friend had told her about a cousin's innocent call to her husband's hotel room in Tokyo that was picked up by a woman with a sleepy voice.

The rumours affected Miss Seetoh not at all, but the guilt did, guilt of the kind that disturbed her to the innermost depths of her being, because it had broken the most fundamental laws of human decency: she had rejoiced over the death not only of another human being, but one whom she was bound by tradition's strongest sanctions to honour and respect. A wife was happy because her husband was dead. The guilt was the greater for the joy being so soon, so real and persistent. It was an unthinkable obscenity, yet to deny it would be intolerable falsehood. Till death do us part. It was bad enough if the widow bounced back to her normal routines too quickly. She had heard of women going back to work the day after the funeral, even remarrying within a year.

A sudden frightening thought had occurred to reinforce the guilt, as she sat quietly reading a novel in her bedroom, in a first delicious taste of solitude: could husbands be wished to death? Could despairing wives' secret wishes, if they were strong enough, cast a spell and induce an accident, a terminal cancer? Miss Seetoh had once watched a TV documentary about a certain aboriginal tribe in Australia; their leader met his death several hours after an enemy from a rival tribe ceremonially lifted his face to the sky in pouring rain and sang out a curse. Heaven forbid! Had her wish, secret though it was, resisted though it was all the way with every decent fibre in her body, been such a curse? Miss Seetoh, who from childhood would go out of her way to pick up wounded birds and kittens and nurse them back to health, was so horrified by the thought that her hand went limp and the book dropped to the floor.

The thought – superstitious nonsense though it was – would not go away. This time it induced a slight shuddering which Miss Seetoh, sitting at the staffroom table ostensibly going over the lesson notes for the following day, hoped no one noticed. She was proud of her capacity for rational thinking, developed over years of serious reading and reflection, against the myth-sodden worlds of her upbringing, first of her ancestor-worshipping grandmother Por Por with its pantheon of frightful temple gods and goddesses, and then of her fervidly Christian convert mother, with its equally bewildering collection of intercessory saints, angels and martyrs. For a while she shuttled between two worlds in conflict, between church holy water and temple-blessed fire, between a gentle god who died to save mankind and a lightning god who directed his bolts against those guilty of filial impiety. Torn between her grandmother and mother, she was saved only by Por Por's dementia which ended the tussle for her soul between the Tua Peh Kong Temple and the Church of Eternal Mercy.

It alarmed her that in the sanity of adulthood, her sound mind could be invaded by the most outrageous childhood superstitions. The fear persisted with another example, much closer to home. She remembered an aunt from Malaysia telling her about a relative who visited a cemetery in the darkest of nights to conjure up the ghost of an ancestor to take revenge on her husband and his family for throwing her out into the street. The husband contracted some fearsome disease and died soon after.

Miss Seetoh vigorously rubbed the sides of her forehead to dispel a headache that always came with bad thoughts, throbbing with vicious intensity. Her memory with its ready store of recollected images, like her imagination with its created ones, came to her rescue. A nun had taught her as a child to quickly picture a certain scene in times of temptation – Good Thoughts wearing white angelic halos fighting Bad Thoughts wearing black horns, and driving them screaming back to hell. The nun had meant the sinful images of sex that young girls were often tempted with; for Miss Seetoh, the one thing to be feared was fear, not sex.

The superstitious dread was soon gone but the guilt of secret exultation, not so easily vanquished, returned again and again. 'I'm free! I'm free!' continued the inward cry, and she continued to beat it down as a shameful truth that must ever be hidden from sight. 'If I ever became a writer,' she thought, 'I could write at length about a woman's journey of guilt.' Women had an enormous capacity for hate and revenge, also for triumph and exultation, and most of all, guilt. Did it have to do with her biology that wracked her body with the anxieties of child-bearing and child-nurturing, or her culture that instilled in her, from the start, the imperative of duty to everyone but herself?

The most frightening image, from a Chinese comic strip that someone had given her as a child, was of a pregnant woman who had gone mad with rage as she roamed the land, looking for her faithless lover, finally killing her newborn and dying in a frenzy of guilt and sorrow.

She had a close childhood friend named Emily who often called her on the phone to sob out the latest cruelty of a callous, philandering husband. One day Emily invited her for lunch, for the sole purpose of revealing yet another of the cruelties: secretly going through her husband's briefcase, she had discovered the receipt for a very expensive diamond pendant from a shop in Hong Kong. In the ten years of their marriage, she said, the angry tears filling her eyes, he had never bought her even the tiniest piece of jewellery. Moreover, she suspected him of siphoning away a large part of the profits from the sale of some jointly-owned shares in the stock market. As divorce became the most likely solution to end her misery, she mobilised the support of lawyer and accountant friends who could advise her on how to get the best out of a financial settlement, how to pre-empt possible cunning ploys by her husband and best of all, how to come up with some of her own.

Miss Seetoh's help was co-opted for an intricate scheme of pre-emption she hardly understood but sympathetically cooperated in. She cheerfully put her signature as witness in an elaborately worded legal document, to prevent the devious husband from laying his hands on a joint property. Her adopted brother Heng, ever savvy about money matters, was aghast. 'You stood guarantor for something involving hundreds of thousands of dollars? You could lose everything, you know, including what is not yours!' He was referring to the four-room flat owned by their mother which would go to both of them upon her death.

Money, money, money – it became the irreducible, rock-bottom reality, the ultimate bargaining chip of husbands and wives, parents and children, siblings, best friends. There were regular reports in the newspapers of family members suing each other over property, the increasing number of cases correlating perfectly with the rise in property prices. 'You want to know what makes a woman stay in a marriage?' said a friend, and she demonstrated with the expert rubbing of middle finger and thumb against each other, the universal language of the miser, the usurer, the profiteer. Miss Seetoh thought sadly, if only money were the real problem in her marriage.

Over steaming beef noodles in the open air café, Emily launched the bitterest tirade yet against her husband who she now suspected of having set up an apartment in London for his mistress, a former airline stewardess who, Emily had found out, was formerly the mistress of a Brunei oil tycoon. Suddenly she paused, her chopsticks suspended in her hands, to listen to the drone of a plane overhead. She listened intently for some seconds and said slowly, 'If that's his plane on the way to London to visit his mistress, here's a wish: may it crash this instant!' Miss Seetoh stared in horror at the look of grim relish on the tear-stained face already raised to witness the fiery plunge from the sky.

And from that moment her guilt was assuaged: never had any wish to be free of her husband included, or could ever include, the wish for his death. Not even injury of any kind. It was just a general wish to be free of her marriage, as understandable as a child's wish to be free of over-strict parents, a student's wish to quickly graduate to the next level and be free of an unreasonable teacher. That terrible image of the aboriginal chief's curse in the rain, of the woman conjuring help from a ghost in a cemetery, would never disturb her again.

'Maria, what are you doing?' cried her mother in alarm. It was odd that her mother, witnessing a clear return of good spirits so soon after her husband's death, should worry about her each time she locked herself in her room. 'Maria, I smell smoke! Open the door at once!'

It was only the burning smell of Maggie's tantalising band of paper, now curled around the rim of a basin. Maria Seetoh watched with a little frisson of wonder as the small flame crept through the first half of the band, leaving a tiny pile of black ashes, and then most unaccountably fizzled to a halt at the second, leaving it intact and whole, surely a foretaste of her new life.

Five

Neither marital curse nor vengeance, thank goodness, had been part of their world; it was too civilised to permit even the raised voice, the crude invective. The husband's clenched fist, the wife's desperate attempts to avoid it and hide her bruised eyes behind dark sunglasses the next day – these would have been both alien and alienating to the world they inhabited. They were the perfect couple, he the epitome of gentlemanly courteousness and gallantry, and she of wifely gentleness and docility. They were said to be inseparable, the ultimate tribute to marital commitment.

The word had a bitter flavour for her. For he expected her to be with him everywhere he went; her physical presence by his side was for him a solid reminder of his control, for her of her subjugation. He liked her to hold his arm or hand tightly, to reinforce the reminder. Her husband had obeyed, with perfect literalness, holy matrimony's call to continue to be joined in one flesh beyond the marital bed. If she got her artistic student to do a cartoon of them, it would probably have the dark humour of painfully conjoined twins. Bondage, not bonding. Marriage, mirage.

As he waved to this or that friend in greeting, as he nodded to this or that fellow churchgoer in Christian solidarity, he exuded husbandly pride. A mere inch taller than herself, he towered with proprietorial satisfaction. If I wrote a book of short stories about married couples, she thought, there would be several on the Owning Husband. In one, the Owning Husband itemised his ownership: these beautiful eyes are to look at me only, these delicate hands are to do my bidding only, these beautiful breasts... In another, the Owning Husband staked his ownership in a roundabout way: see these beautiful jewels that belong to my wife? Well, the diamond earrings were a reward for her obedience, the jade pendant for her...

There would be at least one story about the Trophy Wife. The Trophy Wife cried out, 'Hey, I'm alive, proud warts and all. I'm not to be burnished and polished to perfection!' The Trophy Wife cast gracious smiles all round but looked surreptitiously at her watch to see how soon each loathed outing by her husband's side would end, and she could retire, even if for a short while, to her private world.

He invaded it relentlessly. 'Maria, where are you?'

He made the maid look for her. He would pick up one book after another, from her private store, and read out the titles slowly and deliberately, making a show of mispronouncing the polysyllabic words. *Pe-dah-go-jeee, nooro-psycho-lor-jeee, fun-day-mental phi-lor-so-pheee.* Each book, taking time away from him, became an adversary. He knew about her secret longing to return to the university, to do a postgraduate course. Intellectual superiority was wifely treason. 'Just what are you trying to prove?' She hated the question, loaded with suppressed hostility, unrelieved by the slightest sense of teasing fun, as much as she hated his response when she tried to tell him what each of the books was about: 'So what do you hope to accomplish with these earth-shaking, world-shattering ideas?'

Either by nature or a sedulously cultivated seriousness, he was incapable of humour, except the biting, cynical kind.

He found a letter from a publisher politely declining her request to take a look at her collection of short stories. Refraining from open ridicule, he again asked, in a measured tone: 'Just what are you trying to prove?' Any attempt at a life outside his wishes was an intolerable defiance of those wishes.

Explanation or, worse, argument and protestation, would shatter the already fragile atmosphere, requiring an incredibly long time and an unbearably huge expenditure of energy to start picking up the pieces, one by one. There were no small children for whom, for the sake of a peaceful atmosphere, women readily opted for calm and stoical submission. She had a girlfriend, an extremely intelligent and perceptive woman, who stayed silent through her husband's wild, noisy rantings when drunk and cold, harsh criticisms when sober, for the sake of their four children, aged ten to two.

The modern woman's quandary was more acute than her mother's, or her grandmother's, because being in the ambiguous transition stage between the oppressions of the past and the uncertain hopes of the future, she bore the brunt of both.

More than for herself, the peace had to be maintained for Por Por, her mother and the maid Rosiah, three nervous women in the house, tiptoeing around his dark moods, looking to her for clues as to what to do next. They had to be protected from the fear, which, like a creeping, strangling miasma spread to every corner of the house.

Sometimes the strategy of silence paid off, actually eliciting a sheepish kind of guilt from him. Incapable of saying sorry, he would fidget around her a little, trying to make small talk which she ignored. The worst possible exercise of reparation was a spree of expensive dining and purposeless shopping, ending, as soon as they returned home, with a wild bout of love-making. A man of small mind and large, extravagant gestures alternating between the coldness of the first and the intensity of the second, completely bereft of humour's saving grace, he had, from the very start of their marriage, shriveled up all her creative energies.

Thankfully, these could be brought back to life in her classroom. She once read an article in an educational magazine about overzealous teachers forgetting the real needs of their students; it had the very captivating title 'The Geranium on the Window-Sill Died, but Teacher, You Went Right on Talking!' The geranium on the window sill of her awful marriage would do its own watering and never allow itself to shrivel.

There had been a single fearful moment when that almost happened. When her husband one day said, very casually, about two years into their marriage, 'Dear, there's something maybe we ought to talk about,' her own suspicions were sharpened into the quivering alertness of a small animal poised for fight or flight.

For some time she had known it was coming. *I want you to quit your teaching job.* He left the second part of his wish unuttered. *So that you can stay at home and concentrate on being a good wife to me.* There had been a long preamble about how he was expecting a promotion on the recommendation of Dr Phang, and they would be able to live on his salary, also about how Dr Phang's cousin's wife who was a bank executive readily gave up her job to have more time for her husband. Then he delivered the coup de grâce. *With your being so busy at your job, how can you have a baby?* Her first reaction was an inward screaming protest, for to all the oppressions of her marriage would be added the supreme one of financial dependence, translated into the daily humiliation of stretching out her hand for money to go shopping for groceries, to pay the maid, to buy things for her mother and Por Por, to go for the occasional lunch with her friends.

Without a word, she rushed to the bathroom, locked the door, stood in front of the mirror, stared at the pale, stricken face staring back, and then fell into uncontrollable sobbing. It was a kind of wrenching, wracking misery that she had never experienced before. She was aware of her husband pacing the floor outside the locked door, of his saying, 'Come out, there's no need for all that.' Apparently shocked at her reaction, he never raised the subject again. That night, he made a few attempts to caress her body which was resolutely turned away from him. She longed to go to the spare bedroom, but that further act of defiance would create its own storm of discord which she simply would not have the energy to handle. She had done it once, not daring to lock the door; he had appeared in the middle of the night, a dark austere figure in the doorway, and she had got up and returned silently to their bedroom. In a comfortable, well-appointed apartment that he had specifically taken out a huge loan to buy for her after marriage, the old yearning was still there: if only I had a bed of my own, a room of my own, a house of my own.

She remembered a scene in a movie in which a weary wife, asked what she liked best about her husband, had replied promptly, 'His absence.'

The witticism had at the time amused her greatly, and was readily shared with girlfriends. Later, in the quiet of her reflections, she saw the serious side of the ontological absurdity as it applied to her own situation: her husband's absence from home for a weekend, on a trip with his boss for a conference in Jakarta, was a reality all its own, claiming its own existence and presence. In her imagination, the welcome absence became a solid gift, a magnificent *ang pow* of unending cash, enclosed in the brightest of red gift paper, that she could spend as she liked.

On the happiest spending spree in her life, she returned to the long girlhood walks in the Botanic Gardens, which he never allowed her to visit unless in his company, read for long hours curled up on the large king-size bed now all her own, and, best of all, made an appointment with the reluctant publisher to try to make him change his mind. She made the phone call for the appointment from Emily's house, just in case the maid or her mother let slip the information in her husband's hearing, and there was the whole tedious explanation to go through afterwards. The rare joy of the weekend only emphasised the oppression of the days ahead. I'm not sure I can continue living like this, she thought miserably. The Catholic woman, enjoined to live with her husband till death did them part, could be condemned to a death-like existence till the end of her days.

As a child she had hated the temple visits that Por Por had forced upon her, and the endless visits with her mother during the Chinese New Year season to the homes of relatives she had never seen before, stiff in a ridiculous dress of lace and ruffles that her mother had made on an old sewing machine, with large pockets to receive the New Year *ang pows* which she promptly handed to her mother as soon as they got home, before Heng, even then already on the look-out for gain, could lay his hands on them. In a fit of bad temper, she would, halfway down the road, abruptly remove her hand from Por Por's or drag her feet along the ground as she walked beside her mother. Sometimes she sat down resolutely on the ground and refused to get up.

Her mother would jab her forehead with a forefinger screaming, 'Why are you like that? Do you want to end up like Por Por?'

Por Por who was born and brought up in China was the black sheep who was now paying, with her dreadful premature dementia, for her sins of rebelliousness: there were whispers of her once running away from home to hide in a temple. In a long line of docile females going back to the ancestral country, the bad trait had surfaced in one member, skipped a generation and was now threatening to show itself again. Her mother said, as she would say many times, 'Why can't you be like others? Why are you so difficult?' A warm affinity with Por Por would grow with the years.

The reluctance and hatred were multiplied a hundredfold in the forced visits to his office parties, the lunches given by his boss, the visits to the hospital for his regular health checks, the Bible study classes he conducted, where she sat at the back, squirming at his poor presentation and feeling sorry for him because of the humiliatingly small attendance of four, then two and finally one. It would be too much of an ignominy for him to learn from her some of the skills she had honed to perfection in the classroom. It was a draining, not cleansing pity, and she wanted to run away and never come back. She had kept alive the girlhood hero of her imagination: a paragon of strength, intelligence, high-mindedness, courage and charm, he inspired breathless admiration and respect, never shamefaced pity and embarrassment.

In a roomful of people, she was aware of her husband looking around for her, of his suddenly looking very alert whenever he caught her in conversation with a man. 'How he loves you,' laughed one of her friends at a party. 'My husband won't even notice if I go off home on my own now!'

Love carried its own burden of insecurities. He had won her in marriage at great cost, and he intended that she should pay for it.

St Peter's School with its Christian strictures should be reassuring even to the most jealous husband, but her many hours there gave rise to any number of anxieties about what she could be doing out of his sight.

She had once, in playful banter very early on in their marriage, told him about her enormous charm, if the students were right, for Mr Chin, the maths teacher, and Brother Philip, the moral education teacher, for indeed, she herself was beginning to notice the many excuses each made to talk to her. In the midst of a chuckle, she realised her mistake. She stopped, suddenly looking very foolish, as she avoided the eyes now narrowing in disapproval and the lips tightening in angry silence. With forced jocularity, she went on to talk about something else. It had been a disastrous blunder, calling for the greatest care in its repair. She continued chatting about inconsequential things, she asked if he wanted his favourite Japanese tea, she made a few desultory inquiries about his revered boss, the high-achieving Dr Phang who he once told her with undisguised awe was being considered by the Deputy Prime Minister to join the party and run in the next general elections. Even that subject failed to draw him out of the sullen silence. She was aware, with a sickening feeling, of her small voice now reduced to helpless silence against the chill wall of his displeasure. The silence continued and she made a mental note never to mention any of her male colleagues at St Peter's again.

She was looking at herself in the dressing-table mirror, surveying with a smile the lustrous hair shaken loose from the ponytail now curled upon her bare shoulders. In a school camping trip before her marriage, as she sat with colleagues and students around a campfire, Maggie, always seeking to create diversion, crept up behind her back, and suddenly removed the clip holding her ponytail, unloosing a mass of hair that tumbled on to her shoulders in further demonstration of her natural beauty. Everyone cheered and clapped, including Brother Philip. 'Please, Miss Seetoh, leave it like this, you look so-oo sexy!' cried Maggie, holding the clip out of her reach. There were some minutes of childish fun as the clip was passed from hand to hand. It ended in Brother Philip's, and he returned it to her, laughing.

Her husband was standing at the doorway and looking at her. 'I see you're changing your hairstyle.' *Just what are you trying to prove. What is this all about. What is in your mind. You think I am stupid, don't you.* She hated the questions loaded with the biting sarcasm, born of the endless suspicions. She had no idea that the small casual reference to the putative admirers at St Peter's just a few days ago was rankling so badly. 'Has it anything to do with that admiring Mr Chin and Brother Philip?' She made a mental note never again to refer to any acquaintance so long as it was a male.

Once she was late home from school by a full hour. When his calls home went unanswered, he rang the school, and had to call again because the school clerk said Mrs Tan could not be found.

When he got her at last, he said sternly, 'Where were you? I called home three times and the school twice.'

She had had an urgent, unscheduled meeting regarding some national seminar that her students were taking part in, called at the last minute by Brother Philip who of course she could not mention. 'Then you should have called me at the office to let me know,' he said.

Professing an indifference to literature, he had saved some of her favourite literary quotations to throw back at her. She had tried to explain at length the reason for something she had done – something so trivial she had difficulty remembering it – and he had turned to her and said with a tight smile, 'My, my, the lady doth protest too much!' He had turned her beloved Bard from tonic to toxic.

Silence remained the best option. I live in fear of my husband's daily displeasure, she thought miserably. What sort of life is this? I am truly dying. That night he made love to her as usual, briefly and sullenly, and without a word. Then he turned his back towards her and remained in that position through the night. The spare bedroom called, but she was tied down on the marital bed by a hundred cords of fear tightening by the day.

The next morning, as usual, he dressed carefully to go to the office, again not saying a word as they had breakfast together. He took only a few spoonfuls of the hot rice porridge that was their breakfast every morning.

'Are you aware,' he said slowly, stressing every syllable, as he stood up, and she knew that another paralysing chill was about to descend, 'that for the last few months I have had exactly the same thing placed before me every morning?' Another truth about her unfitness as a wife and homemaker confronted her. She thought, I'm glad I'm not a mother as well. Zero out of three in her report card would be irredeemable failure.

The rice porridge with the pickled leek, the fried anchovies and peanuts, favourite traditional breakfast fare going back through revered generations, was now a symbol of a wife's shameful incompetence and worse, indifference. The preparation of the breakfast was the daily duty of Por Por who took on this one chore in the household with great pride, being incapable of everything else through increasing dementia. The rice porridge, like so many other absurdly small things in their marriage, had become yet one more occasion for marital discord.

She had almost wanted to scream at him: well, dammit, let us know what you want, instead of keeping silent these long weeks and then coming out with all the accusations! The angry words were swallowed back as soon as they formed on her tongue. It was no use. He was sure to respond by referring back to a time when he had mentioned this or that wish, and she had nodded, only to forget it promptly.

Trying to remember each act of disobedience as he dragged it up from his unforgiving memory, only added to the confusion and bumbling which gave the impression of culpability, so that in the end, she always fell back, exhausted, upon a heap of futile words.

The devoted Mr Chin had once managed to persuade her to accept a lift home. She asked to be dropped at a point well away from her house. Days after that, her husband had asked her very casually as they were getting ready for bed, 'What were you doing on Kiam Hoot Road?' and he mentioned the day and hour.

A little tremor of anxiety gripped her, as her memory sprang into rapid recall and remained blank. One of his friends must have seen her and casually told him. Her confused look and hesitant answer confirmed his suspicions, and he said curtly, 'We'll not talk any more about the matter.' What are you implying, she screamed silently. It was always the uncompleted response, locked inside her throat, increasingly charged with bitter anger.

In a dream that night, she taunted him, 'Yes, it was Brother Philip!' He asked, 'Did he do anything to you in the car?' and she said even more tauntingly, 'Of course he did.' Brother Philip became Mr Chin who became the principal who melted into Tony Curtis, in a mocking phantasmagoria of suspected lovers from St Peter's Secondary School. She woke up with a start, to see her sleeping husband beside her, and took care not to make the slightest noise or movement, for even in sleep, a possessing arm would be flung upon her body.

She had made the supreme mistake, one evening, of talking at length on the phone with Brother Philip. School business ended as soon as she reached home; no student had her phone number. The call, about a camping trip that Brother Philip was organising for some students and wanted to consult her about, was actually a welcome diversion. She was aware that her husband was not only listening, but observing her intently. She told herself: remember, keep a straight face, no laughter, no smiles, no sharing of witty jokes or student absurdities, only focused business talk.

He asked, as expected, when she put down the phone, 'What was that all about?' She told him.

'Why on earth would anyone want to consult you on a camping trip to Indonesia?' Sometimes the sarcasm was allowed to end, sometimes it became the trigger for a larger accusation. He said, without looking at her, 'You know the truth? Let me tell you the truth. You are too preoccupied with your schoolwork, your creative writing, your reading all those clever books.' Taking on a life of its own, each favoured activity loomed as a hateful rival. If she lovingly nurtured a little plant in a pot, it would become a rival too.

In remonstrance, she would say, 'But –' and immediately recoiled before the confronting chill of his resentment. He never let the anger get in the way of the unfailing soft voice and civil language, so that her mother, listening anxiously outside their locked door, would think with relief that they had made up and fallen asleep together. In measured tones, his glasses glinting ominously, he reminded her of her persistent dereliction of wifely duty, citing a dozen examples in addition to the porridge episode, that she could not even remember, and she would be silenced for the rest of the day, left to her own vexed thoughts.

The most carefully rehearsed rejoinder to the accusations would be stopped even before the opening word by the sheer weight of the cold anger as he stood in judgement before her.

'I had specifically told you to make out a cheque to Third Aunt. That was ten days ago. She called this afternoon to say she hasn't received it.' But, but. *But it's a huge sum, more than we can afford! Besides, you didn't make it very clear. You said if she were to ask again, and she never did, and so I* – The large sums he was magnanimously dispensing to his relatives and the church charities were an alarming strain on their joint, by no means substantial income.

Her friend Emily had said, 'Every family has its parasites; you can be thankful you have only his Third Aunt in Malaysia.' Not particularly interested in money matters, she was aware that they were spending beyond their means.

Her brother Heng, who tactlessly pried into her finances, had advised her more than once, 'Have a separate bank account, your own money. You never know.' He added, 'Ah Siong is not a gambler or a womaniser, but he likes to act like a big shot, treating his friends and colleagues to dinners and drinks in fancy restaurants. How much do you manage to save a month, the two of you, without any children? Tell him you want to start your own account. I can get my bank manager to get you the best terms.'

He was involved in some businesses which he never spoke about except when he made money, just as he remained uncommunicative about his wife and young son who lived with his in-laws in Malaysia. Their mother had once mentioned that the boy was 'not well', then gestured with finger against lip that no more was to be said or asked about the matter.

Heng called a few days later to find out if she had taken his advice about setting up her own personal bank account. She hadn't. 'Well, don't blame me if anything happens.' His responses to his sister's failure to act upon his advice ranged from a resigned 'I tried my best' to an angry 'well, I wash my hands off you!'

It would be impossible for her to broach the sensitive subject of money with her husband, for his questions, always charged with suspicions, would escalate into a full inquisition that would wear her out.

It was simply amazing – the gap between the outward docility and the inward rage. She lived in a double-truth world. If one day I should write the story of my life, she thought, as she took out her husband's shoes to polish, hating their very sight. She had been doing the daily polishing since he told her the maid didn't do it properly. *I never asked you*, he would have protested. *But you expected it, and would have sulked if I didn't*, she would have replied. *There you are, unwilling to do such a little thing for your husband. You forget the many things I have done for you. Oh? Just name me one. Just one*, he would have sneered. *You are a heartless bastard*, she would have sneered back.

Imaginary arguments went on in her head, endlessly, sometimes continuing into her dreams, because real ones were no longer possible. Imagination, wit, a sense of humour – all were sorely needed if she wrote her life story and described the negotiating of two such different worlds. If, like the meticulous author, she kept little cards to remind her of the incidents to go into her life story, they would bear the most absurd headings: 'Incident of Porridge', 'Incident of (Un)Polished Shoes', 'Incident of Too-Transparent, Green Blouse', 'Incident of Wrong Telephone Number and Pathetic Indian Caller'. She had picked up the phone one evening; the caller had got the wrong number but pleaded with her to hear his story, a terrible one of loneliness and heartbreak, that lasted a full hour. Her husband checked the phone bills not for purposes of economy but for monitoring her calls, especially long outstation calls.

'Would you have listened in sympathy to *me* for an hour?' he had said.

She thought of wives whose energies were channelled, almost effortlessly, into streams of pure attention and devotion, while her husband stood in the aridity of her detachment and indifference. They were well-educated wives who could have had illustrious careers, like Dr Phang's cousin's wife, but chose to be at home to serve their husbands' every wish. During attendance at mass in the Church of Eternal Mercy, sitting beside her husband, she would observe the other wives sitting beside theirs, and conclude they were as loving and compliant as she was indifferent and defiant. Their marriages were peaceful havens, as hers was a storm-tossed vessel far out at sea. It served her right to have embraced an institution for which she had neither talent nor disposition.

She had sworn to love, honour and obey her husband; true to all three vows in the eyes of the world, she had in truth broken them all in the privacy of her own. The outward pretence could not be long maintained; soon he, alert, proud, sensitive, would have to hold her to a true accounting: *did you love me at all? Why did you marry me?*

Six

The silence continued all the way in the car as he drove her to school, and was broken twice, very briefly, by a grievance that was mounting by the day. The car had stopped at a traffic junction that faced a row of rundown shophouses that would soon be demolished to make way for a shopping mall. In an unguarded sharing of secrets very early in their marriage, she had pointed out one of the shophouses as the scene of a silly girlhood romance, where a young man named Kuldeep Singh used to take her for ice cream after school. Her husband had said nothing then, but retrospective jealousy, summoning back the past for present accounting, could be even more fearsome. Thereafter, each time the car stopped at the traffic junction in full view of the offensive house, she would look down, to her left through the car window, into her handbag, anywhere but in the direction of the shophouse, aware of the sideways glance that he was casting at her. Every small act of hers became a test of wifely propriety, subjected to the merciless analysis of a love turned forensic.

That morning, her thoughts being very far away, her eyes inadvertently rested on the forbidden object of the shophouse; worse, the thoughts suddenly took a turn for tender recollection as in her mind appeared an image of herself and Kuldeep Singh in their school uniforms, perched on high stools at the ice cream bar, foreheads almost touching as they sipped, through two long straws, a single glass of ice cream soda. Kuldeep had confessed to being completely broke, but a riffling of the pocket of his uniform, and then of hers, had produced a small handful of coins that was enough to pay for one soda. Out in the bright sunshine, Kuldeep suddenly had an idea, his eyes shining with mischief. He pulled out a small penknife from his pocket.

'See, I'm leaving a mark of remembrance of our happy day.' He carved a large X sign on a corner of the wall near the bar entrance, and had another idea. 'Come here,' he said to her. 'Here, hold the penknife. Like this. Now I'm holding your hand, and we carve together.'

He was duplicating the supreme wedding moment when, in smiling union, groom and bride cut the bridal cake together. 'You're crazy,' she giggled but complied. 'Look out,' she hissed, and they fled. The sign could still be seen, twenty-three years later.

The tiny smile at the recollection had escaped too quickly for her to stop it. Her husband said, 'What was that smile about?'

There was a vast stock of student howlers that she could resort to, and she said, 'I was just thinking of that awful student I told you about, Maggie, and her atrocious grammatical mistakes –', and hated herself for the lie. The stock was cooperatively inexhaustible but was rapidly losing its usefulness.

Her husband said again, more pointedly, 'What was that smile about?' and she lapsed into wordless misery which, in the few minutes before they arrived at her school, became large tears filling her eyes. She made no attempt to wipe them off.

'What are you crying about?' he said, in the closest to a snarl that his habitual politeness would allow. 'One would think that it's *you* who's the victim in this marriage.'

At the school gate, as she got out of the car, the tears having been hurriedly blinked back, she made a feeble attempt at normalcy. She said, 'There'll be a staff meeting that will probably last two hours or longer. I'll be late home. Shall I call you at your office?' and he said, 'You do whatever suits you,' and drove off.

That night the lovemaking was horrible for the intrusion of the afternoon's jealous suspicion which worked itself into what seemed like a manic reclamation of her body. It ended in a wash of self-pity, as he whimpered, rolling off her, 'If I don't satisfy you, you can go back to that Sikh boyfriend of yours.' He was not done. He took the bathos of self-pity to the histrionics of desperate self-abasement, comparing his small build to the amazing, ethnic-joke proportions and prowess of the Sikh, then of the Caucasian male, and cried out, repeatedly and tearfully, 'Tell me the truth; after your Kuldeep, after your Brother Philip, am I a disappointment?'

If she feared a coldly judgemental husband, she was repelled by an abjectly whimpering one. Her marriage had become pure grotesquerie. She got up, rushed to the bathroom, closed the door and expelled her revulsion, which came out in a swift stream, into the toilet bowl.

The bathroom, scene of so many private miseries, had become her most dependable room. Affinity between a lost person seeking protection and an inanimate object offering it could actually grow: in the early hours of a morning, she had sat on the cover of the toilet seat for a full hour, frantically working on the setting of an examination paper due the next morning for the school typist to type and print out. On another occasion, still secure in her hiding place, she had gone through, for the second time, a marvelous story a student in the creative writing class had submitted, and written a whole page of encouraging comments. Both times, thankfully, her husband was still peacefully sleeping when she completed the job and climbed silently back into bed.

The accidental meeting with Kuldeep in a restaurant some weeks later could not have come at a worse time. They were sitting at a table, looking at the menu, and he was telling her about a special project that the admired Dr Phang was entrusting him with over the heads of at least two senior officers. He was in a good mood and summoned the waiter to ask if he could make a special order for his wife's favourite pork rib soup that was not on that evening's menu.

Then Kuldeep strode up to her, bellowing, 'Hey, Maria Seetoh! Do you remember me? Imagine meeting you after all these years!'

Of course she remembered him, at once seeing the handsome beaming confidence superimposed upon the schoolboy's scrawny limbs and untidy uniform. She greeted him joyfully, not daring to return the effusive hug, and instantly turned to her husband to introduce him. 'This is my husband, Bernard.'

But Kuldeep's attention was all for her. 'Hey, Maria, you are as pretty as ever! What are you doing now – we must meet to catch up with all the news and gossip – I am now with Carlton and Wu –' His genuine joy in seeing her, his eagerness to let her in on his good fortune of an eminently happy marriage blessed with three sons and a senior position in one of Singapore's most prestigious law firms, completely obliterated her husband nearby, now dangerously glowering. 'Here's my card, give me your phone number, we really must catch up,' said the irrepressible Kuldeep and left.

In a second he was back, exclaiming, 'Hey, do you remember the X sign we made that day on the wall of The Rendezvous Bar? Remember, we had to run away real fast!' He turned to Bernard, speaking to him for the first time, needing a larger audience for the happy recounting of the past: 'We were crazy! We cut the sign, holding hands like a pair of idiots.' Roaring with laughter, he turned to face Maria again and said, 'You know what? It's still there – we must go back to have a look – we really must catch up –' He had completely ruined the evening for them. They ate the rest of their dinner in silence.

The next day she made use of the two free periods in between classes to go to the library where, under the pretext of consulting some reference book, she could take deep breaths, calm down and organise her thoughts and feelings into some coherent pattern. She had reached a point in her marriage when something had to happen, to rescue her from it. The cage, the net, the bell jar, the dark cave from which no shackled prisoner could escape into the sunlight – all were feeble images for her desperation for release.

At the centre of the tumult was a tiny, tremulous hope: suppose her husband realised that he could not go on in the marriage and decided that a divorce was best? His strong Catholicism forbade that, but suppose his need to be happy was stronger? Beyond the shock of his fellow churchgoers, the parish priest Father Rozario, her friends and, above all, her mother, would be all happiness for her. She would wear the scandal like a badge because it announced the opening of her brave new world.

There were some Catholic couples in the parish who had separated, were no longer living together, but who continued to be devout Catholics. Separation which would still mean the continuance of that hateful MRS would also mean the end of a hateful life. She did not have the strength or courage to initiate the move, but suppose he, coming to the end of the marital tether, did?

A coward's wish. She told her students stirring stories of honesty and courage, and in the privacy of her imagination, the coward's dream played out, one after the other. So: her husband told her they had best live separately, even if the church did not allow them to divorce; her husband managed to convince Father Rozario that they had married under unacceptable circumstances leaving the church authorities no choice but to accept the reason of non-consummation to dissolve the marriage; her husband had found another woman whom he loved deeply and truly, and quietly made arrangements for their separate lives, even paying for her to do her postgraduate degree course at the Singapore University. Each scenario ended with her saying, 'Thank you,' in profound gratitude.

The coward could be capable of self-blame. Too late, yet so soon, she had realised the great injustice she had done him in marrying him. She never loved him, not when she married him, not afterwards. It was possible – a modern, educated, intelligent woman marrying a man even when she did not love him, and thereafter drifting along in a one-sided marriage with all the passion on his side, and all the regret on hers. The modern woman's mother or grandmother had had no choice; she abused hers and then found she had to live with the consequences.

She remembered a survey in which three quarters of the women surveyed stated that if divorced or widowed, they would never marry again. Some gave the most ridiculous reasons for getting married in the first place, the most common being the desirability of the married state itself. *I wanted children. I wanted to get away from over-strict parents. I was tired of society labelling me a spinster. All my girlfriends had already got married. It seemed the right and necessary thing for a woman to do.*

She had a girlfriend who decided to get married because she had won a beautiful bridal dress in a competition run by a woman's magazine, another because the man had a car whereas the other two suitors had only motorcycles, yet another because as a single woman she would not have qualified to buy a government-subsidised flat that she very much desired. She knew of women who got married because they could no longer tolerate the inevitable nosiness of aunts during the Chinese New Year season when unmarried women, regardless of age, were still strictly entitled to receive the traditional gifts of money, 'So when I see you next year, will you be giving instead of receiving *ang pows?*'

There were any number of substitutes for love, revealed by the survey. *I was grateful to him because he had helped pay for my university education. He was the handsomest boy in our group and one day he asked me to marry him, and everyone was so jealous! We were dating for eleven years and one day he said to me, 'We should get married before my grandmother passes away.' He was fantastic in bed! He bought me the most beautiful engagement ring from Hong Kong. He was only one of two persons to get a first class degree from the university, and was offered a scholarship to do a PhD.*

All the absurd causes of her husband's annoyance and displeasure occurring almost on a daily basis – the porridge, his futile calls to her in school, her forgetfulness about this or that, Mr Chin, Brother Philip, her creative writing class, her meetings with the publisher, the shoes not polished right, a wrong telephone call, anything at all – they were laughably trivial, and under different circumstances could have had the opposite effect of creating lively husband-wife raillery. A pet cat fussed over, a little plant lovingly tended – her husband would have crushed them underfoot for taking away the love that should be his. In the absence of love in a marriage, anything could be a trigger for its grievance.

For three years, he had laboured under that grievance. If hate was the other side of love's coin, then his was a huge disc, daily flashed at her, glinting with menace. She told herself she did not, would not, could not love him, astonished at the full range of the brutal auxiliaries. What had she done to him? Within a year, his placid countenance had hardened into a rictus of cynicism and frustration unsoftened even in sleep.

He was exacting a price, and she was ready to pay it. She had done injury to the sacred institution itself, and should, at the least, accord it future respect by never marrying again. If she wanted a new life, completely free of falsehood and all that it brought of confusion, pain and shame, a life as radiant with joy, pride and certainty, as it was now dark with deceit and torment, she would have to begin with nothing less than kneeling before him with a devastating confession of the truth and bow her head to the thunderbolts of his wrath. As he once knelt before her to declare the fullness of his love, she would, by the same ultimate gesture, nullify and void hers. As she was clearer in writing than in speech, she might write him a letter, a very long one, to systematically apologise for the wrongs over three years, beginning with the supreme one of agreeing to marry him. All the others had simply flowed from it. It would not matter if every word in the letter became a bitter pill forced into her mouth, to cleanse her heart of its ills, her soul of its darkness, so that she could rise to a new brightness.

She had once read a story of a woman who was so unhappy in her marriage that she wanted to run away with a man whom she met when she was thirty years old and who became her secret lover. But fear – of her husband, their relatives, his friends, her friends, society at large – held her back; she said goodbye to the lover and continued in her loveless, soulless marriage till her death, thirty years later. Upon her death, she had the following epitaph inscribed on her tombstone: 'She died at thirty, and was buried at sixty.'

In her life she was to look many times, with fearful, honest eyes, into the embarrassing truths about herself. With missionary zeal, even from childhood, she had set out her life's shining goal – to be a really good, a really happy person – and then floundered all the way. Be honest, be authentic, be yourself, she urged her students, and herself turned away from the mirror of the myriad painful truths of her marriage. When she summoned enough courage to do so, they became her own small humbling lights on her own personal road to Damascus.

Did you ever love me? Why did you marry me? At the very end, she was forced to tell the truth: *I felt sorry for you.* Pity was the least acceptable substitute for love. No man would accept it. He flung it back at her. His pride rose to reject it as a lie. He did not, would not, could not believe her. But by then it was too late.

Seven

In July 1989, Maria Seetoh was helping her friend Winnie in a great scheme for a marriage which never took place, just five months before her own which she would never have believed possible.

Winnie Poon, forty years-old, had discreetly found out that the matchmaking agency set up by the government was not interested in single women of her age group, but soon found another avenue for energies exclusively devoted to freeing herself from that maligned label. Trembling with excitement, she secured the help of her two close friends, Maria Seetoh and Meeta Nair, the latter being also her colleague at Palm Secondary School. All three single women took different positions with regard to a status that was increasingly the subject of nationwide concern. Unlike the anxious Winnie, Maria Seetoh, aged thirty-five, cheerfully declared she would always remain a happy single, while Meeta Nair, aged forty-four, claiming a gallery of rejected beaus, wore the derisory label with self-assured panache and noisy good humour. Both women were only too happy to help Winnie in her scheme, Maria out of sheer curiosity, Meeta out of an amiability that included the expectation of witnessing yet one more fiasco in poor Winnie's hapless search for love.

The three women knocked on the door of the little room tucked inside the vast darkness of the White Heaven Temple, and a very old, quavering voice said in an obscure Chinese dialect, 'Come in!' It belonged to a very old, wizened Chinese woman, indistinguishable from a man because of her shaved head and loose yellow robe, sitting at a table heaped with the paraphernalia of her art. Surrounded by curls of whitish, fragrant smoke, her eyes closed and hands clasped upon her chest, she might have been some deity newly descended from heaven to do earth's bidding. It was whispered that she was Singapore's most revered fortune-teller, and had been around for so long that nobody knew her age, only that families had sought her help through three generations.

Maria Seetoh suspected that Por Por in her time had consulted the old woman, and her mother too, before the dramatic conversion to Christianity. Mrs Seetoh Bee Liew renamed Mrs Anna Mary Seetoh, stopped going to temple fortune-tellers, now banned practitioners of the devil's arts, but continued to consult knowledgeable English-educated psychics who must know something of God's mysteries. Neither camp had been helpful in her efforts to make her errant husband mend his ways, or to find out where he was in hiding with his mistress.

Behind the old woman stood a middle-aged man with thick glasses and a dour look. He spoke hesitant but intelligible English and was presumably her translator, as all and sundry from the society's plethora of races and languages came to consult her. It was whispered that even the great TPK had once paid her a visit in the secrecy of night, but then people could have confused her with another illustrious fortune-teller, a monk who lived in Taiwan but flew regularly to Singapore to tell the fortunes of the great and powerful in society, including the political leaders and business tycoons. Or they could have confused TPK, ever the stern, no-nonsense rationalist, with his wife, a gentle, nervous woman who, it was said, was much dependent on fortune-tellers and psychics because of constant bad health. The whole society, it would appear, was in thrall to the power of myth and magic as it was to the power of scientific technology; gleaming glass-and-steel towers comported well with ancient temples and shrines and the occasional makeshift altar at spots where sudden healing springs of water appeared, or an image of the Monkey God upon a gnarled tree trunk, inviting devotees and seekers of winning lottery numbers.

The old fortune-teller in White Heaven Temple, who was said to be as old as the hundred-year-old temple tortoises and who wanted only to be known as Venerable Mother, never asked Winnie any questions, never read her palm or the lines of her face, never required her to cast the fortune sticks or do anything with the immense pile of holy artefacts on the table, including urns of joss-sticks, rows of silk scrolls, prayer bells, golden lotuses, and images of a hundred deities. Therein lay her unique power. Winnie only had to close her eyes, put her hands together in worshipful attitude and state her wish in the silence of her heart. After some minutes, the old one stood up and came to her, laid a withered hand on her head, raised wide open eyes to heaven and muttered something. She nodded to her attendant who came forward with a small casket of ivory discs and asked Winnie to pick one, which he then matched to one of numerous small rolls of pink paper heaped together in a basket. He gave Winnie the paper, Venerable Mother once more closed her eyes, took up her prayerful position under a huge framed picture of a black-faced warrior deity, and the consultation was over.

Out in the sunshine, the three women crowded together to read the message. Maria Seetoh, who instinctively applied the teacher's corrective red pencil to every piece of print, including the little slips of paper in fortune cookies carrying extravagant tributes and promises, always read with suppressed amusement, the inevitable howlers when the lofty idioms and metaphors of one culture were forced into the grammatical patterns of another. She saved the best in a notebook for sharing with students to provide comic relief during particularly heavy-going language or literature lessons.

Out of the many arcane references to bright mountains, roaring seas, bamboo trees that died, bamboo trees that revived themselves, a great white pearl lying hidden in a muddy river bank, one sentence stood out and made Winnie squeal in delight: 'I only had one wish as I prayed – you know what it is.'

Meeta said, 'Alright, alright, we all know you want Teik to propose to you.'

Winnie went on, her eyes shining, 'See this sentence, it says 'Three heartaches gone, then the full heart is rejoicing with the fourth.' You remember all three, don't you, how it didn't work out each time, how miserable I was.'

Meeta said, 'We warned you, didn't we, Maria? All of them useless bums, taking advantage of your generosity. That Benny Ee, the worst of all. Sponge Number One.'

Winnie said, 'Three heartaches over. Then my heart will rejoice with the fourth. And you know what? Today's the *fourth* of July, exactly *four* months since meeting Teik. And you know what, his name means 'bamboo'.' She added, simpering a little, 'He has as good as proposed. Remember the pearl necklace I told you about?'

She was wearing it, and pulled it out of the lacy ruffles of her collar to show it. Every gift from a male acquaintance, no matter how small, was a foretaste of the ultimate one – the formal declaration of love and proposal. Winnie Poon's entire life was organised around that one wish. She looked again at the precious pink slip in her hand, staring wide-eyed at the reference to the pearl. 'How on earth would Venerable Mother know about the necklace?' Picking out each truth revealed by the prophecy on the slip of pink paper was exhilarating, and kept the dream alive.

Meeta later whispered to Maria, 'A cheap one, you know, one of those that you get as a free gift in Y.K.K. Departmental Store if you spend more than a hundred dollars. Seng's sister got it, and gave it to him. I know because he told me.'

She took delight in being the confidante of shy men who went to women for advice, depressed men who needed the warm motherly shoulder to cry on, guilty men who could never unload their guilt to their own kind, and then took her rich haul of men's secrets to share with her girlfriends. 'Without mentioning names –,' she would begin at each delectable session, usually over high tea, thereby preserving the integrity of the confidante.

She took the private sharing about the pearl necklace to a higher level of malice with a conjecture, 'It's the cheapskate's conscience gift, in return for all those expensive ones she's plied him with – all the ties and cuff links and ginseng and I don't know what else. He will soon dump her, you mark my words.'

Meeta had gone along with Winnie to the fortune-teller, as she had on endless urgent errands in Winnie's restive, cluttered life, to give the poor girl, she said, moral support. It was strange support made up entirely of a severe lecture and much scolding afterwards, which the poor girl received with small, apologetic noises and nervous giggles.

'How can you take all that scolding?' Maria had once asked her.

'It's all for my good. Meeta may scold and nag, but she has the kindest heart and will do anything for me!' Winnie replied.

'How can you treat Winnie like a child?' Maria had asked Meeta, in the double confidante's privileged position of shuttling comfortably between the two unmatched mates.

'Let me tell you this,' said Meeta with haughty authority. 'Without me, Winnie the Blue, Winnie the Blur would be utterly –' She left unfinished the statement of her vast redemptive role in the other's life.

In the quiet of her room, away from her mother's incessant chatter, and the distractions from Por Por who could be worse than a disruptive child, Maria wrote a short story which she later tore up as being just too mean. It was about two diametrically opposed individuals – in character, personality, disposition and appearance, down to details of height, build, voice, dress, hairstyle. As Maria wrote, there flashed in her mind the image of Meeta Nair, nearly six feet tall, large and imposing in her colourful saris, with hair perfectly dressed in a sleek bun always decorated with a diamante clip, loud of voice and hearty of laugh, completely eclipsing the tiny, fragile-looking Winnie Poon in her silly little-girl dresses, with her light scanty hair, pale face, thin lips inexpertly smeared with some brownish lipstick, quizzical clown eyebrows and restive fingers always tugging at something. 'I don't know how she ever became a teacher,' Meeta had said once. 'The students show her no respect. I had to teach her the basics of classroom control.'

Fiction coincided perfectly with fact to produce a detailed

description of the terracehouse jointly rented by the two women, which Maria had visited a few times, with the main sitting room wall dominated by images of Hindu gods and a huge framed portrait of the great Sai Baba in the act of administering a blessing, a gigantic garland around his shoulders. Facing the wall was a sideboard on which stood a silver cross mounted on a white marble orb, and a large, leather-bound Bible, both belonging to Winnie.

'You know what all this means?' The liberal-minded Meeta would say to surprised guests, her hand doing an immense sweep to take in the entire panoply of religious objects. A deliberate demonstration of the eclecticism that should rule Singapore society, instead of the narrow-minded bigotry. She said to Maria, chuckling, 'Every morning I bow before my Sai Baba and kiss his portrait, then I turn and bow to the cross. If your Por Por gives me one of her Kuan Yin statues, it too will have place of honour here!' Meeta expected to be invited by the Ministry of National Affairs to be a member of the Council for Religious Harmony. 'I'd love to sit down with those stodgy priests, imams and pastors, and shock them with a truth or two!'

Every day, as soon as the two housemates returned home from school, they changed into casual wear: Meeta into a cotton caftan as colourful as her sari, and Winnie into her flannel housecoat. Each had a clearly demarcated part of the shared house, in an arrangement that roughly reflected their physical proportions, Meeta having the largest of the three bedrooms, the larger bathroom, and the larger share of refrigerator space for her special vegetarian fare, healthful yoghurts and face creams.

Each kept strictly to her apportioned space, but met for afternoon tea and dinner prepared by their jointly employed Filipino maid Philomena, as well as for the frequent consultations requested by Winnie who would knock gently on Meeta's door and ask deferentially, 'Meeta, may I come in? I need your advice,' and the other would emerge, sometimes with a show of weary resignation as she said, 'Alright, what now, Winnie girl,' and prepared to play her role as advisor, mentor and guide all over again.

They had been brought together not only by a social status maligned by the society, but by an agreeable mesh of opposites that complemented and fed each other in perfect co-dependence, like that of the bully and the weakling, the imposter and the gull, drifting naturally together. Out of the enormous differences was forged an unbreakable loyalty and generosity.

Meeta once nursed Winnie through a serious illness, taking extended leave from school to stay with her in hospital when her own sisters were unable to do so. 'I had no time for anything else,' she said later. 'I was running here and there, doing this and that, like a mad woman, just wanting poor Winnie to recover from the operation. My hair, my nails, were a mess. Even Dr Pillay noticed. He said to me, 'Promise me that the next time you come to see Winnie, you will look your usual self.' 'Promise!' She went to offer prayers, on Winnie's behalf, in a Hindu temple.

Winnie, on her part, once saved Meeta's father from bankruptcy by giving her a large sum of money from the proceeds of a rubber plantation left by an uncle in Malaysia. She whispered the sum into Maria's ear, and watched her wide-eyed reaction. 'Don't tell anybody, not even your mother,' she said. 'And don't tell Meeta that I've told you. She doesn't want anybody to know.'

Maria thought with twinkling mischief: 'Well, she didn't say, 'Don't tell your brother,' so it will be okay to tell Heng, watch his face contort with trying to digest the sum and hear him call Winnie a mad woman!'

Fiction departed from fact only in the ending of the story, when one of the women got married, and the other felt so repudiated and hurt that their bond was broken forever. 'Neither of us is likely to get married,' said Meeta. 'I'm so fussy that I'll never find men who will meet my requirements, and Winnie's so keen she frightens them off.'

Winnie did frighten off Teik who not only failed to propose but left Singapore without a word. Weeping silently, incapable of angry recrimination, Winnie left it to Meeta to heap abuse upon the miscreant.

After each failed relationship, Meeta came in to energetically clean up the mess, beginning with the famous scolding lecture, then looking into the messy state of Winnie's finances. '*Aiyoh!*' she would exclaim, laying a dramatic palm on her forehead. 'You wouldn't believe it. I sat down with her for three hours, to straighten out things. That woman could have been cleaned out! If she isn't careful, all that inheritance from her family in Malaysia will be gone.'

She whispered to Maria who felt sorry enough for Winnie to take her out for lunch, 'Relationship? What relationship? It was all in her imagination! He never took her out once on a date. She was the one taking all the initiative, paying for the lunches and dinners, making all the assumptions, buying him those expensive vitamin pills, the expensive Korean ginseng. It was the same with those two others – I can't even remember their names. They took everything, then vamoosed.'

She brought her lips close to Maria's ears, 'Let me tell you this. They took everything except her virginity – they didn't want that!'

'How do you know?' asked Maria, intrigued.

'I know, I know,' said Meeta, giving a knowing wink. When Winnie joined them, she launched on a little homily on women's need to be the hunted, and to take a stance of great aloofness, to whet the chase. 'I blame the government,' she concluded, 'all that fuss about woman needing to get married, and look what's done to our poor deprived Winnie!'

Meeta herself, as Maria privately observed, was capable of the greatest vulnerability of women when they became the hunters: they built a huge superstructure of hope upon a little hint dropped by the man, a little compliment offered in the expansiveness of mood after a good dinner, a cheerful promise to call again that he would promptly forget.

She had occasion to observe this single weakness in the awesome Meeta one evening at the Polo Club to which Meeta, a long-time member, generously invited friends for dinner or drinks, or to watch the monthly movies. At every public place where men walked in and out of rooms, where friends introduced their friends in an ever expanding social circle, both Meeta and Winnie would be completely immobilised into a state of acute expectation as they sat rigidly in their chairs, two statues, except for their eyes moving swiftly here and there, to pick out the presentable male, with an intensity matching that of the predatory lioness crouching in tall grass or the female chimp in oestrus, waiting upon a leafy branch. Completely unlike in every way, they were perfectly united as they looked out for the eligible male in their display of mesmerised anticipation which broke into uncontrolled eagerness as soon as he appeared.

That evening at the Polo Club was exceptional for Meeta's eagerness approaching delirium. There was a good-looking habitué of the club, always seen at the bar, somebody named

Bryan whom she called Byron in teasing tribute both to the resemblance in profile and the aura of romance exuded by his entire person. From the moment she sat down at their dinner table, she was oblivious to everyone else as her eyes did a sweeping survey of the room, then fixed themselves at the entrance. Maria and Winnie began teasing her, but the controlling Meeta Nair was now under the complete control of that one organ of her body, which quickly took on a life of its own, refusing to leave its station at the doorway.

An amusing picture in full technicolor formed in Maria's mind: a stage magician in full regalia of black-and-red cape, top hat and gloves hypnotising Meeta in her beautiful green-and-purple sari and commanding her to do this and that. She walked, bowed, sat, waved her arms, swayed from side to side, lay down on the floor, every part of her body obeying the magician's commands, except her head which moved to a separate command, like a puppet's head on its own strings, jerking and bobbing, twisting and bouncing, to keep the eyes transfixed upon the doorway.

At last Byron made his appearance, a tall, handsome man radiating charm and goodwill as he strode towards the bar in the adjoining room, waving a friendly hand to everybody along the way. By now Meeta's fingers had done their quick check of hair and hair clip, and all her features had tightened into a single expression of hope and yearning; it broke into a burst of smiles when Byron suddenly noticed her and strode towards the table. From then on it was an execution of unabashed purpose that was noticed by the surrounding diners. It embarrassed Maria and amused Winnie who never stopped giggling. Meeta held Byron in the grip of her attention, making him sit down with them at the table, ordering a drink for him, fixing her eyes unwaveringly on him, plying him with a stream of questions and comments which, like a net, held him fast to his seat even as he was looking longingly in the direction of the bar. 'Thanks. Sure, I'll be free for lunch next week; I'll give you a call,' said the affable man, and left hurriedly.

All the way home in her car, the aggressively practical Meeta became the languidly fantasising schoolgirl as she recounted the events of the evening, culminating in that promise of lunch, that promise of a call.

'When he calls, he'll find I'm not one of those easy dates,' she said smiling, as she looked dreamily into the distance. 'Shut up,' she said cheerfully to a car behind, honking impatiently. 'Well, darling,' she continued, still more dreamily, 'as I say, I'm not one of your easy pick-ups, your dime-a-dozen tarts! You'll have to sweat a bit, my dear, and make another call.'

Maria who was sitting beside her in the front passenger seat felt a little poke in the back from Winnie that said, 'Poor Meeta!'

Later that evening, when Meeta was in the shower and out of hearing, she called Maria to say excitedly, 'What do you think? He won't call! You want to take a bet? Did you see how he wasn't even paying her any attention?'

Timid, flustered Winnie had her moments of shrewd observation when she took on a totally different persona, and enjoyed taking revenge for all the humiliations constantly tolerated. Without exactly the ferocity of the worm that turned, she had the satisfaction of the laughing stock sometimes having a few laughs herself. 'He paid more attention to you. Anyone could see that.'

It was always a source of mild amusement to Maria that her girlfriends' boyfriends, at group gatherings, invariably paid her surreptitious attention. One of the men whom Winnie was always picking up and laying claim to, the shamelessly sponging Benny Ee, had actually laid a sly firm hand on her back as he stood next to her for a group photograph.

Meeta would have reported such clandestine acts with uproarious humour to feed her large vanity, watched the look of jealous resentment on the face of her repudiated friend and chortled, 'Dear, dear, don't worry. I'm not a boyfriend stealer. I had enough in my time!' She counted a relative of a maharajah among them.

I don't want all that to be part of my world, thought the peaceful Maria, determined to keep it free of the squalor of petty deceits, rivalries and jealousies. They simply consumed too much precious time and energy. She knew of a group of five women, all securely married, who lunched, played mah-jong and travelled together. They welcomed into their midst a playboy bachelor who, since he dispensed his hugs and kisses openly and equally, became a commonly owned, favourite mascot who could, without any qualms, be introduced to the respective husbands. Thus did the married women enjoy the titillating pleasure of flirting with a handsome, much younger man, with the full knowledge of their husbands. The safety of their married status freed them to tease him endlessly, pull his shirt, pinch his cheek, share risqué jokes, ask him to guess their bra sizes. We know our limits, he knows his, they said; as long as both sides understood the rules, there was all the pleasure to be had, and no harm to be feared. One of them got bolder; when he dropped a mah-jong tile, she picked it up, put it inside her ample cleavage and looked at him challengingly. He made only a show of retrieval and the ensuing merriment meant that the limits were still being observed.

Then he had a secret affair with one of them, and all hell, of women's fury when betrayed, humiliated, shocked and, most of all, threatened with loss of an immeasurable pleasure in their jaded married lives, broke loose. They turned on the traitor and expelled the bachelor from their group. They reserved their greatest fury for the other traitor, calling her all sorts of names. The treacherous pair endured months of acrimonious opposition and punitive action from the woman's husband, which gave rise to all kinds of rumours about an approaching break-up, feeding the insatiable fury. It received no more sustenance and sizzled to an end when the couple finally got married and were obviously very happy together.

Miss Seetoh imagined that if her artist student did a cartoon drawing of her girlfriends, it would be of a screaming horde of women attacking each other in a furious blur of flying hair, fists and high heels, while their frightened-looking prey, with suit and tie askew, crawled away unnoticed.

Less humorous would be the cartoon of the lonely woman parlaying a man's smile, a greeting, a nothing, into massive hope and longing. Maria had heard of a clerk in St Margaret's Convent, a forty-six-year-old unmarried woman named Celestina who told anyone who would listen, endless stories of being courted, each story gathering more tantalising details as it rolled along. Much of the pleasure of teasing poor Celestina was in the seriousness of her answers to the most outrageously teasing questions, 'Well, Celestina, did you accept your surgeon boyfriend's invitation to join him in New York for the conference?' 'Good morning, Celestina. So have you made up your mind about whether it will be the handsome young lawyer or the rich *towkay*?' The teasing invariably ended with the request, 'Well, Celestina, don't forget to invite me to your wedding,' for the sole purpose of eliciting the solemn response: 'Sure. I never forget good friends.'

'I told you it would happen!' Winnie excitedly gave a blow by blow account of Meeta's torment. It had begun on the very next day after the Polo Club dinner, and continued through the entire week, as Meeta returned from school each day to check for voice messages on her phone and found none from the desirable Byron. The phone, both by its silence and its ringing, became a source of great agitation that infected the whole house, unnerving the maid Philomena. Meeta's ears, from whichever part of the house she was in, strained towards it, its silence working up an immense anxiety, the slightest hint of a ringing tone causing a feverish sprint towards it and a crestfallen look as she put it down. The wrong caller came in for some of the pent-up frustration, the nuisance caller for its full discharge. 'You fool, you idiot, you bastard! I'll set the police on you!'

Winnie helpfully suggested a number of face-saving reasons for the broken promise. He was too busy, he had gone outstation for a while and would call when he returned, he had lost her telephone number, he was ill.

To Maria, she said at the first opportunity, 'We saw him! Meeta and I were at Robinson's yesterday afternoon, and saw him in a café drinking coffee with a woman, a very young and pretty woman. It was definitely him. I think Meeta saw but pretended not to.'

Both Maria and Winnie tried to help salvage the badly battered vanity. As soon as she realised all hope was gone, Meeta acted quickly. The reclamation of pride was a systematic affair, beginning with a dismissal of all sympathy from her two friends and a resumption of the old stance of brimming confidence and loud humour. It was followed by vigorous denial of any intention of having lunch with that man in the first place, which in turn was followed by sharp attacks on that individual's character.

Within a week of the episode, Meeta reported, with much gusto, an unsavoury detail of his past: he had left a job, years back, under the suspicion of embezzlement of company funds. He fell woefully short of her high standards, both morally and aesthetically.

'Did you notice,' she said to Maria and Winnie, 'that he has an ugly mole on his right cheek that sprouts bristles, like a wild boar? He has bad breath and speaks with a lisp that makes him so effeminate!' She imitated the lisp and joined in the laughter.

The more she derided him, the easier was the restoration of the lost pride, and exactly a month later she was able to report, with gleeful triumph, that he had waved to her one afternoon, and she had completely ignored him. She went to the Polo Club a few times for the sole purpose of snubbing him, reporting her victory each time.

Winnie whispered to Maria, tittering, 'All bluff, let me tell you! He doesn't remember anything. Yesterday he happened to be at a table near us. She said loudly to me that she had no time to waste on worthless men, and all the time, he wasn't even aware of her presence!'

Buoyed by a new boldness, Winnie shared her discovery regarding the alleged royal conquest. 'Maharajah, my foot! He was some pretentious bum, and they met just once!' She shared another discovery, speaking eagerly behind a cupped hand, 'You know what? Meeta's a virgin, for all her boasting about spending a secret holiday with the maharajah in a desert palace!'

'How do you know?' asked Maria. Winnie, removing the cupped hand, laughed hysterically. 'She said so herself. But not to me. To the great Sai Baba. In a prayer loud enough for me to hear. She said, 'To your Holiness, I offer you the most precious gift of all, my virginity'.'

Maria, in the privacy of her room, laughed so much she had to cover her mouth with her pillow in case her mother heard. If she wrote comedy, she had the perfect raw material: three modern women coping with their virginity, Winnie offering hers on a platter; Meeta variously claiming she had joyously lost it to a mortal and solemnly offered it to a god-man; herself wondering about whether, should her time come, the experience would live up to the breathtaking expectations of romantic novels, or even of Victorian ones, where its loss was signified by a row of coy asterisks. An asset and a prize in the days of their mothers and grandmothers, it had become an ambiguous symbol in a society that was still traditional while claiming modernity. Among the expectations of the men who took part in the government-initiated matchmaking exercise, virginity could still rank high.

Meeta had discovered, quite by accident, that a student at Palm Secondary had the same unusual surname as Byron, and found out that she was his niece. 'You mark my words,' said Winnie secretly gratified that the intimidating Meeta was in the same sad boat of rejection as herself, 'she'll try to befriend the student to find out more about him.'

Maria thought, no, I couldn't handle the complexities of this man-woman thing. They brought out the worst in her girlfriends and would wreak havoc in her peaceful life. Meeta and Winnie with their obsessions about love were quarrelsome and unreasonable; divested of them, they could be such delightful company. The social grapevine was full of tales of rich society women who were so lonely they could not see through the machinations of their young escorts, not even after they were cleaned out of their money. Men and women, whether gawky teenagers or matured adults, whether in their first experience of life or on its last lap, hankered after love and fed on an endless stream of encouragement from the entertainment media, listening to the soulful songs of men who cried out that they couldn't bear to sleep alone, of women who said they waited for the phone call that never came.

Never mind if this many-splendoured thing, enjoyed in the imagination only, was but a pale version of the *real* thing. I'd rather spend my time with my *unreal* books, thought Maria. The Botanic Gardens with their lovely quiet walks, shady corners, their twittering birds and humming insects right in the midst of a bustling city, was a favourite place to bring a book during the weekend and enjoy at least a full hour of solitude.

'Hey, that's an interesting title,' said a young man in jogging gear, looking at her book as he wiped off the perspiration from his face with a towel. 'Hmm, Jane Austen. I had to do her in my first year at the university. Never could take to her!' He recommended himself instantly to her, quite unlike the other fellow, also in the Botanic Gardens, who had said, by way of introduction, 'My name is Professor S.Y. Yong, and I'm Head of the Neurology Department of Raffles Hospital.'

She had responded silently, with a teasing twinkle in her eye, 'Go on, tell me about your salary, your next promotion, your new Lexus.' The jogger was infinitely preferable company. She had chatted with him for a few minutes, but the next time he saw her again in her favourite shady nook, she chatted less and smiled less, afraid to appear encouraging.

A curious thought occurred to her: Meeta and Winnie were close friends by default only. The tenuous bond of their similarity in status would break as soon as one found a partner and waved a cheery goodbye to the other. The co-dependence would sunder even more dramatically if one stole the boyfriend of the other. Then another thought occurred and made her smile, in the gratification of vanity: the supreme irony, part of the hunter-hunted paradox, of eager women being ignored and completely indifferent women, like herself, being pursued.

Both their unhappy affairs behind them, Meeta and Winnie turned to a new subject of interest, eliciting much noisy protestation from Maria. 'No, no! I don't want to hear of it!' she said, stopping her ears against their remarks about the reasonably good-looking Bernard Tan Boon Siong who, from his first seeing Maria in the compound of the Church of Eternal Mercy, had eyes for nobody else.

Eight

'There he is, under the tree, looking in our direction. He's coming towards us,' said Winnie.

'Alright Maria, prepare for another display of gallantry from your knight in shining armour,' said Meeta. 'Shall Winnie and I make ourselves scarce?'

'No, no!' cried Maria in alarm. 'You stay right where you are. Don't you dare go away!'

The situation had taken on the childishness that grown women, in a group, sometimes displayed in the invigorating game of the hunted leading the hunter on a lively chase, and mobilising the help of their friends to form a phalanx of protection against the persistent pursuer. Meeta and Winnie were geared for the fray.

They sometimes helped out in the sale of breakfast food for a charitable fund-raising activity in the compound of the Church of Eternal Mercy, after the Sunday morning mass, seeing themselves, non-Catholics, as doing a favour to Maria who saw herself, already beginning to move away from the childhood faith, as doing a favour to her fervidly religious mother who was in charge of the fund-raising. Maria, to preserve the peace at home, accompanied her mother to the Sunday mass, as well as managed the fortnightly breakfast stall for which, from the beginning, she had recruited the help of the dependable Meeta and Winnie.

The two women, ever on the look-out for interesting males even in church compounds where they were notably scarce, had plenty of opportunity to observe Maria's admirer who had as good as openly declared himself. From the start, he featured in their lively debate about the relative merits and demerits of the direct, unabashed male approach as opposed to the deliberately hesitant, elusive one, both concluding that perhaps this Bernard Tan Boon Siong was making himself too available, and hence less desirable. He spoke amiably to all of Maria Seetoh's friends and deferentially to her elders, even the weak-minded Por Por who was sometimes brought along to church, to give the maid some respite, but it was clear that all the attention to others was but a hurdle to be quickly got out of the way to reach the prize at the end. As soon as he managed to secure Maria Seetoh's attention, or whatever semblance of it was required by civility, all his senses were galvanised into a state of fascinated concentration on that one object alone. Everybody and everything else faded away into the background. This is most embarrassing, thought Maria, I wish he would go away.

He had newly joined the parish, a single eligible male clearly not averse to begin the chase and had, from the very start, settled on Maria Seetoh. Maria's prettiness, freshness of countenance and openness of demeanour gave her the special attractiveness of a girl-child, though she was already thirty-five. Bernard observed her keenly through her every activity at the church: as she sat with her mother in the pew, as she moved down the aisle, row by row, with the collection box, midway through mass (he invariably dropped a large note into the box), and as she walked behind her mother to the communion rail, returning to her seat with bowed head and clasped hands, arousing no suspicion whatsoever that within that body supposed to be housing the divine presence was already forming a secret wish to be free from it.

Once he watched her help Father Rozario conduct some catechism lessons for small children. Her earnest sincerity of tone as she told Bible stories to the row of small faces turned up towards her, impressed him; it would only be much later that he would learn that the earnestness was even then already being claimed by the secret unholy stories of her imagination. Bernard saw a purity he had never seen before, a complete absence of the vanity and pretentiousness he had noticed in some of the women he had courted and abruptly dropped. It was as if he had an evaluation sheet in his head in which one after the other, women were systematically scored and eliminated.

He watched Maria Seetoh with increasing satisfaction. The absence of make-up on her youthful-looking face, her simple pony-tail, her slenderness, her sensible blouses and skirts pleased him enormously. In a short while, indeed within a fortnight, she not only passed the elimination test but rendered it no longer necessary. Bernard Tan was convinced that he had at last found the woman who would make him happy for the rest of his life. After a quick, discreet check with the parish priest Father Rozario who had nothing but good to say of Maria Seetoh and her mother Anna Seetoh, he was convinced of divine endorsement of his choice. The only thing left to do was to hasten the pursuit and bring it to a fruitful conclusion. He did not believe in wasting time.

Such single-mindedness resulted in a purposefulness of approach that no observant parishioner of the Church of Eternal

Mercy could miss. Everyone whispered that Maria Seetoh was a lucky girl because Bernard Tan Boon Siong was eminently eligible, not only because of his academic credentials as a first class engineer from the Singapore university, and professional standing as a senior civil servant in the Ministry of Defence, but, most important of all, as a fine Catholic with sterling moral qualities. For it was known that he had postponed marriage to take care of his sickly parents who died within a year of each other. Even the age was right; he was six years older than Maria. Anna Seetoh's god-sister, a very amiable woman also named Anna, enumerated the good qualities on the fingers of one hand, then the other.

'You are a very lucky woman,' everyone said to Anna Seetoh who had been trying for years to get her daughter married.

'Yes, I am, thank God for His mercy,' said the devout Anna, and did not think that her daughter's feelings mattered in the least. 'You do not know your own mind,' she scolded, 'you have been too long on your own, doing exactly as you like. Who will take care of you when I'm gone? Now, thank God, there's someone,' and she thanked the good God again.

'Help, he's approaching,' whispered Maria to Meeta and Winnie, as they wrapped up the unsold pies and sandwiches to take to an orphanage. 'If he offers us a lift again, I'm going to say we've already got transport. So you back me up.'

But Meeta, who was looking forward to witnessing yet more of love's melodrama being played out, had uncooperatively left her car behind, so the three of them, including Anna Seetoh, piled into the back of Bernard's brand new Toyota, leaving Maria to sit in front with him. That was her assigned place; any other arrangement would have been the most impudent disregard of the man's obvious purpose when he offered the lift.

Later he took all of them for lunch in an Italian restaurant. During the meal, Meeta was her loquacious self, Winnie a silly echoing voice, Anna Seetoh too much in awe of the soft-spoken Bernard Tan to say anything, and Maria acutely embarrassed by it all. She now had the dubious honour of being solely responsible for any act of generosity coming from this noble man at the end of his search.

That evening Meeta and Winnie took turns on the phone to give Maria their impressions. Meeta said with self-deprecatory humour, '*Aiyah*! Winnie and I, and for that matter, your mother, Por Por, everyone else, are just around on sufferance only. We are just pathetic wallflowers!'

She shared the rumour she had heard of a prim and proper minister who wanted to be introduced to a beautiful woman at a glittering function, and for propriety's sake endured the introduction to a dozen unattractive women before achieving his purpose. There was also the memorable episode from a novel, where the hero heroically carried four stranded, rather stout and plain-looking girls, across a river, one after the another, in order to reach the fifth, the prettiest in the group.

Maria laughed merrily at the tales, but dissociated herself from their message. 'Please,' she would say and instinctively put her hands to her ears.

'Winnie, you and I from now onwards should leave poor Bernard to woo Maria in peace!' The contrast with their own situations produced a momentary bitterness: if only their men had shown but a fraction of Bernard's devotion.

'Look, Mother, I'm not going to church anymore, I'm not helping you with the breakfasts anymore, I'm not helping Father Rozario with the Bible stories classes anymore; everything's getting just too ridiculous for words,' cried poor Maria.

She was beginning to experience some of the revulsion of the pursued against the excessive pursuer, and every act of kindness and magnanimity on the part of Bernard increased the desire never to see him again. In every encounter, there was the obligation of gratitude to clothe her words and demeanour with a polite civility that the man was clearly taking for encouragement.

I will say a direct 'No' the next time, she thought, rubbing the sides of her forehead against an onslaught of headaches.

The determination was, alas, betrayed again and again by the combined impact of her mother's eagerness, Father Rozario's smiling approval, her friends' manoeuvres and her own sense of civil reciprocity.

'Why can't I learn to say 'No'?' she moaned. She might have rephrased the rhetorical lament: why couldn't he be less thick-skinned and see that she was simply not interested?

Invariably each nervously smiling response was seized upon as acceptance of the countless offers to give her and her mother a lift home in his car, to take over whatever heavy parcel or bag they happened to be carrying, to hold an umbrella over her head in the hot sun. Her mother, used only to years of abuse and neglect by a worthless husband, could only break into little effusive cries of gratitude.

'How can you blame him,' said Meeta. 'You're encouraging him!' 'No, I'm not!' protested Maria. 'Anyone can see I'm in fact discouraging him.' 'Well, clearly he does not,' said Meeta. The alarm bells screamed in her head, as she sensed the encroachment, so soon to grow into a stranglehold, upon the precious world of private thoughts and dreams that had been hers from childhood. Back then it was a little hiding space on a mat behind door curtains, or on the cool floor under a table, enclosed by a large tablecloth, where, with only her comic books and her dolls for company, she spent long happy hours until dragged out by her mother or Por Por.

Maybe I should write him a note, she thought, a polite note to say I'm not interested. But always, something would happen to paralyse her energies and cause her to be swept further along the powerful stream of his determination. Once or twice, as she was carried along the relentless current, there was a saving branch growing out of the bank that she could grab, a tiny outcrop of rock to leap on to; in failing to save herself, she had created her own dooming fate.

'See, we told you, it is fate,' said Meeta and Winnie who, despite their different religious affiliations, subscribed overwhelmingly to a common belief in an ineluctable force shaping human lives. 'Everything in life is fated. You are fated to meet this man, he is fated to follow you to the ends of the earth, you are both fated to marry each other!'

'It is God's will,' said Anna Seetoh who had been praying for years for her daughter to be suitably married. Two things had happened that confirmed her belief. In a dream just a week before Bernard's first appearance in the Church of Eternal Mercy and his first sight of Maria, she saw herself and her daughter, after Sunday mass, being told by a lady in white, very like the Virgin Mary, to go along a strange road that would lead to their happiness. Then a few days after the dream, Bernard appeared, exactly on the anniversary of the feast day of one of Maria's patron saints, Saint *Bernardette*. Since then, a multitude of significant coincidences had strengthened her conviction, among them the perfect match between the number on Bernard's car plate and the number sequence, when reversed, of the day, month and year of Maria's birth. 'God's ways are strange,' said Anna Seetoh in awe.

I don't believe in fate, thought Maria defiantly. I'll prove that I'm my own destiny. There was a proud quotation from a poem that she had read out to her students; this was the time to live up to its inspirational call to be master of one's fate, captain of one's soul.

'Miss Seetoh,' said Maggie excitedly, cornering her as she descended the stairs on the way to the staffroom, 'You have boyfriend now, right? A friend of mine, he saw you and this guy, quite good-looking and very classy, not like our Mr Chin – hey, Miss Seetoh, so you tell us of romance in creative writing class?'

'Stop talking nonsense, Maggie, and mind your own business!' she snapped.

'Oh ho, ho! Now I know it's all true! No need to be shy, shy, Miss Seetoh!' giggled the incorrigible girl. 'Good for everybody to have love in their life!'

'Where's Por Por?' cried Maria in panic one afternoon. She had taken her grandmother out for a little shopping with the maid and had turned, after paying the bill at a departmental store, to find the old woman missing.

'Rosiah, you were supposed to keep an eye on Por Por!'

They searched the whole store, called loudly, enlisted the help of the sales attendants, but Por Por was nowhere to be found. Once she had left the house on her own and been brought back by a neighbour who had found her wandering in a market. Her escapades could be comical if they involved no danger; one evening she had stolen out of the house and gone to a nearby children's playground where Heng found her sitting on a horse in a merry-go-round.

They caused great concern if she walked through busy roads to get to the White Heaven Temple of which she seemed to retain some distinct memories, or if she got robbed, as happened once when she came home without the jade bangle on her wrist. Heng had since removed the gold chain from her neck and the jade studs on her ear lobes, and left instructions that at no time should she carry more than two dollars in her blouse pocket. The possibility of Por Por lying crushed under the wheels of a bus or inside a deep monsoon drain was a constant nightmare.

In tears, Maria and Rosiah returned home to report her loss and get help for a wider search.

'Maybe you should think of putting her in a home,' said Heng who happened to be on one of his frequent visits, usually to do a check on the apartment, one half of which he would one day inherit.

Maybe I should think of cutting you off altogether from my life, thought Maria angrily. She was always comforted by the thought that he was her brother not by circumstance of blood but of some obscure Chinese tradition that had resulted in his adoption many years ago. I wouldn't want the same meanness to run in my veins, she thought with savage glee.

In two hours, Por Por was back at home, muttering incoherently, led into the house by Bernard Tan who had found her in a side lane near an Indian shrine at least four miles away. It was simply amazing – his uncanny ability to be in every place where his generosity could once more be demonstrated. Maria thanked him effusively, her mother invited him for dinner the next day, cooking the most extravagant meal equal to any Chinese New Year Eve banquet, the church encounters intensified with him now sitting next to them in the pew, and bouquets of flowers started arriving for her with cards filled with the most heartfelt sentiments of respect, regard and affection. Bernard had taken his pursuit on a breathlessly rising trajectory of ardour, that would surely soon peak with the realisation of his dreams.

He invited her for a movie and dinner date, the first time they would be out on their own together. Father Rozario had said to her, 'Bernard is one of the finest, most god-fearing men in the parish.' The god-fearing virtues were less commendable than a few things she was beginning to notice about him: he was utterly sincere, never said anything fatuous, was unfailingly polite to everyone, including lowly waiters, petrol pump attendants, maidservants. He spoke impeccable English.

Through habit she had developed an enormous capacity to smile politely through male bombast: she had seen her mother nod encouragingly through her father's beer-sodden promises of making big money and buying her a big house, even while he was in hiding from the loan sharks, sometimes waking his family up in the night to run to yet another secret location.

In her student days in the university, she had been the object of interest of a fellow undergraduate who basked in his self-given name of Valentino, and in his reputation, also self-initiated, as the biggest heart-throb on campus. He took his boasting to an incredible level of braggadochio that no longer had any connection with reality and that at the same time, was suspiciously inaccessible to verification, since none of the conquests were girls on campus.

There was a Francis Sng, a fellow parishioner of the Church of Eternal Mercy, who talked endlessly about his job, his salary, his good standing with his boss, his sheer good luck at selecting the right stocks in the market that were now yielding amazing dividends, the devotion of his mother and aunts who regularly fed him the most expensive and healthful herbal brews from Korea, completely oblivious to her suppressed yawns. She had only been out once with the obnoxious man, on a church outing, during which he chose to sit next to her, his large, sweaty face and loud voice obtruding upon her attention all afternoon until she made an excuse to go to the washroom and returned to take another seat. If on a Repulsiveness Scale of one to ten, he and Valentino scored a nine, the quiet-voiced, well-mannered Bernard Tan was out of that hall of male infamy altogether.

She asked him about the heroic time when he took care of both ailing parents, and was impressed by his simple modesty. He had nursed both of them to the very end, and had been particularly close to his mother who had died from a very painful liver disease. 'It's difficult to talk about those times,' he said, 'and if you don't mind, I'd rather not.' She wanted then to reach out to touch his hand. But no, she thought, that might give him the wrong impression.

Nine

'Can we stop here for a short while?' said Bernard, slowing down his car along a small gravel path, and for a moment, as she looked out into the surrounding darkness and saw tall trees silhouetted against the night sky, she had a wild thought that he was going to kiss her or do something alarming.

Years ago, when she was still an undergraduate at the university, she went on a date with someone on a motor scooter; he took a different, unfamiliar route to the campus coffee house, stopped in a dark spot with shady trees, got down from his scooter, and kissed her. She was about to resist his advances when, in the most unexpected way, her attention suddenly became diverted by the sight and sound of a couple in a nearby bush, and then of two more couples, in different parts of the secluded spot, all clearly too engrossed in their activities to notice any onlooker. It was intriguing new knowledge in her innocent world which she would have been happy to acquire without help from that stolen, disgusting kiss.

Bernard had managed to persuade her to go out for a second movie and dinner date which she secretly swore would be their last, for she was now completely convinced that she could never marry him. His intensity was beginning to frighten her. To the discomfort of the evening was added the sudden fear of an attack of passion; both feelings vanished in a gasp of astonishment when he laid a small blue velvet box on her lap, opened it and revealed the most beautiful diamond ring she had ever seen. 'I got it from Tiffany's,' said Bernard not with arrogance but in appreciative acknowledgment of her taste and worth. 'The salesgirl was kind and patient enough to help me select it. I hope you like it.'

He took the ring out from the box and picked up her left hand to slip it on the engagement finger. It was at this moment that astonishment gave way to panic which mounted by the second.

'No, no,' she gasped, and as she did not withdraw her hand, Bernard deftly slipped on the ring.

'Don't worry about the price, I needn't tell you,' he smiled, and promptly told her.

'Oh no,' she said again, her powers of resistance still locked inside her cold limbs, her stuttering tongue. For a moment she found herself in the grip of an experience as amazing as it was intimidating in her simple, ordered life, an experience tantamount to a life-or-death matter that required her to quickly commandeer all her resources of clear thinking and honest feeling to deal with it.

'From the first moment I saw you, I knew you were the one for me,' he said fervently. 'I couldn't wait for the day of our engagement, and it has come.'

He had a rich repertoire of the suitor's language, and he dealt it out, systematically and with feeling. Her mind was working quickly, to enable her to break out of the paralysis of movement and speech. This was not her understanding of how a woman got engaged and married, her feelings unconsulted, the whole affair circumstantial only, finalised and closed with the formality of a ring. The deep-seated, long-standing fear of losing her world and her freedom, akin to the primordial aggressive safeguarding of territory, asserted itself powerfully and she said, in clear distinct tones, 'Bernard, I thank you very much, but no, please no, we can't be engaged.'

At this stage, still completely convinced that he was at the end of a long, laborious but divinely blessed mission, he said, 'We could wait a little longer if you like, though I don't see any need for that.'

She felt a rising tide of annoyance at the presumptuousness, which gave an edge to her voice as she said, 'You don't understand. I don't want to be engaged to you. I don't want to marry you – or anybody.' Capable of only the gentlest remonstrances, she surprised herself by the brute delivery of truth.

By the light of a faint moon in the sky, she saw his expression change quickly to frowning puzzlement. 'But wasn't it clear to everybody that we were serious about each other? Weren't you encouraging me all the way?'

The word elicited the sharp response that she had used for Meeta's teasing accusation. 'Oh no, I wasn't encouraging you at all,' she protested and was almost tempted to let out the second part of the protestation lying silent upon her tongue, 'You chose not to see all those signs of discouragement; you almost forced upon me those lifts in the car, those gifts to my mother and Por Por, those –'

Years later, she would be even more painfully aware of how the very same acts and words could have completely different meanings for men and women, accusing each other across an enormous chasm of misunderstanding.

'I don't understand,' said Bernard very softly, as if talking to himself. He turned to her and said, with a hint of pleading in his voice, 'All those times we were together –' It was his turn to leave the utterance unfinished, fearful of being dealt another of truth's humiliating blows.

There was silence for a long while, as he stared out into the night. A man with a disposition to be magnanimous towards others, and an unshakeable belief in his own worth, he was now reeling from the sheer incredulity that a woman on whom he had lavished all that magnanimity and who therefore must be aware of all that worthiness, could reject him. Having sedulously built up a whole superstructure of intention, purpose, understanding and expectation, he now saw it crumbling before his eyes.

His face stark and taut from the sheer incomprehensibility of it all, he at last said, very slowly, 'Listen, I want you to understand this. I am a man of principle and honour. I want to get everything right. I don't play games.' He made a final attempt to confront the devastating reality and challenge it. 'Surely you don't mean what you just said. Surely you're not telling me that –' he began, and she cut in to say with a rush of breath, her heart beating wildly with the urgent need to hasten a bizarre episode to its end, 'No, I'm not interested in you.'

She saw his stricken face, and suddenly felt a surge of pity that made her stretch out her hand to touch his, saying with all the kindness of tone she could muster, 'I'm so sorry.'

He moved his hand away abruptly, and continued staring into the distance, his whole body rigid in the shock of his discovery, the veins throbbing fearfully on his neck and temples.

The courtship had been an enormous investment of time, money and energy, impossible to envisage losing. Trying to save it, he made a last desperate effort – a reminder to her of the magnitude of his gift, and a gentle reproach for her disregard of it, 'One would imagine any woman would be grateful to receive a twenty-thousand dollar ring –' Instantly he saw his mistake for she replied with some hauteur, 'It would make no difference if it cost a hundred thousand dollars.' Her tone belied the mounting terror of a situation spinning out of control; only outwardly was she in charge, dealing one pitiless blow after another.

Meeta had often said to her, shaking her head, 'You may be so intelligent and well-read, my dear, but you're as naïve as a child in the ways of the world.' She was not naïve; she had an instinctive sense, as well as the inner strength, for doing the right thing, the worthy thing. Could he hear her heart thumping so hard she could faint any moment?

She removed the ring from her finger and held it out towards him. 'I want to thank you again for your generosity –' she began and then all was confusion, which would, in the years to come, be a fearful memory that would return again and again in her dreams.

She saw him, in a whirl of white-faced fury, grab the ring from her, get out of the car, stand by the side of the gravel path and in a mighty swing of his arm, fling it far out into the darkness of sky, trees and bushes. The image would be permanently seared into her memory – the man, the gesture of angry despair, the brooding night sky, the silent forest trees. He returned to the car, breathing heavily, and without a word drove her straight home. 'Bernard, I'm sorry –,' she quavered, now in tears, but his car had already roared away.

That night she had a dream in which, in slow motion, she saw the arc of the flung diamond traversing the night sky, like a silvery trail of spittle from the bared jaws of a great night predator as it sprinted, with easy graceful movements of its long lean body, after its prey.

'It cost me a fortune, did you know that?' Bernard shouted in rage. 'Do you know I'm now in debt to the loan sharks?'

'I never asked you,' she said calmly and then added, 'let's start looking for it. We won't leave till we find it.'

They cut their hands on sharp branches, pricked their fingers on thorny bushes, brushed giant ants off their clothes, all to no avail. Father Rozario, then her mother joined in the torrent of rebukes. 'It's all your fault! You're the most selfish person on earth! You're a cold, unfeeling bitch!' Then suddenly she saw the diamond, glinting beautifully in a patch of mud.

'There it is! Look, Bernard, your diamond!' She picked it up from the mud and handed it to him joyfully. 'What will you do with it now, Bernard? Will the shop take it back? You must get back your twenty thousand dollars. Your mother needs it for all those expensive operations. You should never have bought me the ring in the first place, Bernard, because I never loved you. Aren't you glad I've found it?'

In the dream, speech, loosed from its moorings, bore her truest thoughts and feelings along a joyously flowing current. In the dream, she stood fearlessly facing the others, ankle deep in mud. Livid with fury, Bernard grabbed the ring from her, and flung it into the darkness a second time. 'Oh no, oh no,' she screamed. 'You go look for it again,' roared Father Rozario, 'and this time I will have it. It goes to the orphans! Shame on both of you!' Her mother was crying and drumming her chest with anguished fists. The well-populated dream admitted one more inhabitant. 'How do you know it's a real Tiffany ring?' sneered Heng. 'It could be a cheap fake for all we know. Show us the receipt, Bernard.' Bernard ignored him and faced her.

'Maria Seetoh, you are a curse in my life.' He picked up a wet branch and struck her across the face. 'Since I met you, my life has been a living hell!'

Someone let out a shriek which was powerful enough to punch through the dream and yank her up into the reality of sweat-soaked pillow, rumpled blanket, pounding heart. She sat up, her hair fallen in tangles over her face, her hands pressed against her ears. Her mother came knocking on her bedroom door, 'Maria, what was that noise? Are you alright?'

The next day was Sunday, and she did not see Bernard at church. Her mother saved a barrage of anxious inquiries for firing as soon as they reached home, and she wisely chose not to mention the Tiffany diamond ring, now lying somewhere in a forested area near a small path that had no name. Till the end of her life, Anna Seetoh was never told about it.

From the maelstrom of feelings that crowded the dream, she pulled one out for special safekeeping and solace: her own proud self-assertion which she had expressed to Bernard as they stood in the mud together, and she handed him the ring, 'I'm free now.' Gifts if they came loaded with sinister purpose were promptly given back, even in childhood. There was an aunt who once pushed a coin into her pocket whispering something about not telling her mother what she had just heard, and she instantly pulled out the gift and returned it, before running away. *I'm free now.* In the murkiness of the dream, the declaration, as she made it repeatedly to Bernard, had stood out in the clarity and intensity of relief and celebration, and was now even more powerfully felt in the reality of waking.

It would give her the necessary strength in the days ahead when she would have to begin the tedious work of dismantling the huge edifice of expectations that everybody had built around them. Her mother, Father Rozario, Meeta, Winnie, the curious parishioners of the Church of Eternal Mercy, the inquisitive Maggie, even her brother Heng, even Por Por who in her lucid moments might demand to see the kind gentleman who had found her wandering and brought her home – all of them, at some time or other, in one way or another, would be told the truth, if only to have the peace of mind to move on to a new phase in her life.

She had learnt a valuable lesson. A woman had to be mindful of her words and actions if they were not to be construed as encouragement. She had made a dreadful mistake which, fortunately, could be corrected. Her imagination supplied an image that made her smile: a large pile of garbage in the yard, created by her own stupidity and carelessness, which she must clear quickly in a massive spring cleaning exercise before the Chinese New Year, if the gods were not to be offended. Soon the gods were appeased, for the rubbish was all gone. She loved the slate made blank once more, the chalkboard cleared of all its clutter, for writing on anew.

It would be a truth that needed telling only in its broadest outlines, without mention of the ring, and she would tell it with a firmness and finality to preclude all further questions and speculations. She was once more in charge of her life. In my new life, she thought, meaning of course her inner world only, I would admit no one. Maybe only Por Por.

A fearful object in her dreams, where it was flung into the distance, dug up from mud, caught in a roaring torrent, pulled out from the throat of some forest predator, amidst a chaos of tears and curses, the ring was the subject of much quiet wonder in her waking hours. Nobody would believe my story if I wrote it, she thought. Mortals stamped their love on monuments of marble that towered into the skies for all eternity; lesser mortals with money to spend bought diamonds that had the same enduring power. That Tiffany ring would lie unclaimed under dead leaves long after she and Bernard had passed away. Or it would be dug up, hidden inside huge clumps of soil, and then dumped into a pit, once the bulldozers moved in to clear the forest for the new developments that were springing up all over the island. Or its fate would take it to a muddy ditch that, with the rainy season, swelled into a stream and flowed out to sea, casting it to the very bottom, its resting place for all eternity, testimony to the sad story, that could not be told, of a man who loved a woman who could not love him back.

Within two days, she had broken the promise to herself, and told the story. The seductive romance of love's twenty thousand -dollar tribute had suddenly come up against the brute calculus of life's realities. She had to act quickly, to find the ring before anyone did.

Ten

The project, as she was later to call it, had begun, as with so many things, with the irrepressible Maggie. Two days after the ring incident, Maggie stood outside the staffroom, asking to speak to her, indicating that her presence was urgently needed.

It was the luckless school gardener whom everybody called Ah Boy, for whose sick wife Maggie had months before collected a small class donation. Now it turned out that the poor woman needed a very expensive operation. A few thousand dollars, whispered Maggie, relishing her dramatic role of the savior when she should be busy preparing for the approaching school examinations. Could Miss Seetoh speak to the principal? If he declined to help, could she pass round the hat among staff members? Maggie on her part would try to get some help from her mother. She looked intently at Miss Seetoh, studying her reaction. 'Two thousand dollars for the operation alone, and money, money for the stay in hospital, for this and that, for good food and medicine which they can't afford. My heart feel so much pity for them, I want to help, even if other people don't want,' said the girl who had sensed yet another opportunity for self-worth to rise above the daily contempt.

Between her habitual sense of caution whenever she was approached by Maggie, and a genuine desire to help Ah Boy's wife, Maria felt a weary helplessness that suddenly vanished with the image of the diamond ring lying in the forest. Thrown away because of her rejection, it was surely hers to claim upon change of mind. She instantly saw it shining in a brilliant arithmetic of hope. The twenty thousand dollars that it had cost, even if reduced to half that amount upon resale, would exceed the cost of the operation for the poor woman and provide decent meals for the entire family for months; she remembered Maggie telling her the daily fare was instant noodles or cheap broken rice. Meeta had a very wealthy socialite cousin who might be prevailed upon to buy a Tiffany diamond that she could claim had cost her twenty thousand dollars when she had paid only ten, or nine or even eight for it. The object of love's bitter controversies, now lying rejected in some deserted spot, could become a gift of life itself.

As the idea of such a transformational role for the fateful ring grew, so did the excitement of mounting a search for it. Maggie, now in the reverse position of receiving confidential information from a teacher, was wide-eyed and speechless in trembling awareness of her privileged position. It took her some time to digest the amazing nature of Miss Seetoh's recent experience and the central role she was about to play in the equally amazing aftermath. Once she did, she swung into a state of full preparedness, vowing to Miss Seetoh she would tell no one except her boyfriend who, having been a scout, would be very familiar with the enormous challenges of the forest and its dense undergrowth.

'He is very smart. Even two days lost in Cameron Highlands, can find his way out. He can surely find your ring, Miss Seetoh,' said Maggie and added, breathless with admiration, 'I can't believe it. But I would do exactly like you, Miss Seetoh. If you don't love a man, what for to accept his gift, even if cost one million dollars? Miss Seetoh, I'm proud of you!'

The search party, to cover the immense area of forest, would have to include a few more capable men, all to be sworn to secrecy, all to be provided with proper instruments of search such as small hacking knives, spades, digging sticks and even torches to penetrate the dark tangles of undergrowth. The task, in its sheer magnitude, promised unimaginable thrills for Maggie; she wrote down a list of the things needed, together with a clear plan of action while the mathematics lesson was going on, slipping out as soon as it was over, to proudly show the list to Miss Seetoh. Throughout she maintained an elaborate secrecy that was soon noticed by the students and teachers who wondered why she was always summoning Miss Seetoh from the staffroom with such urgency. In the staid atmosphere of St Peter's Secondary School, a little conspiracy was developing, with the school's most controversial teacher and most disreputable student at its centre. Ah Boy was immediately approached, briefed and recruited by Maggie, all during the brief school recess. The sole beneficiary of a massive enterprise, he understood little of the details beyond the need to get his brother's help, and do whatever the kind teacher and the kind schoolgirl asked him to.

The richly promising arithmetic of the project intrigued Maria enough for her to sit down and work it out systematically on a piece of paper. She recollected Meeta and Winnie telling her about the cleaning woman in their school, who had to take care of two mentally retarded children on her meagre wages, and decided that the ten thousand-dollar yield from the hunt should be divided equally between her and Ah Boy. The once-in-a-lifetime opportunity for her to do good in a big way had a satisfaction all its own, and she meant to make maximum use of it.

The anticipatory gratification was equal to that experienced when she was eight years old and joined other children helping an old vagrant who wandered from kampong to kampong in search of fallen coconuts lying unclaimed, ripe fruit from trees still unplucked, eggs snatched from under hens if they wandered out of their coop for the laying, even a dead chicken newly run over by a lorry that might still be cooked and eaten. They would all run to the vagrant if they found such a prize and lead him to it, a noisily triumphant group marching ahead of a somewhat bemused old man in rags, a comic Pied Piper replay in reverse, that made the watching adults smile. There was an unspoken code of honour by which no finder should keep the prize; if he or she did and was found out, the penalty was to compensate the vagrant twice over when he next came to the kampong. Sometimes when there was nothing for the looting, she would feel sorry for the old man rummaging in the large rubbish bins, with his many dirty bundles strung on his body, and shyly offer him a coin from her money box.

Meeta and Winnie were delighted with the magnanimous scheme of rescue, and readily joined it. 'You know what, God's hand is at work,' said Winnie devoutly. 'I just heard yesterday that Ah Lan's older daughter got ill again and needs expensive medicine.'

'We have to go in pants,' said Meeta. 'There will be thorn bushes and jungle insects. I will wear my Punjabi trousers.'

In the end, the search party grew to seven in number, all ready to find the lost treasure at the earliest possible opportunity before it got lost forever, driven deeper into the ground by passing animals or washed away by rain. It was a project of unprecedented novelty, adventure and opportunity, enough to give Maria one of her famous headaches and make her look forward to a speedy, successful conclusion.

The reality was far from the theoretical simplicity of staking out the area of search, and fanning out efficiently, in twos or threes, armed with the spades and sticks. As soon as the search party got out of the van that Maggie's boyfriend had borrowed for the occasion, they gazed in dismay at a vast densely forested area stretching endlessly, which Maria was not even sure was the right location, having only a very dim recollection of the gravel path where Bernard had parked his car that evening. 'I remember there was part of an old wire fence near it, covered with creepers,' she said suddenly, and to everyone's relief the fence was soon found to allow the search to begin.

'Wait, we have to do something first,' said the capable Maggie. 'Miss Seetoh, show where Mr Bernard stand exactly when he threw the ring,' and then she and her boyfriend, standing on the indicated spot, flung a small pebble each into the forest, to gauge the distance of the treasure from the path.

'How on earth –' said Meeta in dismay, looking at the surrounding impenetrability of trees, creepers, bushes. 'Talk about the needle in the haystack.'

'What shall we do, Maria? We'll never find it,' said Winnie freeing her foot from a tangle of ground creepers.

Maggie said, assuming the position of leader, 'We all here already. Might as well look. No time to lose.' She carved out the area of search, assigning the largest, most difficult terrain to herself and her boyfriend.

Maria called off the hunt after two hours. 'It's no use,' she said. 'We're all tired, let's get back. I'm sorry. Thank you, everybody.'

Meeta whispered, 'That Maggie. I don't trust her. I saw her give her boyfriend a kind of signal. That diamond could be in his pocket now. He looks like a gangster.'

A day later, Maggie voiced exactly the same suspicion to her: 'Miss Seetoh, I saw Ah Boy's brother, he whisper to Ah Boy, and then both of them, they get very close together, like hiding something, they look around to see if anybody see them, they don't know that I am behind a tree, watching them. Maybe they go to pawnshop and pawn the diamond now, no need to share with the cleaning woman. Do you want me to confront Ah Boy and ask? I will say Miss Seetoh very angry with his dishonest action.'

'Oh no,' said Maria, suddenly very tired, burdened by a new heaviness of heart that she could not share with anybody.

Years later, she would remember the episode, not for its futile search but for the larger futility of human effort, in all its contradictions of vanity and nobility, trust and deception, longing and frustration, symbolised by Bernard's diamond ring taunting its seekers from its hiding place in a vast forest. She saw Bernard in the exclusive jewellery shop in Robinson's Building, selecting it with the help of the salesgirl, writing out a cheque for it, constantly looking down, as he drove to pick her up, to check on the precious blue velvet box lying beside him on his seat, his heart glowing with an anticipatory joy that was only exceeded by the subsequent misery. In the course of a single day, they had both ridden on the wildest waves of human feeling, he of hope and despair, she of shock and pity.

All over the world, down through the aeons of time, men and women met, then watched, in dismay, their dreams colliding with each other and crashing to the ground. Did her father and her mother have similar dreams which later, like angry beasts, turned upon each other? She remembered seeing their wedding picture which her mother later tore up and threw away; beyond the propriety of looking solemn for the occasion, her mother, in her white satin wedding dress, veil and pearl necklace, already had the sad expression of loss and betrayal.

As a child, she had heard hints of Por Por's dark past when a suitor rejected by her parents because he came from a different dialect group, later met her secretly in a temple. When her father found out, he sent her away to live with a relative in a distant village, but allowed her back, still stained with dishonour, to marry a simple-minded man who could be bribed to sustain his opium habit. Men and women met, turned away from each other, then met again, in a compromise of dreams, condemning themselves to a lifetime of unhappiness by their own mistakes or allowing others to do so by theirs. The story of men and women, from time immemorial, was written in sweat, blood and tears. For each happy journey where love safely reached its destination, there must have been many ghastly wreckages along the way.

It was good that she and Bernard had not reached that point of irrevocable commitment. Two basically good people, both wanting only to be happy and to do good in life, they had crossed paths and, in a single colossal moment one dark night in the middle of nowhere, had become each other's torment. Through the turmoil of her thoughts and feelings, appeared again and again one compelling image: Bernard's face that evening as he stood by the forest, white and taut in the indescribable pain of holding the returned gift, now mocking the giver. She had remembered only the fury when he returned to the car, that was many times amplified in her dream that night; now two days later, she saw only the desolation of utter despair. And she was the cause of it all. A stupendous sense of responsibility shook, then depressed her.

She was already weeping silently, when they got ready to leave the forest and get back into the van parked on the gravel path. Meeta, mistaking the tears of pity for those of disappointment, said, 'Never mind, my dear, you tried your best.' Winnie said, 'It's all fated,' and Maggie said, 'I don't understand. Maybe someone find it already. Never mind, Miss Seetoh. We all tried our best.'

In their united effort to console poor Maria Seetoh, they were silently united by a single puzzling thought – how a woman who was pretty without being beautiful, charming without being dazzling, could have inspired such an amazing display of male adulation twice over, first in the purchasing of a twenty thousand-dollar diamond, fit for the fabulously rich or royal, and then in its peremptory discarding, as if her rejection had reduced it to a worthless trinket. Such a superordinate demonstration of love existed only in the imagination.

The true explanation, said Meeta, as she and Winnie later discussed the matter at length and came to the same conclusion, must lie both in Bernard Tan's deceitfulness and Maria Seetoh's naiveté. Meeta said, 'No, it's just not possible. That man must have exaggerated the value of that ring. Maria is so unworldly she'll believe anything. Sometimes she's even more naïve than you, Winnie! Only *towkays* and tycoons can afford such a gift. And they would never throw it away. They would keep it for the next mistress. He's only a civil servant with a salary.' Maria

Seetoh, through her central role in a drama of love far removed even from their wildest fantasies, had created an intolerable dissonance in their minds.

'Dear Bernard,' she wrote in a letter that evening, 'I feel compelled to tell you about what happened two days after you threw the ring into the forest. But first let me tell you again and again how sorry I am about the pain that I had caused you. I wanted so badly to apologise when you took me home, but you had already driven off. It could have been the need to wrest some good out of this very sad episode in our lives, that I had a plan to search for the ring, sell it and use the proceeds to help a number of very needy people. I felt you would have approved of the plan, since your generosity towards the poor is well known; in any case you would not have disapproved of it. I organised a discreet search yesterday to find it, but alas, it is irretrievably lost in that vast forest. It would have given me so much satisfaction to be able to tell you that your valuable ring helped two very needy families. May I wish you every happiness.' Regularly storing up interesting events in her own life for the telling or the writing of stories, she was consigning the most momentous one of all to memory's dust-heap with a one-page letter.

One little vestige remained to tease her mind, again related to the potential saving power of that large sum of money. If Meeta and Winnie were right about Ah Boy and Ah Lan not being fated to benefit from her kind intentions, would that mysterious force have favoured someone who was in equal need of financial help? V.K. Pandy, in a lawsuit for defamation that the great TPK had brought against him, had lost a huge sum of money, at a time when his wife was undergoing expensive treatment for cancer. She saw herself striding hurriedly towards him in that spot of infamy in Middleton Square, pressing an envelope of money into his hands, and then quickly turning and walking away. But the double insult to Bernard would have been too daunting: his gift, rejected by the woman he loved, used by her to benefit an opposition politician he detested.

'What on earth –' She had just finished the letter, and was staring at Bernard as he stood dripping wet on the doorstep. In the short distance from the open car park to her apartment, he had been drenched by a sudden, torrential shower. Her mother, Por Por and the maid had gone to bed, leaving her to face what could well be a ghostly visitant making its appearance on the stroke of midnight.

'Forgive me,' he said when it should have been herself, still pained by the memory of his anguish, to say those words. He asked forgiveness for his bad behaviour that evening, for throwing away the ring in a fit of temper, for driving off in an even greater fit, when she had tried to speak to him.

As he spoke, calmly and simply, a hundred turbulent thoughts raced through her mind, among which was a question that was answered as soon as it arose: Suppose he proposes that we start all over again? No, a very firm No. Then I'll offer him a hot drink, a towel for his wet hair and clothes, and sit down with him to wait out the rain. As soon as he leaves, I'll throw away that letter.

'I was going to write you a note,' he said, 'but I changed my mind and drove here instead. I was hoping you would still be awake.' Letters unwritten, letters unread, letters torn up – they were supposed to help failed speech, but were themselves failures.

'Oh Bernard –' she said, deeply moved and reached out to touch his hand. She was startled to see him holding out to her a small thick square of some silky stuff which she then recognised as a ring purse. 'Oh no,' she thought in panic, expecting a bizarre replay of the awful scene that night by a forest.

'It's my mother's,' said Bernard, opening the purse and taking out a gold ring, set with a small piece of carved jade. She remembered, as a child, seeing a similar ring on Por Por's finger, and being allowed to feel the carved surface of the dark green jade. 'She left it as a memento when she died. I would like you to have it as a token of my deep regret for causing you so much distress.'

He added, in a little apologetic murmur, 'It's rather old-fashioned, with little value beyond the sentimental one for me. But I will be very happy if you will accept it.'

She said again, 'Oh Bernard —' and was unable to go on. Her first thought was, 'Oh my God, after that twenty thousand dollars, he would have no more money for gifts,' and her first feeling was an overwhelming pity, as she stared at the once proud, sensitive man, now wet from the rain, standing before her humbly offering his most valued possession.

Within a month, she had married him.

Eleven

Years later, she would remember the honeymoon for two small incidents that had nothing to do with it. Both had to do with children. Childless, she found much pleasure in their presence, or simply observing them from afar, happy inhabitants of a world of innocence until their time came for entry into the complicated world of experience.

Taking a walk along one of the peaceful country roads of the lovely Cameron Highlands in Malaysia (Bernard had said in a flush of generous promise, 'That's all I can afford for the present; for our second honeymoon, I'll take you to Europe'), they came upon a scene of distress. A little boy of about four was sitting on the ground with a bad cut on his forehead, and his mother who looked very young was wringing her hands and making small sounds of panic as she looked around for help. It was a simple matter for her and Bernard to effect a full rescue, which they did promptly. She cleaned the child's forehead with tissue paper from her handbag and wrapped her scarf around it; then Bernard carried him to the nearest hotel where his wound could be properly attended to by the resident doctor. 'My, young man, you are heavy,' said Bernard, not exactly complaining.

She had to suppress her amusement as witness of a running drama between the precocious, self-assured child and the silly, helpless adult. Assuming a stoical silence as his wound was being attended to, the little boy ignored his mother's plaintive noises until she raised a wail and he turned a cool bandaged head towards her to say with some sternness, 'If you don't mind, the doctor says must not make noise!'

The same day, along another road, they came across a woman wheeling a double-pram in which her twin babies lay sleeping under snowy white coverlets; it took just a friendly smile from her for Maria to ask if she might look at them. The woman glowed with maternal pride throughout the few minutes that Maria gazed upon the sleeping infants, uttering little delighted sounds at their cherubic beauty, a whiff of heaven upon earth, until they grew up, learnt language, learnt to use it to deceive themselves and others. Bernard said, pressing her arm affectionately as they walked away, 'I couldn't help looking at your face. You'll make a wonderful mother, you'll give me lots of beautiful children,' and when he added with something of a suggestive smile, 'They say the best babies are made during the honeymoon,' the magic of that encounter with the sleeping infants was gone.

So soon had the sense of unease set in, of something very wrong with her marriage, that it frightened her. There were stories of brides who tore off their veils and threw away their bridal bouquets at the very altar itself, at the same moment that they threw away their lie, and faced, wild-eyed with elation, a stunned congregation. These were mainly stories from the movies. Some years ago, Meeta told her of a cousin who was marrying again after divorcing his wife of sixteen years. At the very last moment, he changed his mind, destroyed all the wedding invitations that were just about to be sent out, and humbly asked his wife to take him back, saying God had made him see the truth.

Her own story had none of the drama of Hollywood or divine revelation. It was the old one of marrying without love, and thereafter suffering the consequences. It did not have the excuse of the matchmade marriage where the bride submitted all the way, first to parents, then her husband, then the in-laws in a large household where her feelings counted less than her ability to produce heirs. Lovelessness, from choice, not society's strictures, was inexcusable and incomprehensible. She had made the greatest mistake of all, for pity was the weakest foundation upon which to build this most enduring and awesome of human institutions. Pity was no substitute even for friendship, duty, empathy. Disguised as love, it had to maintain the pretence, allowing only for a ghost of a marriage, or its parody. Pity was its own nemesis. She had done Bernard an incalculable injustice.

'Hey, that's Dr Phang,' whispered Bernard, directing her attention to a tall, handsome man and a very attractive young woman who looked young enough to be his daughter.

It was the second last day of their four-day honeymoon, and they were in a restaurant for dinner. Bernard's attention was now given fully to his well revered boss in the Ministry of Defence, while hers, at one glance, took in the sharp contrast between the man's handsomely graying maturity and the woman's vibrant beauty brimming in a voluptuousness of red sweater, black tights and a multiplicity of gold and silver trinkets. Bernard instantly stood up to go and pay his respects, but not before informing her, in a whisper, that Dr Phang had recently re-married and this must be the new wife who was from Hong Kong. There had been the hint of a scandal;

the first Mrs Phang was a highly respected university lecturer who had borne him a daughter, and the second was said to be a minor starlet or model, twenty years his junior. Bernard, disliking gossip in general, loyally refused to talk about this part of his boss's life and concentrated only on the remarkable achievements of the man, an acknowledged superstar in the civil service firmament, who was sometimes consulted, it was said, by the great TPK himself. Frowning on sexual scandals in the lives of his aides, the prime minister was prepared to overlook them if they were brilliant men who could advise him on the economy or national security.

Throughout the introductions and pleasantries, she was aware of the illustrious Dr Phang giving her a quizzical glance or two, as if trying to square prior knowledge with present evaluation. What had Bernard told him about her? If her proud, sensitive husband confided in anyone, it must be this man who was both boss and friend.

In the midst of much small talk, Mrs Phang suddenly pointed to the wedding band on Maria's finger and said, 'Very good idea. Never wear expensive jewellery on vacation,' and went on to describe, with round-eyed wonder, how an aunt had lost a very expensive emerald ring, costing exactly the same amount, in a hotel in Hawaii. It would have been a reflection of Bernard's immense trust in his boss, as well as of his own need for privacy that at the same time that he had confided the astonishing story of the ring, he had withheld its second half.

This was exactly the melodrama that would have appealed so much to Mrs Olivia Phang that she would have insisted on its full retelling in the restaurant. She would have listened to it wide-eyed and breathless, interrupting with little cries of delight and admonition by turns. Her husband could already be regretting that he had told her at all; Maria saw him giving her arm a slight nudge as she was about to make more comparisons with her aunt's expensive jewellery, and her instantly clamping her mouth shut before giving him a playful nudge in return.

But the partial telling, while it saved his pride, hurt hers. She did not care about the opinion of the boss's wife, but it vexed her that this man who struck her as eminently superior in looks, speech and manners to every other man around, should attribute to her, even if only in the privacy of his thoughts, the lowest of motives for marrying. Why did it matter to her what he should think of her, when she had no wish to see him again?

In an urgency of need to throw off any aspersions of falsehood, she seized the first opportunity to tell him the whole truth. The next day when the four of them were walking through a famed flower garden, and she found him walking beside her, she at once set about repairing the damage to her reputation. In two minutes she was done. Then she realised her mistake. His astonished look showed he had not known about her rejection of the gift and her husband's own angry rejection of it in the forest. She would always remember how he looked that afternoon, as the habitual smile was momentarily suspended for a look of amazement mixed with puzzlement. Her husband had always exercised a fine circumspection in the telling of secrets about himself, even with the most trusted friends. 'I lost my head and bought her a ring I could hardly afford,' would have been harmless, even pleasant self-deprecatory secret-sharing with his male friends, resulting in no more than laughing male camaraderie. 'She rejected it, and I threw it away' would have invited shock, unwanted sympathy and worst of all, the pity reserved for the greatest humiliation a man could suffer – not only outright rejection by a woman, but his being driven to insane action by it.

The earlier vexation was replaced by an overwhelming confusion, as she saw her massive betrayal, even if inadvertent, of her husband. In trying to save her pride, she had ruined his with the person whose opinion he cared most about. The pain of the confusion made her turn pale and feel ill. Dr Phang was watching her closely, not in judgement but with genuine concern and goodwill.

He said very quickly, for his wife was walking towards them, 'Don't worry. Nobody will ever know,' and touched her hand reassuringly.

'Can I trust him?' she wondered. 'What an awful blunder. Now things are going to get more complicated than ever with Bernard.'

'So what was it like?' Meeta and Winnie with their usual prurient curiosity, the usual crude nods, winks and nudges, were sure to ask her. She would resort to their own easy jargon to put a stop to all the inquisitiveness: so-so, okay, no big deal. The truth was she blamed her own ignorance and prejudices based entirely on a few childhood incidents that should have been of no consequence in a woman's path to maturity and fulfillment in sex.

When she was a little girl of eight and playing hopscotch with two friends of about the same age, the unruly kampong urchins, led by a brutal-looking boy of fourteen, suddenly surrounded them and herded them into a disused hut, where they tried to pull off their underwear, having already stepped out of their own. She had a terrified glimpse of raw, turgid male power, quivering with menace, before all three of them screamed so loudly that someone came running to investigate and the culprits fled.

Then when she was about ten, her mother took her on a short ferry trip, when they were seated on a wooden bench opposite a man who was lounging on his seat, with his legs wide apart, his trousers unzipped, staring at them menacingly.

She remembered her mother bending down and hissing to her, 'Don't look,' then pulling her up by the hand and hurrying away to another bench at the far end of the ferry.

Back home, her mother made her spit three times into the drain, each time accompanied by a loud cry of '*Choy!*' which she knew was some kind of countervailing curse. Then her mother washed her hair in water purified by flower petals, refusing to provide any explanation and all the time muttering to herself that men were evil, doing their evil thing in public. That night she had a bad dream in which she alone faced the man in the ferry, and stood transfixed as he pulled out from between his legs one snake after another, and tossed them at her.

The childhood incidents could have been so much light-hearted sharing between husband and wife on honeymoon. Their honeymoon, she noted with dismay, was the start of a serious exercise of reclamation and restoration on the part of her husband: he had worked so hard, endured so much, suffered such great material loss that the work of self-compensation had to begin without any loss of time. Their roles should now exactly be reversed: she to do all the giving, he to receive all the attention and adulation, beginning with the claims of the marital bed. If there was the greatest possible mismatch between a man's small build and quiet demeanour, and his sexual passion, it was her husband's, she noted with awe mixed with anger because it was a passion that excluded hers. In the cosiness of the honeymoon room, as he claimed her body, at any time of the day or night, working through his appetite energetically and methodically, she thought, with mounting panic, that she, Maria Seetoh, experienced graduate teacher of English language and literature in modern-day Singapore, was no different from her mother who squirmed under her drunken father, and her Por Por who, it was said, was dragged to the bed of her opium addict husband and told to remain there, naked, till he was ready.

Her mother would have passed that awful test of a woman's pristineness; her Por Por, if she had lost it to that lover during the temple trysts, could have been punished with death in the ancestral country. She herself had let out a little scream of pain in the darkness, and winced to see the satisfaction on her husband's face, and hear the satisfaction in his voice. He said, caressing her, 'I too kept mine for you, you know,' making her wince even more. For now, to the huge financial investment of the ring, there was the libidinal one of the preserved manhood, an awful double debt to pay.

She returned from the honeymoon sick in mind and body, and her husband, ever attentive, took several days' leave to take care of her. When she recovered, he said eagerly, 'Guess what? Dr Phang has invited us for dinner with him and Mrs Phang at The Pavilion Hotel.'

There was a moment during the dinner when the man, with the debonair mane of greying hair and boyish smile, had the opportunity to whisper to her, 'You don't look well. Take care of yourself.'

She thought he looked at her with pity, and understood what it felt like to be the object of this most unwelcome of human offerings. She said to him, with all the pride she could gather, 'Thank you. I'm alright,' before Mrs Phang came up to say breezily, 'That's a pretty dress. But I wish you would wear some make-up, my dear! You would look even prettier, wouldn't she, Bernard?'

Twelve

It had always been the suspicion of the intellectual elite as well as the diplomatic community in Singapore that both the national TV and newspapers, always serious in their dissemination of news and highlighting of national problems and solutions, occasionally allowed themselves the indulgence of humour without losing the seriousness. They did this through the simple principle of contrast, by juxtaposing news and pictures of the great TPK with those of his hated political opponent, V.K. Pandy, for instance, between the awesome prime minister speaking into a forest of microphones against an array of international flags at the United Nations, and the pitiable opponent in his lonely corner in Middleton Square, waving his pamphlets at the lunchtime crowds hurrying by.

On another occasion, a TV news programme showed the prime minister in tuxedo receiving the highest honour from a business community in the United States, followed by a picture of V.K. Pandy in untidy shirt and crumpled trousers loudly arguing with a traffic policeman.

A national campaign on the proper use of English, the necessary language of trade, technology and international relations, which was initiated by TPK himself and launched amidst great fanfare in the media, was yet another occasion for highlighting the astounding contrast between the prime minister and the opposition member who dared to challenge him – TPK's impeccable use of Oxford-marked English and V.K. Pandy's deliberate, persistent use of Singlish, the awful localised variety, completely unintelligible to the international English-speaking community. Indeed, Singlish was the special target of the campaign which had kicked off with a pledge by schools and colleges to take corrective measures.

The principal of St Peter's Secondary School, upon receiving official notice from the Ministry of Education, immediately called a staff meeting to work on a plan of action with clear objectives and time frames to replace Singlish with proper, grammatical English in both the writing and speech of students.

He had a video recording of TPK's TV appearance, played out on a big screen in the auditorium during the school assembly, in which the prime minister, looking as severe as when he had warned Singaporeans of the danger of not marrying and producing children, warned them that if their standard of English continued to deteriorate, business with the international English-speaking community would suffer. The prime minister referred to official letters and memos in the civil service which failed to convey their meaning because they failed to observe the basic rules of English usage. He made no mention of Singlish, but it was understood that this was the real culprit, being a low form of spoken English with liberal admixtures of the local languages that was utterly incomprehensible to the foreign visitor and tourist. Hence Singlish became the single target of an intensive nationwide campaign called 'Use Proper English' launched immediately after the prime minister's TV appearance.

As the campaign against Singlish intensified, so did V.K. Pandy's perverse use of it. At one parliamentary sitting, he asked his questions in loud, deliberate Singlish, lacing it with low marketplace Malay and Hokkien colloquialisms, making everyone squirm and prompting the Speaker to warn him against levity and disrespect. Throughout, TPK looked away angrily, outraged by the presence of the untidy, loud-mouthed Indian with the ever-present whiff of alcohol clinging to his clothes in the august precincts of Parliament House, surely an intolerable insult to the dignity of government.

V.K. Pandy was a politician by default, elected by the people at precisely a time when there was public anger with what was perceived as an overweening arrogance of the leaders.

In a noisy rally just days before the election, V.K. Pandy had warned of even greater arrogance and disregard of the people's feelings, attracting large noisy crowds. Furiously punching the air with his fists, to wild roars of approval from the crowd, he asked again and again, 'Why do they treat us like children? Why do they treat us as if we don't have minds of our own? You know why, dear fellow Singaporeans? Because we apparently don't have minds of our own! We have become a nation of fools and idiots! They say, 'Don't have so many children' and then they say, 'Don't you dare have more than two children!' and we say, 'Yes, yes, we obey.' I say, wake up, wake up before it's too late!'

He had been elected on a wave of anti-government sentiment that would have voted in an illiterate trishaw peddler, a circus clown, a monkey. In a post-election TV appearance, TPK, livid with rage, vowed that if Singaporeans chose to vote irrationally, they would have to learn a lesson or two about social responsibility.

By and large, the leadership was not unduly worried about the people's choice of V.K. Pandy over their more academically and professionally qualified, and certainly more competent, hard-working candidate. It would only be a matter of time before these unthinking people woke up to their mistake and saw the man's sloppiness and utter incompetence as a leader, before they realised that under him, their constituency was getting dirtier, poorer, more disorderly as others were getting cleaner and more prosperous; they would surely then kick him out as hastily as they had voted him in. A newspaper editorial had referred to him as a thorn in the side of the body politic.

It was by some kind of tacit, civilised consensus among the society's wags that no joke about politicians should include their families. Occasionally, in the circuits of private sharing, a riddle would surface: what did the great TPK and the wretched V.K. Pandy have in common that neither would admit? Answer: a sickly, superstitious wife. Both Mrs TPK and Mrs Pandy, it was whispered, sought help from a variety of traditional supernatural sources, with or without the knowledge of their avowedly rational husbands. Indeed, went the rumour, in their desperation they once crossed over into each other's territory: Mrs TPK seeking help from a famed Hindu priest, and Mrs Pandy drinking blessed temple water brought to her by a Chinese friend.

Not satisfied with his championing of Singlish in Parliament, V.K. Pandy stood on a box in Middleton Square and delivered an hour's oration, deliberately in pure Singlish, on why it should not be abolished in favour of standard English.

'What is this? Singlish our natural Singapore language. Otherwise how can Indian man speak to Malay taxi driver; how can salesgirl speak to one another? We all not University professors, you know, we all not educated in Oxford, we are simple working people! Why bring back Queen's English, I ask you? We still have colonial mentality or what? Our Singapore how can call itself independent sovereign nation when still want to speak language of colonial master? Where got any pride? Any national identity? Still want to lick boot of foreign master, eh?'

Some in the hurrying crowds paused for a short while to titter; the majority continued to hurry on, just in case there were secret surveillance cameras to provide indisputable proof of guilt by association.

The principal called Miss Seetoh to his office. The gravity of what he was going to say forced him into a few awkward preliminary pleasantries which were pure inanities, making Maria look down in embarrassment.

'Mrs Tan, your choice of Cameron Highlands for your honeymoon was a good one. My cousin is going away on a vacation with her husband, and I recommended – ' His smile was at odds with the deepening frown on his forehead as he came to the business at hand, 'Mrs Tan, it has come to my attention –'

Maria thought, 'I see Teresa Pang has been at work again.'

'Mrs Tan,' said the principal, trying to tone down the reproach in his voice, 'you know that we are in the midst of a national campaign to stamp out Singlish, and you are encouraging its use. That, as I'm sure you'll understand, is not acceptable.'

It must have been the play submitted by the two new students in her creative writing class. They were from the Commerce class that had never shown any interest in literature, much less creative composition, but from the start Maria had been impressed by their eagerness to participate fully in all the class activities, as also by their perfect compatibility as a working pair, always sitting next to each other, conscientiously making notes, whispering in urgent consultation, finally passing up their work as a joint effort, signed by both, in an artistic intertwining of initials, like royal monograms. Whether a short story, a play or a poem, their combined work showed a level of maturity and creativity that must have been the result of the unusual combination of intimacy and discipline.

They were two fifteen-year-olds named Mark Wong and Loo Yen Ping, a shy, soft-voiced couple who looked very much alike in their slenderness, pale skin, neatness and quiet demeanour. They stood out in an educational setting that discouraged any pairing among the boys and girls for two reasons: it was a serious distraction to studies, and it could lead to immoral behaviour. Mark and Yen Ping, always getting good grades for their class work as well as for their exemplary behaviour of politeness to their teachers, courtesy to their schoolmates and decorum towards each other, had effectively removed both causes for censure. Indeed, they did not at all fit the picture of the actively dating teenager who was much cause for parental alarm, for they had never been seen even to hold hands, in or outside the school.

Maria thought with some amusement that their image was more in keeping with that of babes in the woods, hardly out of childhood, clinging to each other in a large, unfriendly world, or that of those ideologically united, intense young couples of Mao's Cultural Revolution, wearing the asexual drab uniforms.

'Miss Seetoh,' whispered Maggie with a chuckle, 'do you think they ever kiss each other? I think they don't know how. Somebody must teach them!'

Maria thought of herself and Kuldeep Singh, vibrant with animal energy, sipping soda on high stools, and wondered about this unusual, over-achieving pair in her creative writing class.

They had confided their dreams to her: Mark wanted to go abroad to do a course in media, despite his mother's ambition for him to do business administration; Yen Ping wanted to be a writer, but would be a teacher first to support her parents. Between them was an unspoken bond of deep regard, understanding and trust that could have no place for the crude experimentation of teenage passion.

Maria once saw them sitting on the steps of a school staircase, Mark helping Yen Ping to re-plait her hair, both going about the operation with the same earnestness as when they sat in the school library doing research for an assignment or comparing notes in the creative writing class. It was a picture of young romance that was both amusing and touching. As Mark handed Yen Ping her hair-clip, they noticed Miss Seetoh's presence. She hurried away, looking down, suppressing a smile at the surprising manifestations of young love. She remembered two of her classmates from Secondary Three, aged fifteen, completely nondescript, completely forgettable, who, she later learnt, were forced to leave school and get married at sixteen when the girl got pregnant.

Mrs Neo said, 'I say it is not all healthy, their not mixing with others. Brother Philip, being the Moral Education teacher, should counsel them.'

Teresa Pang said, 'Why don't you speak to Maria Seetoh about them? She seems to be encouraging them a lot.'

Maggie had disliked them from the start, less for their standing out as a couple, than for the good comments from Miss Seetoh on their creative writing assignments, which her own efforts never earned. Unable to reveal the secret of her major role in the hunt for Miss Seetoh's diamond ring that dark night in a forest, she contented herself with spreading the general information that only she knew Miss Seetoh's secret life.

She was not about to let her favourite teacher forget her contribution that night, for ever so often, she would whisper to Maria, 'Miss Seetoh, I hear Ah Boy's brother bought a scooter. Where got the money? I think he and Ah Boy found the ring and sold it,' and 'Miss Seetoh, you think maybe the ring still there? Shall we do another search?'

Feeling her position as favourite slipping, she directed her anger at the upstarts, writing a savagely satirical story about a couple who pretended to be one for the purpose of hiding their true sexual orientation, he being gay and she lesbian.

Miss Seetoh, with much matter-of-fact casualness said, 'Maggie, that was an interesting story. If you clean up the spelling and grammar, I could use part of it as an example of vivid narrative.'

From the start, Maria had had some misgivings about the extensive use of Singlish in the short play submitted by Mark and Yen Ping, being constantly reminded of its infamy in the campaign posters put up in the school. It was precisely this use that made the dialogue in the play come alive, resonating with the rhythms of everyday Singaporean speech in the home, the shops, the workplace; indeed, she had never come across a play or short story that carried such an authentic local flavour. The more she thought about it, the more she realised that the couple had real talent, discovering the dramatic value of Singlish before even she, a qualified literature teacher, did.

The story of the play was even more intriguing. It was about a young couple whose families disapproved of their relationship and tried to end it. Maria knew that Mark's mother, a divorcee and a sophisticated, widely travelled business woman, disapproved of her son's relationship with Yen Ping whose parents sold soft drinks in a food centre, and wondered if their play, with its overtones of a Romeo and Juliet tragedy, came dangerously close to open rebellion. Maria had wanted a contribution from her creative writing class for a school concert, and thought the best hope came from this talented duo, publicly so shy and deferential, but privately, in their little world of intense intimate understanding and sharing, amazingly innovative and daring.

'Oh no, oh no, Miss Seetoh,' cried Yen Ping, blushing furiously, her eyes wide with horror.

'This play's only for you, not even for the rest of the class,' said Mark. 'Miss Seetoh, you can use it anonymously in class, as an example of a point you want to make. But not for a school concert,' adding shyly, 'if you like it, Miss Seetoh, that's enough for us.'

Thus had Maria used it in class as an example of the literary value of the much maligned Singlish, and thus probably had Maggie gone to tell Miss Teresa Pang who then went to tell the principal.

'Mrs Tan,' said the principal, 'will you give me the undertaking that in future you will not allow the use of Singlish among the students?'

It would have been the most futile of exercises to explain to him the role that the localised variety could play in local writing, for it had now taken its place, together with laziness, complacency, racial intolerance and a low birth rate, as the enemies of economic survival and progress.

Maria said 'Yes' dispiritedly and the principal was emboldened enough to administer a sharp pinch to the vanity of his best English language teacher who could also be the most difficult, by saying with a casual laugh, 'Mrs Tan, all those grammar mistakes in vivid pictures that you have on your classroom walls. I find it difficult to believe that as a strict English language teacher, you can tolerate, even encourage Singlish!' He waited for a response, ready to turn the compliment he regularly paid this teacher for achieving good examination results into another sly deflation of her ego.

But Miss Seetoh said nothing. It would have entailed just too much energy and patience to explain, much less to justify, the use of Singlish to this most conscientious of civil servants. For him, the linguistic villain stood irredeemably condemned, first because denounced by the great TPK, and second because embraced by the opponent, V.K. Pandy.

It was only to Brother Philip that Maria could show that brilliant play by Mark and Yen Ping. 'I read it again last night,' she confided, not mentioning that she had to get up from the bed very quietly so as not to wake her husband, and slip into the spare bedroom to give the script the full attention it deserved, 'and I think it's a real pity that such a clever little play can never be staged because the dialogue's in Singlish.'

Brother Philip said with a smile, 'They're unusual, aren't they? Commerce students who have a love of literature and theatre. Fortunately, there's you to keep their talent alive.'

He had been long enough in Singapore to have picked up Singlish, with its plethora of easily identifiable interjections, inflections and hybridised innovations, which he sometimes used to amuse his students. '*Aiyoh*! Why you all so *bodoh*, ah? Or you got no moral values, is it? I give up, *lah*!' In the atmosphere generated by the aggressive national campaign to eradicate its use, it would be unwise even to use it for light-hearted exchanges.

He and Maria had hilarious tales to share, in private, about the inevitable excesses when a whole nation was galvanised into instant action by the great TPK's warnings. The newspapers ran guides for Singaporeans eager to improve their English, by pairing each expression in Singlish with its proper, standard British counterpart, duly checked with the British Council, helpfully indicating each error with a large cross and its correct form with a large tick. TV presenters, in the mistaken notion that if Singlish pronunciation was bad, then foreign pronunciation must be good, accordingly read the news with exaggerated American or British accents. All over the island, schools took the battle against Singlish even into the canteen and playground during recess.

Meeta and Winnie became language vigilantes, moving among their students at Palm Secondary School to listen to them and impose fines of five cents per Singlish expression. Meeta said in confidence to Maria, 'Winnie – and a whole lot of others. All making grammatical mistakes right in front of their students without realising it. I had to pull her aside and quietly point out her errors.'

The fear was that students from English-speaking homes might notice the mistakes, report them to their parents who would write irate letters to the newspapers about badly trained teachers being the source of all the trouble. One mother had written a letter that was both a complaint about a teacher and a compliment to her young son, aged six: the teacher had told her students to close the tap, and her little boy had gone up and said politely, 'Miss, the correct expression is 'Turn off the tap'.'

Thirteen

She was so glad that Brother Philip's call had come when her husband was not yet home. He had called her on impulse, he said; their discussion that morning of the effectiveness of Singlish in Mark and Yen Ping's play had suddenly given him a thought which he now posed to her as a challenge: would she collaborate with him in the writing of a play (the moral message, incumbent upon him as the moral education teacher, would be incidental only) in which the monologuist was someone like herself who was familiar with the whole continuum of English language varieties, from formal and literary to colloquial and low marketplace, sliding in and out of each variety with ease, as the situation required. Brother Philip got more and more excited as he elaborated on his idea.

He said, 'I can already see you, Maria, speaking in correct formal English to a team of visiting inspectors from the Ministry of Education, then sliding down to a less formal form with your students, then to pure Singlish as you whisper some urgent instructions to the school gardener Ah Boy who can be very slow-witted, and then back again to standard English as you once more face the principal and the inspectors. Can you see what a hilarious play it will be? Just right to make the concert a lively event!' The normally soft-spoken, urbane Moral Education teacher was displaying the refreshing enthusiasm of a schoolboy about to work on a pet project.

It was difficult to keep the thrill out of her voice even as she said No. No, the principal would never approve of such a play. She left unsaid the fearful thought: a collaboration with him, necessitating hours spent together, including on the phone, most likely in the evenings when her husband would be home, would be an utter impossibility. She looked at the clock: at least ten minutes before he was expected home, a precious stolen ten minutes of happy, spontaneous chat. She told Brother Philip about her small, secret collection of stories that a local publisher said he might consider publishing.

His call, inducing a very happy mood in her, soon induced a clever idea of her own. It had all the promise of sparkling mischief, inspired by a recollection of something she had once read which had amused her greatly. A writer who could not spell, simply got round the problem by writing a story that was written by a writer who could not spell, thereby legitimating all the spelling mistakes in the story, indeed investing them with a kind of lunatic brilliance.

She would write a short story entirely in Singlish. It would be in the form of a monologue by an uneducated taxi driver who had learnt English by listening to it as it was used in the streets. The monologue would alternate between complaint and exultation, as the taxi driver talked gloomily about the tedium of his job on the one hand, and eagerly about how easy it was to overcharge the tourists, on the other.

It was based on a real conversation with a taxi driver many years before, and his speech, loud and friendly, came back in every vividness of detail: '*Aiyah*! What to do, must work hard in

Singapore – pay this, pay that – our government very money-face, I tell you! Lucky got tourists, easy to charge them more – the Japanese with their yen, don't know how to convert to Sing dollars – one day – *aiyoh* – gave me fifty dollars –'

She smiled as she recollected her encounter with the shrewdly loquacious cabby, dressed in a T-shirt bearing the proud logo 'Come to Singapore – Paradise on Earth!' who apparently made it a point to talk incessantly with his passengers to size them up. Her mind throbbed to the sound of his voice, to the robustness and earthiness of the local idiom that would never go away, despite the official strictures, because, unlike these, it grew from the ground, spontaneously and effortlessly and thus became part of the people's sense of themselves.

As the story shaped in her mind, her excitement was too great not to be shared. Her husband was on the sofa reading the day's newspaper and she was seated beside him; he always liked her to be by his side as soon as he returned home from work. Her physical presence was not enough; if she had a faraway look in her eyes, he pulled her back into full attentiveness to him.

'What are you thinking of?' he said, and she turned to him and said, her eyes sparkling, 'I've just got an idea for a wonderful story; it's going to be written entirely in Singlish, it's about a taxi-driver –'

He looked at her and said with a puzzled frown, 'You mean you're not aware of the campaign? I'm surprised, you being an English language teacher –' From that day on, he took his place with the principal, with her colleagues at St Peter's except Brother Philip, with Meeta and Winnie, with all civil servants, with all publishers who would be afraid to publish anything if it contained a single item of Singlish, all ranged in a formidable phalanx of disapproval, facing her as she stood defiantly on the other side of a wide chasm, ranged with V.K. Pandy and the student pair Mark Wong and Loo Yen Ping. 'You snob, you think you're so clever,' they shouted at her, and she shouted back, 'You herd!'

The story in her head cried out to be written. She listened for her husband's snores; they came soon enough, and she hurried to the spare bedroom and the small table where she wrote furiously for an hour before she saw him opening the door and standing at the doorway.

'What are you doing?' he said. She said, 'Oh, just completing some school work.'

This would be the beginning of a routine of small lies, to calm, placate, avert a reproach, prevent the setting in of one of those bad moods she was beginning to dread.

'You teachers are given free periods precisely to complete your work at school and not have to bring it home, aren't you? I thought that was the main reason for women going into the teaching profession, so that they would have time for their families.'

His discontentment with her had already set in; it was beginning to eat into him. Why couldn't she be like other wives? Why did she steal away from him even in sleep?

Would she dare? She would. This time she shut herself in the bathroom, sat on the toilet seat, and managed to finish her story before it lost its momentum. 'What were you doing so long in the toilet?' he asked. So he was not asleep after all. She chose to say nothing; silence was less wearying than explanation.

Brother Philip said, returning her the script, 'Fantastic. I enjoyed it thoroughly. It ought to be published. Why don't you put together your stories and bring out a book? Try a foreign publisher, if your local one isn't interested. It will be his loss!'

To her dying day, she cherished the warmth of the encouragement. She said, suddenly feeling very happy, 'Thank you. Maybe one day. One never knows.'

'Next week, I shall be in Dr Phang's team on a very important and sensitive mission to Jakarta,' her husband said, his voice a constricted mix of pride in the bestowed honour and disappointment that his wife was not going to be impressed or to miss him.

Other wives waited eagerly for their husbands' return from trips abroad; his wife seemed glad of his absence. He suspected that she would have been unhappy if he had decided to extend their honeymoon and delayed her return to school by even a few days. Already, for Bernard Tan Boon Siong, the returns he had expected from his marriage were not at all commensurate with the vast effort he had put into it; everyday he saw evidence of his horrible miscalculations.

'I can see you're going to relish three days on your own,' he said with a sharp little laugh. He came home that evening to announce something for which he watched her reaction keenly: 'Dr Phang's wife and the other wives will be going. There will be a special programme for the wives because of Dr Phang's status. I would like you to come along too.'

There could be one thing he could salvage from his marriage: its public face. In public, by his side, with her pretty looks and gentle demeanour, she was the perfect wife and he was in charge.

'They don't have to work, I do,' she said with some spirit.

'You don't *have* to work, you know that very well,' he said. 'How do you think I'll feel, being the only man not accompanied by his wife?'

'If you like, I'll apply for leave,' she said wearily.

'Not if you go reluctantly. Do you know,' he added, and she knew that the angry frown and the taut white forehead would remain for the rest of the evening, 'that you do everything reluctantly where I am concerned?'

In bed that evening, she had tried, for the sake of keeping the peace for her mother, Por Por and the maid, to induce a good mood in her husband. But pretence always took a toll on both spirits and physical energy, and turned everything into a fiasco.

He snapped, 'You don't have to pretend you like that thing and wear it just to please me. I'm not stupid, you know. I can see through falsehood straightaway.'

It was an item of lingerie as ridiculous in its mystique of lace, straps and strings as it must have been in its price. She had no doubt her husband had bought it upon the insistence, and with the help, of the incorrigible Mrs Olivia Phang: she could never wear it with a fraction of the seductive eagerness which that happy woman, never happier than when she was by her husband's side, must bring to her entire wardrobe of foreign-made lingerie.

The sight of the black lacy item on her body suddenly infuriated him. 'Take it off,' he said. 'Give it to me.' He got up from bed and flung it out of the window. She would remember to get up early and retrieve it before anybody found it.

Maria thought, relieved at not having to hide her relief since her husband had already left for the trip, 'Three days. I shall have time to look at my story again, maybe write another.'

She was turning more and more to the world of her imagination for solace, to balance the bleakness of the reality. There was a price to pay; the imagination sometimes spilled over into the dreams at night and heightened the terror.

She was somewhere in the Botanic Gardens, in a secluded spot hidden from sight by bushes and trees. 'That's a nice nightie you have on,' said Dr Phang, and he made to touch the lacy straps on her shoulders. 'Why, you're crying. Tell me,' he said gently and laid her head on his shoulder. 'It must be that Bernard. He's such a pain in the ass. You are completely mismatched. I saw that in Cameron Highlands, on the first day of your honeymoon. Do you plan to leave him?'

She said, 'I can't! I can't!'

'Why not?' he demanded, but she could only continue weeping and repeat, 'I can't!'

He bent down to kiss her. 'You know, beneath all that docile exterior lies so much unused love. You were never meant for a life of solitude, my dear.'

They heard the sound of approaching footsteps. Bernard was shouting, 'Alright, come out, wherever you are. I've caught you. I've got grounds for divorce now. Caught you in the act, you bitch, you slut!' For she was standing before him, naked, the lingerie on the grass.

'Who was that with you?' He pulled somebody out of the bushes, yelling triumphantly, 'Got you! I knew it was you all along. I'll set the police on you for seducing my wife.'

'Yes, go ahead, you bastard,' said Brother Philip, also naked. 'She came to me for comfort because you never gave her any!' and knocked him to the ground.

His dreams which he never told her must have had their own share of terrors; she would wake up suddenly to long drawn-out groans, incoherent bits of angry conversation, an arm suddenly flung out in the darkness, and would instantly sit up to soothe him, stroking his forehead, rubbing his chest, bringing him a cup of hot water, whispering calming words into his ears, as to a child in delirium. Kindness was no substitute for love either, and retreated at once if mistaken for passion.

As soon as he sat up, looked around, realised it was only a bad dream and saw his wife beside him, all gentle solicitousness, he would break into something like a sob and pull her towards him in a return of hope and yearning, and she would inwardly recoil, in a return of guilt and desperation. It was an impossible situation they were in, the dreams at night being now an extension of their torments by day. Through her own fault, she had become the best exemplar of that warning about marrying in haste and repenting at leisure: only the haste she had married in had nothing to do with passion, and the long, grey vistas stretching endlessly ahead were not of repentance, since she had done nothing wrong, but of regret for an act of sheer folly and stupidity.

On the first anniversary of their marriage, he said with a wry smile, 'Why don't we give each other the best anniversary present ever?'

She dreaded the sarcasms that often followed the statements or the questions delivered with slow deliberateness for effect. 'Why don't we see a marriage counsellor, since we're going nowhere?'

She knew his pride and sensitivity would never allow a full unburdening of secrets, whether to strangers or family, whether to professional counsellors or close friends. Only his sharp-eyed Third Aunt, on a visit sixth months into their marriage had pulled her aside to say, in a poignantly brave attempt at English, 'My Ah Siong. He so thin. He not happy. You got take care of him?'

He liked to come up with unusual statements and suggestions for the sole purpose of provoking a reply from her, of breaking into her long silences: 'Why aren't you pregnant yet? Maybe the fault's all on my side. Why don't we seek medical help?' 'Should we think of adopting?'

She wondered why desperately unhappy women continued to stay on in their marriages, and concluded that it was not the oft claimed folly or lack of self-esteem. It was simple calculation: every unhappy woman had an abacus in her head in which she constantly did the sums of gain and loss, of continuing in the marriage or walking out. The most daunting cost lay in taking the initiative: suddenly she would have to face and justify her decision, not only to her husband but the entire support system of relatives, friends, colleagues, fellow church members. When a woman married, it was not just to an individual but a whole community. Even the much steeled woman would quail before the hideous prospect of facing the shock and disapproval, disappointment and sorrow of such a force whose first duty would be to argue her down and help her save her marriage. Think of your children, they would urge. Think of this. Think of that. What would people say.

Then of course there was the question of money. She had heard of couples who continued to be under the same roof because they could not afford another. One couple had had separate bedrooms for decades, communicating through their two children or notes stuck on doors.

In the end, it was easier for an unhappy woman to simply give up and resign herself to her lot in life. Taking stock of that lot, she could improve it in small ways – focusing on the children, going out more with her girlfriends, taking up community work. One woman she knew took up mah-jong and in the end came to rely completely on its compensatory solace. The tiny light at the end of a very long blistering tunnel would come when the children were grown up, started working and give her the financial independence she needed from her husband. But by that time, she would be an old woman, like the poor woman who suffered for thirty years in her marriage and revealed the truth in the sorrowful inscription on her tombstone: 'She died at thirty, and was buried at sixty.'

The daunting problems of children and money were not hers, yet there was no lightening of the heaviness of heart. Maria thought sadly: I would have no support whatsoever in my decision. Do I have the strength to stand all alone? An act of adultery, constant abuse, wastrel habits, a serious dereliction of husbandly duty – all these would be comprehensible because they were in the expected order of things, and be given due consideration. But lovelessness?

'Why, Maria,' everyone would exclaim, 'you're such a good, loving wife, always tending to your husband's needs. And Bernard's such a good husband. Anyone can see he loves you with his whole heart and soul!'

Her mother would be hysterical: 'Are you mad? He bought this apartment for you! He doesn't drink, gamble or womanise. You are his whole world. Do you know how many women would be glad to have Bernard as their husband? Why must you be so difficult?'

Fourteen

The owl's cry in the dead of night – she had heard it only once as a child, and it had remained a terror ever since, despite the weaning from the ancestral superstitions starting from the girlhood years in school, despite even the strong, enlightened stance of reason in adulthood. In the morning her mother asked her, then the maid, if they too had heard it, to confirm the final sign in a long series of an imminent death in the house.

Por Por had not been behaving like herself, a welcome sign only in the case of very old and sick people, that their release was in sight. Watching Por Por suddenly becoming quiet and subdued, sitting by herself in dark corners for long hours, she remembered the many tales she had heard – of the kindly, gentle old neighbour, aged eighty, who turned nasty and cursed everyone in the household for a whole week before he died, of the nasty mother-in-law who suddenly stopped scolding her long-suffering daughter-in-law and died actually holding the young woman's hand. It was as if they needed to give warning of their approaching death in the most conspicuous way possible – a total reversal of personality and temperament. External signs like the owl's cry, a sudden discharge of scent into the air of pale nocturnal flowers, even the sound of knuckles knocking on coffins, were all but secondary warnings.

She bent down and looked into Por Por's face, offered to take her shopping, to the playground, to the White Heaven Temple, and watched in dismay as the old woman silently and resolutely shook her head, like a dispirited child, to each offer. Bernard, whose kindness in searching for and bringing her grandmother back home almost three years ago she would never forget, joined her in trying to break through the thick silence that the old one had wrapped round herself, like a warm, comforting blanket. Both were able, just for a while, to step out of their world of silent conflict, growing more fearful by the day, to stand side by side as a pair in a unity of concern and compassion for another.

The pleasant thought was interrupted by a sombre one: could tension between two persons in a household spread outwards, like a dark and pestilential cloud, to infect others? Could even very young children in their cribs and cradles succumb to slow, silently spreading adult poison?

She spoke about the owl's cry to Bernard, and he dismissed it, as he regularly dismissed the superstitions of elderly relatives like his Third Aunt, as just so much of the traditional nonsense forbidden by the Church. Nowadays he turned every statement, every question, no matter how innocuous, into yet one more painful reminder of the hopelessness of their marriage, a continuing supply of fuel for an angry furnace that needed to be fed constantly. She waited with weary resignation and it came as expected, accompanied by a bitter laugh: if the owl's cry was a sign of *his* impending death, it would be no bad thing. She thought grimly: wallowing in self-pity only made a person sink deeper in the regard of others.

She wondered how much her memory had been influenced by her ever active imagination to fix permanently in her mind the recollection of a little girl who had died the morning after an owl's cry was heard. The girl and her mother had rented part of a room in a large rundown house with many rooms, endlessly partitioned by a greedy landlord, to take in as many as possible of the near destitute that regularly came with small children and belongings hurriedly stuffed into baskets or wrapped in sarongs. To this house her father had once taken her, her mother and Por Por in one of his frantic attempts to escape the loan sharks. She vividly remembered the thin, sickly-looking, sad-eyed little girl who was about the same age as herself, always wearing ragged, oversized clothes and rubber sandals, and sleeping with her mother on a dirty mattress in a tiny corner of a room.

In the middle of the night, at least six people woke up to the long, drawn out cry of the owl, and in the morning they looked upon the cold stiff body of the little girl on the mattress, and the mother squatting beside her, crying softly. She remembered her parents quickly packing up to leave, her mother pressing some money into the hands of the weeping woman; within a day, the house of death had been emptied of all its tenants.

No, it was nonsense. No bird's cry would take her Por Por from her, and no change of behaviour in an old woman who habitually swung from one mood to another, like a temperamental child, should be cause for alarm.

Then Por Por suddenly emerged from her solitude to launch upon a series of activities that were alarming, not for any portentousness but for sheer danger to her life. She managed to slip out of the house several times, displaying the cunning of a sly caged prisoner intently watching for the smallest slip in vigilance of the prison keeper. She was on one occasion found near a Hindu shrine and on another, near her favourite haunt, the White Heaven Temple. 'Por Por, you could have been killed by all those cars and buses, don't you understand?' said Maria in tears, examining her for injuries. Bernard had once suggested putting her in a home, the best and most comfortable in Singapore, but spoke no more on the matter when he saw his wife's distress.

Then Por Por's escapades took on a strange focus and urgency that only later Maria understood, in a return of all the old fears of tradition she thought she had left behind. Heng had managed to track the old woman down at the White Light Temple where she seemed to have gone with a special purpose. 'What's that? Show me,' he ordered, but she insisted on hiding something behind her back. It turned out to be nothing alarming, only a joss stick that she must have taken from one of the many urns in the temple.

'Por Por, what are you doing?' Anna Seetoh asked as she saw the old woman stirring some ash in a cup of water with a spoon. The maid said it was ash from the joss stick; she had been trying to make a mixture for some time, like a small child engrossed in make-believe cooking.

'Por Por, what on earth –' Maria had opened the bedroom door in response to the frantic knocking.

The old woman was holding the cup of joss stick water and walking towards Bernard who had sat up, fully awake.

She put the cup to his lips, saying clearly in her dialect, 'Drink this, it will cure you.'

The strange incident could have been dismissed as yet one more harmless eccentricity of demented old age if it had not been followed by a similar one, this time while they were having breakfast. Por Por walked straight up to Bernard, removed a packet of something from her blouse pocket, and said, 'The gods have blessed this. Wear it close to your heart. It will save you.'

The packet contained some dried marigold petals which Maria instantly recognised as those from a garland that Por Por had some time ago removed from a stone god in a Hindu shrine and which she and the maid had hastily put back.

If Bernard experienced any frisson of terror in being singled out as one in dire need of supernatural help, he showed no sign of it, merely receiving the packet calmly and murmuring something to humour the old woman. Por Por watched with keen intensity; when he did nothing with the saving gift and continued eating his breakfast, she burst into a frenzy of scolding and had to be led away. Maria watched with mounting anxiety.

The ancient fearful world of darkness and owls and portents had come back to trouble her, and distilled into a single deadly chill that froze all power of speech and thinking, exactly a week later, when she had a call from the office of Dr S.K. Chiang to whom her husband went for his regular medical check-ups.

Dr Chiang said, 'I need to speak to your husband; it's urgent.'

She said, her mouth suddenly very dry, 'What's wrong? Could you tell me, Doctor?'

Dr Chiang said, 'I really would like to speak to your husband personally. Tell him to call me as soon as he can.'

She made a frantic call to his office where he was having an important meeting and could not be interrupted. 'Please tell him it's extremely important,' she begged the secretary. He came on the phone, none too pleased about having to leave a meeting that he was chairing. 'Alright,' he said when she told him. 'I'll call Dr Chiang after the meeting.'

'Will you let me know as soon as you can?' she asked, and he could not resist the opportunity to say, with the habitual hard-edged cynicism, 'Why this concern for me all of a sudden?'

'Please let me know,' she pleaded. 'Alright,' he said in a softened tone.

She did not want to share her fears with her mother, in case they turned out to be unfounded: her imagination, in a wild flight of hope, pictured her husband coming through the door talking with unaccustomed good humour about wrong prognoses and alarmist doctors.

If she could, she would have shared her fears with Por Por, to draw out the explanation for those weird actions that now seemed like some dreadful portent. She looked at Por Por who was looking at her with the quizzical half frown of someone trying hard to remember something. An old woman rapidly losing her mind, who had suffered much in her youth, who must have a huge store of secret hopes, dreams and passions that would finally go to the grave, unknown and unfulfilled, together with that frail body: were women like Por Por, at the last stage of their bitter lives, given the gift of the owl, the harbinger of death? Were they also given the power to avert doom? The image of Por Por offering Bernard the saving joss stick ash from her temple, and later, the holy flower petals from an alien shrine would not go away. In different circumstances, could Por Por have become like the powerful Venerable Mother in the White Heaven Temple, dispensing hope to the hopeless? The dark forces of tradition that modernity's vanguards of education and technology claimed they had routed, were unroutable.

At the sound of the key turning in the lock, she rushed to the door to face her husband. He did not look at her; his pale taut face told her everything.

'Dear –' It was the first time in their married life of nearly three years that she had used any term of endearment to the man she had promised to love, honour and obey, elicited by none of these imposed vows, but a natural compassion that swelled and overwhelmed her. 'Dear,' she said again and took his arm. She said it in the fullness of heart; if her heart had never had any place for this thing called love for which men and women supposedly married, it could at least enlarge now to fill itself with kindness.

Kindness was superior to pity, to sympathy, to empathy, maybe even to love itself, for unlike any of these, it was never self-serving but translated immediately into action to help, relieve and comfort the sufferer. No other human feeling had been compared to milk, for indeed it was one with that life-giving sustenance: she saw herself, from that moment onwards, being impelled by this purest of motives to do everything for her husband. If love was a talent she did not have, kindness was the compensating gift of which she had been blessed with plenty.

'Dear,' she said, and her husband turned once to give her a brief forlorn look that said, 'Too late.'

They were dreary days which she would remember with much sadness, filled with anxious waiting never rewarded with good news. The prognosis, confirmed by two other cancer specialists, was even worse than expected. There was an initial period, expected in such circumstances of shock and disbelief, when the sufferer lashed at all and sundry in the sheer incomprehensibility of it all. How could Dr Chiang have failed to detect the cancer in all those regular check-ups? How could it have spread so rapidly and virulently without notice? All those expensive tests, all those reassurances. Anna Seetoh, always awed by her son-in-law, readily joined him in castigating the doctor.

There was a moment of wavering faith when Bernard turned his cynicism in another direction, dismaying the parish priest Father Rozario who had come to comfort as soon as he heard the news.

'Father, why does God punish those who have always served Him faithfully? Can you explain that?' His tone of grievance was by turns plaintive, savage. For a while, the very sight of life itself was too cruel a reminder of his impending loss of it, so that visitors, by the mere fact of their being alive and in good health, gave offence and were not welcome.

Facing death, he hated the living. Por Por, her mother, herself, the maid Rosiah, the delivery boy coming in with the groceries, the caller on the phone, the TV news presenter – each, as he saw and heard them, still a participant in the greatest human enterprise called life, must have squeezed out of him, again and again, the wrenching cry, 'Why me?'

It would only be a matter of time, thought Maria, before he turned upon her, in blame's desperate escalation: 'Cancer is brought on by stress, as the medical literature has proved. For the last three years, I have never been so stressed in my life.'

When the accusation came, in all the remaining bitterness that had to be expelled from his system, she received it humbly, thinking only of the relief it gave him. Third Aunt came on an urgent visit, pulled her aside and said in a rebuke she was able to receive with equal humility because it bore no malice, only love of the suffering man: 'I told you my Ah Siong not happy, so thin. Why you never take care of him? Why you never tell me?'

Fifteen

It took some time for her to absorb the brutal ultimatum of death's sentencing. Four months, the doctors had said, at most six. But what about those cases she had heard where the patient, given some months, lived on for years? What about those who beat the disease altogether? The doctors, understandably, were wary of giving false hope. She knew her husband knew, but that deadly piece of knowledge would never be openly brought up, as if its mere mention might hasten its fulfilment. In a house of death, the word was assiduously avoided, both by the sufferer and those in timid attendance on him.

Anna Seetoh, who never spoke much to her son-in-law, used the same neutral terms whenever she had to say something to him: 'This soup is good for giving energy.' 'This oil is good for massaging the arms and legs.' She stuck to the language of hope, 'When you get well,' but abandoned it when talking privately to her daughter, 'When Ah Siong dies, what are you going to do?'

Father Rozario, in charge of preparing his parishioners for death, did not have the luxury of circumvention. He asked Bernard's permission to make an announcement of the illness after his sermon, so that fellow parishioners at the Church of

Eternal Mercy might start novenas for his recovery. Bernard managed a small sharp laugh, his proud, sensitive nature recoiling from an outpouring of sympathy from people he hardly knew, or cared to know.

'It's alright, Father. Your prayers are good enough. Besides, as you can see, I'm still well enough to go to church on some days.' Later Father Rozario said to Maria and her mother, 'We can have our own private prayer gatherings here, with a few close friends of Bernard's choice. We will all pray for a miracle. It *will* happen, with Bernard's acceptance of God's will. That in itself is a miracle, you see.'

Maria thought, I will join in all the prayers, in all the storming of heaven for a miracle, even if I believe in neither. Indeed, for the past year, even as she accompanied her husband to church and joined him in the partaking of the holy sacraments, she was aware of a falsehood that simply could not be sustained in its enormity. The comforting God of childhood, the benign presence whom she greeted, both upon waking and sleeping, with words of love and adoration, as taught by her mother, was now a vague irrelevant presence far removed from the exigencies of everyday living. It did not need the combined impact of those TV news programmes she watched to emphasise the irrelevance – of whole villages washed away in a hurricane, of innocent families clinging to each other and their bundles of belongings, fleeing brutal soldiers, of children walking around on stumps, their legs blown off by hidden mines when they went looking in the fields for scrap metal to sell.

She had thought she could write stories about God and that particular group of His creatures He had singled out for special loving mention, but it would have been too painful. She thought she could write about the little children she often read about in newspaper reports, who were washed away in deadly typhoons, crushed by tons of mortar in earthquakes, or died from disease, poverty, starvation and constant abuse from adults, while an omnipotent, omniprescient and omnibenevolent God was presumably looking on. Her stories would have bristled with a hundred frantic questions, fired uselessly into the vastness of divine indifference: why did they have to suffer? What wrong had they done? What did that promise mean, the promise that had begun with a rebuke to the adults to stop making a fuss, and to suffer the little children to come to Him, to touch His divine person as only children could, climbing upon the divine knees for a hug, fighting to be in the divine arms for a cuddle, for of such was the kingdom of Heaven?

If He existed, she thought, she could count on this perfect love to understand her timidity, very much like a child's, and to forgive all that pretence of going to church, receiving the sacraments, conducting catechism lessons, as one would smile at a child's desperate whistling in the dark or telling fantastical tales to hide his fear; if He did not, all that pretence, as a purely human coping mechanism, was quite acceptable.

In his illness, Bernard had some good days when he would go to church, in complete reconciliation with his God after the initial outburst of anger. 'You needn't come along if you don't wish to,' he said to her. Was he aware of her increasing alienation from the religion in which they had made their marital vows to love till death did them part, or was he simply being considerate, aware that she was juggling the demands of both the job in school and the caregiving at home? For the first time in their married life, she had difficulty detecting his tone, to act in accordance with his wish; the line between cynicism and civility had become blurred by the muffled, laboured speech and the habit, from the beginning of the illness, to look down or away each time he spoke to her.

Silence served her as well now as it did in those days of quivering confrontation; it was the silence of kindness, giving much peace of mind, not of resentment, throwing her whole being into turmoil. As they made their way into church or out of it, her husband leaning on her, a shrunken version of his former proud, confident self, it was no longer pity she felt for him, but something transcending it, enabling her to fend off the pitying looks cast in their direction and turn to him even more attentively.

She had taken to speaking to a rapidly disappearing God as if He were still the solid presence of her childhood years: 'God, if You're still around, I'm going to Holy Communion now with Bernard because it pleases him, and he's very ill, and that's no sacrilege, is it, God?' After a while, the silent messages of apology and excuse became tedious and stopped altogether, as she joined the prayer group from the Church of Eternal Mercy, led by Father Rozario, saying prayers and singing hymns, first for his body, and as it rapidly deteriorated, for his soul. There was a wall mirror in the room where she could see herself kneeling with her mother and the prayer group from the Church of Eternal Mercy, holding a hymn book, her mouth open in song and prayer, the expression on her face perfectly harmonised with that of the others in an outpouring of love, goodwill and hope. The sight always induced a sense of surreality, as if she were a detached presence looking upon another Maria, created for the sole purpose of making a dying man happy. When her husband died, this false Maria would too. She felt not the slightest twinge of guilt for the outward appearance of worshipful trust and the inward reality of hardening disbelief and isolation that would soon make her a shocking prodigal daughter of the church. For kindness, like a powerful mantle, covered all sins, even those of lying and sacrilege.

Years later, in the quiet of reflection, she would try to understand this strange period in her life, when the contradictions of her inner and outer worlds had all come together in one huge disjunction and irony, mocking, then cancelling each other out – the selfless kindness to her dying husband meant to compensate for the great unkindness of having married him without love, the open display of a religious fervour that had long ceased privately, the tremulous awareness that in the darkening shadows of a house of death, her hopes of a radiant new life were being born. Por Por placed a stool beside Bernard's bed and sat there, looking at him and making strange little noises. Anna Seetoh said to the maid, 'Take her away, don't let her disturb Sir,' and Bernard who was lying very still, opened his eyes and said, 'No, let her stay.'

When Maria entered the room with a flask of hot ginseng tea for her husband, it was to look upon a strange little scene of perfect amity, where an old, demented woman and a dying man who did not speak each other's language were clasping hands.

'Tell her,' said Bernard with a smile on his thin, pallid face, 'that she made really good rice porridge for my breakfast.'

Maria thought, the tears coming into her eyes, 'If I could love him for nothing else, I could love him for this.'

Why, in the midst of the determination to be all kindness to her husband, did she still have the unkind thought that even as he lay dying, even as he showed kindness to others, he meant to continue to exact full compensation for the misery she had caused him? He was actually the most considerate of patients, submitting stoically to all the painful and tedious procedures required by the doctors and nurses, choosing to suffer additional discomfort rather than deprive anyone in the household of sleep or rest, accepting, with grace, the hours of massaging by his wife and mother-in-law.

'Maria,' he said. 'I would like you to help me choose a fitting quotation from the Bible for my obituary.'

This was the first time he was referring directly to his approaching death; for the first time too in his illness, he was looking at her with the hard look of a returning pride that meant to reclaim itself.

'How would you like me to do it?' she asked.

'I would like you to go through the Bible and find something that you think will be fitting,' he said, looking closely at her. The old habit of wary suspicion came back.

'A trap,' she thought. 'He's laying a trap for me.' Was he going back to the old habit of turning her words into an accusation, a wry comment on the failure of their marriage? Her choice of a quotation, any quotation from the holy book, would be sufficient grist for his bitter mill.

She played safe by presenting to him a collection of the most common quotations in the obituary pages of *The Singapore Tribune*: '*I have fought the good fight, I have kept the faith, I have finished the race.*' 'What about that?' she asked.

His mind was regaining its cynical sharpness even as his body was declining. 'I'm not so sure about finishing the fight yet,' he said pointedly, and her suspicion about a two-fold punishment in getting her to refer to the Bible was confirmed: he wanted to compel her to have recourse to a book she no longer believed in, and he wanted to remind her of her role in his misery through no less than the pronouncements of God Himself.

Just when she thought that her kindness and his acceptance of it were providing a comforting closure to the tragedy of their marriage, he sought to reopen the old wounds. *Oh Bernard, Bernard.*

'What about this one?' she asked. She had written it out in large print for him:

'I will wait patiently for God to save me,
I depend on Him alone.
He alone protects and saves me,
He is my defender, and I shall never be defeated.'

She realised her mistake, when he was immediately provoked to turn the prayer of praise into one of complaint: 'God, You never protected or saved me; You never were my defender. I could have borne any cancer, God, but what cancer can be worse than a loveless life?'

They were alone in the room; he did not want to discharge the bitter sorrow of his marriage into other ears. She murmured something about having to leave the room for a while; she rushed to the old comforting sanctuary of the locked bathroom, in a desperate effort to beat back the old anger and revulsion. For a few minutes, she stood before the bathroom mirror, clutching the sides of the sink, looking upon the whiteness of her knuckles.

When she returned, her husband who appeared to be wide awake said, 'Well, have you found one yet?' and she wearily rolled out for him the entire feast of heaven's promises: *'The Lord is my Shepherd, I shall not be in want'*; *'Surely goodness and mercy shall follow me all the days of my life and I shall dwell in the house of the Lord forever'*; *'In My Father's house, there are many mansions.'* He was less interested in the prospect of heavenly sojourn than of earthly remembrance in his wife's mind. 'Why don't you write the obituary yourself?' he said, and she knew that all the Bible searching was only a preamble for the ultimate rebuke which had its own preamble of extravagant praises. 'You are an extremely creative, widely read person. You are a teacher of English language and literature. You are going to be given the Teacher of the Year Award.' The intensity of purpose gave a new clarity to his voice, a new brightness to his eyes. 'Surely you will be able to come up with a first class obituary for your husband. It could be in the form of a poem, or even a very short story.'

Carried away by the discharge of so much emotion, he began to splutter, and she rushed to give him a drink of warm water. The small act of concern by no means blunted the sharpness of the taunt which continued to spiral upwards on a new spurt of energy.

'Will you swear eternal love to the deceased? Will I live forever in your heart? Will you spend your days waiting to join me on that eternal shore, etc. etc.' He fell back on his pillows, exhausted. She thought sorrowfully, 'When will all this end?'

His anger was spent at last; the taunt, like an angry flame that had flared up, died down as quickly. He said, looking at the large pile of unmarked scripts on a nearby table that she would work on during those hours when he was asleep, 'That's a lot of work you've brought home. You must be very tired. I am too. I'm going to close my eyes and rest for a while.'

She fell asleep in her chair, and had the most troubling of dreams. Her husband walked through the door, waving a piece of paper in his hand. His face was bright with excitement and joy. 'You'll never guess!' he shouted. 'Dr Chiang was wrong. All those doctors were wrong. They made a mistake. I don't have the disease after all. The X-ray shows no tumour!' Her mother cried out, 'A miracle!' and was joined by several women in the prayer group who cried out, 'Thanks be to the Lord! Our novena of supplication to the Holy Virgin Mary has saved him!' Bernard turned upon all of them to say scornfully, 'Miracle, my foot! There's no such thing. You can all pray till the cows come home. The doctors made a mistake, that's all. I could sue them, you know. Sue them for all the anxiety they caused us.' He came to her and held her face in his hands in a tight grip. 'Hey, is that a look of disappointment I see? Yes, it is! You are disappointed that your husband is not going to die after all. Isn't it bad enough that you don't love me, without wishing for my death?' He struck her across the face with the X-ray document, then chased her around the room. 'I will outlive all of you!' he shouted triumphantly. 'I have suffered enough, and mean to be happy from now onwards. Do you hear?'

He caught her, and held her with one hand while he pulled out something from his shirt pocket with the other. 'The greatest mistake of my life!' he cried, waving the Tiffany ring before her eyes. 'Good thing I managed to find it. With the help of Maggie.' The girl appeared from behind a door, dressed in a sexy nightdress, simpering. 'I've been good and honourable all my life, and what has it brought me? Nothing. From now on, I'll be selfish. I mean to have all the sex I want. You hear that, you cold, unfeeling bitch?' And he struck her again.

She awoke with a start, almost falling off her chair, and saw her students' work scattered on the floor around. She heard her husband say, 'Come and rest with me,' and he made place for her on his bed.

Sixteen

Dr Phang's visit was the most welcomed because her husband was most cheered by it. On the verge of entering the next life, he seemed more interested in the affairs of this one, and, in his frail voice, asked his boss about a number of pending matters in the office. Was the deputy prime minister still making his regular visits to the department? Who would be the delegates for the coming conference in Bangkok?

Maria said, each time the visit ended and Dr Phang bade a brief goodbye in his usual cheerful manner, 'Thank you. I hope you'll come again soon. You cheer Bernard up, like nobody can.'

She was grateful to this man. Her pitying kindness was the wrong kind, only emptying out her poor husband's pride; his boss's, tactful and gracious, put back some of it. For Dr Phang had one afternoon brought the draft of an important ministerial paper and consulted him on it. A faint flush of restored pride had actually animated his pale face and sunken eyes, and given a new strength to his voice. The incident would have given her far more pleasure if he had not thought to use it against her, as she was arranging the pillows to enable him to sit up.

He said slowly, without looking at her, 'It's good to know that I'm appreciated.' It was not only the cancer that was consuming him but his own obsessive torments which, with the clarity that the last deathbed moments were supposed to bring, he was casting at her door: see what you have done to me. I'll make sure you don't forget.

She had thought once of a desperate move to remove that even more virulent cancer – explain the whole situation to Father Rozario or Dr Phang, tell the whole story of the colossal failure of their marriage and her part in it, with the unflinching honesty that she would never again be called upon to show. Throw herself at their feet and plead: you know my husband best, tell me what I should do; better still, you take over where I have failed. She could imagine their shocked faces as she looked into their eyes and repeated the centerpiece of the entire melancholy narrative: 'I never loved Bernard.'

Father Rozario would likely try to save the situation by saying, 'But you were a good wife. You were faithful. You were loyal. You've done your duty very well,' and she would have to say, 'But Bernard and I were both romantics in our own ways. We both saw that it was not the real thing, and we are both suffering for it.' As for Dr Phang, she could not imagine his reaction. He must have married both times out of love, first to the intellectual woman, and then to the flamboyant model.

It was an existential impasse beyond the counselling power of any priest or good friend.

The idea was abandoned as soon as it arose, for the possibility of complicating a situation already so hideously complex was simply insupportable. She would not be able to survive the heinousness of one last blunder, one last accusing look from her dying husband that said, 'So this is your coup de grâce? You want to destroy my standing with two of my closest friends in the world?' The bizarre Gordian knot of their marriage, with its many impossibly twisted strands, could only be undone by the swift, cruel stroke of death's sword that would leave its own wound on her long after her husband was gone.

By now she understood and accepted the final state of her dying husband's feelings towards each of those committed to being with him in the remaining weeks of his life on earth: genuine love of his Third Aunt, high regard for his priest and his boss, continuing active anger against his wife, and tolerance of everyone else. She alone of all the inhabitants in his world stood denounced and unforgiven, because upon her alone he had placed the highest stakes and lost. If it was true that stress caused cancer, she alone was responsible for the death of his body too. There could be no greater devastation. His deathbed balancing of accounts could not take the usual gentle course of seeking forgiveness. Instead, forgiveness was something for him to give and even then only conditionally – she had to come as a true penitent.

The only penitence she was capable of was the bruising honesty unacceptable to his pride: 'I beg forgiveness because I married you after those terrible events connected with the ring that made me feel so sorry for you.' She could twist the act of contrition to suit his pride, 'I beg forgiveness because I realise now that I've loved you all along but was just too carried away by my career and other interests,' and in the process give him some measure of satisfaction while committing the greatest falsehood in her life. She thought grimly, I will not let the close of your life blight the beginning of mine.

One thing she was clear about: she would redouble her acts of kindness and compassion towards him, and if they fell uselessly against the great wall of his unresolved grievances, she would not be daunted.

Kindness, not convertible into love, still converted into an incredible amount of physical stress and personal sacrifice – her colleagues and students in St Peter's had expressed alarm at her loss of weight, her loss of spirits. It gave her some satisfaction that the price she was paying for her injustice to her husband was by no means small. She knew of women who put their dying husbands in homes and hospices because they could no longer cope with the terrible physical exertions of the caregiving.

It would be her own private purgatory, very much like that awesome state of punishment with its cleansing flames, prior to admission into heaven, by which she would have to fully discharge her debt to her husband, down to the last farthing, before being allowed to enter a new life of pure joy free from the treacherous pitfalls of love and marriage. In bidding a final goodbye to him, she would also be walking away from that institution for which she had been so woefully unqualified. If the fervent masses and prayers offered by Father Rozario, by her mother and the church prayer group, earned for Bernard's soul immediate entry into heaven, she and her husband would be entering their respective paradises at the same time.

The thought struck her with such force that she paused in her marking of students' scripts to dwell on it as Bernard lay in fitful sleep beside her. Meeta and Winnie had told her of caregiving spouses for whom the sense of relief when it was all over was in proportion to the stress suffered. Winnie's cousin who had cared for a particularly difficult husband bedridden after a massive stroke, even described it as her hallelujah moment. 'I was almost ashamed I could feel such relief,' she had said. 'I went on a cruise with my girlfriends, looked at the gulls circling in the sky and said to them, 'You know, I feel freer than you!' '

It was that perilous word again. Women from time immemorial sought freedom in its every form, and if they won it through the death of a spouse, felt guilty and were ashamed of having betrayed the ideals of wifely duty that society had held up for them. Freedom stood opposed to the sanctity of marriage and had become a bad word.

But the future, increasingly showing itself in tantalising glimpses, would not be allowed to intrude upon the present. And the greatest duty of the present was to allow her dying husband to go to his death in the only way he wanted – to discharge upon her submissive head all the years of grievances she had caused him. For him only this restoration of equilibrium would bring peace to his tortured soul.

Dr Phang had an idea which she took up eagerly, to allow for a bright spot in the terrible gloom of those days. It would be Bernard's birthday in a few days; if it happened to be one of the good days when he could get up from bed, would he like a celebration lunch in a private room of the Pavilion Hotel? It would be a short outing only, and everything would be done for his convenience and comfort.

Maria said to Dr Phang, with the tears coming into her eyes, which they did very frequently in those days, 'Thank you so much. Would you tell him, encourage him?' and had to mention that on no account must he give the impression that she had anything to do with the idea, as that would only meet with opposition.

Dr Phang looked at her and said quietly, 'I understand.' How much did he understand of the awful complexities of their marriage? How much had Bernard told him?

She would be taking extended, no-pay leave from school soon, to be on round-the-clock duty by her husband's bed.

It was unfortunate that Bernard's birthday coincided with the celebration of Teachers' Day in school, when she knew she would be given a special award for her work in the steady improvement of the English language examination grades over the years. She would make known her wish to leave the celebration as soon as she could to be in time for the all-important lunch at the Pavilion Hotel.

It would appear that the whole school was in a conspiracy to be kind to her during this most difficult time in her life. Even Teresa Pang came forward with a few kind words and offers to take over some of her classes. At a time when she was anxious to quickly get done with the various ceremonies of the festive day and rush home, everybody seemed to be making demands on her time and attention. Brother Philip stopped her briefly as she was hurrying along the corridor to say, 'You may no longer believe in the power of prayer, but I'm praying for you and your husband.'

She said, 'But I do believe in the power of kindness. So continue to pray for me, and thank you so much.'

'Miss Seetoh, I want you to meet the most important person in my life,' said Maggie and she pushed forward a young girl of about twelve. 'This is my sister Angel. She is in Mansor Secondary School. Today a holiday in her school, and I have brought her here so can introduce you. Angel, this is Miss Seetoh, the most wonderful teacher in the world I tell you about!'

Maggie slipped in and out of the many roles she took upon herself; she was playing this one, of older sister or surrogate mother, with greatest pride and enthusiasm, suddenly looking older than her years.

The younger sister who was extremely pretty, said shyly, 'Hello, Miss Seetoh,' and held out her hand.

'I give her the name 'Angel'; don't you think it suit her? Her old name 'Ah Choo' – *yuks* – so low-class and common; I told my mother I want change it. Now her name, in school register, is 'Angel',' cried Maggie, smoothing the girl's hair with such a display of maternalistic pride that Maria wondered, as she had wondered many times, about the home background which the girl was so assiduously keeping hidden from her teachers and classmates.

Maggie confided in hushed tones, 'You know what, Miss Seetoh, my little sister Angel, she's very bright, only her English not so good. I want to get her into St Peter's Secondary School, so you can teach her, Miss Seetoh. I will go to see the principal and the inspector of schools at the ministry. Angel, she must go to the university. I not so good, cannot study well, will go to work after GCE O Level, but Angel, she is very intelligent girl, must go for further studies!'

The award-giving ceremony would start in twenty minutes. Maggie suddenly took her by the hand and, followed by Angel, dragged her into a small room sometimes used as a private study room by students and teachers.

'Maggie, what on earth –' she began, noting the girl's look of eager intent and Angel's excitement which she was trying to suppress by pressing her mouth with both hands. Inside the room, she saw Mark and Yen Ping, unlikely companions in any prank devised by Maggie and yet just now looking as if they were close co-conspirators in some worthy plot.

Maggie said, 'Miss Seetoh, today your special day. We want to make you look beautiful when you go up to receive award from the principal. You are already beautiful but we want to make you look like film star!'

The purpose of the ambush into the private study room was clear as soon as Maria saw, laid out on a table, an assortment of make-up items. 'Oh no,' she said laughing, 'you're not going to put all that stuff on my face!'

'Please, Miss Seetoh,' begged Yen Ping, and Mark joined her in her entreaties.

It turned out that the idea, in the oddest way, had originated with this shy, pale-faced girl who was far removed from the world of make-up and glamour as the pig-tailed, jacket-wearing girls of Mao's Cultural Revolution must have been. It had come about in a roundabout way that reflected how in a Christian school the ancient superstitions it sought to eradicate were very much alive.

Yen Ping told Miss Seetoh that when she was about fourteen, an aunt who worked in a beautician's parlour and was involved in various community activities, made her go on stage one evening to sing a song with some other girls during the Festival of the Hungry Ghosts. The transforming power of powder, lipstick and rouge extended to behaviour, and she sang with unabashed ardour and thrilling confidence before a large crowd, enjoying herself thoroughly. There was a picture of her at the event, completely unrecognisable even to family.

'You know what, Miss Seetoh,' said Yen Ping, her eyes shining with excitement. 'The evil spirit could not recognise me anymore and I was cured of my asthma!'

If there was any superstition that was the most laughable, it was this belief that the evil spirits who roamed the earth with malicious intent were so stupid that they could be deceived by the most superficial of disguises. Mothers protected their precious male children by giving them female names or making them wear earrings. There was a special evil spirit who killed healthy, able-bodied men in their sleep; those wishing to be left alone went to bed wearing their wives' sarong, lipstick and nail polish.

Yen Ping said, 'Miss Seetoh, you may not believe this, but my mother took me to one doctor after another for my asthma, but it was no use. Then after my aunt put make-up on my face that evening, my asthma disappeared. She took me to a temple medium who told us that the ghost who used to trouble me for years could no longer recognise me and left.'

Together with Mark, she came up with her plan, 'Miss Seetoh, if you put on make-up today – it is a special day of spirits – the bad spirit causing all your misfortunes will go away and your husband will be cured.'

Years later Maria would remember, how in her little world of St Peter's Secondary School, the Christian prayers of Brother Philip and the ancient practices of Yen Ping's ancestors, coming from opposite directions, had merged into one large, warm, comforting power sustaining her in her hour of need; for her, they would never clash but be perfectly harmonised by their common intention of goodwill and kindness.

While it would have been easy to reject Maggie's aim to make her look like a film star, it would have been impossible to disappoint the gentle Yen Ping who was looking at her in trembling expectancy.

'Alright,' said Maria, and everyone yelled with delight before Maggie took charge of the entire proceedings, and the rest were contented to assist by following her instructions to do this or that – stand watch at the door to see no one was spying, fan Miss Seetoh since it was a hot morning, get ready comb, hairbrush, lipstick, eyeliner and a myriad appurtenances that supposedly formed a woman's survival kit in a world dominated by men with an eye for beauty.

'Would you please hurry, the ceremony will start soon and then I have to be off!' urged Maria, as Maggie worked furiously. The girl never looked happier as her fingers worked expertly on her teacher's lips, cheeks, eyes, eyebrows, finally taking off the ponytail hairclip, and letting the lush hair fall down to her shoulders. She had a special brush to tease the hair into a riot of soft waves framing the face. With a dramatic bow, she held up a mirror for Miss Seetoh to look at her new self.

Maria gasped. 'Talk about evil spirits!' she said. 'I don't even recognise myself.'

Maggie said, 'Never mind evil spirits. You look like a film star!' Angel, completely infected by her sister's exuberance, was clapping her hands in delight.

Mark said admiringly, 'You know, Miss Seetoh, you look like the actress Gong Li. Maybe even more beautiful.'

There were tears in Yen Ping's eyes. As a final touch, Maggie produced a beautiful, expensive silk scarf and draped it round her neck. 'Sorry I can't give it to you, Miss Seetoh,' she said, 'but you keep it as long as you like.'

If she did not have to rush away so soon, she would have responded, with warmth and wit, to the students' enthusiastic reaction to her new appearance as she stood on stage in the school auditorium and received the award, a wooden plaque with gold inscriptions, from the principal. After the initial stunned silence, they broke into loud cheers and scrambled to have a closer look at Miss Seetoh. A few of the more rowdy boys let out wolf whistles. The principal managed to say, with great propriety, 'You see how they are all responding to your new look.'

She said, 'It isn't a new look that I'll wear to school everyday. Some crazy students gave me this makeover on a whim.'

The anxiety of wanting to be in time for the lunch at the Pavilion Hotel, of wondering how her husband was taking all the stress of the outing, and whether Dr Phang had ordered special food for him, caused her to keep to herself, for the time being, yet another student howler guaranteed to enliven life at St Peter's. The class prefect enjoined with the task of deciding on a suitable inscription for the plaque, had made the mistake not only of taking up valuable space with the completely unnecessary mention of the ornamental tablet itself, but of misspelling it, so that Miss Seetoh, for being the best English language Teacher, was awarded, as a token of deep appreciation by all her students, a 'plague'. Maria was so amused she almost let out a laugh. The mistake had gone unnoticed even by the teacher in charge of school trophies and medals; held up high in the air by Miss Seetoh in acknowledgement, it was probably unnoticed by everyone. She had only time to point to it surreptitiously to Brother Philip, saw his face crease in a broad smile and then rushed away.

There were deadlier demons than Yen Ping's evil spirits to vanquish; she had no idea how a student's caring act of the silly makeover could unleash a torrent of emotions that would end all hope of anything like a peaceful closure for both herself and her husband.

There had been no time to remove the make-up; she would realise its treachery only later. Right now, as she entered the private room in the Pavilion Hotel and everyone looked at her with surprise, all was good-natured jocularity.

Mrs Olivia Phang cried out, 'Oh my, oh my, how beautiful you look! I could hardly recognise you!' She turned to her husband and said teasingly, 'Darling, if you keep looking at Mrs Tan like this, I will get very jealous!'

Her mother said, 'What happened, Maria? You've never worn make-up in your life', to which Mrs Phang said very loudly, 'But don't you think she looks simply beautiful? I'm glad she's taken my advice at last to pretty herself up for her husband.'

Then she said to Bernard, 'You've got a very glamorous wife, Bernard – beats all those socialites in the glossy fashion magazines! All the more reason for you to get well and keep an eye on your wife. Otherwise, all the men will be chasing her!'

Carried away by the gratification of her useful advice to Maria, and unmindful of the constricted smile on Bernard's face, she laughed merrily into her perfumed handkerchief. Maria briefly acknowledged the presence of the two other guests for the lunch: Bernard's colleagues at the Ministry, whom she must have previously met but could not now recognise; they were staring at her as much as decorum would allow.

She had to get the explanation out as quickly as she could. Mrs Phang said, 'Well, your students have certainly done a good job. Tell you what, Mrs Tan, I can introduce you to my beautician and my hairstylist. He can do wonders with your hair. Bernard, you lucky man!'

Without looking into her husband's face, Maria knew the damage was already done; she could hear the words screaming inside his head: what are you trying to prove? Why have you chosen to taunt me publicly, on my birthday? Indeed, to the outsider, the radiantly beautiful wife could only increase the pity towards the husband and fuel speculation about a very merry widowhood.

'Come, time to cut the cake!' said Mrs Olivia Phang. 'Mrs Tan, you come and hold your husband's hand while he cuts the cake, just like a bridal couple. Here,' she called to a waiter, 'you take a picture of all of us.' And she led the others in the birthday song.

Days later, Dr Phang brought the birthday picture to show her and her husband. It showed both of them with wan smiles, their hands clasped over a beribboned knife held over a large chocolate birthday cake. Together with other photographs of themselves, it would have no place of remembrance in her heart.

Back home, she went straight to the bathroom and scrubbed off every bit of paint and powder.

'I see you've removed that make-up,' said her husband, as she got ready to massage his legs. 'So it wasn't for me that you went out of your way to make yourself beautiful.'

It would have been futile to remind him about that silly student caper; in his mind, the image of her flaunting her beauty in public was yet more fuel for his unquenchable self-pity. 'Go and put it on again.' The peevish perverseness to goad her all the way provoked, for the first time, a sharpness of tone in the sickroom. She said, 'But I don't have make-up. You know I never use it.' Maggie had actually slipped the stuff into her handbag with the words, 'You try it yourself. Very easy. Practise. You look better than some of our TV stars.'

'There you are, you see,' he said, 'you never do what I want you to.' And it was then that despite her determination to submit to all the torments with unremitting patience and kindness, she lashed out bitterly, 'Why are you so unreasonable, Bernard? I'd already explained that it was all some silly students' whim. Why are you so bent on making me miserable?'

He said, closing his eyes, 'I'm tired, I want to sleep. Leave me alone now.'

Seventeen

Dr Phang said, 'I had to tell you all that because I think he wished it.' A reluctant messenger with an accusatory message from a dying man to his wife, he kept his imperturbable demeanour but dispensed with the engaging smile.

They were outside the sickroom, standing near the door that was only half closed to allow her to hear any movement from her husband who appeared to be sleeping peacefully. She looked down, with a heaviness of heart, while Dr Phang looked anxiously into her face. Her mother passed by; she threw them a sharp, angry glance on behalf of a dying man whose wife and best friend were talking together in unseemly intimacy just outside his room. Later she would say to her daughter, 'Why does he come so often? Is it to see Ah Siong or you? You want to have people talking?'

Dr Phang's conveying of the message was as brief as he could make it, the chief point of which, in Bernard's own words, was her culpable encouragement of him all along, leading to the enormous commitment of the Tiffany ring. He would never, ever have flung it away if he had not been so devastated by her sudden inexplicable change of behaviour. And she would never have changed her mind about him if it had not been for that Brother Philip. A Christian brother in charge of moral education in a Christian school? He had as good as seduced her. There was proof. She talked in her sleep. She uttered his name. Not once but a few times. Dreams never lied. Dream-talk was incontrovertible proof. He had never confronted his wife with the proof of her sinful liaison out of sheer shame and respect for the Church and Father Rozario.

Oh Bernard, Bernard.

As Maria listened, she was swept up by immense waves of anger alternating with pity, pulling her in different directions, a helpless marionette between two maniacally competing puppeteers. It was heartbreaking that near the end of his life, her husband's tormented mind should be further visited by hallucinatory demons who viciously scrambled together past and present – he had not known about Brother Philip till after their marriage. The fiends smeared the line as well between truth and suspicion – she never talked in her sleep, and if she did, he would have awakened her to fling the incriminatory evidence in her face. The faintest shadow of proof had been sufficient to unleash his anger; the cry of a lover's name in sleep would have discharged it like a cannon and crushed her without mercy. She thought she was done with anger, but it rose to wrestle with the pity, and left her exhausted and numbed. Angry on behalf of Brother Philip, now co-villain, she thought: a person on the brink of death should not feel licensed by that fact alone to make wild accusations against the living.

She was aware of Dr Phang looking intently at her, as if waiting for an explanation: what was he thinking? What thoughts was he forming about her? It no longer mattered; she had no more strength for explanations. She said nothing, still looking down.

He reached for her hand and said, 'You're okay,' and it was at this point that the tears, held back with great effort, burst forth, and were instantly suppressed, making her body tremble all over. He had needed no explanation to continue to believe in her. *You're okay*. A commonplace banality of assurance, it comforted her as no avowal of trust and regard could. She made no effort to wipe the tears that were now freely coursing down her cheeks.

He reached out to hold her, and she rushed into his arms, pressing her face on his shoulder, like a frightened child desperate for protection and comfort after a long pretence of brave whistling in the dark. *You're okay.* In her confused and confusing little world, her husband, her mother, her brother, all looked at her and thought her mad, perverse, wilful, difficult, obdurate, selfish. They would never have said to her, 'You're okay.'

By the time they appeared at Bernard's bedside again, she had wiped away all her tears and appeared calm and composed. A deep peace, such as she had not felt for a long time, filled her heart. Bernard was still asleep. They sat on two chairs in a corner of the room and began talking, in whispers, so as not to disturb him. Dr Phang had more to say; he was done with the tiresome message of the dying man and was now concerned with practical matters: would she need his help for the onerous matters that had to be attended to upon the death of her husband which, according to the doctors, would be quite soon? The mere mention of the eventuality still brought on a sense of surreality, still sent little shuddering chills through her body.

The church people – they were very kind – would see to all the funeral arrangements. Her brother Heng was efficient and would also be at hand to take charge of other matters. She saw Dr Phang's hesitancy in bringing up a sensitive point: yes, financially she would be alright. She had some savings and if necessary would sell their apartment which had seen a huge jump in price since its purchase, pay off the rest of the mortgage, and move with her mother and Por Por to live in her mother's small apartment now being rented out with the approval of her brother Heng, who jointly owned the property with her.

They spoke softly, their heads almost touching. There were still a few moments of talking together before he needed to take his leave, and their conversation, even if unseemly in a room of the dying, took a lighter turn. 'Olivia has been talking of nothing but your new look at the restaurant lunch; you looked stunning,' he said smiling. It would have cheered her more if the compliment had made no attribution to a third person. The vanity of memory years on would preserve only the latter part of his statement. Now she felt light-hearted enough to want to extend the cheerful sharing; she told him the joke about the students presenting her with a plague for all her good work for them. He laughed out loud. She felt impelled to tell him a few more. There was one about the great TPK, and she told it before realising the horrible faux pas: Bernard had spoken several times of his being a protege of the prime minister, of being earmarked for political grooming and high political office. She apologised, and he held out a hand to stem the effusive apology. No need for that, he said, for he liked the joke very much and could himself produce a few, even more irreverent, ones.

Then he confided in her a secret which nobody, not even Olivia knew: he was seriously thinking of leaving the Ministry of Defence for another job. There had come a point in his life when he wanted change. 'I might start another political opposition party, to keep V.K. Pandy company,' he said, and when he saw her eyes round in astonishment, laughed again and said, 'Just joking. Political life is not for me!'

Oh, how she wished for them to be in circumstances where they could talk freely with each other, share views, reveal private dreams. Now there were these awful barriers between them. 'You know, I would love to be a writer,' she confided in her turn, and told him of her ever active imagination already filling itself with lively people and incidents that were just waiting to be spilled out upon the pages.

The conversation could not be allowed to go along its dangerously light-hearted path in a house soon to be visited with death; both dragged it back to the sombre decorum it had begun with.

He said, 'Don't forget. Let me know if you need help.' He gave her hand a reassuring squeeze and rose to take his leave.

She did not even dare say, as she normally would, 'Thank you, and please come again,' fearing to betray a greater need than her husband for the comfort of this man's presence.

Her husband stirred but continued to sleep peacefully. For the first time in many days, she had leisure to allow her thoughts to roam. Powered by her imagination, they took on a life of their own, bounding off in all directions like small animals let out of their cages or pens, eager to explore every corner of an exciting new world. Her new world had not yet taken on any clear shape, but in leaving behind the old one of confusion, distrust, anger and misery, it was already bright with promise. For one thing, she was looking forward to returning to the regularity and comfort of her life at St Peter's. Into her memory a hundred images of recent events crowded and competed for attention – the Teachers' Day celebrations, Maggie, Yen Ping and Mark, the astonishing make-over, Maggie's young sister

Angel, even the unappealing Mr Chin, coming up awkwardly to make courteous inquiries about her husband, Brother Philip and his kind words when they met along the corridor. That man's image would be dearer for being connected with a special pain: how could he have been dragged into the sordidness of her husband's suspicions? Had she, in fact, inadvertently done him a disservice by talking about him with so much affectionate regard, as to place him in that unsavoury light?

Meeta and Winnie – she would be happy to re-connect with them, get into their world of man-hunting and gossip and superstitious nonsense, and as quickly get out of it back to her own. Meanwhile, she was grateful to them, during this difficult period, for having Por Por over at their house for part of the day and taking her mother out for occasional lunches. Kindness everywhere! Her new world would be full of it. You could go so wrong with love, but never with kindness.

If she could train her thoughts to steer clear of her husband, they could be exclusively directed towards a future that beckoned with hope. So great were those little flutterings of anticipatory excitement that they carried their own seeds of guilt. They coalesced around one wish that lit up everything around it. She would write a book, and another and another. Her world would be centred on her life, and her life would be centred on her writing. There would be a neatness, an order, a peace in her world as could never be found outside it, in the madding crowd of husbands and wives, men and women constantly misunderstanding each other.

As soon as she had the time – even in her thoughts, she skipped direct reference to the awful reality of death and its concomitant hassles, from the funeral arrangements down to the last details of administrative and legalistic procedures regarding something she had no knowledge of or inclination for, known as the deceased's estate – she would set about this supreme, defining task. She would begin by looking into the heaps of notes and drafts of stories she had written and put away over the years, and see if they could provide the beginning of a collection of short stories, or even a novel. Might she not do a course or two on creative writing, perhaps even go abroad for the purpose? She had heard of summer schools in universities that offered such courses. Brother Philip's words of encouragement came back to warm her heart.

One thing was certain. She could never write a story, even if heavily disguised, about her husband. If writing was a form of escapism, there was no world greater than the one she had shared with him for three years that she wanted to escape from. She thought of his ring lying in a dark forest, its brilliance lost under layers of mud and dead leaves. Perhaps years hence, as an old woman for whom the years would have softened the terrible guilt, shock, pity and anger and transmuted them all into one overpowering desire to tell a story, she would be able to sit down and begin it with the words: 'This is the strange story of a man who loved a woman, and bought her a diamond ring so expensive he was in debt for years. She did not want it, so he flung it away where it could never be recovered. Nevertheless, she married him, and had a greater debt to pay, because she did not love him.'

When she told Dr Phang about her secret yearning to be a writer, was that smile one of encouragement too, like Brother Philip's? Images of the boyish grin on the different occasions when she had witnessed it, causing a flurry of friendly crinkles around his eyes, came flooding into her mind; she sorted them out in the order of the pleasure they had given her, beginning with the one in the restaurant when she had stood before them all, blushing furiously in her new look, her face expertly made up by Maggie, her hair tumbling upon her shoulders, a multicoloured silk scarf draped around her neck. That smile of admiration was precisely replicated only a short while ago, when he had briefly referred to the new look; was it to deflect the admiration that he had to make mention of his wife's name?

She kept the best image for the last, like a child delaying the opening of the most cherished present while all the time looking longingly at it. For years it would remain in her memory, his comforting her in his arms while the healing warmth of his simple assurance permeated her whole being: *You're okay.* She would remember vividly the pattern of lines on his shirt on which her face was pressed, the very smell of his closeness. The image would remain free of the angry taint of scandal that her mother, increasingly watchful of them, seemed determined to daub it with: he's married, you're married. He has a second wife, your husband is dying. Just what do you think you are doing?

She would ever remember his head thrown back in laughter at the funny plague joke, their turning quickly to look in her husband's direction to make sure they had not disturbed him, and then continuing to laugh together.

'What was that smile about?' Her husband had awakened, and was looking at her. Apparently he had been looking at her for a while; his voice was very weak, but he spoke slowly, enunciating every syllable, as if to make sure she heard. She suddenly realised with horror that she had been smiling to herself for at least a full five minutes, a wifely obscenity by any standard. But she could still answer his question truthfully, and say, with an attempt at smiling casualness, 'It was the funniest misspelling but nobody noticed it,' and went on to describe the gaffe in detail.

'Tell me about that smile.'

Numbly she clung to the rejected explanation, saying in a bathos of desperation: 'If you don't believe me, I'll show you the proof' and went at once to get the plaque. She held it before his eyes, drawing attention to the misspelling, hating him and herself all the while for the hideous pretence of a casual tone against the cold ruthlessness of his judgement.

'Take it away,' he said, 'and come and sit here.' She pulled up a stool and sat beside him.

'No, here,' he said, and indicated the bed itself, 'so that you can hear me better.' She sat beside him, looking down, weighed down by misery.

'No, look up, look at me.' He was preparing for some important proceeding that had all the marks of climax and finality in his judgement of her. White, wan, sunken, he already looked like a spectre returned to exact revenge in full measure. 'I want you to listen to me and not ask any questions until I allow you to. It is important business I have to settle. Very important, and it can't wait.'

He lay back on his pillows exhausted with the preparations of settling this business that he had been clearly working out in his mind in the last few hours. Conserving his energy for the final stage of his deathbed campaign, he lay very still, his eyes closed. When they opened, they shone with a preternatural brightness that frightened her. Such a brightness, she was told, was a deathbed phenomenon, a final flare of energy and affirmation before death took over and reduced the body to a lump of cold, rigid matter. She reached out to touch his hand, but he moved it away from hers. One of the most painful recollections of their married life would be his moving away his hand each time she stretched out hers. Perhaps that was her instinctive expression of pity and he had learnt to loathe it.

'I was ready to forgive you everything, even the fact that you never loved me.'

She cried out in agitation, 'That's not exactly true, Bernard! I loved you in my own way –' She was prepared to get as close as possible to the truth he desired without violating the truth she lived by. *I loved you in the way I knew how. I wanted so much to make you happy. I tried to do everything you wanted me to.*

He said, 'I told you not to interrupt,' and went on, 'I was ready to forgive you your affair with Kuldeep Singh –' She opened her mouth to let out a cry of protest, and he put up a warning forefinger. 'Don't think I didn't know about your secret meetings at that old shophouse, to look over that love sign you carved together.' *Oh my God. So this is what's eating you up. The delusions that the dying mind feeds itself on! Not content with the present, it forages the past. Why didn't you ask me? But then, would that have been of any use?*

'A friend saw you both at Hoot Kiam Road together and had the kindness to tell me.' *Just what is it, for goodness' sake? You can't be hallucinating, for you're speaking with a clarity and purposefulness I've never seen before!*

'But I was ready to forgive you your infidelity. Even with Brother Philip.' *Oh no, oh no, don't bring in Brother Philip!*

'You will understand how painful it is for me to know that my wife is committing adultery with a man committed to serve God with a vow of chastity. Now I know why you spent such long hours in school, why he made those phone calls to you in my absence, why you called out his name in your sleep.' It was impossible not to break into the outrageous accusations with her own outrage.

'How dare you, Bernard,' she cried out, 'how dare you even think of that? Are you mad –'

It was no use. He was past listening to her. If a hundred voices had broken in on her behalf, they would have simply washed over him uselessly. He was launched on a mission of saving himself that must begin with emptying himself of all the grievances that had accumulated in his system; he was now pulling them out, in a continuous stream, black and poisonous, determined not to leave behind the smallest residue. Exhausted, he fell back again on his pillows, but managed to gather enough energy for the climax of the purge.

'I didn't think I could forgive you this – you cannot have an idea of the pain it's causing me – but since I'm going back to my God, I will. I forgive you your affair with Dr Phang.' She let out a scream, but only an inward one which, like the flapping wings of some monstrous bird, beat furiously upon her ears, mouth, eyes, suffocating her. *I'm not having an affair with Dr Phang! If you saw anything just now, he was just comforting me. Why don't you let me explain? Oh my God, how can this be happening to both of us? What have we done to deserve all this pain?*

'Give me a drink of water.'

It was bizarre, she, the accused, carefully spooning water into the mouth of her accuser, moistening his dry lips, wiping the stray drops on his chin, waiting for him to revive, to go on to the next stage of accusation and deliver the final judgement. To the outside observer, it was the universally touching sickroom scene of unstinting wifely devotion, the wifely arms propping up the dying husband. She saw her mother standing anxiously at the doorway and waved her away.

'I want you to answer each of my questions with a Yes or No. No buts. No explanations. Just Yes or No.' He had turned the sickroom into a courtroom, and stood over her as the ruthless prosecutor armed with the most deadly questions, like arrows in a quiver, to be fired one after another in quick succession.

'When we were in the Cameron Highlands walking through some gardens with Dr and Mrs Phang, was there a time when he and you broke away to have a private conversation on your own, well away from myself and his wife?'

'Yes'. *But I was only telling him about the ring incident which in any case you had already told him about. There were certain things I just had to tell him.*

'During the birthday celebration at the Pavilion Hotel, did he, at any time, admire your new look?'

'Yes.' *But so did everyone else. It was all in good fun.*

'Did you put on the make-up for him?'

'No.' *I had already explained that my students did it as a joke. Why don't you ever listen to me?*

'You're lying. But never mind. Next question: this afternoon, when you and Dr Phang were standing together outside the door, thinking I was sound asleep, did you embrace as lovers?'

'No'. *So you were only pretending to be asleep, to spy on us? My God, what sort of a person are you?*

'You're lying again. When you both returned to the room and sat over there talking, were you already planning to meet as soon as my funeral was over?'

'No.' *Bernard, you are mad, raving mad!*

'Final question. When you smiled just now, looking so happy, not for an instant, but for a long while, were you thinking of Dr Phang?'

'Yes.' *But not as you think, Bernard! I was thinking of a whole lot of other things as well – my students, my friends –*'

'That's all I need to know. I will instruct Heng to tell Dr Phang that he's no longer welcome here. Now I want to rest. Leave me alone.'

She burst into hysterical weeping. 'This isn't fair, Bernard!' she screamed. 'Hear me out. I insist that you hear me out!'

But he had put a pillow over his face with one hand, and was dismissing her with the other.

Eighteen

'Dear Bernard,' she wrote in her letter. It would be the second of two letters she had written to him, both unopened and unread. The first, on that fateful day when he appeared at her doorstep soaked in rainwater, she had decided to tear up and throw away; this second one would be laid beside him as he lay in his coffin, in the funeral parlour of the Church of Eternal Mercy. She would have to do it quickly and secretly when nobody was looking, when Father Rozario and the members of the church prayer group were not around saying prayers for him, when her mother who had since his death spoken to her only stiffly or angrily, was not watching her.

'Dear Bernard,' she wrote in her clear, neat hand. 'I wish this could be the kind of letter that I've sometimes read about, written by a wife to her dead husband, full of love and longing, recounting the tenderest of shared moments, ending with the yearning wish to meet again on some distant shore. Alas, alas, this is no such letter. As you must have long suspected, I no longer share the beliefs which comforted you in life and death; I now stand outside the protection and solace of the Church and must from now on brave the disapproval and disappointment of Father Rozario, our fellow parishioners of the Church of Eternal Mercy and my own mother. Your funeral mass will be the last religious service I will attend. If, as a spirit looking down and seeing only with the eyes of truth, you are shocked by my having taken part in all those devotional exercises of the prayer group around your sickbed while in this secret state of disbelief, I have to beg your forgiveness and say that I did what I did simply to preserve the peace and harmony in a house already so melancholic with the sad circumstances of your sickness and suffering. Hence this letter will have none of the solace that religious faith brings, and also none of the solace from the loving, longing wife that, to both our regret and sadness, I have never been.

I have decided to tell you in writing what it was impossible to tell you in speech during the months of your illness, indeed, in the three years of our marriage. There was so much that we should have talked over, but each time we tried to, we reached an impasse almost with the first sentence, so deep was the problem underlying our marriage, so bad had things become, right from the beginning. This is my last opportunity to tell you the whole truth, and although I don't believe that the dead live on and know what is happening in the lives of those they leave behind, who knows? Right now, as I've said, your spirit may be hovering about somewhere, and since death is supposed to open all eyes and remove all falsehood, then I hope that this letter will open yours to the falseness of your shocking accusations in the last hours of your life – oh, how I regret that the last time we were together carries no memory of tenderness and kindness – as well as open mine to my own falseness in marrying you without that one thing you craved from me till the end.

There is something I simply have to tell you now regarding the ring – oh, that Tiffany ring which had brought both of us nothing but pain and confusion! I did in fact tell you in a letter but I threw it away on the stormy night that you appeared on my doorstep. I had tried to look for the ring with the help of friends and students, but unsuccessfully; I am telling you this now only because you might have wanted only Dr Phang to know about it. I had made known to the search party only those details as would explain the rather strange circumstances of the search. Neither my mother nor my brother Heng knows about the incident. You have always been a very private and sensitive person guarding each secret, and I've regretted the decision of the search because it had necessitated letting other people in on the secret. If it's any comfort to you, each and every one of them has been sworn to secrecy on the matter.

Another matter on which I need to clear myself – you see the self-serving purpose of this letter! – is related to those appalling accusations of infidelity. If you had been suffering the hallucinatory delusions of the dying, that would have lessened the shock. But oh Bernard, it seemed to me that those accusations had less to do with hallucinations and more to do with your profound anger against me from the beginning of our marriage, an anger that became so focused and unremitting as to become an *obsession* – yes, an obsession, Bernard, in its picking on everything, whether from reality, imagination or pure conjecture, to feed itself on. It simply wanted nothing to do with the brutal truth that I did not love you as you wanted me to, a truth that neither of us seemed able to deal with, going round and round in futile, agonising circles. It would have injured your pride so seriously that you chose anger instead, and it would have required an honesty so bruising that I chose the easier way of doing nothing instead. Your anger easily found a jealous target in any man I appeared to like, and could not be satisfied till it had exploded in a storm of accusations against me. Of course I liked, and will always like Kuldeep Singh and Brother Philip and Dr Phang. I was going to say that I regretted mentioning them to you or even meeting them at all, for the tremendous pain they caused you, right to your last breath, but no, life goes on for me and the people I have met, and the real regret should be yours, for such unaccountable jealousy. If we had both faced the truth of our unfortunate marriage squarely, we might not have saved it, but, more importantly, we would have saved our sanity and integrity. To my dying day, I will regret my cowardice in taking the easier path of staying the course and not rocking the boat, of wanting to make everybody happy, of ignoring the ghastly gap between the peaceful, harmonious exterior that fooled everybody and the private turmoil that ruined both of us. To my dying day, I will regret that I did not have the courage to stand before you, packed suitcase in hand, and announce, 'Bernard, I made a mistake in marrying you, and since both of us are suffering the results of the mistake, I'm leaving you before things get worse.' If you had suffered great shock then and raged and ranted at me, if you braved the humiliation of a failed marriage before your priest, friends and colleagues and endured the pain, since you have a gentle nature, of punishing me severely for my mistake, that would have been a hundred times better because it would be more honest than what we went through. After a while, we seemed locked inside a hell of our own making, from which only death, either yours or mine, could have freed us. What an awful, awful fate for any married couple, what a terrible indictment of this impossibly demanding institution called marriage. If Fate – or God – had not taken you away, and our marriage had gone on, how long could it have endured? Over time (as we both must have seen in some marriages) we might have accepted each other for what we were, no longer upset by the absence of that elusive thing called Love, and learnt to appreciate its poorer cousins by whatever name they are called – kindness, comfort, companionship, accommodation, duty, tolerance. Again I say, what an awful indictment of this tyrannical institution called marriage. But Bernard, both of us were ever romantics and idealists, and could not have settled for less. It must have been our passionately romantic nature that proved to be our undoing. Alike but different in its domination by different impulses, it had drawn us to each other, yours by warm generosity and mine by warm compassion. If only the romantic urge had been moderated by that rather less exotic but more dependable thing called honesty! You would have said to yourself, 'I love her, but she's not reciprocating,' and walked away, even if dispiritedly. I would have said to myself, 'What your heart is feeling is only pity, not love,' and not committed myself to any man till I could tell the difference. It will be a lifelong lesson for me, thanks in part to you, that I will have to understand the heart better. Someone once said that the heart has its reasons which reason cannot understand. Heart, head, reason, unreason – I will have to learn not to let all get into a sad, messy, treacherous tangle again.

I ask for your forgiveness, Bernard, not for any wrong done, but for a terrible mistake made, all the more terrible because it involved not just myself but another, and who knows, how many others? I'm thinking of my mother who appears unable to forgive me because she believes I am to blame for your unhappiness, for bringing her great shame. I ask for forgiveness also for failing to undo the mistake while there was time. We are shocked by, but should really admire, the groom or bride who, just as the priest announces the last chance for anyone to stop the marriage, suddenly becomes his or her own impediment: 'Stop! I've changed my mind!' and walks away. I had sometimes wondered what your life would have been like if you had married the right woman. With your generosity and her love, your marriage would have been so happy. If you are now a spirit up there, cleansed of all earth's taint, freed from all its burdens, duly rewarded for your pains and kindness to others – for you were always kind to me in making sure I was well provided for, buying a lovely apartment for me, taking care of all my material needs, and you were more than generous towards Por Por, my mother and brother – then a heaven of peace, love and happiness is what you deserve and what I wish for you.

Maria.'

The letter had to be slipped in before the coffin lid was lowered; the coffin had a glass window through which she gazed, with much sadness, at her dead husband, looking peaceful and composed, a white pearl rosary entwined in his clasped hands. So vast and bewildering were her thoughts, like storm waves heaving and breaking upon each other, that even years later, she would have difficulty in teasing them out one by one to put together as a coherent narrative.

Outwardly, she was the gently mourning widow; inwardly her thoughts began to race in a fury of unholy conjectures that would have appalled Father Rozario and the fellow parishioners. Where was her husband's soul, if there were such a thing as a soul? Had he already appeared in judgement before God, if there were a God?

To each his own, she had often thought with reference to the countless differences among people, whether these be of personality, character, belief or lifestyle. Suppose a person's post-death existence were also an individual, personal thing, meaning that Por Por would join her ancestors in the realm of Sky God and Monkey God, her mother would ascend to the Christian heaven with its multitude of angels and saints, and she, disbeliever, would be simply consigned to oblivion, as easily as her ashes would be lost in the vastness of sky and ocean. Where would the soul of her husband be at this very moment, as she was looking at him in his coffin? Deserving neither immediate entry to Heaven, earned only by the very saintly, nor condemned to the fires of Hell, inhabited only by the truly wicked, he would most probably now be in Purgatory, the intermediate waiting place for a thorough cleansing of minor sins. Two questions intrigued her. Would the minor sins include unfounded husbandly jealousy? Secondly, since the living on earth could help their loved ones get out of Purgatory faster through their prayers, would she be expected to do what all grieving widows did – arrange with the priest of the parish church to offer special masses, especially on occasions such as the anniversary of his death and the Feast of All Souls? Her mother would expect her to do so. Well, she would do so, to please everyone. Pleasing everyone, keeping the peace – that would be her way of remaining in the world, while no longer being of it.

Her mother and Heng came up to her and pulled her aside, saying in urgent, lowered voices, that they had to speak to her on a very important matter. The looks of intense discomfort and anxiety on their faces, presaging bad news so bad it could not wait, sent little tremors all over her body. She was convinced it had to do with her husband. She thought: he has suffered much; please don't let anything disturb his peace.

It would appear that he was determined to disturb hers. Apparently, he had made two decisions just before his death, without her knowledge, both reflecting a rage that would not die with the body. The first was reported by Heng, the second by her mother.

'Just what was going on between you that he had to do this?' demanded her brother in a mixture of shock, anger and disgust. The disgust was directed mainly at the new beneficiary in her husband's will: he had got his lawyer to change it a few days before his death, naming his Third Aunt in place of his wife.

'The apartment is now at least thirty per cent more than when he bought it,' Heng said, his face taut with incredulity. 'Why would he suddenly want his aunt to have it? She's in her seventies, living in Malaysia. Her horde of relatives will all be clamouring to have a share of it.' His anger was that of a family member needing to protect his own against a greedy world.

Her mother looked at her with a mixture of sorrow and vexation. 'Maria,' she said tearfully, 'what will people say?'

Her brother asked her again in mounting exasperation, 'What on earth had you done to make him do such a drastic thing? I've never heard of such a thing.'

She replied with cool hauteur, suddenly incensed against him, her mother, everybody, the living and the dead. 'It's none of your business, Heng.'

Almost tempted to say, in a surge of spite, 'Why don't you mind your own business and take care of your poor wife and son?', she calmed herself with a decisive defence of her husband, 'Listen, both of you. Bernard was free to do exactly as he liked with whatever he possessed.'

Outwardly defending his action, she tried to curb the inner tumult that left her trembling: 'Bernard, if you can hear my thoughts now, was it necessary to go so far in your revenge? But you are achieving the purpose you intended; you have thoroughly poisoned my family against me.'

Her mother pushed a sheet of paper at her, on which something had been written. She recognised her husband's handwriting, though it was a weak scrawl. 'Ah Siong really loved you,' Anna Seetoh whimpered. 'This proves it. How could you?' She must have been thinking of that treacherous embrace outside the sickroom.

There was something frightfully unreal about the self-composed obituary that he had scrawled and instructed his mother-in-law and brother-in-law to insert in *The Singapore Tribune:* it was cast in the form of a grieving wife's tribute to her husband, affirming love, remembrance and yearning for all eternity. *Loved eternally by your ever devoted wife, Maria. Dearest Bernard, in my heart forever.* The extravagance of love was no less obscene than if it had been a discharge of purest hatred. Her husband had in effect forced upon her a public avowal of love that was a savage mockery of its absence in their marriage. For ten years, according to his instructions, it would appear, on the anniversary of his death, in Singapore's leading newspaper. For ten years, she would look upon the photograph of her husband, smiling gently, and below it, the breathless proclamations of her love and loyalty, and be thus reminded of what a terrible failure she had been. He had left Heng a substantial sum of money to take care of the cost of the quarter page insertion, big enough to attract the attention of even the casual newspaper browser. How was it possible that a dying man's last energies, despite the exhortations of his priest to prepare his soul to meet his God in the next world, could be so entirely devoted to the planning of a revenge to take place exclusively in this one?

With rising anger, she suspected a more sinister intention: if, during the ten-year period of public professions of undying devotion, she was seen with another man, or married or had an affair, she would forever stand condemned for hypocrisy of the worst kind. The Black Widow. The Blackest Widow. If he was no longer around to point an accusing finger at her, let others do it on his behalf. She thought that revenge of this extreme kind which reached beyond the grave existed only in dramatic, sensationalist literature and movies; now she, Maria Seetoh, most ordinary of mortals, school teacher and aspiring writer, who only wanted to be happy in life and do no harm to others, was being touched by the deadliest of dead hands. If fact overtook fiction, her own life story would be in the realm of the fantastical.

She managed to retrieve the letter from the coffin and return it to its place beside the dead man after adding a post-script:

'Dear Bernard, thank you for not letting me have the property, since to benefit in any way from your tragic death would have brought guilt to my new life. Guilt there will be, in proportion to the happiness and freedom I know I will be enjoying, but it should be just that much and no more. Besides, I couldn't bear to continue to live in a place that holds such sad memories. As for the remembrance notices over the next ten years, they will be just ten years' worth of falsehood in which, thankfully, I have had no part. You have upset me so much, Bernard, that you will allow me my own kind of revenge, though I wouldn't use that word. From now onwards I will not want to be known as Mrs Tan Boon Siong.'

Nineteen

What a lovely sight, she thought, my eyes could feast on it forever. From her bench in the shade of a tree, one of those lovely ones in the Botanic Gardens that not only provided shade but a delightful, soothing scent from its clusters of tiny white flowers amid a riot of the greenest of green leaves, she watched the children by the fish pond, absorbed in the various delights provided by a large body of water teeming with hungry fish unafraid to swim right up to the edge, right up to their small fingers holding out bread crumbs, their little outstretched bodies held tightly by smiling parents. A young woman wheeling a pram stopped close by the water's edge to allow the infant who had just awakened from his nap, to look upon the lively scene, which he did with gurgling interest.

A little girl who was clutching a plastic bag of biscuit crumbs was squealing with delight for having spotted a turtle among the fish; a little boy of about four with a thin serious face was giving the correct answers to an over-earnest mother turning the entire Botanic Gardens into a classroom: 'What is that, Kevin?

'A fish.'

'What's that, out there, look!'

'A duck.'

'Spell 'duck'.

'D-U-C-K.'

'Look up there, on the tree branch. What's that?'

'Butterfly.'

'Butterflies. So many of them. Clever boy!'

A sparrow hopped very close to her feet, pecking at something on the ground. Another joined it, then a third. She watched them with interest, wondering at their very thin legs and tiny feet, like matchsticks that would never snap, but could be depended on to carry them through any harshness of weather in their briefly appointed existence on the earth. The lovely, slender may-fly with its beautiful transparent wings lived exactly twenty-four hours, during which it was born, matured, mated, gave birth and died. How long did a sparrow live? There must be something special about these birds to be singled out for mention in the divine lecture admonishing those who worried unnecessarily: Divine Providence took care of all living things, including these humblest of birds, for not a single one of them fell to its death without divine knowledge.

Here in the Botanic Gardens, Providence had appointed little children, with their generous bags of crumbs, to be its assistants to make sure its precious sparrows never fell dead from starvation. 'Providence', like 'God', capitalised, but with the relative pronoun 'it' in lower case, unlike the towering male supremacy of 'His'. Ever since she stopped going to church, she had been content to think in terms of abstract nouns – Providence, Power, Force, Energy, Source, Being, indeed, anything, as long as it was vague enough for that unknown entity out there, or in here, that was nowhere and everywhere. She did not want it to have a gender, an ethnicity, a home country, a face, a voice, a personality, for that had caused all the trouble in the world. Someone had once said that those who abandoned God were left with a God-shaped hole that nothing could fill. Hers was being richly filled with all manner of things that did not even have names.

She made a slight movement with her feet, but the birds went on pecking, unperturbed. There were now four of them, and she wondered whether they were a family, the two smaller-sized ones being nestlings taken out for their first lesson in independent foraging. Her eyes caught sight, a short distance away, of a group of three sparrows furiously tearing away at something on the ground that looked like a dead lizard. She looked closer: oh no, it was a dead bird. One of the sparrows was ferociously pulling out, through a mess of feathers, an intestine that looked like a very long worm. Those divinely favoured creatures were cannibalising their own. She moved to another bench, determined to see nature only at her benign best, not savagely red in tooth and claw.

A skinny brown squirrel appeared from somewhere, scurried to a spot under her bench and made off with something, probably a nut, or a bit of a child's biscuit. She looked up into the sky and saw a huge flock of white birds, their bodies moving in perfect group synchronisation like a single playful organism that changed rapidly from one shape into another, now stretched out into a row of pennants streaming in the wind, like the beard of an awesome warrior god riding out to battle, now gathered into itself to look like the round-headed friendly ghost with a tail, seen in comic books. That too dissolved, in a matter of seconds, to form – surely it was her vanity that was distorting her vision! – the letter M. Her name writ large in the sky, if only for one fleeting second.

It had been her vanity, right from childhood, to believe that when she cried, nature shed tears too, sending down, if not a torrent, at least a tiny drizzle. A fallacy by no means pathetic, it had become part of a dependable comfort kit in her long hours of solitude, Rain, sun, sky, cloud, grass, the birds of the air and the lilies in the field – she had co-opted them all for her own safe, happy world. Stare hard enough at the clouds, she was told as a child, and they will form any picture you like. She only looked out for letter formations of her name; if there were none, she created them, needing only small lengths of white cloud to work with, like pliable plasticine, to shape into any letter of her full name. 'Look!' she would tell her mother or Por Por. 'That's my name in the sky!'

As a child, she had had her birthday celebrated only once. Her mother had bought a cake and iced her name on it. She was so thrilled she could not bear the cake knife to break up the five pink letters arranged in a rainbow curve. In the end her mother sliced off the whole top portion of the cake for her, to keep the name intact. She wondered how she could bear to spoon up her name and eat it. Could she keep them in a box forever?

'Don't be silly,' said her mother laughing.

Then her brother Heng stole up from behind her with a large tin spoon and plunged it right into the middle of her name. She screamed. Her mother did nothing to punish the culprit; Anna Seetoh's constant anxiety about what people would think of her had invested the adopted child's position with special privileges. Heng always got away with the naughtiness and later, the viciousness of boyhood pranks, laughing to see all the scolding, pinching and slapping directed elsewhere. When he made further devastation of her name on the cake, she rose in full fury. While she had submitted to his hair-pulling and arm-smacking, his raiding of her small store of coloured pencils and coins in her coconut-shell money-box, she could not let him get away with the mutilation of her name. She chased him with such fury that he ran away in fright; when she caught him, she smashed a surprisingly strong fist into his face. He ran howling to Anna Seetoh who subsequently calmed him down with a fistful of coins.

From that day on, he never bullied her again. Her mother would never tell her why she had adopted him, why he had had very little share in the family's privations as they moved from place to place to escape the loan sharks, but stayed comfortably with his biological mother whom he called 'Auntie'. Years later, when she reminded him of the incident of the cake, he feigned a forgetfulness not consistent with the bribe of money.

She looked at the giant gnarled trees towering skywards, that had existed in brooding silence for hundreds of years before they became part of a garden constructed for the pleasure of a tired city; in them surely resided a pantheon of deities that had never left their abodes in nature for the man-made churches, temples and shrines of the city. Here in this loveliest, most peaceful spot in her world, the feathered, furred and finned denizens of nature came up, unafraid, to be fed and stroked by children.

She got up from the bench and walked to a nearby gentle slope where she lay on the grass, stretching out her arms and legs to luxuriate fully in its warmth and scent, a solitary mortal on the face of the earth, at one with all the life nourished by it and nourishing it, animal, vegetable, human, divine, and who knows, also the tiniest of tiny specks of life in a universe so vast that Earth would have perished and returned to primordial dust by the time it was visited by a sister planet separated by breathlessly unimaginable light years. A small grasshopper flew into her hair and got entangled in the long strands spread out on the grass. The more it struggled to escape, the more deadly became the trap; she sat up and carefully freed it, hair by hair.

'Foolish thing!' she laughed, and cast it back into the air.

A wedding group was busily posing for pictures under a large tree. The bride's long white dress with a full skirt and her long veil of net, held by a diamante tiara, were being carefully arranged for the camera by her two bridesmaids, both dressed in pale pink. The bride carried a bouquet of yellow and white orchids, smiling gamely in the heat under her thick make-up that was being constantly repaired by a powder puff held by a middle-aged woman in a cheongsam, whose own make-up looked very much in need of repair. The bridegroom in a smart grey suit and red tie was smiling broadly throughout, and readily acceded to a demand yelled out by one of the watching guests, 'Kiss, kiss!' for the last of three different bridal poses for the cameraman; to loud applause, he clumsily turned his bride around, pushed aside her veil, and planted a quick kiss on her lips.

Giddy with happiness and new mischief as she sat on her bench watching them, she could have cupped her hand and shouted out to the newly married pair, 'Hey, I offer my condolences!'

If they had shouted back angrily, 'You, sour grapes, you!', she would have joyfully told them her story, like the man in the myth who, when he was forbidden to tell his secret, ran out to a field of corn and whispered it to them, thereafter investing them with ears.

The Botanic Gardens was clearly an even more popular place for trysting couples who might or might not end up marrying; on her way to the fish pond, she had passed several of them in secluded spots in the various poses of happy love, from the shy tentativeness of hand-holding to the aggressive demonstrations of full-blown passion checked only by the law's prohibition against public disrobing. One very young-looking couple, probably students, had dispensed altogether with discretion; they were nestled, fully clothed, against each other on the top of a grassy slope, and then, locked tightly together, rolled down the slope, laughing all the way.

Oh, how happy I am, she thought, and realised she had not used that word in the present tense for a long while. I *was* happy. I *will* be happy. She wanted to summon the entire romancing, loving, lusting, marrying population of the Botanic Gardens to come before her for a lecture: Are you sure it's love? Otherwise, don't! For goodness' sake, don't!

The book on her lap lay unread; she was content to watch the people around her, their faces temporarily cleared of all the stresses of negotiating life one day at a time in a city increasingly stressful, as they took in long draughts of the invigorating air and broke into smiles at the antics of the little ones around them, wrestling with each other on the grass, rummaging picnic baskets, running after their hoops and balls.

A little boy of about three stopped before her, uncertain about how to rescue his bright red ball that had rolled under her bench. He stood before her, a forefinger inside his mouth, looking intently at her. She bent to retrieve the ball, then smilingly handed it to him.

It must have been her bright, encouraging smile that inspired the little fellow to launch upon his own initiative of friendly self-introduction.

'My name's Randal,' he said, 'I've got a blue boat. And Spiderman.'

She was delighted. 'My name's Maria,' she said. 'I don't have a boat or Spiderman, but lots of books. You like books, Randal?'

But Randal's interest had taken a different turn. He took her hand and led her up a grassy slope, to where a woman was sitting on a bright mat surrounded by an assortment of picnic cups, plates and boxes.

'Oh there you are, Randal,' she said. To Maria, she said smiling, 'I hope my boy hasn't been bothering you?' It was part of the continuing delight of the encounter that she accepted the invitation from the friendly woman to sit down for a sandwich and a drink of juice.

The delight climaxed in the most unexpected way. As she was walking back to her bench, she saw, some distance ahead, Randal emerging from behind a clump of trees. Surely that was not possible! A little boy with the supernatural power of bilocation, who could simply appear and disappear at different spots as he chose? A child's ghost, or more accurately, a doppelganger, in a popular recreational spot even before daylight had gone? She had heard tales of the ghosts of Japanese soldiers seen wandering in the gardens, more than half a century after the war, recognisable by their distinct uniforms and caps.

She stared, then realised, with a smile, how unnecessary had been those wild conjectures, as soon as she saw a woman emerge from behind the trees to say to the child, 'Ryan, you feel okay now?' and adjust his shirt and pants.

She turned to have a look at the picnic scene she had left behind and saw, as she expected, the other twin. Randal saw them, shouted, waved, then got up from the picnic mat and came running towards them. When the two little boys stood before her, perfectly identical from their round heads, large eyes and stocky legs to the precise shade of green of their shirts and socks, she burst out in delighted laughter.

She had a tremendous love for children, and this would be one encounter she would remember with pleasure for a long while. She would share it with her students in her creative writing class, perhaps using the subject of identical twins to provoke any number of dramatic stories, whether comic, tragic or purely farcical. She could see Mark and Yen Ping's faces lighting up with the challenge, could foresee Maggie readily responding with a particularly salacious story of a man worn out by the demands of his partner, unaware that he had been sleeping with her twin too.

The woman who was clearly the twins' maid said, 'This happens all the time. Even their parents sometimes can't tell them apart.'

Randal, clearly the more talkative and extrovert of the two said, 'I have a mole on my neck, Ryan has a red mark on his shoulder!' and proceeded to show Maria the means of identification.

Her visit to the Botanic Gardens that day was destined to be dominated by Randal; it could have been dominated by someone who would certainly have been a much less welcome presence. She was looking up from her book when in the distance she saw and recognised him: he was the jogger who, some time ago, had stopped by to comment on the Jane Austen novel she was reading, and then stayed to chat. He represented the world of men that she wanted to have nothing to do with from now onwards.

Dr Phang had written a brief note: what was that strange message from her brother Heng all about? Why was he told not to come for the funeral? Would she see him as soon as she could to explain what was happening? Brother Philip's condolence card caused no anxiety. 'I look forward to your return to St

Peter's. Meanwhile, take care and keep well. My prayers are with you.' Kuldeep Singh, Dr Phang, Brother Philip – each, through no fault of his own, would, for the time being, be anathema to her. They would have no part in her thoughts, much less in her new life. Each, in due course, would come to understand why. Meanwhile, no new man would be allowed into her world, whether solidly mortal like the sweating jogger or ethereally distant like the god-man Sai Baba unabashedly adored by Meeta in both her waking and sleeping hours, whether a dull, plodding presence like Mr Chin at St Peter's Secondary School or that machismo-exuding guy whom Winnie continued to dream of and consult fortune-tellers about.

She looked down again, burying her face in her book, and when she looked up, minutes later, the jogger was gone.

A little dog managed to break free of its leash and ran towards her, leaping up on her legs and arms in a frenzied celebration of freedom. Its owner, a young man in his thirties, ran up, apologised, then saw there was no need to, for she was laughing as she bent over to have the little terrier repeatedly lick her face. Back on its leash, it kept straining towards her, yapping loudly.

'What's your name, sweetheart?' she shouted as they left, and the owner shouted back, 'Alex! But if you're talking to my dog, his name's Laiko!'

'Well, goodbye, sweethearts both!' she yelled back.

Alex returned with Laiko. They looked at each other, each delighting in the other's friendly wit.

He said to her with a sparkle of interest in his handsome eyes, 'Hey, you're one of the happiest persons I've seen. Probably the nicest too. I hope you come here regularly? Laiko and I do.' He looked at her closely. 'Coffee? There's a nice café just outside.'

The Botanic Gardens – it would always be a place of calm and peace for her, and where there were men who took an interest in her and began pursuing her, there could be none of that. She would not even risk the beginning of that interest.

'Thanks a lot; not this afternoon though. Maybe another time.' She was ever mindful about saving male face.

'Another time, then,' said Alex. 'Bye!'

She thought, I think I'll buy a little dog. Her mother's apartment that all of them would soon be moving into was far too small for a pet; perhaps she should just continue to enjoy the delightful antics of Meeta's and Winnie's dog, a playful Alsatian with the impossible name of Singapore. They had bought it together as a puppy to be a watchdog; Meeta was the name-giver.

'Singapore, come here! You're bad and you stink!' Meeta would say loudly, with mischievous intent to alarm her next door neighbours, a prim and proper couple in their seventies who had, on their sitting room wall, a framed picture of the prime minister with a map of Singapore in the background.

Meeta said that Byron had told her she was guilty of infringing some law akin to lese majesty and could be hauled into court for an offence only slightly less than tearing up the Singapore flag. Meeta said if she went to jail, she could be assured of at least one visitor.

'Well, you can count on me,' Byron had said. 'No, I meant Sai Baba,' said Meeta.

On her way out of the Gardens, she passed a favourite spot for children, a circular paved playground with a ground fountain at the centre, comprising thin jets of water that shot up playfully in obedient response to the stomping feet of children, and then proceeded to chase them and wet them like playfully writhing garden hoses held by adults. She stopped to watch the squealing children, alternately running away from and submitting to the jets, refusing to be led away by parents worried about wet clothes, hair and shoes. Suddenly she felt a small hand tug hers. It was Randal and he dragged her right into the orbit of the teasing jets.

'Ryan's a cry baby,' he said disapprovingly as Maria caught a glimpse of the other twin tearfully watching his mother remove his wet socks. 'See, my hair's all wet!' he said proudly.

'Wait a second,' she said and left her book safely dry on the ground while she returned to join him in childhood's pure, untrammeled celebration of life.

'Can you do this?' asked Randal, and he lifted his face and opened his mouth wide to receive a jet of water.

'Of course I can,' she said and succeeded after the third attempt. 'Can you do this?' she asked, doing a little gypsy dance to the rhythm of her clapping hands.

Randal clapped, hopped about and fell down. She joined him on the ground, and they began to splash water on each other. She was aware of someone standing near her and watching them. It was the jogger who looked both amused and intrigued.

'Is this your boy?' he asked, and she said instantly, 'Yes!' to pre-empt any interest from one whom the Botanic Gardens, despite its vast size, seemed determined to throw in her path.

'No!' cried Randal. 'She's not my mummy. My mummy's there!'

It was wonderful – the sense of solitude in the vastness of the Gardens, as dusk fell. She stood very still, relishing the moment, the single overpowering sense of oneness with all of creation. The grasshopper, the sparrow, the fish, the turtles, Alex and Laiko, Randal, the bride, the jogger, the young mother conducting lessons in vocabulary and spelling for her little son, the young lustful couple rolling down the slope – every single one of them was responding to life's imperative to be happy. The great chain of happiness-seeking could be extended downwards to include the tiniest organisms inside each of their bodies, for surely even these primordial forms of life sought their own kind of happiness, and upwards to include the deities of Providence residing in those huge ageless trees, for surely even gods needed to be happy. When the Gardens closed for the evening, only the mortals would have to leave and resume their lives in the city. Would the bridal couple, years hence, look back with regret upon that day of joy; would the young lustful couple soon go their separate ways, or remain together, even more separated by those awful conflicts that invariably arose between husbands and wives as they went through the various stages of their marriage that society had red-flagged as mid-life crises or seven-year-itches?

'Should I do it?' she asked herself.

She was back at the fish pond, standing at the water's edge. She had in fact gone to the Gardens with that special purpose, but had forgotten it in the midst of all the wonder and joy. She opened her waist pouch and took out her wedding ring, a plain gold band. She looked at it for a while, then threw it some distance from where she was standing. It landed with a soft *plop* in the water, and in the next second was lost forever, buried deep in the ooze at the bottom of the pond.

'Maria, where's your wedding ring?' her mother would ask. Or might not, given the unusual nature of all that had happened.

If asked, she would say simply, 'I lost it,' and still be telling the truth. Her mother had a friend who wore her dead husband's wedding ring on a chain next to her heart for the twenty years before she joined him in death; beside that devoted wife, she must stand as the blackest-hearted widow.

'I no longer care what people think of me,' she thought with the old defiance.

She had noticed, some days before her husband's death, that he was no longer wearing the wedding band. If it had slipped out of his skeletally thin finger, and had been found by somebody, she was glad it had never been returned to her. Perhaps that somebody was his devoted Third Aunt whose last words of sharp rebuke to her, after the funeral, had been interrupted only by a bout of convulsive sobbing.

There was another ring to dispose of, that would not be the object of any inquiry from her mother for she had never been told about it. She took out from her waist pouch the gold ring set with the carved jade piece, the valued memento from his dying mother that her husband had given her that fateful evening, and for a moment wondered if she should have returned it to his Third Aunt. But the tedium of having to explain how it had got into her possession in the first place would have simply drained all energy from her. She gave it a last look, then with a mighty swing of her arm, flung it far out into the pond. Again, it fell with a soft sound before being swallowed up by the pond waters, now dark and less friendly-looking. While all her late husband's effects had been left in the apartment for his Third Aunt to dispose of as she wished, the two rings carried too much of the past not to warrant a special kind of disposal for closure.

Also to put an end to those unpleasant dreams in which her husband, either alive or dead, or both, as in the odd way of dreams, stood before her as accuser and judge. Lying at the bottom of the pond, the rings would, over the years, be ignored by generations of fish and turtles and ducks that in any case would be too well fed by children coming daily with their parents and maids to enjoy the peaceful loveliness of this most precious spot in Singapore.

Twenty

It was the object of the society's greatest fear, and the schools were its permanent abode from which, like the legendary ogre that terrified a whole village until it was slain, it had dominated the lives of Singaporeans for as long as they could remember. The G.C.E. O Level examinations, which nobody would dare attempt to slay, loomed over the entire national landscape. So deeply had the fear of not passing them been ingrained in students that a whole sub-culture, fuelled largely by parental concerns, had grown around it, from a flourishing industry centred on the provision of private tuition and exam study aids to a prevailing mindset that a person's potential or actual worth, whether in his career or personal life, could be gauged by the number of distinctions or credits scored in the examinations.

The gauge could be said to apply to the next world as well, for it was reported that in the funerary ghost-paper house for a certain deceased Singaporean male, there was, in addition to the usual appurtenances of furniture, car, kitchen utensils, maidservants, a computer, TV and CD player, a ghost-paper G.C.E. O Level certificate replete with distinctions and credits.

Teachers in the schools were acquainted, first-hand, with the parental anxiety as soon as the results of the school preliminary exams were announced, for these were supposed to predict the results of the all-important nation-wide G.C.E., to follow in a matter of months. Some mothers came crying, some came with bribes cleverly disguised as donations to a school fund or charity, all pleaded with principals and teachers to ensure good results, with the stark reminder that their children's entire future depended on it. The young Singaporean couple's life was regulated by the educational needs of their children, from getting them into the best kindergarten, the best primary school, the best secondary school, and seeing that they passed an array of school and national examinations, right from the first year, through the third and sixth years, culminating in the fearful G.C.E.

Maria Seetoh knew a couple from the Church of Eternal Mercy who had four school-going children and systematically organised their priorities for allocation of resources and attention around the child who happened to be preparing for the examinations. Thus, at the beginning of the month, when the father handed his pay packet to his wife, she would instantly rip open the envelope and count out the exact sum needed for the child's examination fees, private tuition fees, cost of exam aids and guidebooks, and dozens of bottles of 'Essence of Chicken' as well as the best Korean ginseng for the long hours of night study; it did not matter how much money was left for the entire household expenses and needs of the other school-going children who were by no means resentful since each would have his or her privileged turn. By the time the last child sat for the examinations, the father who had suffered a mild stroke and had been given a job with a much lower salary, was in debt. The mother who had little education understood its value enough to be ready to take on a part-time job washing dishes in a restaurant if it helped in securing a place for her child in that special crash course, conducted outside school hours by enterprising teachers-turned-tutors, that were guaranteed to improve exam results.

Meeta told the story of the mother of one of her students who, after having done all that was humanly possible for her son, went on to secure the help of the supernatural. Moreover she wanted to maximise that help, thus adopting a shrewd eclecticism by visiting, in turn, her church, an old Chinese temple reputed to have a thoughtful, motherly goddess, and an ancestral tomb, and returning home with, respectively, a bottle of holy water, an amulet and a joss-stick. It was only in the examination hall that her son noticed a small cloth amulet sewn into the sleeve of his school uniform, which was really at odds with the wooden cross he carried in his wallet. Which of the two forces proved to have the greater influence on his G.C.E. results was not known.

The G.C.E. phenomenon could be explained simply by the fact that Singaporeans took the cue for much of their behaviour and thinking from the great TPK. For some reason, the prime minister had settled upon the possession of a full G.C.E. O Level certificate as the starting benchmark for personal worth and integrity, as was demonstrated in two major policies. Firstly, the government organisation that had been set up to matchmake single Singaporean men and women, made it clear to them that to benefit from the various free matchmaking activities, such as tea dances, they would have to possess that certificate; the condition was clearly based on the assumption that below that educational level, young Singaporean men and women were incapable of producing and raising intelligent children for the country's economic future. Ideally, parents should be graduates; realistically, the organisation was prepared to settle for less. Secondly, if a Singaporean aspired to join the government political party, the certificate was again the very minimal qualification for entry; unless supported by incredible experience and sterling qualities, it would not have stood a chance beside the plethora of competing academic qualifications from Harvard and Cambridge.

TPK and his ministers had drawn scathing attention to the fact that V.K. Pandy had to sit *twice* for the G.C.E. O Level examinations to secure a *partial* certificate, whereas their own party candidates could boast of distinctions in a wide range of subjects, which in turn had opened the doors to the highest institutions of learning, both at home and abroad. Following the shameful revelation of his low academic standing, V.K. Pandy wrote a letter to *The Singapore Tribune* in which he reminded Singaporeans that a former protégé of the prime minister, a Dr Yong, whose academic credentials blazed with a PhD degree, two Masters', a First Class Honours and an eight-distinction G.C.E. O Level, had been on the run for years to escape corruption charges involving millions of dollars, whereas he, V.K. Pandy with no G.C.E., had, with patience and hard work, successfully built up a business that would still be running if he had not been prosecuted and fined several hundred thousand dollars on charges of defaming the government. When his small printing shop had to close down, V.K. Pandy's wife, it was said, put on a white sari of mourning, let down her long hair, stood in front of the closed shutters and threatened to commit suicide. The letter was not published by the newspaper, and V.K. Pandy put it up, in enlarged print on a placard mounted on a stand in his favourite spot in Middleton Square. 'No G.C.E. doesn't mean No Integrity!' was the caption.

Employers who, like the schools, were ever alert for signs from the leaders, also demanded good G.C.E. results before they would even call up applicants for interviews. Thus the position of an examination which continued to be designed, set and marked by examiners of a former colonial power, long after that power had left, became unshakeably entrenched in the national landscape.

One of Maria's friends, Emily, had one day brought along a young, pretty relative who worked as a sales assistant in a departmental store to join them for lunch. Swee Hoong needed urgent advice for a problem related to the G.C.E. She was being courted by three men: one was fairly well-to-do, being a contractor and driving a Mercedes, but he had no G.C.E.; the other, a technician, was far less wealthy but much handsomer, and had only a partial certificate, scoring a credit only for Chinese language; the third was reasonably well off, lived in a semi-detached house, drove a Mercedes, had a full certificate and a very successful business as an undertaker, revealing that last, discomfiting fact only very late in the courtship. Despite society's top ranking of the G.C.E., it occurred with just too many competing variables in the young woman's calculus to sort out and come to the best decision.

'Well, which one do you love?' Maria had asked.

'I don't know, it depends,' she replied.

'Which one is most likely to be unfaithful?' Emily asked, remembering her own husband's disgusting infidelities.

'I don't know,' she said gloomily.

'Tell you what,' said Maria brightly. 'Why don't we do things systematically, like the government's systems engineers, that is, we assign a value to each of the attributes of wealth, looks, possession of Mercedes, G.C.E. O Level, character, etc., add them all up, and see who scores the highest!'

In the end, the undertaker was the loser; not even his valued certificate combined with his semi-detached house and Mercedes could trump the *yuk* factor of his occupation, which, however, might conceivably convert into an eager *wow*, if he had possessed, additionally, a penthouse, a Lexus and a verifiably huge bank account.

Over the years, the more enlightened among Singaporeans had drawn attention to the flaws of an educational system so dependent on paper certifications and called for urgent redress if young Singaporeans were ever to become creative, independent-minded and in tune with a rapidly changing world. 'Are we aware,' went an anguished letter in the Forum page of *The Straits Tribune*, 'that while our students abroad excel academically, they rank appallingly low in creative thinking and personal and social skills?' But fear was too valuable, indeed, too essential an instrument to discard: take it away, dispense with the exams, said the teachers, and students would no longer have any motivation to learn.

In any case, the fear of exams was of a piece with the political climate in the society; without fear, said the great TPK, nothing would get done, people would slacken, they would spit on the streets and litter public places, unruly elements would come out of the woodwork to cause disruption and disorder, opportunistic foreign elements would enter and create mischief, and Singapore, from a much admired city-state, would be no better than the many failed societies in the region and the world, permanently mired in chaos and corruption. Use the cane, said TPK, and if it doesn't work, get hold of a bigger one. His most quoted pronouncement was that he would rather be feared than liked.

Singaporeans, are you aware that forty years ago, you lived in slums that had no proper sanitation?

Are you aware that our streets are among the cleanest in the world?

Do you know that every one in three Singaporeans owns his home?

Aren't you pleased that we have the lowest crime rate in the world?

Aren't you delighted that Singapore has been ranked as the most successful economy in Asia?

We are Number One!

Are you happy?

Nobody thought to ask that question; instead of the enthusiastic 'Ay, ay!', Singaporeans might have looked puzzled, or looked uneasily at each other. Maria thought, maybe I could write a little collection of satirical stories, beginning with one on the decreed power of the G.C.E. O Level Certificate: a school principal, against the promptings of her heart, turns the school into a virtual boot camp to secure good exam results, the students suffer enormous anxiety, and the school suddenly finds itself in the midst of a political storm when its poor exam results coincide with a spate of student suicides.

I will have to persist in my hypocrisy and use the very instrument I despise, thought Maria Seetoh, if I want to get my students to pass those wretchedly intimidating exams. As English language teacher, she felt the brunt of the intimidation, for English language had highest ranking among the subjects; a poor grade in the English language paper would render the entire certificate quite worthless for getting into the junior colleges, and thence into the university. The road to higher learning, a good career and a happy, successful life in the society was unremittingly laid out for the young Singaporean, and the burden of launching him upon that road fell largely on the English language teacher.

There was also the plaque presented to her as a token for her role in improving the English language results of St Peter's Secondary School over the years; now she would have to outdo herself. Her special concern was for a group of students who came from purely dialect-speaking homes and environments; they were sure to do badly in their English paper, being incapable of writing a grammatically correct sentence if it exceeded ten words.

One of them whose name was Hong Leng, a very thin boy with a large Adam's apple and grave-looking eyes behind his thick glasses, stopped her one afternoon as she was walking to the staffroom and said, 'Miss Seetoh, I very scared. I can get distinction in maths and science and commerce but I sure to fail in the English paper. That mean I fail whole exam. Can you give me extra homework? Or extra coaching?'

The boy was one of those desperately hopeless cases every English language teacher invariably encountered and eventually gave up on. Maria looked at him sadly, already seeing the ignominious F9 in the certificate when he came to school to collect it some months after the exams.

She said lamely, 'I'll see what I can do, Hong Leng,' meaning she could do little. It was difficult to shake off that look of despair which followed her all the way home.

The next day, as she was walking out of the school gates, a very thin, worn-out looking woman approached her. Speaking in dialect she introduced herself as Hong Leng's mother, and then, to Maria's horror, she whipped out of her tattered handbag a large envelope, half opened to show the wad of dollar notes inside, and tried to press it into her hand. Bribery of a teacher in any form was a highly culpable act, to be reported instantly; Maria felt nothing but pity for the woman who was probably a cleaner at some restaurant or shopping centre.

She said severely, 'You must never do that again,' walked on miserably and in that moment was fired by the determination to do whatever it took to get Hong Leng to achieve at least a passing grade in the English language paper of the G.C.E. O Level exams.

The examination system had suddenly become that monster in the cave, which, if it could not be slain, could at least be avoided and outwitted. Maria Seetoh, she told herself, Hong Leng's mother has thrown at you the greatest challenge of your teaching career, and you have to accept it. The greatest challenge, she suddenly realised, had nothing to do with the ideals of her chosen profession and everything to do with brute bread-and-butter realities.

What she called the Eureka Moment, when the odd bits floating about in her imagination suddenly came together to form a complete story, sometimes happened when she was doing the most mundane things, such as sweeping the floor or brushing her teeth, as if her wildly soaring muse needed to be dragged down to earth. She would then pause, wide-eyed, to let the newly born story scroll through her mind, committing it to paper, in quick notes, as soon as she was free of the day's tasks. The equivalent of that magical moment came as she was sipping coffee, well past midnight, after poring over a stack of past G.C.E. O Level English Language papers, scrutinising the wide range of composition titles and topics offered to candidates to see if she could comprehend the unruly foe, study its every sinister feature and come up with a method to dodge its moves. Feeling that delightful cartoon flashbulb lighting up inside her head, she said excitedly to herself, 'I can help poor Hong Leng.'

A strategy had suggested itself which, being so much at odds with the ideals of an institution of learning, she would have been acutely embarrassed to use in her role as teacher. But as secret tutor to Hong Leng over the two months just before the examinations, she would have no qualms about taking on the role of an educational Machiavellian armed with pure savvy and cunning to best that G.C.E. tyrant.

'Alright, which composition topic must you absolutely avoid? Show me,' she demanded, having worked out what she called a schema of salvation for Hong Leng.

The boy who came during the weekends for the extra coaching absorbed every instruction with fervid attention, taking down notes copiously, asking questions eagerly. By now he knew the kinds of titles that he had to avoid, like poison, said Miss Seetoh, because they were far too difficult for him, and would condemn him to a straight F9.

The first stage of identifying the most deadly features of the enemy was crucial. They were the argumentative topics that asked about the good and bad points of having national zoos, of depending on the tourist industry, or of abandoning traditions, the descriptive topics that required him to describe his ideal home or the ideal library; the abstract topics with deceptively simple one-word titles like 'Love', 'Happiness', 'Dreams'. Conceptually and linguistically demanding, the topics must have been designed by the examiners for the elite few from very privileged English-speaking homes, who, at fifteen or sixteen years old, were already capable of mature thinking and expository writing. They were clearly not at all meant for the rest of the students from the high-rise, government-subsidised flats, who if they chose these composition topics would flounder from the opening sentence.

Hong Leng, with five sample past examination papers spread before him, duly ruled out, with a red pencil, all the treacherous topics. That left a few out of the dozen or so provided. They were the friendlier, less demanding narrative topics requiring the candidate to provide a story for the given title. The titles were generously broad, to allow the candidate to come up with a simple story, within the limited time given, from personal experience or pure imagination: *'Write about the happiest day in your life.' 'Write a story with the title 'Too Late!' 'One evening, as I was getting ready for bed, I heard a strange sound....' Continue the story.' 'Was there a time when you made a serious mistake and suffered the consequences? Write about it.'*

Maria said, 'Hong Leng, tell me again what you must do as soon as you look at the exam paper.'

Hong Leng said confidently, 'I must cancel out all the dangerous topics'.

'Good. What must you do next?'

'Look at the narrative topics, choose one and circle it in red.'

'Then?'

'Then I must underline the key words in the topic.'

'Okay. Now show me which key words you underline in this topic.'

The procedural meticulousness could save a student's composition from that fearful F8 or F9 grade. For one of the greatest exam disasters was to 'go out of point', by which a student missed an important word in the question or misread it, thereby submitting a composition that could well be construed by the annoyed examiner as a pre-prepared piece of work.

Irrelevance, possibly indicating cheating, could thus carry an even greater punishment than weak grammar.

'Describe a recent occasion when you suffered a disappointment.'
There was a student, some years past, who had not been mindful of the key word 'recent', and had written about a real childhood experience six years ago. She was one of the best students in her class and had been expected to get a distinction. Her poor grade created a flurry of activities, initiated by her shocked parents, that ended with the school writing to the Cambridge examiners to make an inquiry, and their subsequently conducting a proper investigation that unearthed the serious mistake that the student had made. Singaporeans could be apathetic about public or political issues, but be roused to extreme passion and action when their children's educational well-being was threatened.

For years, the story made the rounds of the schools as a cautionary tale. Some teachers had developed a method of instilling so much fear about 'going out of point' that their terrified students never made the mistake again: their ruse was to write a huge, ferocious 'F9' across each page of the offending composition with a brutal red marker, and pin it up on the classroom news bulletin board for public humiliation of the offender.

Hong Leng, by prior acquaintance with the monster's deadliest feature, would be able to avoid it. There were other dangers to be taken into account.

'Alright, Hong Leng, how much time did you take to do this composition?'

The boy, in working on the extra compositions at home, had to be trained to write the required two or two and a half pages within the allotted one and a half hours. He was slow, and at the first attempt, had managed only a three quarter page, but was steadily improving. What would be the use, explained Miss Seetoh, of producing a first-class introduction to your story, going on to a first-class first paragraph and then hearing the exam invigilators announce, 'Five minutes more!' or 'Time's up!'? Time was another foe to reckon with.

'Alright, Hong Leng, tell me, what tense form should you use throughout in your story?'

'The past tense, Miss Seetoh.'

'Good.'

'What's wrong with the tense form in this sentence:

'During the last holidays, my parents visit Malaysia –'

' 'Visit*ed* Malaysia', Miss Seetoh.'

'Good. Remember, after you finish your composition, to check all your verbs, and see if they have the past tense form. You know what verbs are, Hong Leng?'

'They are the doing or action words, Miss Seetoh.'

'Good. Now tell me, how long should each of your sentences be, Hong Leng?'

'No more than ten words, Miss Seetoh.'

The shorter the sentence, the less chance for students like poor Hong Leng to make grammatical errors. Complex and compound sentences were death traps. No examiner could punish a student for short simple sentences even if these were uninspired and uninspiring, but they would apply the ruthless red pencil to long, sophisticated sentences that were sure to succumb to the traps of English grammar and syntax.

Maria thought: for Hong Leng's sake, I'm going to subvert the very purpose of the examinations, to undermine its role as a true test of merit. She would of course always have nothing but contempt for those who tried to get hold of exam papers before their release, using any means, including bribery, to break the traditional tight security enforced upon these all-important, life-affecting documents. It must be the dream of every lazy, incompetent, irresponsible student to know all the exam questions beforehand, get expert help for the answers, learn them up, write them out with a flourish in the exam hall and then sit back, for the remaining time, to watch the other students slog away.

There had been a case, in Meeta's and Winnie's school, of an attempted break-in; the exam papers, kept locked in a safe in the principal's office, were saved from theft only because the school night-watchman doing his rounds had spotted the intruder who instantly fled. Beyond the sheer desperation of such attempts, the annals of exams must be filled with all manner of cheating.

Did the final stage of her strategy in helping Hong Leng, smack of cheating too, because it involved actually preparing answers beforehand?

'Hong Leng, I want you to think of three or four happy or positive experiences in your life and also of unhappy or negative experiences.'

All the narrative questions in the exam paper invariably asked about each or both of such experiences. Hong Leng duly came up with two lists.

'Now Hong Leng, I want you to write out short paragraphs, as many as you can, describing your feelings, pleasant and unpleasant. Describe your joy, surprise, excitement, gratitude, affection, admiration, love, and so on, as well as anger, disappointment, fear, frustration, distress, despair and so on.'

The suggested feelings covered virtually the entire range relevant to the entire corpus of narrative topics, possibly for the entire history, over generations, of the paper; there could not be a greater offer of guarantee. Miss Seetoh, armed with this certainty, set Hong Leng a large quantity of homework which the boy worked at most conscientiously and enthusiastically. The next, and final, step was for her to correct all the grammatical and other mistakes in the submitted compositions, then hand them back for Hong Leng to study meticulously, even learn by heart, for reproducing in the exams. The trick was to knit together some of these pre-prepared paragraphs into a full composition, and hey presto! a reasonable credit was assured. She had discovered the formula for passing an exam, thus undermining its integrity and her own as a teacher.

The boy's joy must not be diluted by guilt. The stack of marked paragraphs now in his keeping, Miss Seetoh explained, were all his own work, for she had merely corrected their grammatical and other mistakes, therefore if he made use of them in the exam, he would be in no way cheating. Maria Seetoh thought: *I* am the real cheat. She, teacher of English and literature, enjoined with the purpose of inculcating a true love of the subject in her students, of preparing them for life, had reduced that noble purpose to the passing of exams. She was helping to turn out a conveyor belt of exam-smart students who would find good jobs in the society and be absorbed into the rules-governed, unquestioning, unthinking culture that the great TPK favoured.

'Really, I don't care much,' she said to herself in the mirror, in the privacy of the bathroom. Lately she had taken to talking to herself, to help clarify her own thinking. She had become two selves: the public persona as she engaged with others in the world with its many perils, and the private person as soon as she returned home and became absorbed in her own, dear world of private thinking and feeling. Be in the world, but not of it, was the advice of the holy book she had left behind but never forgotten for its occasional insights into the day-to-day struggles of decent men and women. Be pure as the dove, but at the same time, be wily as the serpent. How much of the dove and how much of the serpent had she been as wife, and now as a teacher?

'I don't care,' she said again defiantly, 'as long as I'm happy.' And she had not been as happy for a long time.

Hong Leng passed the English language paper in his preliminaries and actually scored a strong credit in the G.C.E. O levels. On the day he collected his results, he shyly presented a 'Thank You' card to Miss Seetoh overflowing with effusive gratitude (with three grammatical errors, she sadly noted). Every year, long after he had left school, he would send her Christmas and Chinese New Year cards. He landed an extremely well-paying job in a computer firm, writing to tell her about it and to add, with self-conscious pride, that he was going to get married soon to a wonderful colleague. 'I will appreciate very much for your kindness to attend my marriage,' he wrote. When the prime minister lamented the poor standard of English in formal and business letters, he could have had, in mind, Singaporean users of English like Hong Leng.

'Are you happy?' she asked him.

'I am very happy, Miss Seetoh. And I thank you for your unstinting help you gave me to get my G.C.E. O Level.'

One day Maria was surprised to get a call from Hong Leng who asked her whether she could conduct courses for his staff to improve their English. He added, rather shyly, that she would be well paid for it. She said 'No' instantly, for by that time, in her solitude, she wanted little to do with a world that reminded her of her days at St Peter's Secondary School.

Twenty-One

Dr Phang is bad news, her head told her. Beware that man, said her heart. If head and heart were investigated by those instruments of science that told only the truth, there would be no registration of suspicion or anxiety, only the firing sparks of pure elation. Even the mention of his name, much less the recollection of the deep gaze of his eyes or the touch of his hand, would elicit that reaction, properly belonging to lovers only, which the sensitive instruments monitoring heartbeat, breathing or pupillary enlargement could instantly pick up.

No, she would not, could not cross that line; she would be a friend only. Crossing that line: how did the act of sex, that very first time when the woman decided to abandon all the rules of the game enjoined on her by her mother with the unshakeable backing of society, give in to the man's pleading and go to bed with him, become such a crucial, irrevocable decision, resulting in a commitment with so much emotional, if not legal, baggage? In the time of her mother and Por Por, that one act of sex could be revealed to the world by physiology: how many heartbreaking stories she had heard about the woman betrayed by the broken maidenhood and the visibly swelling belly that caused her enraged family to cast her out. Por Por was saved only because the family face had to be saved.

Suppose the modern, educated woman, free from all those ancient perils, decided to disregard her mother and her society, adopt the man's attitude and said she did not at all want the baggage, only the excitement of the game? 'Wonderful,' he would say. 'We think alike. Let's go to bed. No commitment! No strings attached! Perfect!' The perfection would not last beyond the second, or third or tenth coupling, perhaps not even beyond the moment the man rolled off, stretched out languorously on the sheets and heaved the huge satisfied sigh of eventual conquest.

There was the story of a married playboy businessman in Singapore who had secretly tried for years to seduce the beautiful Taiwanese mistress of a fellow businessman. He eventually succeeded with a vanload of her favourite red roses, left the petal-strewn bed triumphantly and never visited it again; later he succeeded with another reluctant lady, in only half the time of the previous attempt, without the need, moreover, for roses. Research studies had shown that the average life span of an affair was a paltry eighteen months.

'What's the matter?' he would demand. 'Why are you crying?'

And she would sniffle, ' I can't bear to think that in a short while, you'll be up, dressed and ready to go home to your wife and fly off on holiday with her next week.'

'You know I can't go on holiday with you.'

'You could if you really tried.'

'Now stop crying and come to me again, there's a good girl.'

'I can't bear that you carry your wife's photo in your wallet and her framed picture is on your office desk.'

'You know I can't do that with you. What's the matter with you? I thought we had agreed there would be no commitment.' The forbidden word would have to be uttered at some stage. 'For goodness' sake, are you jealous that I sleep with my own wife?'

The classic quandary had been made much of in the movies and popular literature, where even the most forbearing woman succumbed to that dreadful green-eyed monster that eventually devoured her. They also made much of the woman's classic strategy to force her lover to a commitment with the simple declarative sentence that would never lose its fearfulness for the man: I'm going to have a baby.

Maria thought, smiling to herself: I could never stoop to such a strategy, the lowest of the low, involving a falsehood of such magnitude. What lies women told on men's account! In a Chinese movie that she saw as a young girl, Por Por had difficulty explaining to her why the female protagonist wore a small cushion tied to her belly, and she remembered she was aghast at the extent of the deception.

The high ground of her sexual morality, if she were honest enough, had its slippery slopes: she was already being tantalised by that trick, inspired by history's royal mistresses and concubines, whereby the wily lady led the besotted king or commander up an enchanted garden path, strewing along the way an abundance of soft endearments and kisses, only to stop at the line, saying sweetly, 'No, my lord, not yet,' and smiling to see him driven mad with desire. When the enchantress finally did cross the line, securing a crown, a place in history, or a position of superiority in a household of lesser wives or concubines, she might find, alas, that her lord's desire thereafter rapidly declined and could, within a royally appointed thousand days, turn into rabid hostility satisfied with no less than a rolling of her head, after which he rubbed his hands together and got ready to start the whole cycle of intoxicating infatuation and lust all over again.

Romantic love tried to solve the problem for romantic women: get out of the game completely, because you will only end up the loser. So let the men love you across an impassable gulf, let them love you in a frozen picture on a vase that permanently captures that moment of male yearning, let them love you in poetry and song that will never die. Stay dressed. Wear a chastity belt of your own making. Love in the Platonic abstraction might be the romantic woman's only game. Such an alluring but physiologically intact woman must be as familiar as her sexually accommodating sister in human experience, to have gained lexical recognition: she was defined as a *demiviurge*, the ultimate femme fatale.

Maria looked at herself in the mirror, admiring the expertly subtle, undetectable use of lipstick and rouge that was already making her colleagues and students at St Peter's take a second, wondering look at her. With the last bit of colour, as she capped the lipstick, closed the powder compact and made adjustments to her hair, she was also putting finishing touches to a new phase in her life. It stretched before her, shimmering with thrilling possibilities. Suddenly, at thirty-nine, newly widowed, she was entering the intriguing world of men, a world that had been so confusing and cruel to poor Por Por and her mother, that had failed Emily and thousands of other women, enticed young girls like Maggie and mature women like Meeta and Winnie, and might just live up to the dreams of incurably trusting and loyal girls like Yen Ping who would have but one true love in her entire life.

Amidst the avowals that no men would be allowed to enter her brave, new post-Bernard world, because they would only complicate it and bring misery, was the realisation that, if she managed things well enough, their entry might actually enhance it. She was not creating a new world; she was merely staking her claim on one that that seemed decreed for women alone, which, from girlhood, they had confided about endlessly to each other, or into their diaries, breathless with anticipation and hope. When she was an undergraduate in the university, even as she preferred solitariness, she took great interest in the incessant buzz of speculation among her girlfriends, about who was dating whom, who was serious about whom, who was poaching whose dates, etc. She had had very little experience of that domain, preferring to concentrate on her studies and her love of literature; the disastrous, but fortunately brief, period of courtship and marriage to Bernard of course did not count and could be dismissed as an anomalous experience best forgotten, though it had provided her with new knowledge of herself, and a new awareness and confidence that would surely stand her in good stead in the future. With the strategic purposefulness that she had guided the student Hong Leng to success in the examinations, she was approaching a crucial test she had set herself in her pursuit of happiness. She did a little reenactment of that happy dance with Randal amidst the sprays of water in the Botanic Gardens. World, here I come! she thought with girlish tremulousness. Head and heart: each should be allowed its promptings. That was the advantage of the latecomer to the game of love, unlike the callow sixteen-year-old.

Head and heart: the male had a third force which the female had to reckon with, well below either but superseding both, allying him with the raging beast in musth, sniffing out the promising female, ready to lose tusk or antler to win her. When she was a little girl listening in on adult conversations despite being repeatedly shooed away, she heard her mother and the neighbourhood women comparing men to the lustful barnyard cockerel that chased every hen. The childhood incidents when she had been forced to look upon throbbing male power, rearing its ophidian head in readiness to strike, first in the group of exhibiting kampong urchins who had enticed her and her friend into a shed, and again when an unzipped male sat opposite her and her mother in a ferry, would have no place in her romantic memory. Her honeymoon was no honeymoon because she had secretly cringed throughout to the incessant demands of male desire. She had read, with incredulity, of worshippers of Priapic power during religious festivals, who, despite being endlessly brutalised by it, actually knelt before its symbols cast in solid stone or clay, reverently touching and caressing them.

Her world would accommodate only male desire when it was civilly clothed and softened by kindness and tender regard for female needs. How could she ever forget the embrace that day outside the sickroom when she had felt so safe, so understood and loved by a man? Memory captured and cherished every sensuous detail – touch, sight, smell – of that embrace. As a child, she had often heard of the dead as being safe in the arms of Jesus; she had not wanted to wait for death to enjoy the happiness of being enfolded by those arms in their long white sleeves, of being held close to that loving bosom, pressed against that benign face with the soft brown eyes, the shoulder-length brown hair and gentle beard. A god in male form was ever a woman's comfort; she could also look up to his representative, the priest, and seek solace in a warm enfolding by those caring arms. The gods in mythology who came to earth to rape mortal women, the men of God whose cassocks hid unbridled lust – these too had been banished from her world.

During those moments of deep contentment nestling in the divine arms, she would cuddle her favourite doll which would in turn cuddle its baby doll, which had its own tiny infant formed by a knotted handkerchief, in an endless nesting of love, like those lovely Russian dolls, one inside the other, that she had once seen in somebody's house. Meeta with her frequent night dreams of the venerable Sai Baba would understand a woman's need for touch, whether from divine or mortal beings, as would Winnie who largely favoured the mortals, cheating though they were. Touch me, said the yearning woman, and found, too late, that she had been completely misunderstood by the man.

There was a young girl in her school, years ago, who was made pregnant by a neighbour, a married man with four children, who lived two doors away in a block of flats. Why did you allow him to do that to you? she was asked. I felt so safe and loved each time I cried and he took me in his arms and comforted me, she replied. Did the wily, calculating Maggie know where to draw the line so that she could go on with her school life? Was she already teaching that young sister called Angel whom she loved so much to do the same?

Each encounter with Dr Phang drew her closer to the line; perhaps the thrilling challenge, on her part, of seeing how much she would be in control, and, on his part, of seeing how soon she would capitulate, kept both of them in that deliciously trembling prelude to an affair that still had no name. It was as exciting as it was unreal, a man and a woman locked together in a daring, exhilarating suspension of reality that would come roaring back with a vengeance because the man had a wife and a family who had the support of society. She was thirty-nine, and he fifteen years older, and they were playing a game that men and women must have played since the establishment of that institution called marriage with its many relentless rules that cried out for suspension, if only for a brief while, because they were so hopelessly contrary to the unruly passions of head, heart and gonads.

'Why is he calling you so often?' said her mother, with the same disapproval that she had when she first asked about the frequency of his visits during her husband's illness.

Anna Seetoh noticed the lighting up of skin and eyes when her daughter rushed to pick up the phone, the guilty cupping of hand over the mouthpiece. The tragic circumstances of her son-in-law's death would always be associated with the treachery of her own daughter and his own best friend. Her suspicions were confirmed with the phone calls that usually came at odd hours and lasted briefly, as expected of a man in guilty evasion of detection by his wife, and with the secret meetings that she was sure took place in some hotel. One of these days, she would search her daughter's room for incriminating evidence.

On behalf of her dead son-in-law, she felt she had to ask her wayward daughter outright, 'Are you having an affair with that man? Heng says he's absolutely sure you are.' Maria said angrily, 'It's none of his business; just leave him out of anything that concerns me.' The antagonism against Dr Phang of that adopted brother of hers had less to do with affairs than with money; he would always be aggrieved that the large sum from the sale of the apartment left by Bernard to his Third Aunt had gone forever outside his reach into the pockets of her greedy relatives in Malaysia. Apparently he was having money problems in the various businesses he would never talk about, in the same secretive way he remained about his wife and young autistic son living with his in-laws in Malaysia; the thought of never being able to tap into a little of that vast amount must have increased his resentment against the sister whose folly had caused all the trouble.

'Are you having an affair?' demanded Anna Seetoh. 'Tell the truth and shame the devil.'

'Well,' said Maria airily, 'the devil can be duly shamed; there's no affair,' adding, with the perverse need to shock a parent who had been dominating her for too long, 'but I don't promise there won't be one.'

Anna Seetoh gave a little shriek. 'Then you will be committing a mortal sin!' she said in a mixture of anger and sorrow.

'The rules no longer apply to me,' said Maria with cool defiance.

'Don't you care what people will think?' pleaded Anna Seetoh. She announced shortly after, 'I'm joining Father Rozario's pilgrimage to Lourdes next month,' clearly with the intention to earn enough spiritual merit to cover the prodigal daughter.

'Mother, I didn't mean to upset you,' said Maria, giving her a hug which she brushed away. 'But I'm happy, at least for now. Aren't you happy that I'm happy?'

'There's no future with a married man,' said Anna Seetoh stiffly. 'One of these days his wife will find out. How do you know she hasn't already set a private detective on you? And Ah Siong has not been dead a year. For God's sake, Maria, do you know what you are doing?'

Maria hated it when she was dragged down from the soaring clouds of a vertiginous joy and pinned to the ugly realities on the ground. 'Mother, please leave me alone,' she said with firm finality. 'I know what I'm doing.'

'I certainly hope so!' snapped Anna Seetoh, and in the next breath whimpered, 'I shall pray for you.'

It was a happiness rich and brimming, once guilt and anxiety were banished with the simple decision not to cross the line, and it spilled over into a cheerful disposition towards everyone.

'You look very happy,' said Brother Philip with shrewd perceptiveness.

'I don't know whether I have a right to be so happy,' said Maria with a cryptic evasiveness that only increased the good man's curiosity. 'Perhaps one of these days I could unburden myself to you.'

'*Unburden*? You're sure that's not a Freudian slip, my dear?' He had taken to using that little endearment when talking to her, and she was not sure whether it was simple avuncular geniality or something else.

Dear Brother Philip, she thought. Of all the inhabitants in her world of St Peter's, she enjoyed his company most. If he were not protected by that vow to be ever chaste, would he too have been drawn into her increasingly rambunctious world?

A beneficiary of the new, light-hearted magnanimity was Mr Chin. Meeta said what he had done to her was so disgusting nobody should take it sitting down. The man had one morning during recess, when he happened to be sitting beside her in the school canteen, invited her for lunch in a newly opened restaurant in town that was famous for its dim sum. He spoke at unnecessary length on the excellence of the dim sum to cover his embarrassment at having plucked up enough courage to ask her for a date, and she apologised, with unnecessary effusiveness, for declining it. She saw the deep flush of shock and humiliation spread on his face and had an instant inspiration to save it.

'Won't you join me for a cup of coffee in the staffroom later?' she said sweetly, assuring him that there was enough in her flask for two. Colouring even more deeply, he declined, walked away and never spoke to her again.

Within a week, he had launched his own face-saving campaign. He spread the story that Maria Seetoh, out of sheer loneliness in her newly widowed status, had invited him for coffee; he had politely turned her down and had been avoiding her since, fearing to get involved with someone who, since her husband's death, was no longer the same person. Besides, she had lost all her fresh beauty and looked haggard and worn out. The story accreted all manner of tantalising details along the way: Miss Seetoh had invited him for dim sum, Miss Seetoh had invited him to her home for coffee, Miss Seetoh was clearly setting her sights on him.

'The cheek of him!' Meeta had exclaimed. 'Maria, you should have countered his story with the truth. How can you let him spoil your reputation like this?'

Brother Philip, the only one to whom Maria cared to tell the truth, responded with a silly limerick scribbled on a scrap of paper during a staff meeting and surreptitiously passed to her:

There's this man who, ahem,
Fell for a lady called M,
But she only sniffed
And he was so miffed
He wished her a life of mayhem!

Maria scribbled back a response: 'Laughter postponed. Coffee after meeting?'

Winnie told the story of a Mr Beh, a Chinese language teacher, who mistook her kindness in making coffee for him every morning in the staffroom, for infatuation.

'I wouldn't touch him with a ten-foot pole!' she giggled. 'No looks, no personality, bad teeth, a worse gossiper than a woman!'

Dr Phang soared above the dull, mean-minded Mr Chin and the unprepossessing, gossip-mongering Mr Beh as Olympus above dung-hill, as white knight on horseback above the lowly, load-bearing minions on foot. He was bad news because his extraordinary charm broke the calculating machines of self-protection inside women's heads, and caused them to throw all sensibility and caution to the winds. If asked why they had succumbed to his charms, knowing full well he was married and had had affairs throughout his more than thirty years of marriage to a good, decent, home-loving wife from a good family, they would have said, 'I don't know,' meaning that they were unable to explain the huge gap between the astutely deliberative apparatus of head and the hopelessly unreliable apparatus of heart. If the situation had been reversed, and it was a woman who had cut such a huge swathe through swooning men, she would have had the charge of witchcraft laid at her door: she must have had recourse to time-tested charms and potions for making men fall desperately in love with her, for making them increase their potency in her company and losing it as soon as they climbed back into their wives' beds.

Dr Phang's charm was as far removed from the dark forces of tradition as his abundance of wavy silver hair, gentle eyes, beguiling smile, witty speech and permanently relaxed air were from the artifices of the poseur at cocktail parties, or in glossy advertisements. Women ever loved the au naturel in a man; Dr Phang, in his looks, bearing and demeanour, down to the last endearing mannerism of running a hand, in moments of puzzlement, through the film-star locks, or throwing back his head in a hearty laugh, had it in abundance. Women who did much thinking about how best to give excuses, offer explanations and present arguments, loved Dr Phang's habit of dispensing with all three. He is so spontaneous, he makes you feel completely relaxed, they said. He behaves like a gentleman even to the office boys and the cleaning women, they said, and instantly contrasted him with those arrogant high-fliers and top-achievers in the civil service whose arrogance only showed their insecurities.

In a note after Bernard's funeral, he had asked why Heng had told him not to attend it, but when he met her for the first time, months later, over lunch in a restaurant, he never referred to the subject and instead plunged straight into the sheer enjoyment of her company. She had been prepared for a lengthy, tedious time of endless questions and explanations, of their moving cautiously around each other's sensitivities, of saying something and then, for answer, listening to what was not, could not be said. To her utter surprise and delight, the lunch was all pleasant, light-hearted talk and laughter.

The note asking for an explanation could not have been a stratagem, as the man was incapable of any. All he had was his enormous self-confidence and brimming exuberance to turn a potentially discomfiting situation into a completely enjoyable one. Dr Phang, she concluded, was the true hedonist who never let the intrusive *why* of the past and the tiresome *what* of the future intrude upon the pure enjoyment of the present, whether it was playing golf, hiking with his daughter in Europe, drinking with his buddies in a pub or trying to seduce a woman over a meal in a restaurant. It was said that as an undergraduate he would spend much time, during the examination season, playing the drums in a band, while his friends swotted, despaired and lost weight, and then, to their disgust, emerge with top grades.

At work, his massive intellect, which had impressed his superiors right up to the Minister of Defence and the great TPK himself, came up with such brilliant ideas that the leadership, ever conservative and austere, was prepared to overlook his philandering ways and invite him to get into politics. It was said that at some time or another, every ministry had sought his views on this or that major national project.

'I don't know, let me think about it,' he would say, settling himself comfortably in his chair with his feet on the table and closing his eyes; shortly afterwards, he would come up with the most insightful ideas.

Head, heart, the libidinal urge: each, kept apart from the others, had its own vibrant energy because all were governed by a prodigious, unapologetic lust for life.

The great TPK had seen enough of yes-men to appreciate his firm No to many a request or invitation. 'I am not suited for a political life,' he had said, and, paradoxically, became rated by the leadership as the most suitable. Only Dr Phang, it was said, could have got away with doing what he did some years ago. He had absented himself from a very important state function because his daughter, who was then studying in London, was distraught over something and had called him urgently; he had immediately taken leave to fly to be with her. The Prime Minister, who was known to chastise those who put their personal concerns above official duties, actually inquired about the distraught daughter upon his return; perhaps he was thinking of his own sickly wife needing more of his time than he could spare. The rumours about his devotion to his wife of thirty years had a somewhat softening effect on the hard, callous image that he presented to the world. Those severe eyes, that belligerent jaw, that raised forefinger of threat and warning – they all melted, it was whispered, into a soft centre of pure tenderness and concern when he attended to her, covering her feet with a warm blanket, bringing her the most expensive ginseng brew.

He would deal with Dr Phang's philandering in an appropriate way: once he got the man into politics, he would issue him the stern warning that he invariably issued to all his ministers and members of parliament, 'It's your own business, but once it becomes a public scandal, there'll be no mercy.'

At least one wife of an errant minister had written to the prime minister about her husband's shenanigans; he was dropped from his ministerial job soon after and dispatched as ambassador to some obscure European country. Olivia Phang, if she even remotely suspected an affair, would likely not just send a letter but ask for a personal appearance before the prime minister to plead for no less a punishment than complete disgrace, to be commensurate with the love she had given him.

The man's unique hold on women must ultimately lie in his love of them, even if only ephemeral, even if only physical, but still to be called love, if women so hankered after it. Here was a man who would unabashedly say he could not do without women, thus paying them the supreme compliment. Definitely not husband material, one of the women he had loved and left had sniffed, and then had to admit sadly, but definitely lover material. No mere rude, crude Casanova, he deserved that epithet which women used for the ultimate lover: *sensitive*. And the ultimate tribute was that he was *naturally* sensitive to their every mood, need, desire, there being none of the pretence that women so hated. Effortlessly, Dr Phang made conquests; only he did not see them as such, but a celebration, on each occasion, of the sheer enjoyment of the woman's company, a perfect meshing of male desire and female need. He put her on a pedestal; it did not matter if she had soon to vacate it for another. It was said that he had so charmed a French woman he had met in a plane to Europe that after their single rendezvous in a Paris hotel, armed with no more than a recollection of his name and appearance, she came to Singapore to look for him.

Dr Phang had got married at the early age of twenty-two, for the sole purpose of sex, to a shy young girl of the same age, chosen for him by his strongly conservative Christian parents who would have beaten him to a pulp if he had joined his friends in their secret jaunts to test their manhood in the sleazy haunts of his home town in Malaysia. The effects of the conservative upbringing did not last long in his marriage: before long, his shy, intellectual, conservative wife must have been no match for his enormous energies and the affairs started, first with the pretty girls in his office, then, over the years, with women who came into his social circle and women outside the circle who came crashing into it, like his present wife, a model from Hong Kong whom he had met by the merest chance. It was through sheer tenacity, or her striking sexuality, that she had got him to divorce his wife and marry her. Where other men would have floundered through a mess of emotional and legal wrangling, would have wrestled with guilt, remorse and shame, Dr Phang simply sailed from his first marriage into his second amazingly calm and in control, remaining on good terms with his daughter, his ex-wife and his ex-mistresses. It's impossible to be angry with that man, they would say. There is not a single snide, mean bone in his body. He is always generous, helpful and caring. Other men? They behave much, much worse. They can't hold a light to his candle.

The enviable Teflon Man, ever undamaged. If he had been the president of the most powerful nation in the world, or the leader of the most powerful religious organisation, the onerousness of office, and the responsibility of handling crises and calming a nervous world, would not in the least have detracted from his cheerful imperturbability and joie de vivre. He would have gone to play a game of golf, or made love to a woman, in the midst of an international crisis and woken up the next morning to see an abatement of the crisis. Life was a game which he played with relish by rules he bent with saucy impunity.

Maria thought, this man bears a charmed life. The goddess who presided at his birth must have left at his cradle a mega gift of luck. The classic Byronic hero was said to be mad, bad and dangerous to know, except that in his case, the madness, badness and danger were all on the side of the poor pursuing woman. If she wrote a book about him one day, she would call it 'The Man Who Loved Women', a generous euphemism for that insatiable lust ranked high among the Seven Deadly Sins, depicted sometimes as a horned, goat-footed, bright-eyed man playing a merry pipe. A man's lust, unaccompanied by a brilliant mind and an engaging manner, turned women off; dressed in both, it brought them scrambling over each other to his bed. Olivia Phang, young and beautiful and wealthy after a very profitable divorce from her first husband, with her impeccably manicured nails, must have clawed her way right to it, shredding the competitors along the way. Now she, Maria Seetoh, by no means as young, beautiful and wealthy, was being courted by this man. Vanity made the thought alone intoxicating. Was hers the next scalp he would wear on his victory belt?

She was glad that Olivia Phang and her mother were helping her in the drawing of the line, the first through her vigilant monitoring of her husband's activities, like a small animal with sharply quivering nostrils, and the second through simply being in the house virtually all the time, thus ruling out a major trysting venue.

Sometimes Anna Seetoh sat by the table with the phone, in a form of self-inflicted punishment that required picking it up, hearing the hated interloper's voice and saying to her daughter, 'It's for you,' without being able to add, 'You're playing with fire.'

'You're playing with fire,' said Meeta.

'I've only seen him once,' said Winnie, 'and I must say he's a charmer. No wonder you've fallen for him, Maria!'

'He must be such a refreshing change from that awful husband of yours and that boring, childish Mr Chin,' said Meeta.

'Oo-oh, now you know what it's like to be in love,' said Winnie. 'But he's so much older! Not old enough to be your father, but definitely so much older. Think, Maria, when you're forty-five, he'll be an old man already!'

'Winnie, you're being your usual silly self,' said Meeta. 'Don't you know that the older some men get, the better they look, the sexier they become?'

She mentioned a gentleman at the Polo Club, seventy-three years old, and as dandy and debonair as ever.

'I've never heard you speak with such feeling about any man before,' said Winnie. 'Oho, our cold, detached Maria Seetoh in love at last!'

'I understand his Hong Kong wife is a shrew. I tell you, Maria, you're playing with fire!' cried Meeta.

'Dearie,' giggled Winnie, 'have you slept with him yet?'

'Tell you what,' said Meeta suddenly, in a display of that supreme female illogicality that could turn a warning in an instant into its total opposite of enthusiastic encouragement. 'If you have no place to meet your beau, we could lend you ours occasionally. Winnie and I could spend an evening at my sister's, and we'll take the maid with us as well as Singapore who may bark too much and spoil your fun. You can have the whole place to yourself. And shut the windows; the couple opposite are real nosy parkers.'

Twenty-Two

A birth, a death, an affair: St Peter's Secondary School, being society's microcosm, duly replicated its human events with all the attendant human feelings of joy and sorrow. Mrs Kee, one of the maths teachers, had given birth to a baby boy after a succession of four daughters, and Sister Elizabeth, the chemistry teacher who had been diagnosed with womb cancer a year ago, had passed away.

The birth and the death could be talked about at St Peter's; the affair would have to remain secret to avoid society's censure, even if it was only at that stage when the strict technicality of the uncrossed line put it beyond the censure. But society could still warn. It had its favourite metaphor of playing with fire, the imagery simultaneously capturing the consuming flame of foolish passion and of the other kind of flame, eternal and seasoned with brimstone, that folly deserved. Maria was sure, if she could read the mind of Brother Philip or the sharp Mrs Neo or even the principal who sometimes gave her quizzical looks, she would see the question in vivid letters rolled out in a scroll of judgement for all to see: 'Maria Seetoh, barely a year after your husband's death, are you having an affair?'

Affair, liaison, relationship, infatuation, amour – it was happiness, by any name, thought Maria with defiant joy. She could not recall a time in her life, whether as a young girl or as an adult, when she had been so happy. Mentally she applied to her happy state the modifying adverbs she had taught her students to use instead of the overused, unimaginative 'very', selecting only those that went beyond mere modification to scale the greatest expressive heights: so she was *supremely, ecstatically, phenomenally, indescribably* happy. Never mind if it was happiness of the dubious kind that would not stand up to the moral scrutiny of Father Rozario or her mother or the principal. Or of the inferior kind celebrated in popular love songs and Valentine cards that relied exclusively on cheap rhyming words such as the fervid 'true'-'you'-'blue', 'moon'-'June'-'soon', 'kiss'-'bliss'-'miss' clusters of silly juvenilia. A teacher of creative writing who sternly forbade her students to use those dreadful clichés, she now recognised that the happiness she was experiencing was translatable into exactly the cheap banalities of the airy walk, the singing heart, the starry eyes.

Meeta said, looking at her with eyes narrowed in intense probing, 'How come you're looking younger?'

Her mother was less kind.

'Maria, don't think I don't know. I heard you singing in the bathroom just now. And your mind seems far away, like it's thinking of something else.' She could not resist tagging on the fire warning.

Being in love, it was said, was something purely chemical, a throwback to life's primordial origins, back even to ancestors that were rough and scaly, crawling out of mud in response to the mating call, or that were delicately winged and beautiful, flying unimaginable distances on a pheromone-scented trail. Love, raw and pristine, unabashed and unstoppable, was well before the time of thinking and calculating, giving rise to the only explanation for unaccountable attraction between two people: love's chemistry. In Nature's grand scheme of things, its only purpose was procreation and its strategy was to offer a reward in advance for all the pains. Human beings soon dispensed with the procreative burden but cleverly kept the reward. So a woman in love was buoyed up on a tide of wondrous chemicals, with no price to pay. A clichéd happiness was still happiness, to be savoured as long as possible.

Being in love and loving were not the same thing, the first being a temporary and intense state of suspended reality, the second, in its firm rootedness and commitment, being the exact opposite. The apportionment of reward was unfair: the loving woman, guided only by devotion and loyalty, was often weighed down by sadness and disappointment, while a woman in love, ignoring all duty and responsibility, had a face that radiated happiness and walked with a light step. Did Por Por, meeting her lover secretly in the shadows of a temple, sing and dance to that kind of love? Even her mother, while being courted by her father who was handsome and generous both with words and gifts to women, must have felt that tremor of heart and limbs.

As a young girl she had overheard her mother telling a fellow worshipper from the Church of Eternal Mercy how disgusting it was that a couple living in sin could dare sit in the church pews and look happy. The thinking modern woman who was clandestinely in love dispensed with morality altogether and just needed to say to her head, 'Hush, be quiet; just leave me alone for a while.'

A *moral vacation* – that was what every one of those pious

worshippers of the Church of Eternal Mercy needed, she chuckled wickedly.

'That's right,' said Meeta. 'Stop thinking for a while and enjoy, enjoy! You're no longer young, you know.' According to her mood of the moment, Meeta encouraged, warned, lectured, empathised, scolded. Her mood depended very much on the elusive Byron of the Polo Club, whom, according to Winnie, she was still intently looking out for each time she dined at the club.

'Seize the day, girl!' she would urge. 'Carpe diem!' Or 'They're all alike, those bastards. Only thinking of themselves.' Or ' You be the one in control. You play hard to get, and they get harder! Ha! Ha!'

In love, one could be amoral but not apolitical. She whispered to Maria, 'You know, our Winnie the Blur is so blur I have to explain the joke to her.'

There was no blurring in Winnie's keenness of observation.

'Our Meeta talks too much. She's pining for that guy who doesn't care too hoots for her. One little look of encouragement from him, and she'll jump into his bed. Just you see!'

She had her own advice for Maria.

'A woman needs a man, whatever she may say. There is nothing like love,' adding dreamily, 'love is a many-splendoured thing.'

Winnie's head, even as she was standing in front of her class and teaching her subject of history, throbbed with romantic definitions and pronouncements picked up from the movies and popular literature that came out more easily than the dates of wars or imperial dynasties. Alone in her room she listened for hours to the mellifluous voice of Frank Sinatra and Dean Martin celebrating or bemoaning love; she had seen the movie

Love Story four times and made the proclamation that love meant never having to say sorry so many times that Meeta forced her to stop.

Maria thought, it must be real happiness. For it was of the abundant kind that spilled over into goodwill for all around her, even the contemptible Mr Chin who either met her smile with a very constricted one or looked away. It made her listen patiently to Mrs Kee's story about her baby boy, a tale that had become tiresome to the others in the staffroom who swore they had heard it, and seen the photograph of the baby, at least half a dozen times. Mrs Kee, normally talkative, became doubly so with the birth of the precious male child whom she and her husband had given up hope of having after the four daughters, telling anyone who would listen how they had tried everything, from special medicinal herbs imported from Taiwan to special times and conditions for making love. One of her listeners took prurient interest in Mrs Kee's intimate revelations and himself revealed a certain traditional technique, amazingly gross and involving the ubiquitous ginseng, about how to make a male child.

While Mrs Neo rolled her eyes upwards and quietly left the staffroom, while Teresa Pang smiled forbearingly and continued marking her students' exercise books without looking up once, Maria Seetoh not only listened but said the appropriate things to add to Mrs Kee's pride and joy.

'Miss Seetoh,' gushed Mrs Kee, 'I know you are very good with English. Can you think of very nice words for my son's birthday?'

The first birthday of the only male grandchild in the Kee family would be celebrated in style in one of Singapore's best Chinese restaurants, and there would be a huge birthday cake on which only the most illustrious words, in both English and Chinese, would be inscribed.

'I will get special Chinese translator to translate your words,' said Mrs Kee by now quite breathless. The whole event would be videotaped.

Maria obliged, but declined very politely to be among the guests at the celebration.

Out of deference to Mrs Kee's superstitious fears, she kept from her the fact of the visit to Sister Elizabeth's wake in the funeral parlour of the St Francis' Hospice. Mrs Kee's eyes would have dilated in horror, for any connection with a house of death, even if many stages remote, would have been an evil impossible to risk in the protection of her newborn. There were malignant spirits everywhere, and they were most potent if associated with a corpse. Mrs Kee even avoided the mention of Sister Elizabeth's name, and had nervously waved away the staff member who had gone round collecting money for a joint wreath and message of condolence in *The Singapore Tribune*.

Looking upon Sister's body in her coffin, her hands gently folded upon her chest, with a rosary entwined round the fingers, Maria instantly thought of her dead husband in exactly the same prayerful pose in his coffin, almost a year ago. What a long way her feelings had travelled since! She must have gone through the entire human gamut – bitterness, anger, pity, shock, sadness, despair and then relief, hope, surprise, excitement, wonder, joy. Head and heart had made the journey together in mutual reliance, whatever the tumultous conflicts along the way. Thinking with the heart, feeling with the head: the line that separated them was constantly being blurred.

She was suddenly struck by the irony that had attended each death, as if the powers out there, whether they had a habitation and a name among mortals or remained unidentified and distant, sometimes acted like malicious mortals themselves and wanted the last laugh. Poor Sister Elizabeth dying of womb cancer when her womb had been chaste all its life; and poor Bernard, dying in the bitterest of beliefs that the friend he most trusted had betrayed him with the woman he made most sacrifices for, beside his very deathbed, before his very eyes. Was it a continuation of the irony that it was precisely his hideous accusation that had drawn their attention to each other, who else might have gone their separate ways and never have bothered to see each other again after his death?

Thoughts of a discomfiting nature could not be permitted to stay at a time when the heart was allowed its ascendancy. They were easily swamped out by the new happiness that continued to cast a benign glow around everyone in the classroom, the staffroom, the canteen, along the corridors, down the staircases. It wanted to shine most warmly on the person who seemed most in need of it, but was rejected all the way.

Maggie, for the first time that Maria could remember, looked troubled and unhappy, avoiding her when usually she would seek her company and attention, sometimes very obtrusively, such as cornering her on her way to or out of the staffroom, or out of the school gates. The girl was now frequently absent from school and had stopped attending the creative writing classes.

'No, nothing's wrong, I'm okay, okay!' she would say with a sharp laugh and proud toss of her hair when Maria sought her out on one of the days she had turned up.

'Maggie, something's wrong, you must tell me,' she said solicitously, recollecting all the rumours of her mysterious family background that she determinedly kept secret.

'I tell you, nothing wrong, so stop asking!' she said sullenly and walked away.

Her troubles were probably related to the beloved younger sister Angel who, oddly, accompanied her to school on some days, and spent the time at a table in the students' canteen, reading her books and comics and writing in copy books, before Maggie picked her up after school and they went home together. On one occasion during recess, Maria had seen the two of them eating from a plate of noodles in the canteen. The sister was thirteen, but Maggie was coaxing her to eat and even fed her a few mouthfuls, like a child. The canteen woman whom everybody called 'Auntie Noodles' was generously re-filling their plate.

Maria watched, deeply moved. When she walked towards them, Maggie looked up sharply, instinctively put a protective arm around the bored-looking Angel and assumed a cold hard defiance to beat off any question.

'Maggie,' said Maria. 'Shouldn't Angel be in her own school? Why is she here with you?'

A sudden thought occurred to her, causing her eyes to dart all over the young girl's body in a search for marks and bruises: was the older sister protecting her from parental abuse? It broke her heart to think that the student who liked and trusted her most of all, had suddenly stopped doing so. Her concern came up against a wall of chill resistance: 'Miss Seetoh, I appreciate very much if you not interfere in my affairs.'

She spoke to Brother Philip.

He said, 'Maggie once told me that it was unfair you were giving all the attention to Yen Ping in your creative writing class. She said you always used Yen Ping's stories as examples, never hers.'

'Oh my God,' said Maria and a load immediately lifted off her chest. Here was a problem with an easy solution. For a while she had feared having to make a police report about child abuse, going through those dreadful formalities she had heard about, such as having photographs taken of the bruises cleverly inflicted only in hidden places, including the chest, stomach, upper thighs, working out with the principal, the discipline master and other relevant staff about how to keep the matter from the inquisitive Chinese language newspapers, to protect Maggie's privacy, and worst of all, testifying in court. She was so glad she did not have to be part of that huge, messy, pitiful, detestable world out there that she caught glimpses of in the newspapers and on TV.

She grasped Brother Philip's hand in a rush of relief so great it had to be instantly expressed in light-hearted sharing and laughter. She told him that Maggie's stories were so ridiculously, fantastically sexy that they could not be used as examples in the creative writing class; otherwise the principal, receiving complaints, would send him to investigate.

'Well,' said Maria, once more in a happy mood, 'I'm prepared to use them now, to make the girl happy. And if you come investigating, dear Brother Phil, I'll make you sit down with the rest of the class and join in the discussion!'

She told him that she was once tempted to pass on to him one of Maggie's boldest attempts, a very risqué and amusing story about a businessman and his karaoke lounge visits, in case the moral education teacher of St Peter's needed diversion from his many onerous duties.

'My dear Brother Phil,' she said warmly, liking the sound of her new form of addressing him, 'you could learn from Maggie's rich vocabulary of sexual terms! Maybe you could even use them for one of your delightful limericks.'

She had grown very fond of Brother Philip with his ready wit and quiet, gentle wisdom, and was not above teasing him in a way that would have appalled the prim and proper principal. She paid him the supreme compliment: 'Never, never ask to return to your native Ireland. I'll miss you.'

'Why are you looking at me like that, you mischievous girl?' he once said, and she liked the mischievous twinkle in his own large, kindly eyes.

He would never know the chilling thought that had for a moment gripped her: what if her dying husband, in his wild delusions and suspicions, had actually scribbled a note of complaint to the principal of St Peter's Secondary School, accusing his moral education teacher of having an affair with his wife? Past that danger, she could see its humorous side: Brother Philip in the white brother's cassock, looking puzzled, and herself, in bright unseemly red for a widow, with explanations at the ready, standing side by side in the principal's office, while he stood facing them, his hands tightly clasped behind his back, clearing his throat with elaborate deliberation before saying in a very precise, formal tone: 'It has come to my attention – ' There were many things she could share with dear Brother Philip, but not those shocking suspicions, nor the shocking dream she had had, of them together in the Botanic Gardens, discovered naked by her husband.

When she next saw Maggie, she said brightly, 'Maggie, write me a story. I miss reading your stories,' adding, 'Hey, Maggie, what about coming over to my place for lunch this weekend? Here's my new address. I moved a while ago. You can bring Angel if you like.'

The girl said, 'Thanks,' without enthusiasm. She received the slip of paper bearing the new address with a limp hand and looked away.

Maggie was in school the next day, and was passing Yen Ping along the corridor when she did something that quite shocked Maria: she spat at her rival.

Yen Ping, with the help of the ever devoted Mark, had recently won a prize in a short story competition, and Maria had enthusiastically read out the prize-winning story in the creative writing class, unaware of driving the thorn of rivalry even deeper into poor Maggie's side. Maria was to learn later from Yen Ping that it was symbolic spitting only, not full expectoration, but it was shocking enough in its crude malice to warrant a rebuke.

She strode up to Maggie and said sternly, 'I saw that. You have to apologise to Yen Ping. At once.'

Maggie looked down sullenly; Yen Ping looked upset and tearful. Maggie, probably thinking of Miss Seetoh's kind invitation to lunch, a unique enough gesture from a teacher, relented and said, 'I'm sorry.' 'Now I want both of you to shake hands.' In her days at school, the nuns made every quarrelling child, whether the offender or victim, extend a hand of reconciliation. Maggie and Yen Ping shook hands, neither looking at the other. Maria had a sudden thought: she too should be extending a conciliatory hand to all those she had upset or wronged in her life: her dead husband, her mother, Mr Chin, Olivia Phang, the great TPK himself for her intense dislike of him, despite all that he had done for Singapore. Only for Olivia Phang would the apology entail an assurance and a promise: 'Don't worry. There isn't any affair. It's a silly little flutter that will run its course, like a fever.'

She told Dr Phang about Maggie the next time he called her on the phone. He listened with chuckling interest, as he had to the comical incident of the plaque. One story led to another; Maggie's life, even the little she knew of it, was a rich compendium. It was weird; there were a hundred questions she wanted to ask him, and she was instead telling him school stories and gossip. What exactly did her brother Heng say when he called to tell him not to attend Bernard's funeral? What else had Bernard confided in him that he had not told her? And Olivia? Surely it was without his wife's knowledge that he was making all those private calls inviting her to join him for lunch in town? What if she saw them, or somebody saw and told her? How did he elude those ferociously vigilant eyes? And his feelings for her? Exactly what did he want from her? What about all those rumours she had heard about the smitten women in his life? His ex-wife? The daughter he seemed to love most of all? His standing with the great TPK? The promise of a political career? The rumour that he had actually made a secret donation to V.K. Pandy when the poor man was ordered by the courts to pay the great TPK three hundred thousand dollars for defaming him? If he had political ambitions, surely he was also playing with fire. But he had privately disclosed to her, before Bernard's death, that he was thinking of leaving his high position in the Ministry of Defence. What were his plans now? He had confided in her then that he needed change and adventure. Was his present affair-in-the-making with her now part of that adventure?

A woman's questions for a man she was interested in were voraciously retrospective and prospective; like a hundred probing tentacles they stretched beyond his present to dig into the smallest crevices of his past and reach for the most elusive hiding places of his future. If she was wise, she would keep all the questions locked up in her head and never permit any to roll out upon her tongue. For she would never be satisfied with his answers; she would, when alone by herself, examine each of them in its every detail and nuance, under the relentless microscope of suspicion and jealousy, and then come up with even more questions to ask.

A man hated a woman's questions; it always made her querulous and unreasonable, bringing out the worst in her. The answering of a mere fraction of the questions would set in motion an intolerable deluge of explanation, argument, confrontation, taking them round and round in tortuous circles. Above all, a woman's tears unnerved a man; if he was helpless against them, he hated them even more.

Dr Phang, the undamaged Teflon Man, had a simple solution: if the questions arose, he dismissed them with that alluring boyish grin or put a genial male finger on the protesting female lips; if they did not, he pre-empted them permanently with his cool, relaxed demeanour that said, 'No, please don't; they will spoil everything for us.' A woman was mollified if her mouth, opened wide for recriminations, was stopped with a gentle kiss, if her arms, ready to flail in rage, were grasped and locked in a tender embrace. Even abusive, battering husbands could get away with the strategies of appeasement. Women themselves admitted they were their own worst enemies. They seldom admitted that they were guilty of the worst double standards – condemning other women for illicit liaisons, excusing their own as something unavoidable, fated.

Some of the women accused him of being a coward, of being in denial, of taking the exasperating ostrich head-in-the-sand approach; the majority actually preferred the unreality of the silencing manoeuvres to the reality of an open, shouting match.

They said the first left happy memories long after everything was over, the second only a bitter taste in the mouth. The first might not solve the problem, the second always made it worse. Talk it out, said the counsellors, let everything come out in the open, shout, scream at each other, and you will feel the better for it. They did not know how wrong they were; most men and women felt exhausted and drained, not purged and cleansed.

Emily had told her that she once wrote out all the questions she wanted to ask her wayward husband and forced him to answer them, one after the other, screaming if he demurred or hesitated, even making him go down on his knees and swear on the Bible. The experience took such a heavy physical, mental and emotional toll on her that she went into deep depression soon afterwards. 'Nothing changed really,' she said bitterly afterwards. 'I wasn't at all proud of what I did.' Her husband had something of Dr Phang's cool unflappability; all her screams and curses and tears simply washed over him, like water off the proverbial duck, and he emerged from the storm to go out of the room and bring back a glass of water to stop her fit of coughing.

At their very first lunch together, some months, after her husband's death, he made it clear to Maria, in that famously effective strategy of deflection and silence, that their presence together, so precious because it would be necessarily limited to quick lunches in one of the lesser known restaurants and coffee-houses in town, would brook no intrusion to detract from its pure pleasure. 'Precious'? Why? How? Her vanity cried out to hear the reasons. He had once said to her, 'You know, I enjoy listening to your stories! You are a born story-teller!' But surely he sought out her company for more than her story-telling prowess? Again her vanity wanted to hear more. 'Necessarily'?

Why so? Did his wife already suspect something? What would he do if she did? Suppose she had already engaged a private detective?

A woman developed very long and sensitive antennae to catch the mood of the man she was interested in, and they reliably relayed to her the signals. No questions, no demands for explanations, no accusations. Words could so easily kill joy which was as fragile as it was precious. The only permitted use of language was to enhance the pleasure of the present, which, like a cool, quiet room with a silken bed, should remain oblivious of the loud knocking from outside. The annoying whys of the past and what-ifs of the future were crude barbarians at joy's gate, best ignored.

'I love talking to you,' he said, by which he meant mostly listening while she talked and told her stories. Sometimes she wondered, as he made surreptitious attempts to touch her hand across the table or caress her foot under it, if he was listening at all. Surely it was his way of biding time; he had his own line, not of danger but conquest and victory, and with each phone call, each lunch meeting with her, he came closer to it, with the mighty anticipation of the fevered bull elephant or moose.

She thought, 'Ah, you evil, exasperating, egoistical, intriguing, wonderful, irresistible man. You're okay.'

The spillover effects of her exuberance had to touch poor Por Por, now hopelessly demented but still as trusting as a child. She had no idea that her concern for her grandmother could lead to family conflict. Por Por had asked to have back her jade earrings, her jade bangle, her gold chain. Maria, remembering that her brother had taken away all the items of jewellery after the old woman was almost robbed in her wanderings and given them to their mother for safekeeping, now asked for their return. She explained that since Por Por was mostly at home now, watched over by the maid, she should be allowed to wear all the jewellery she wanted to make her happy. Anna Seetoh instantly looked uncomfortable.

She murmured, 'They're not with me anymore.'

'What do you mean, not with you anymore?' said Maria sharply, and the suspicions which were quickly forming in her mind were as quickly confirmed.

Heng's many money problems had caused him to do reckless things, including pawning all Por Por's jewellery.

'How dare he!' exploded Maria. Pawning was as good as selling off; Heng would have neither the means nor inclination to redeem it. She said angrily to Anna Seetoh, 'Tell me, Mother, has he been borrowing money from you too, or rather, demanding it? Come on, tell me. Now it's your turn to tell the truth and shame the devil!' She was all up in arms now.

It turned out that the truth was much worse. Anna Seetoh had even borrowed money for the errant adopted son; it was a substantial sum. Maria said, hot tears coming into her eyes, 'How can he do this to you and Por Por? What on earth is happening? I thought he was not doing too badly in his businesses, whatever they were. Remember he was always boasting about making profits here and profits there?' Anna Seetoh clearly needed a full unburdening of horrible family secrets, in the same way that she needed a full confession of the week's stock of sins, even if very minor, at the confessional in the Church of Eternal Mercy.

She said, not looking at her daughter, 'You remember that Por Por had a large biscuit tin in which she kept all the *ang pows* that we had given her over the years?'

Every Chinese New Year, Por Por's main delight was to receive the gifts of cash from family members, which she instantly put into her pocket, happy as a child. Maria remembered the pitifully rusty, square biscuit tin holding all the money that the old woman possessed in the world, which she kept under her bed. 'Is that gone too?' Her mother nodded and said tearfully, 'He's in debt.' Months back, he had gone into a risky business venture in China with a friend that was supposed to make millions for them; very soon after, he lost all his money, as well as all contact with the friend. Anna Seetoh delivered the last bit of bad news in a lowered voice, 'He's been gambling. He says the loan sharks are after him.' Maria thought of the long-suffering wife and the autistic son whom she had seen only once, years ago, when she had gone on a visit to Malaysia with her mother and Por Por, a sickly, unhappy child who sat huddled on the floor with a plastic bag of coloured balls, breaking into occasional tantrums and hitting the sides of his head with tightly clenched fists. His mother, always haggard-looking, would rush to him and rock him in her arms till he calmed down.

Distant shadowy figures who had little part in her world, her sister-in-law and nephew now provoked deep pity. She made a mental note to enquire after their welfare and arrange to send them some money; now all her anger was directed at the feckless, irresponsible brother. 'Listen, Mother,' she said, 'you are not to give him any more money for his gambling, do you hear, not one cent. Have you spoken to him?' Her brother would never speak to her, except in the position of advisor, dispenser of knowledge, fault-finder about her naivete in money matters.

Anna Seetoh realised her mistake as soon as she said, 'Heng thinks that if Bernard had not willed the apartment to his Third Aunt –' for Maria instantly said, raising her voice, 'How dare he! And how dare he assume that if the apartment had come to me, he would have any share in it?' She had never despised her brother as much as she did now.

She looked at her mother, still sniffling into a piece of tissue paper, and wondered if this was the right time to ask her the question that had been in her mind for years: was Heng her real brother, rather than the claimed adopted one? As a child, she had caught enough adult whispers to suspect that Heng was the son of one of her father's mistresses, who had abandoned him at birth. The infant had then been brought to her mother, to be brought up as an adopted son. Her mother, already incensed by her husband's infidelities, had refused until he had, by way of compensation, bought her a flat and given her a sum of money, his generosity coinciding with a period of prosperity in some shady business that would never come his way again. The boy was as nasty as any sibling could be, and she was glad that he had spent many of the childhood years with his real mother who had unaccountably reappeared in his father's complicated life. No, thought Maria, I would prefer to think of him as an adopted brother rather than one related by blood; I don't want any of that nastiness flowing in my veins.

The next time she saw him, she was shocked by his appearance. He had lost weight, looked haggard and depressed. The old arrogance was gone.

She felt sorry enough to press some money into his hands, for which he said humbly, 'Thanks.' Anna Seetoh whispered, shaking her head, 'It will go into the fruit machines at the Manis Club, or the horse races or the 4-D.'

Heng had apparently, after having once won a fairly substantial amount at the national Four-Digits lottery, begun to have dreams of a colossal win that would wipe off all his debts. He had begun to take on the irrational behaviour of the big-time lottery dreamer, fervidly seeking lucky numbers in his dreams by night and in the most improbable events by day. He threw away hundreds of dollars on a single bet in pursuit of that elusive jackpot. Anna Seetoh confided that he had taken Por Por to a temple to pray before a deity reputed to give winning numbers, and had made reckless bets based on her age, the age of an old neighbour who had been knocked down by a lorry, the number on the registration plate of the lorry, the number he made his son pick up from a box of counters, a number randomly picked up from a scrap of newspaper stuck to the sole of his shoe. He had gone mad.

Maria thought in self-reproach, 'Was I so engrossed in my own affairs that I had no knowledge of what was going on?'

He asked Maria rather sheepishly, not looking at her, 'What was Ah Siong's exact age when he passed away?', actually taking out a piece of paper and a stump of a pencil from his pocket.

She said, white with rage, 'You disgust me. Go away.'

Dr Phang said, in a call that evening, 'You sound depressed,' and she said, 'I am. Family problem.'

He said, 'Would you like to tell me about it?' and she replied, 'No, it's not a pretty story; I'll try to forget about it.'

'Tell me anyway,' he said. 'I like the sound of your voice, the brightness in your eyes, whatever you're telling me.' *Suppose I ask you all that I've been dying to ask from Day One? Suppose we sit down and talk?*

The question of course could not be given utterance; she had learnt to fully cooperate with his strategy of deflection. What was it about men and women that it was so difficult to sit down for a good, honest talk?

'Let's have lunch again, sometime next week,' he said.

'Yes, let's,' she said eagerly. He could lift her mood from dark despondency to singing elation. Could love or infatuation or whatever it was called become an addiction, like Heng's gambling, like the drug habits of Ah Boy, the gardener's son, that Maggie had once told her about? Addiction had no use for talk, only the next fix.

The day which had begun badly was fully restored in its joy.

The next morning when she walked into the staffroom after a lesson, she saw a note placed under her teacher's record book, recognised Brother Philip's handwriting and smiled. It contained a limerick:

There is a Brother named Brother P
Who is as naïve as naïve can be,
When asked about the birds and bees,
He said, 'Why, yes, if you please,
They're welcome for my plants and trees!

Maria thought, unable to hide the smiles that were inviting curious looks from Mrs Neo and some others, 'Maybe I love Brother Philip, but am only in love with Dr Phang.'

Twenty-Three

From the doorway of the dispensary on Middleton Square where she had gone to get some cough medicine for Por Por, she looked to see if V.K. Pandy was at his usual post, with his pitiful pamphlets, with the even more pitiful unspoken message of despair written all over the shabby appearance, the unruly beard, the piercing bitter eyes searching the faces of all who passed by: 'See what the great TPK has done to me. Now I have lost not only my business, but my political career. And not a single one of you has the guts to stand up for me!' Some time after he had sold his business to pay the huge sum to settle the defamation suit taken against him, he had been found guilty of tax evasion, had once again been hauled into court and fined a sum which instantly put him in the category for disqualification from membership in Parliament. When he lost his parliamentary seat, it was said, V.K. Pandy sat down on the floor and cried like a child. That night he got drunk in a beer shop and had to be taken home by the beer shop owner. The case of his dismissal from parliament was not reported in the local papers but when *The International Courier*, based in Bangkok, reported it at length, the paper was slapped with a court order for defamation and had to pay a fine, after which it learnt to be more cautious in its dealings about Singapore.

V.K. Pandy was not at his post, but the space his presence carved out in the bustling square remained empty, being avoided, by habit, by the crowds hurrying by. It was as if an invisible V.K. Pandy was there, still captured on the secret relentless surveillance cameras, and nobody wanted to take any risk of being seen with him. There were a few who took the risk, albeit circuitously, after hearing about the poor man's financial misfortunes; their strategy was to send someone, a child or a maid, to go up and casually drop an innocuous-looking envelope containing the donation money beside his pile of pamphlets. Singaporeans were ever kind, responding generously to reports about families suffering the loss of the sole breadwinner, foreign workers left in the lurch by thieving contractors who had made them pay large sums to come to work in Singapore's construction industries, a seriously ill child whose parents were too poor to pay for the expensive medical treatment. Kindness to them sometimes won praise in ministerial speeches on social cohesion, as kindness to political opponents never would. There must have been enough secret donors for V.K. Pandy to put up a small placard that said 'Thank you, kind Singaporeans.' The bitter lines around his mouth must have added sadly, 'But not brave enough to be kind openly.'

Without V.K. Pandy waving his pamphlets and loudly calling out, the familiar circle of empty ground looked eerily empty and silent. Maria, watching from the dispensary, felt a sudden heaviness of heart, weighed down equally by sadness and pity. She was thinking of V.K. Pandy's wife whom she had never seen but only heard about, a woman sick with cancer and perpetual worry for her now bankrupt husband. At what point in her anger was she driven to get out of the house, go out into the streets, stand in front of the closed shutters of their modest printing shop and weep loudly to protest the injustice against her husband, wearing the white sari and long dishevelled hair of mourning? People had passed by quickly; they had to avoid looking at her too.

Maria noticed a figure striding across the square towards V.K. Pandy's spot; indeed it cried out for notice, being dressed in the costume of a huge chicken, with bright yellow feathers and a very long, sharp orange beak; it had the friendly familiarity of Big Bird in the popular children's TV show. Jerking its head up and down, it held up a placard mounted on a stick, which Maria could not read from her distance. There being a Kentucky Fried Chicken outlet near the square, which was very popular with the lunchtime crowd, her immediate thought was that Big Bird was there for some promotional stunt. As soon as she had that thought, she smiled to see how delightfully wrong she was.

The figure who was probably a male, given the height, build and energy of movement, stopped at precisely the spot made familiar by V.K. Pandy's presence, held up his placard and began to prance around with comical strutting and flapping chicken movements and sounds. *Cock-cock-cock-quawk! Cock-cock-cock-quawk!* On the placard were the words in bright red which Maria could now read distinctly: 'Chicken – that's what we are, Singaporeans!' and below them a sentence which she could read only partially but understood perfectly, for the word 'fear' in it was highlighted. The demonstrator stopped his crazy dance briefly to pass a small camera to one of the passersby, a middle-aged man in neat shirt and trousers, with a request to take a picture of him. The man backed away, laughing nervously as he raised both palms and began waving them about in a frantic gesture of refusal; a young woman with blonde hair, in tourist hat and sunglasses, stepped forward and offered to take the picture.

A few passersby had gathered to watch; one, a young man with long hair tied in a ponytail, and gold ear-studs, began imitating the squawking sounds and movements, flapping huge imaginary wings and lumbering behind Big Bird with exaggerated clumsiness, causing the crowd to break out in laughter. Despite the presence of the large beak fastened around his mouth, Big Bird's words of denunciation came out with amazing clarity, filling the square and drawing more curious onlookers.

We're comfortable and we're fearful!
We're rich and we're fearful!
We're safe and we're fearful!
We're Chicken Licken, Chicken Stricken,
The sky's falling, and we don't even know it!
Chicken Licken, licked clean of our freedom
Chicken Stricken, struck dumb with fear
We say Yes, Yes, Yes, because No, No, No
Means more, more, more fear
Fear of losing our job, our promotion, our son-in-law's
promotion, our bonuses, our upgraded housing estates,
our good life
Fear of bringing the taxman beating at our door, crying
'Foul Fowl! Off to jail you go!'
Chicken Licken, Chicken Stricken
The sky is falling
And we can only go quawk quawk, quawk quawk!

Fortunately for Big Bird intent on delivering his message in full, the police arrived on the scene in twenty minutes, longer than the usual efficient five or ten, to effect the entire operation of issuing a note of warning to the offender, confiscating whatever paraphernalia of offence they could find, hauling him off to the police station since his offence was deemed serious enough, and dispersing the crowd. Apparently they had had no forewarning of Big Bird's demonstration in Middleton Square, but one of them was alert enough to spot the camera held by the tourist and instantly confiscated it.

Maria looked in the newspapers the next morning for any report on the incident; there was none. Demonstrations were rare; there had been one about a year ago, to protest some government policy, which was widely reported in the local newspapers; *The Straits Tribune* made much of the fine imposed on each of the three demonstrators, clearly as a deterrent to future troublemakers. But every tiny incident of a political nature which did not make it to the media created rumours that circulated underground in the private gossip of the coffee shops and cocktail parties: the chicken demonstrator was V.K. Pandy himself. That accounted for his absence in the square that day. Maria doubted it; the man was too skinny for the robust looking figure she had seen, and his voice was nowhere as loud.

She had as many questions to ask V.K. Pandy as she had for Dr Phang, and one of them brought together the two men, whose worlds could not be more different, in an intriguing possibility – was it true that Dr Phang, civil servant and poster boy of the great TPK, had secretly donated a large sum of money to help V.K. Pandy in his financial woes? There were other questions of a more immediate and urgent nature: what was he going to do now, what was happening to his poor cancer-stricken wife, was it true that the great TPK once called him 'vermin', was it true that he was going to get out of politics permanently, return to his native village in India and retire there?

There was a question for herself, for which she had no answer: for all her sympathy for V.K. Pandy, why did she not have the courage to come out from her safe peeping place inside the dispensary and join the crowd cheering Big Bird? Such questions came during what she called the mirror moment, when she stood before the mirror in her bathroom and took a good hard look at herself. She had started the practice, secretly, from the first year of her marriage to Bernard, and now, as then, fear featured large in the self-questioning. If it was not fear of the great TPK, was it fear of the principal's displeasure, especially after he had issued another stern reminder to the teaching staff, clearly aimed at her, not to have anything to do with opposition politics? Whether of the powerful TPK or of the principal of St Peter's Secondary School, it was still fear, and she was as much trapped by it as any of the Singaporeans derided by Big Bird. Big Bird himself had hidden his identity under an elaborate, all enveloping costume; he too was not free from fear. It was a whole society in thrall; it was mirror time for a whole society.

I have a headache coming, thought Maria, the headaches being an excuse to get away from too much thinking.

She was glad that only heart needed to be engaged in the following days. She and the maid went on a shopping trip to one of the large departmental stores with a section well-stocked with costume jewellery, and came back with very convincing-looking jade earrings, bangles and gold chains. Por Por laughed with happiness as they put the various items on her, and stood before a mirror, admiring herself like a vain child decked out for a party. In her quavering voice, she sang a song in the dialect of the village of her childhood in China, making delicate movements with her hands and fingers. Anna Seetoh gave practical advice, with the same sad expression as when she had received the devastating confession of her adopted son's gambling debts: Por Por must not be allowed out on her own. The bad people out there would mistake all that worthless stuff for the real thing. Anna Seetoh left unsaid a bitter thought: she did not want to have one more family disaster to cope with. Why was the Holy Virgin Mary not answering her prayers?

She woke up at five every morning to be in time for the early morning mass in the Church of Eternal Mercy, remaining on her knees throughout the one hour of the service, praying for her son, her daughter, her mother. She prayed *to* her late son-in-law, believing him to have served his purgatory and gone to heaven where he was in a position to help his loved ones on earth, among whom, in his new saintly state, he must include even his sinful wife.

'No, there's no need to accompany me,' said Anna Seetoh brusquely to her daughter, adding, 'what's the use. You stopped believing long ago.'

'I told you, Mother,' said Maria patiently, 'it's bad weather this morning, and it's a school holiday. Besides, it's your birthday, and after mass, we can go for breakfast to Tai Kee Restaurant for your favourite pork porridge.'

Anna Seetoh was about to say No again when a thought suddenly occurred to her which made her say instead, 'Alright, if you wish.'

This could be the Holy Mother's answer to her prayer to bring back the prodigal daughter, or at least a prelude to the answer. She said, 'Suppose Father Rozario thinks you've come back; suppose your godma and the others ask. What shall I tell them?'

'Anything you like,' said Maria cheerfully, 'but this morning you're going to have the best birthday breakfast!'

The last time she was at a service in the Church of Eternal Mercy, her heart was heaving to the tumult of a hundred conflicting emotions as she looked upon her husband's coffin and joined in the prayers for the repose for his soul. Now it was muted in its joy only by the surrounding sombreness of the small early morning congregation, still sleepy-faced, comprising mainly the middle-aged and the elderly bent over their prayer books, responding to the priest in low murmurs.

Her own prayer could not come from any book, only from a heart determined to be kind: God, if you really exist as everyone believes you do, could you do something for Mrs V.K. Pandy? Also Maggie and Angel. Maybe even Mrs TPK. For it was said that the prime minister's wife was suffering from some strange illness or combination of illnesses that Singapore's doctors seemed unable to cure. Maria thought, what an irony that all the money, all the best medical help at her husband's disposal – it was said he had brought in top medical consultants from London – could not help her. She was seldom seen outdoors; Winnie had once seen her in a departmental store, accompanied by two maids, at the furniture section, buying some bolsters, looking too old, bent and fragile for her age. She was said to be a very good, kind woman, as compassionate as her husband was ruthless. Dear God, if it is true that you care for every one of your creatures, you must help poor Mother, and Brother Heng and Por Por and the maid Rosiah who says her husband is squandering all her hard-earned money on a woman who is using black magic on him. Maria then remembered Rosiah's sister, living in a small village in Indonesia, whose woodcutter husband had died from a fall, leaving her with four young children. And a fellow maid Rosiah had told her about who was very unhappy working for an abusive employer but had no choice but to stay, being in debt to the agent who had brought her to Singapore.

Her heart went further afield to embrace a man whose plight she had read about in the papers – a villager from Pakistan who had come illegally to Singapore to work as a construction worker after selling his farm, and had been brutally exploited by his employer; when he was seriously injured at work, the employer, on the pretext of taking him to a doctor, drove him to a deserted area and threw him into a ditch where, fortunately, his feeble cries for help were heard by someone who happened to be passing by. Her heart, now fully launched on its journey of connection with fellow human beings, wandered even further to ask God's help for the survivors of a cyclone in the Philippines, the grieving families of a coal mine disaster in China, children on the brink of starvation in a war-torn African state, their skeletal legs hardly able to support their bloated bellies covered with flies, the victims of a savage mass shooting in Washington that wiped out a family of five, including a baby of ten months.

All this while, her head remained silent, holding back thoughts that might disrupt the heart's free roaming. God, if you exist. If you are truly a Creator worshipped by his creatures as all powerful, all good, all loving. If you are the someone in the great somewhere, celebrated in those hymns of yearning, who hears every word. Why, why, why? In the drowsiness induced by Father Rozario's monotonous chanting and the billows of incense smoke coming from his censer, all the large existential questions disappeared into her own ridiculously trivial one: should she, or should she not go to bed with Dr Phang? She felt too sleepy to answer the question and surrendered herself to the overpowering soporific effect, as to a narcotic, of the morning gloom and chill inside the Church of Eternal Mercy. She was having a strange little dream in which she was standing in some desolate-looking school compound, surrounded by naked, flag-waving children, when she woke up suddenly to the sensation of a sharp nudge in her side and an abrupt jerk of her head. She opened her eyes to see an amused smile on her mother's face, which made her smile too.

She had to work hard to make Maggie smile again. The day before the appointed lunch at her place – Anna Seetoh had kindly offered to fry noodles and bake a cake for dessert – she saw an envelope addressed to her, laid on her teacher's record book, and pulled out a note saying 'Miss Seetoh, owing to unforesee circumstance, I am not able to have lunch with you this Saturday. Please accept very sincere apology from me. Maggie.'

There was no mention of the story she was submitting for the creative writing class, in a separate envelope, written on three sheets of paper, also laid on the record book. At a glance, Maria could see it was one of those hopelessly atrocious love-and-sex stories that seemed to be Maggie's staple; as she put it back into the envelope she was determined to put it to good use in the next creative writing lesson, when she would remember to assign only second place to Yen Ping. The two girls were still avoiding each other, Maggie with a toss of her head, Yen Pin with her eyes on the ground.

She saw Maggie in the canteen, again with her sister Angel, again eating at Auntie Noodles' table, and said, 'Maggie, I hope you will be around next Thursday, we're going to have an interesting class discussion,' but the girl only smiled faintly and looked away.

Maria was almost envious of Auntie Noodles for being the only one in the entire world of St Peter's Secondary School whom Maggie would talk to. Brother Philip had said that when he asked her to his office and tried to get her to talk to him, she looked straight ahead all the while, as impassive as a statue.

Maria said, 'Brother Phil, thank you for telling me about the rivalry with Yen Ping. To think I could have been so blind all along.'

Brother Philip said, 'So despite her campaign of resistance, she's given you a story. It must mean something.'

Maria sighed, 'Totally horrible. On a subject I wouldn't tell you about, dear Brother Phil, because it would make you blush. And written in the worst clichés. But I think I understand Maggie better now.' It was her last hope to restore the girl's mood. Perhaps then she would open up and allow her teachers to help her and her sister.

They were in his car parked in a deserted area outside the Botanic Gardens. It was the first time they had met in the evening; the question as to whether Olivia Phang was away on one of her visits back home to Hong Kong could not be asked. She thought, with some amusement, about the classic 'one-thing-led-to-another' explanation that men and women gave for the best intentions gone awry, when lurking passion, beginning with something as innocuous as a sip of wine together, a smile, a sharing of a joke, could escalate into the breathless rush into the bedroom. But men and women were ever disingenuous about that first one thing that had led to all the others: the choice of a venue away from all prying eyes.

Here they were, in a car, in a dark isolated area marked by tall trees and bushes, with nobody in sight except other parked cars at discreet distances, all united in a delicious conspiracy of amatory intent. It had begun with a dinner in an obscure café outside town.

'A ride?' he had suggested, 'If you like,' she had said, with no idea where he was going. It was amazing how much of their exploration of each other's intentions and sensitivities were in casual, crisp monosyllables.

When she was thirteen, she went on a church outing by the sea and one of the picnickers, a good-looking boy of sixteen, had issued an invitation of a vaguely clandestine nature. He said, pointing to a cluster of rocks a short distance from shore, 'There are interesting shellfish to pick there. Would you like to come with me?' The boy spent at least ten minutes searching for non-existent shellfish, all the while holding her hand tightly, but he had accomplished his purpose of being alone with the prettiest girl in the picnic group, and she had experienced a special thrill in stealing away from her mother's side for a secret rendezvous. Now, thirty years later, she was feeling something of that girlish sense of adventure.

It was a situation that was bringing her closer to the line which she knew she would be crossing at her peril, but how many women had not succumbed to the thrill of a peril? One thing led to another. Before I knew it. It all happened so fast. I really didn't know what I was doing. Women would afterwards wonder at how easily they gave in and learn that passion had its own unstoppable momentum. Now she understood why the nuns in the Convent of the Holy Infant Jesus where she had her education, and the Christian brothers in the boys' school just next to the convent, were always warning their respective charges: stay away from temptation. Better still, stay away from the *occasion* for temptation.

Their occasion, in a locked car in a dark isolated spot, completely safe from a prying world, was replete with both promise and peril. The line to be crossed had become an edge on which she was standing and looking down tremblingly into an abyss. For Dr Phang, there was no tremor, only the sense of an exhilarating free fall. He was as far removed from those loud, uncouth males boasting of their conquests in bars and locker rooms, as an Ariel playing a romantic tune on a harp was removed from a slouching, slobbering Caliban. While having his morning shave or combing that handsome head of hair in front of the mirror, he might just pause for a while, look hard at himself and allow a quick self-congratulatory smile outside the range of his wife's detecting eyes. For him the mirror moment of honesty had only to do with keeping faith with life's instincts for pleasure and joy.

He was all for making use of the stolen moments to do what the open daytime meetings at the restaurants and coffee-houses forbade. He said, wrapping her in his arms as soon as they were parked and had only the faint light of a few stars in the sky to show the outlines of their faces, 'What's with that pensive look?' If she insisted on asking irksome questions, he was ready with a quick answer about Olivia being away in Malaysia and returning in two days. There was clearly something troubling her, and he sat back and prepared to listen, a firm hand on her thigh.

'Today's the first anniversary of Bernard's death,' she said. 'Did you look at the obituary pages of *The Straits Tribune* this morning?'

'Yes, I did,' he replied. She could see him over his morning coffee reading the words under Bernard's photo in the 'In Memoriam' notice, exactly as Bernard had dictated them to

Heng on his deathbed: *Loved eternally. Forever in my heart. Your beloved wife, Maria.* Words of love and devotion, in a scheme of revenge that would work itself out over the next ten years.

She had the same urge to correct the falsehood now, as she had been intent almost four years ago, when they had all met on their honeymoon in the Cameron Highlands, to do away with the false impression that Dr Phang might have had about her marrying on account of a twenty-thousand-dollar diamond ring. A cheap woman, a lying woman – that impression of her by anyone, let alone that man – would have been intolerable to her pride.

She told him the ghastly truth about those words of undying devotion announced to the world, and realised, with dismay, that she would have to repeat the tiresome explanation to Meeta and Winnie who would by now have seen the notice and could already have left their shocked inquiries in the voice mail of her phone. To no one would she reveal the new truth, something to which she had responded first with disgust and then with relief, that there would be no more of the remaining nine commemorations enjoined by Bernard, for Heng had spent all the given money on his gambling.

When her mother told her, she had merely replied, 'Tell him to sell the niche next to Bernard's, if he likes. I have no use for it.'

In the last month of his illness, Bernard had bought two niches in the columbarium next to the Church of Eternal Mercy, the second one presumably for her.

'Today's his anniversary. Aren't you going to pay your respects at the columbarium?' Anna Seetoh said. 'At least go with some flowers.'

Maria knew that her mother had just returned home from an anniversary mass for Bernard. She said, attempting a smile, 'I think I might as well keep my 'lost sheep' status all the way.'

Her mother had told her that in one of his sermons on lost sheep, Father Rozario had specifically mentioned her. The good priest and the entire congregation of the Church of Eternal Mercy could have any ill impression of her; she would make sure that Dr Phang did not.

'Yes, it was rather odd, but I guessed,' he said briefly. 'Bernard was incapable of any straight thinking at that time.'

Then apparently glad to have disposed of the talking, he resumed the passion, pulling her to him and nuzzling her with anticipatory eagerness. His passion had no need of the soft enveloping darkness, the heavy scent of night flowers, the gentle hum of small insects, nor the suggestive low moans coming from some of the other parked cars. He was kissing her ardently and the hand that had been caressing her neck moved down slowly, tentatively, checking for the slightest sign of resistance. For under no circumstances would the gallant man force himself on a woman.

'Well, it's not my night,' he said with a sigh of resignation as she suddenly broke free of his arms with a start and a small scream. She had heard some rustling sounds in a nearby bush and caught sight of a moving shadow with a tiny flicker of light that moved with it. There would always be the annoying Peeping Toms prowling around lovers' haunts with their furtive torchlights; she had once read about a sick voyeur who charged into a parked car and dragged out the couple, injuring the man with a knife and attempting to rape the girl.

Their evening was over, and they tried to make light of it. Maria said, 'You don't want the papers tomorrow to carry this headline, do you: 'Dr Benjamin Phang, protégé of the great TPK, caught naked in car with teacher from St Peter's Secondary School!'

He said, 'Come to think of it, you've never called me by my name.'

He was 'Dr Phang' officially, 'Benjamin' to his colleagues, 'Ben' to close friends, 'Benjy' or 'Darling Benjy Boy' to Olivia, in a rapidly ascending scale of intimacy. Whatever her present relationship to him, the address should, at the least, have been somewhere between the formality and the intimacy. Meeta, according to Winnie who liked to listen at her door or peep through the keyhole, was addressing the holy god-man Sai Baba as 'Dearest Baba' and 'Darling Baba' while waiting to use the endearments on mortals. Winnie herself used all manner of pet names for the many men who came into her life, which became abusive nicknames as soon as they got out of it.

'Isn't it odd that you're still referring to him as Dr Phang?' said Meeta.

'Even after you've slept with him?' giggled Winnie.

She had shared her secret with them for no other reason than that they had always shared theirs with her. Women were a sorority of incorrigible secret sharers. But she was getting a little tired of their company, their peevishness and querulousness, and beginning to decline the invitations to dine with them at the Polo Club.

'For goodness' sake,' said Meeta. 'Stop all this playing hard to get! Your dream man will get tired of waiting and leave you for another less difficult woman.'

She told the crude joke of a Priapus turned shrink, literally. ('Have to explain that again to our Winnie the Blur!')

'He will have no shortage of women,' said Winnie. 'I take

back what I said about his age. Few men in their fifties, look, oh my, oh my, so-ooh distinguished and sexy!'

They would not be able to understand her reason. Perhaps she herself could not either. It probably had to do with the complicated business of calibrating that fine line of the crossing which kept shifting. The austere formality of 'Dr Phang' instead of the casual familiarity of 'Ben' or the surrendering endearment of 'Dearest' or 'Darling' helped in the calibration.

Vanity, thy name is woman. For the modern thinking woman, the name had to be vanity plus caution plus self-preservation plus control plus a hundred unnamable drives, motives, instincts, intuitions and what women liked to call their astute sixth sense, forming a Gordian Knot impossible to untie into its numerous strands. Men liked to tell women that they were like the caterpillar with its countless legs; as long as the creature ignored them, it walked along smoothly and happily; as soon as it became conscious of them, it got itself all tangled up in a knot. *Complexity, thy name is woman.* Or simple confusion.

'Why don't you ever address me by my name?' he asked.

'Alright, I'll call you Benjamin, if you like.'

'You're a very complex woman,' he said, giving her nose a tweak. 'You think too much. Too much cerebra, too little viscera.'

She liked his pithy use of language, as he did hers.

'Alright,' he sighed, as they drove away. 'Next time it has to be a warm room, with a silken bed.' She liked it when he remembered all her fanciful expressions and used them when she least expected it.

'Well, if we're not going to do anything, you might tell me a story,' he said. 'I'm like a little boy all over again when I listen to your stories. You are my Sheherazade.'

Maria said, 'She nearly lost her life to the wicked sultan.'

He said, '*Nearly*. But in the end, he married her because he could not do without her tales.'

'Alright,' said Maria, thinking that this man would never be in such a state of dependence on a woman. 'I'll tell you another one I've just made up about poor V.K. Pandy, but I warn you, it's a silly story that will go someday into a book of children's stories.'

She had been inspired by that incident of Big Bird that day in Middleton Square, as well as a scathing comparison of V.K. Pandy, to a prancing circus monkey, in a newspaper some time back. In her story, a crowd of Singaporeans went all out to protect Big Bird from the police in a big chase which ended with the police catching their target, only to scratch their heads in bafflement as they at last caught their prey, pulled off the Big Bird costume and faced a real monkey turning its indecent, reddened backside to them.

Dr Phang said, 'I must remember to tell my daughter that story; she'll love it.' Then he said, 'That man's supporter will be allowed to go free this time, but not another time.'

Did the protégé of the great TPK know much more than he was prepared to admit? Was he among the very few in the inner sanctum of trust who could put in a word for the much hated opposition dissident? What did it say of his magnanimity that in addition to secretly giving money to the much beleaguered V.K. Pandy, he was prepared to risk the prime minister's displeasure on his account? For the great TPK was known to fall into an apoplexy of rage at the mere mention of that despised man.

Maria wanted to ask: surely all this kindness towards V.K. Pandy has got nothing to do with high moral principles, because you have none? Dr Phang had instead what even the great TPK ultimately trusted more – a natural honesty born of the impulse to be happy and to bear goodwill towards the whole world.

For the first time since they met, her heart ached to a fervent wish: *if only. If only he were not a married man.* If her mother had heard the wish, she would have cried out, 'Ah, Maria, you've come to your senses at last! It's immoral to go with a married man!'

For many women, morality was suspended for the duration of an affair, and after the affair was over, could be brought back to give it closure: I did something wrong. I am sorry. I wasn't thinking at the time. The conscience, in any case, was a pliable organ at the mercy of head and heart. Hers was exceptionally vulnerable in the presence of this extremely seductive Dr Phang who must have tamed his a long time ago. He had more than once hinted to her that if she wished, they could have occasional vacations abroad – in Europe, the United States, South America, South Africa – that would not be *interrupted* in any way. He was so enormously attractive to women precisely because he was so avowedly *amoral.*

Twenty-Four

The sudden departure of the principal of St Peter's Secondary School provoked speculation which, for the time being at least, had to lie silent beneath the proper public response of polite acceptance of any decision taken by the Ministry of Education. The Ministry promoted deserving principals in secondary schools to senior school inspectors or administrative officers in the various departments of the ministry headquarters, or transferred them to larger, more prestigious schools and junior colleges. The sudden decision to let the principal of St Peter's go on 'indefinite leave' was only slightly less foreboding than the decision of a 'suspension' which would mean that he was being investigated for some serious misdemeanour. What wrongdoing could the principal be possibly guilty of? He was an exemplar of professional and ethical conduct and had been so long at St Peter's that he was simply known as 'the principal'; many among the staff did not even know his full name. Besides, he had unfailingly shown support, expected of all school principals, for all government policies on education and gone beyond that to laud all other government decisions, whether on the promotion of marriage among eligible Singaporean singles or the punishment of those who chewed gum and stuck them on the seats of buses and trains. In political matters, he had been most enthusiastic in his prohibition of even the mention of V.K. Pandy in the classroom. All the newspaper cuttings of ministerial speeches put up on the school bulletin boards for the students' edification could only confirm the ardour of his support. He was the ideal civil servant.

It fell to the vice principal, a small, nondescript, hard-working man with a nervous twitch, to make the announcement to the whole school, which he did with great difficulty, confirming the suspicion that something serious must have taken place to plunge the poor principal into disgrace. What it was, nobody dared discuss openly; Maria noticed small groups of the staff huddled in urgent discussion from which she, the maverick teacher, was necessarily excluded.

The vice principal, a week later, introduced the new principal, a Mr Ignatius Lim Song Kooi, who, without any reference to his predecessor, launched into a long speech about how he was determined to make St Peter's one of the finest schools in Singapore. He had a bright smile for everyone, a hearty laugh and a readiness to talk about his rapid ascent up the ranks in his chosen career in education, which he spoke of fervently as a mission and a vocation. He spent his first day meeting the staff over coffee and cake and interviewing them individually afterwards, and the following days visiting every class in turn. Each visit began with a singing of the school song by the students standing up very straight, which he listened to very attentively, nodding amiably throughout. After he congratulated the students on their inspiring rendition of the song, he launched upon an enthusiastic lecture on living up to the high ideals of both the school song and motto. He made it clear that everyone was welcome to come to him with any problem, any time in his office.

Maria thought, I'm going to miss the principal, realising with a start that for the first time in her many years in the school, she had heard his name mentioned in full: Augustine Tan Chee Kuan. She had a burning curiosity to find out the truth of his disgrace. That would come only after the task of regaining Maggie's trust and finding the truth, probably heartbreaking, about her family circumstances that could be destroying her. Her school programme was full, and for the first time, had nothing to do with exams but unhappy persons gone into silent, troubled retreat.

Maria cast a glance around the students getting ready for the creative writing lesson, and was relieved to see Maggie sitting at the back, looking down resolutely, and Yen Ping and Mark two rows ahead. It would be the first time that Maggie's story would be used for class discussion. The girl was proud and sensitive. Maria had spent considerable time working out an agreeable balance between the need to please her by, first, emphasising the creative elements in her story while suppressing the really awful ones, and second, by drawing attention to the worst clichés without embarrassing the poor girl who wrote and lived by them. She knew that Maggie, like a small quiveringly alert creature, would detect the remotest hint of condescension or patronage and rise to strike with her sharp responses.

But no strategy of balancing could have out-manoeuvred Maggie's purpose to shock everyone with her story. The outrageous tale was already outlined in the brazenly raw title 'How Dirty Uncle Joe Lost his Bird' and could not be read out to the class without extensive prior censorship and editing. Maggie had written, using incredibly crude imagery throughout, about a lecherous middle-aged man trying to seduce a pretty young girl who, at precisely the moment of danger, grabbed a pair of scissors and executed her bloody act, leaving Dirty Uncle doubled up in agony, his hands pressed on his now vacant crotch, hopping madly about and swearing. Of the half dozen words he used to describe her, 'bitch' might just be permitted in the reading out of the story. 'You think this punishment enough?' screamed the young girl. Of the numerous invectives she used, none was replicable in class. 'You think I not suffer and suffer because you are so dirty and always try to touch me? Even when I asleep, even I take my bath, I have to watch for you, you dirty old man!' 'Oh no, oh no,' screamed Dirty Uncle, as he saw her open the window and fling out his manhood, now no more than a tangle of bloody bits, like discarded offal on a butcher's chopping block. He screamed even more when he heard loud quacking sounds outside the window. The girl looked out and watched four ducks fighting over the offering. She said smiling, 'Good. Now you will not disturb me any more, you wicked, evil, sinful, dirty Uncle!' Maggie must have built up her stock of stories from those she regularly heard from her mother and the other lounge waitresses, gathered together in their free time to drink and laugh at the men whom they would, after their brief respite, have to start pleasing all over again.

Stripped of the lurid imagery, Maggie's story was still stunning in the sheer daring of its theme and dialogue. Peals of laughter erupted in the classroom, in which Maria joined readily, at one point wiping the tears off her eyes. One of the students, a bright-eyed girl with long plaits, collapsed in a wash of merriment upon the back of the boy sitting in front of her; another, a mischievous-looking boy with a pimply face cried out 'Dirty Uncle Bird! Dirty Uncle Bird!', using a ruler to beat rhythmically upon his desktop.

Maria was about to call a halt to the rowdiness and explain that saucy stories like Maggie's were alright for the creative writing class but not for the G.C.E. O Level English Language paper when she saw Maggie look up with an expression of such concentrated fury that she stopped suddenly, said, 'Maggie, wait –' and the next moment rushed to stop the girl make a dash out of the classroom.

She yelled, 'Wait, Maggie, come back!' but the girl was gone in a flash. Maria said, 'Oh dear, oh dear,' and stood helplessly at the doorway, wondering what to do next. She returned dispiritedly to face the class, now quiet and looking at her for the next stage of action in the unfolding drama.

One of the boys volunteered to go and look for Maggie. 'Oh dear,' Maria said, quite pale with the shock of the sudden turn of events. 'We have upset Maggie. We shouldn't have laughed so much. She must have thought we were making fun of her story.'

'What about her making fun of our stories?' said the bright-eyed girl with long plaits. 'You remember when I read out my story, she kept giggling and making all sorts of comments?'

'But it was such a funny story, Miss Seetoh!' exclaimed the pimply boy. 'I never laughed so much in my life!' The laughter began again. Emboldened, the boy said, 'Hey, Miss Seetoh, tell Maggie her story is good enough to be made into a movie! She'll become very rich! That part about the ducks gobbling it up – ha, ha, ha!'

Maria said, 'Be quiet,' then looked at Yen Ping and Mark who had remained silent throughout; they seemed to have withdrawn into themselves, not self-consciously as the school's most celebrated pair but gravely as if that position was bringing its own insurmountable problems.

As soon as she was free, Maria went in search of Maggie. She was nowhere to be found. In the canteen, Auntie Noodles said that Maggie had picked up her sister and they had both gone off, without their usual meal of noodles.

'Did she look upset?' asked Maria anxiously.

'She was crying,' said Auntie Noodles.

'Did she say anything to you?' asked Maria and dreaded to hear the answer, 'She said Miss Maria Seetoh made fun of her and her beloved sister Angel.'

Maggie did not come to school the following day, nor the day after. After a week, Maria, sick with remorse and worry, went to Brother Philip for help and advice. She was met with the worst possible news. Maggie had left the school, with no intention of returning.

Brother Philip showed her the letter addressed to him: 'I Maggie Sim Pek Ngoh, am no longer student of St Peter's Secondary School, because it is stinking school. The principal, the teachers, the students – they all stink. Miss Maria Seetoh, she stink most of all!' Maria burst into tears.

'I really want to see her again, to explain everything. She misunderstood me so badly.'

Brother Philip offered to drive her to Maggie's home to do the explanation. He said he would be wearing shirt and pants, not his robe, to avoid attention.

The school administrative officer gave them Maggie's address from a register, saying, 'This may not be the correct address. She changed it three times.' Some months back, when a school counsellor went to the last given address, she was told by a middle-aged couple there that they were Maggie's relatives, with little connection with the girl or her family. The couple mentioned The Blue Moon Lounge in an infamous part of the town where Maggie's mother worked.

'That's where we'll go next,' said Maria with determination. 'Dear Brother Phil, I'm sorry to involve you in all this mess. But I simply have to find Maggie.'

Mrs Neo and Teresa Pang were already heaving sighs of relief. Good riddance to bad rubbish. They added that if that troublesome girl had not left on her own, the new principal would make her, for he was clearly a man of action who would not tolerate a fraction of the nonsense that the old principal did.

The search was fruitless. Nobody at the Blue Moon Lounge had heard of a woman with the surname Sim or with daughters named Maggie and Angel. Or they were co-operating with her and Maggie not to reveal anything.

'Don't cry,' said Brother Philip soothingly. He offered her a large white handkerchief which he took out of his pocket. She continued to sob convulsively.

All, all gone wrong in her world, when she had only meant to be kind. But it all boiled down to her insensitivity. How could she have not noticed Maggie's distress?

Brother Philip drew her gently into his arms and patted her back. 'You're alright,' he said. Soon she stopped crying and continued to lie in the comforting protection of his arms, a safe warm spot in a horrible world. *You're okay. You're alright.* All her life, she needed men to tell her that.

Brother Philip was one of the very few at St Peter's who could tell her about the situation regarding the principal. He was being investigated by the Ministry of Education following a complaint, in an anonymous letter, about unprofessional, unethical conduct: he had awarded the contract for the building of an extension of the school library to a contractor without the proper procedures laid down by the Ministry; the contractor turned out to be his brother-in-law. Now disgraced, he spent all his time at home and would likely lose his principal's position even if he were allowed back into education; if found guilty of corruption, he could even be sent to jail, for corruption among civil servants, said the great TPK, was the beginning of rot in a society and would never be tolerated. Singaporeans remembered that years back a junior minister had been charged with accepting the bribe of a free vacation to Indonesia for his whole family plus an Italian leather armchair, and had, during the period of suspension, committed suicide by hanging himself.

Maria thought, poor principal. I'll miss him. She asked Brother Philip if he had seen him since. 'Once,' he replied, 'he looked much thinner. He looked sad and subdued. He did not welcome visitors.'

'Do you think the charges are true?' asked Maria.

'Who knows?' shrugged Brother Philip.

Maria thought that the last person she would link with her greedy, money-desperate brother was the principal of St Peter's Secondary school. Venality, corruption, sordidness – from the great murky ocean outside, they washed up on the shores of an institution dedicated to learning and noble ideals.

Also heartlessness and cruelty towards young love. Yen Ping and Mark asked to see her privately. They met in a corner of the school library after school. Each looked nervously to the other to begin confiding their troubled story. It seemed that Mark's mother had found out that they were serious about each other and had immediately stormed into the school to complain to the principal. Maria could imagine the woman, insufferably loud and arrogant, with her heavy make-up, perfectly coiffured hair and designer clothes, standing before Mr Ignatius Lim, waving her manicured hands about, dropping hints that she was the niece of the Deputy Minister of Trade and Business, disdaining to refer to her son's girlfriend's parents other than as working class people with whom she had nothing in common. 'I have plans for Mark to go abroad and study in the best university,' she said, 'and I would like you as the principal to see to it that there is no more nonsense going on!' Before she left, she opened her handbag, took out her chequebook and made a donation to the school charity fund, saying with a smile that St Peter's could always count on her support. As soon as she left, Mr Lim sent for Mark and Yen Ping and reminded them that no pairing was allowed in schools. 'I will be keeping an eye on you,' he said with a great show of geniality. 'Any more complaints and I might have to do something drastic. You strike me as very sensible young people. So stop being naughty and concentrate on your studies!'

'We will not be attending your creative writing class anymore,' said Yen Ping tearfully. Mark revealed that his mother was already making plans to transfer him to another school. Yen Ping revealed that the angry woman had made a visit to her parents, at their drinks stall in Siah Street Market, and delivered an ultimatum: if their daughter persisted in distracting her son from his studies, she would take the matter to the Deputy Minister of Trade and Business who could revoke any business licence at very short notice. After she left, Yen Ping's mother gave her daughter a sound scolding.

'Why do you have to get mixed up with those rich, snooty people? Their world is not our world!' Her father said, 'Stop seeing him, we have our pride.' They were saving up to send her to a university of her choice. All she had to do was to study hard and get good grades in the exams.

Maria thought that the entire ugly affair was saved only by the purity of the two young people at its centre. They were like two radiant spirits standing on a vast expanse of seashore, untouched by the detritus all around. Mark and Yen Ping said, 'Miss Seetoh, we want you to know that we have enjoyed and benefited from your creative writing classes, and that our feelings for one another will always be the same, despite what is happening,' then turned to look affectionately at each other and moved closer for the merest contact of fingers. She had to pull them down from the high clouds of their love to the hard realities on the ground.

'How will you continue to see each other? There will be risks.'

Again they looked at each other. The resourcefulness of pure, young undeterred love could not be underestimated.

'We have thought it over,' they said. 'We accept that we can't see each other as much as we want, but we have ways. Besides, we can always write to each other.'

Ways? Maria thought of secret meetings in ice-cream parlours, that she and Kuldeep Singh had dared, and in the Botanic Gardens where she had seen the young couple, in school uniform, unabashedly locked in each other's arms at the top of a grassy slope, then rolling down together in joyous laughter.

She was taken aback to be so decisively included in their scheme of secret love.

'Miss Seetoh,' they said, 'would you be able to give us private tuition in English language to prepare us for the exams? We could go to your place once a week.'

Private tuition to do better in the exams was the best stratagem to make even cautious and suspicious parents throw all caution and suspicion to the winds. She could already see Mark and Yen Ping, looking as pure and innocent as ever, seated side by side at a table, holding hands under it while she tutored them. Parental threat from both sides was clearly drawing them closer to each other and too close to an edge far more dangerous than hers because they were so young.

Maria suddenly remembered the incident, so long ago, of her two classmates, both aged sixteen, who were forced to get married when the girl got pregnant.

The reliable alarm bells in her head rang loudly on their behalf, and she said, 'Perhaps we should all sit down and have a good talk one of these days. I see problems.'

'Yes, Miss Seetoh,' they said, adding, 'we trust you.'

Yen Ping said, blushing deeply, 'Miss Seetoh, I know what you're thinking. But Mark and I are not like that. We've talked things over. Our plan is to study hard, get good university degrees and then get married. Our parents would have no objections once we prove that we are really serious about each other and our future together.'

Maria could only give each a hug. 'Bless you,' she said, the tears coming into her eyes. She noticed they came too easily these days.

'So you have only distress stories to tell,' said Dr Phang. They were once again parked in the dark isolated spot outside the Botanic Gardens. By now completely attuned to each other's mood, they were assiduously avoiding even the slightest possibility of conflict or tension; he made no demands and she asked no questions.

There were always her stories – from school, from home, from the realm of pure imagination – to sustain the neither-here-nor-there state which had its own piquant pleasure. He said, 'My turn to tell a story,' and asked whether as children, they had a common fear experienced by all Chinese children exposed to the terrifying pantheon of gods in the mythology of their ancestral cultures before the moderating, calming effects of Christianity, the common religion of conversion.

It was the terror of the mightiest god in the pantheon whose supremacy was embodied in his name – Tua Peh Kong – whom children remembered as the largest, most decked-out statue with the most elaborate altar in temples that their mothers or grandmothers took them to.

Maria said, her eyes bright with happy recollection, 'I remember the Tua Peh Kong in the White Heaven Temple that my Por Por used to take me. I would hide behind Por Por and peep at the ferocious eyes, the black beard, the glittering warrior costume, the sunburst of swords on his back.'

Dr Phang's Tua Peh Kong was seated on a gold throne, one booted foot on a pile of screaming demons, like a bunch of writhing earthworms. As a boy, he would wake up screaming from nightmares of Tua Peh Kong which continued even after the family converted to Christianity and formally denounced the superstitions of their forbears.

The best part of the story was in the connection with the great TPK.

'The happiest coincidence of initials,' smiled Dr Phang. 'Have you ever wondered why the prime minister is seldom referred to by his real name – Tang Poon Kim? Singapore's Tua Peh Kong sits astride his throne, striking terror in all hearts. He makes use of the Thunder God to hurl the bolts of his fury against his enemies and throw them into disarray. If V.K. Pandy leaves Singapore and returns to India, that will be the sixth dissident to flee from his wrath.' Maria thought, now I know why I'm so much attracted to this man. It was not only his good looks and his charm, but his position as a maverick, like herself, remaining in the system, yet out of it in spirit, taking delight in cocking a snook at the powers that be.

She said, her eyes sparkling, 'I challenge you when you next meet up with TPK to tell him about his godly status.'

'I already have,' he said chuckling. His canny charm must have been even more finely calibrated to the great TPK's mood; the austere prime minister, it was said, was not without a sense of humour in private, albeit a wry one, and it was no bad thing to catch him at a moment when he was in need of some light diversion and tell him, 'Sir, Singaporeans say you're Tua Peh Kong; their children and grandchildren down the generations will know you only by those fearsome initials!'

The great TPK might even have let out a smile before resuming the task of tapping on Dr Phang's brains for this or that national project.

Maria said, by now all delight, 'If I write a book, any book, it must have a place for Tua Peh Kong. His image will be a blend of our respective childhood nightmares.'

He had never seen her in such a light mood. He swept her into his arms and whispered in her ear, 'Well?'

Let's go to bed. Let me take you to bed. Shall we? How about it? Would you like to come up and see my etchings? The wording of a proposition, if clichéd or crude or stale, might dismay the romantic woman. This man dispensed with them all by a single bold, rising inflection. Heady with the light-heartedness of the evening, after an extremely vexatious day, she responded with her own insouciance,

'Alright, we'll not keep the silken bed waiting. Now I'm going home to my plain one – alone.' She could see his broad smile in the enveloping darkness; it remained through the ensuing flurry of serious suggestions.

He would be going on a trip overseas, in a fortnight's time, with a team of colleagues for a conference in Europe; he could go earlier, or return later, on his own, and meet her in a hotel in London or Paris, whichever suited her. Meanwhile, he would be too busy to see her.

Twenty-Five

A fortnight of eager anticipation that was betrayed by a light step, a flushed skin, a secret smile. The marks of a woman being in love surely had to do with the anticipation, or recollection, of the first kiss, the first nakedness together. Sometimes while having a cup of coffee by herself in an open café, she would look in pleasurable idleness at people passing by, singling out women betrayed by those chemical manifestations, whether walking by themselves or beside their lovers, never their husbands, oblivious to the rest of the world. The element of secrecy always sweetened the anticipation.

Once she was in a taxi that screeched to a sudden halt in front of a dreamy-looking girl who was playing with strands of her long hair, gently twirling them round her forefinger. When the taxi-driver leant out of the window to scold her, she merely glanced at him and continued her serene, smiling walk across the road. Maria watched with amusement.

The taxi-driver turned around to remark, 'Thinking about her boyfriend, that's why. These girls, they think, oh, my darling, oh my darling, when I see you again? When you make love to me again? They are very big danger on the road, I tell you!'

Maria asked, 'Have you ever felt like this in your life?' and he replied, with a roar of laughter, '*Aiyah*, so, so long ago. When just in my twenties. She was *ronggeng* dance girl from Thailand. Very pretty. So-oo sexy!'

'Did you marry her?'

'What, no, *lah*! How can. My mother found me girl from her hometown in Malaysia. Married now for thirty-two years! Two sons, two daughters, five grandchildren. Ha, ha, ha!' The taxi passed a small street where outside a rundown coffee shop, a number of elderly men sat on red plastic chairs round old wooden tables. 'Miss, look at the old *ah peh* there, drinking coffee,' he said. 'You know what? They are sixty, seventy years old, yet dreaming of young sexy mistress! One *ah peh*, seventy-five, found young girl from China. Suddenly he look younger, in love, have sex. But only one year. She took all his pension money and went back to China!'

'Well, has it happened yet?' asked Meeta and Winnie, and the moment she said, 'Soon, soon,' she regretted it for the two women, incorrigibly curious, would now be impelled by their own kind of anticipation to call her constantly to check.

Brother Philip said astutely, 'Maria, these days you are forgetful. It can't be the bad kind of forgetfulness since it comes with all those smiles.'

She thought, 'No, I can't bear to tell him. He might lose all respect and regard for me.'

He kept his promise to take her to the Blue Moon Lounge in another attempt to find Maggie; it too was fruitless. Brother Philip said, 'I think they're lying. Maggie's mother was probably peeping from behind some curtain and wondering if we were from the anti-vice squad.'

She found a note from Maggie in an envelope addressed to

her at St Peter's. It said: 'I know you and Brother Philip trying to find me. Don't waste your time. If you really want to see me and make apology for what you have insulted me and my sister, meet me at the Chantek Café on Slim Street at 7.35 tomorrow evening. Do not bring Brother Philip. Do not be late. My boyfriend will pick me up at 7.40 for dinner and take me for important appointment in town. If you not punctual by 7.45 latest, I will be gone, and I will not see you again. Maggie.'

There were the marks of proud assertiveness of her new position of power as the one being eagerly sought – the terse language, the laying down of precise conditions of time and place of their meeting, the reference to a boyfriend at her beck and call.

Brother Philip said anxiously, 'You think it's safe for you to go on your own? It will be rather dark. And I'm not sure what the new Maggie is like, back in her world that she's been keeping secret from us.'

'Bless you, dear Brother Phil,' said Maria. 'I'll be alright. And I'll tell you all about it.'

As it turned out, when Maria next turned to Brother Philip for advice and help, Maggie's matter would take second place to a host of others that threatened to engulf her. Now, in a mood of the kind for which the language of romance drew ridiculously extravagant comparisons with blue sky, blue ocean, billowy clouds, eternal birdsong, she walked airily into the Chantek Café at precisely the appointed time, looked around and saw no Maggie. She knew, with certainty, that the girl had arrived in time and must be hiding behind a shop façade somewhere to make her wait. She waited a full ten minutes, after which she saw Maggie enter the café and approach her. The signs were not promising. The girl's face bore the same intense anger as on that day when she had fled from the creative writing class. But she was determined to be conciliatory all the way; if she was going to make any mistake now, it had to be one on the side of kindness and forbearance.

She said, 'Maggie, I'm really, really sorry. I can explain,' and the girl said, with a toss of her head, 'Okay, you explain. I listen.'

Apparently, Maggie had no interest in any explanation; she had long since come to her own conclusion about the incident and had called the meeting purely to unleash her fury. Again and again, she accused Maria of making fun of her and her sister Angel, at a time when she needed the help of the teacher she trusted most to help her through a crisis. Again and again she said, 'Miss Seetoh, how you can do such a thing to me?'

'Maggie, stop, for goodness' sake, you have to stop and listen to me,' cried Maria, grasping her hand, as if that could stop the torrent of words coming out of her mouth.

She said angrily, 'Don't touch me!'

'Maggie, why do you bring in Angel? There surely is some misunderstanding. I was only reading out your story to the class. I'm so sorry if we laughed. We were not laughing at you, Maggie, only at the funny story. This has happened many times in our creative writing sessions, remember?'

She saw Maggie's eyes suddenly fill with tears. 'Miss Seetoh, I tell you the tragic story of my sister Angel, how we both desperate, how I have to protect her and keep her in the canteen till I go home with her, and instead of help us, you make fun of us, and encourage whole class make fun of us! Even if my sister got killed, you all will laugh and make fun of her!'

'Maggie, what on earth – '

The girl was mad; she was talking incoherently. Nothing could be more disconnected than the hilarious story she had written and the tragic one she was revealing now. Only one thing was clear – the deep distress connected with the younger sister whom she loved so much. Maria would ignore the incoherence and concentrate on helping the poor girl unburden her heart. She reached out for Maggie's hand which once again moved away abruptly.

'I say not to touch me,' said the girl. 'Miss Seetoh, you stink. I thought you are best teacher in world and I can trust you and share secret with you. Now I know you are like all the rest. Only laugh and make fun of me and my sister. Look down on us, like we are dirt.'

Maria said very slowly and calmly, 'Maggie, I really don't know what you're talking about. Why don't we calm down and you explain everything to me. Tell me about Angel and how we can help her.'

'Too late,' said Maggie haughtily. 'Now I depend on myself, not anyone in the whole world. Angel is safe now. I find a place for her to stay because I can find work and earn money. If I depend on world to help me, Angel by now raped and I kill my father and don't care if police come after me and lock me in prison!'

Suddenly the picture of Maggie's dark mysterious world began to shape, and its connection with the strange story of Uncle Joe and the dismemberment, to emerge. It was still an unclear picture; what stood out with certainty was the girl's need for help, disguised as a proud insistence on a full-blown apology in a public place.

Maria said, 'Maggie, I just can't tell you how sorry I am for upsetting you that day. I was so wrong. Will you forgive me?'

The girl stood up, by no means mollified. 'Miss Seetoh, I go now. We are not friends any more. I was so happy before because I trust you and you trust me and you even tell me secret about the diamond ring, I the only student that day in the searching group. But now everything change, Miss Seetoh. I don't want to depend on anybody. I will work, make money and give Angel good education. She will go to university. Then nobody will harm her. Goodbye, Miss Seetoh.'

'Maggie, wait, please wait – ,' but the girl had disappeared, as quickly as she had that day when she ran out of the classroom. Maria cursed under her breath. 'Dammit, there's a limit to how far I'm prepared to go, even for you.'

'Go and find out more from Auntie Noodles,' said Brother Philip.

It would only be much later that Maria understood how the need to disguise pain in a story could distort the disguise beyond all comprehension. Auntie Noodles told a story of incredible anguish that Maggie had confided in her. Maggie and Angel never knew their real father, the man they called father was their stepfather, one of several men in their mother's life, one of whom could be Angel's real father, making the girls only half sisters. It was a pitifully tangled web of relationships sometimes discovered in dysfunctioning households visited by counsellors anxious to help. The father who held odd jobs and had tattoos of dragons on both arms often came home drunk; for as long as Maggie could remember, he had tried to molest her as soon as her mother was out of the house. When she threatened him with a knife one evening, he simply transferred his attention to her young sister whom Maggie protected fiercely. There was a dangerous one-hour period when Angel would be home from school and be alone with the drunken man; Maggie solved the problem by making her sister go to St Peter's and wait for her in the canteen. At night they slept huddled together, Maggie's ears ever alert for the rattling sound of the doorknob, the sight of the lurking shadow under the door. Her dream was to get her G.C.E. O level, find a job and remove herself and her sister permanently from the dark, perilous world of her parents. Her mother cared little about what was happening; after her work at the Blue Moon Lounge, she sometimes came home and joined her husband in his beer-drinking, sometimes laughing merrily together, often quarrelling loudly and throwing things at each other.

Maggie despised her mother. She told Auntie Noodles that she sometimes spat at her. Upon her sister, right from babyhood, she had lavished all the love she never knew, while using all the wiles she had, to beat off any threats to the little world of safety she had carved out for themselves. Auntie Noodles hinted that Maggie sometimes joined her mother in the Blue Moon Lounge to make some money to spoil her adored little sister with gifts of clothes, toys and colouring pencils. Maria had the saddening recollection of that day in school when Maggie complained of a heavy period, making a great show of a fistful of sanitary towels; she had probably been just discharged from one of the government clinics for an abortion that had not gone too well. Auntie Noodles said, tapping the side of her head with a forefinger to demonstrate Maggie's shrewd mind, that the girl had once talked about looking out for a rich man, even an old one, to marry, for a job with a G.C.E. O level qualification would not support Angel through university.

Maria read the infamous story again, scouring it for telling details. Then she showed it to Brother Philip.

'Read it,' she said, 'and tell me if it was really a cry for help. Idiot that I was, I missed it.'

'Don't be too hard on yourself,' said the kindly brother. He laughed so much over the story that Maria was provoked to laugh too. She remembered the precise moment when she had bonded with the strange, overaged, most disliked student in St Peter's Secondary School; it was the moment she saw the truth of her entire life flashing before her eyes in the inspired words on a playful strip of paper: *Mrs Tan is no more. Long live Miss Seetoh!* She told Brother Philip about it.

He said, 'Don't worry about that girl; she'll do well in the world. She has more savvy than both of us combined.' He asked, 'What will you do now?'

'Nothing,' said Maria. 'Clearly she doesn't want to have anything more to do with me.'

The opposite was true of Yen Ping. The girl looked forlorn on her own, though she tried to put on a brave front. Mark Wong's mother had made good her threat and transferred him to the St Paul's High School; she had him driven every morning to school and brought home every afternoon in a chauffeured car, with strict instructions to the chauffeur to double up as private detective and watch out for any girl trying to meet up with her son.

'Miss Seetoh, can I see you for a moment?' Yen Ping needed constant encouragement in her studies, in her attempts at creative writing, in her need to fight the sadness of the greatest loss in her life. 'Miss Seetoh, I love Mark very much, and I will study very hard so that we can have a good future together.' 'Miss Seetoh, I received this letter from Mark; would you like to read it?' 'Miss Seetoh, I've written this poem for Mark. What do you think of it?'

Young love was so pure, simple, uncalculating.

She had but one call from Dr Phang since their last meeting, and it was to tell her, very quickly, that his departure for Europe would be postponed by a week. He said, 'Looking forward so much; you have no idea how much,' and hung up.

The road, it was said, was better than the inn, the travelling better than the arrival, the anticipation, if it was fed by the dreams of languorous sleep, far sweeter than the reality.

They were lying, not on the silken couch of pleasant jesting, but some kind of sofa in some kind of place that did not at all resemble a room, for she could see some pillars in the distance, festooned with plants, and hear the low hum of insects. They were laughing like happy children, their nakedness covered by a white bedsheet.

He pulled it over their heads, snuggled even closer to her and said, 'There, isn't that nicer,' before his hands did a slow, luxurious exploration of her body and invited hers to do the same of his. He was a very handsome man, driven by the vanity of a regular regimen of thrice-weekly workouts in the gym.

She said, 'Meeta and Winnie say you are the most distinguished man they've ever seen. They think you take great pains over those fantastic Richard Gere locks.'

He lifted her hand to let her fingers run through them and said, 'They make Olivia go crazy. You should see her in bed.' She said, 'Let's not talk about Olivia. But first a question. Do you love her as much as you love your daughter?'

He said, 'Here's the truth. I love my daughter most of all. No woman can come even that close to her.' He showed a precise inch between thumb and forefinger.

She said, 'I understand that perfectly. In the end everything boils down to biology, you see. It's nature's way.'

He said, 'Hey, you read too much and think too much. No wonder poor Bernard couldn't come up to your intellectual level. He passed off a paper as his own, but I could see your hand in it.'

'Don't talk about Bernard.'

'Alright, I won't talk about Bernard if you will not talk about Olivia.'

She remained silent for a while, before asking with some anxiety, 'You think they can hear and see us?' For now they were in a parked car in a dark area and could see the shadowy forms of people moving about in the distance. He gathered breath, then released it in an explosive expletive, accompanied by a crude raised finger. 'That's what we should say to them.'

She wanted to laugh but instead said reproachfully, 'Why, Benjamin, that's not like you! I've never heard you use any vulgarity!'

He said, 'I use them enough in the office when I get frustrated. I swore once at our great Tua Peh Kong, and he swore back. But hey, you're calling me 'Benjamin'! At last. Why don't you call me 'Ben' or 'Benjy'? I would love the sound of that.'

It was at this point that the ever vigilant mind, never asleep even when the rest of the body was, pushed through the unreality of dreams with its own reality to sound a grave warning. It said to her, as she lay pressed against him, murmuring with pleasure, 'Are you sure you want to cross the line? He will ditch you as soon as he gets up, puts on his clothes, returns to his wife and starts to look around for another conquest to add to his crown of victory. The man's a bastard. The man's bad news.'

She thought, I'm not that much of good news, either.

'Hey, why that serious look all of a sudden?' he said, tickling her chin with a blade of grass he had plucked. They were lying on a stretch of grass, still naked, under a large tree beside a pond in the Botanic Gardens.

She said, 'Here's a riddle. Two guesses. What lies at the bottom of the pond?'

'No idea. Anyway, who cares?'

'Well, two rings.'

'Who cares?' he repeated. He held up her left hand and slipped an imaginary ring on the engagement finger. 'You're engaged to me, Maria Seetoh. I pronounce you fiancée and dearly beloved.'

'Enough of rings,' she said and made a great show of removing the imaginary one. 'From now onwards I am a free woman, wearing no ring of subjugation.'

'Why do you women think we subjugate you? You're as much in the game as we are!'

They fell into a long silence, during which he traced, very slowly, the contours of her right breast, then her left with a forefinger. 'You have a beautiful body,' he said. They were silent again.

Then she said, 'I have a horrible sensation that Olivia is hiding somewhere with her private detective and watching us.'

'I thought you had promised not to bring up her name. Anyway, have no fear,' he said jauntily. 'I've packed her off to Hong Kong. She'll be so busy shopping with her mother and sisters she will forget to return to Singapore!'

She said again, this time even more nervously, 'I have a horrible feeling that Bernard is hiding somewhere, watching us and ready to pounce at the right moment.'

'He's dead, you silly girl. Now come to your beloved Benjamin.'

'I know he's dead, but I know he's somewhere here, ready to pounce.'

'Well,' he said, in a burst of laughter, 'why don't I do the pouncing for him,' and the next moment he was on her and in her.

The sensation caused a loud pounding in her heart and ears, and she woke up. Lying very still in the darkness, she was aware of the warm convulsions of pleasure gripping her entire body, reaching to its every shuddering corner and crevice. She thought with a smile of Winnie's shameless listening outside Meeta's bedroom door to catch the wild moans and thrashing movements that could last a full five minutes. Perhaps at this very moment, she and Meeta were in a sisterly camaraderie of the dream-induced throes of pleasures. She was thankful, since her mother's room was just across the corridor that she did not have the telltale unruliness of Meeta's night dreams. Even worse, the room that Por Por shared with the maid was next to hers; it had thin walls and Por Por was a very slight sleeper, roused even by the distant bark of a dog or the honking of a car.

Twenty-Six

Even the mere sight of a letter addressed to her brought unease.
When V.K. Pandy, without a word, handed her a brown
envelope with her name written on it, she felt a little frisson
of alarm. She had, as usual, after her visit to the dispensary in
Middleton Square, walked up to him, in the most casual way,
and bought his pamphlets, gesturing, with a smile, for him to
keep the change. Each time he would say, looking at the money,
'Oh my, my, are you sure, Miss? Thanks, Miss.'

He looked shabbier and thinner than ever, and on the few
occasions when she had actually stopped for some minutes to
talk to him, he had launched into his usual diatribe against the
great TPK for ruining his life and possibly bringing about his
wife's cancer.

'The Almighty God is just after all,' he said bitterly, referring
to TPK's wife's numerous health problems. 'As you Chinese say,
Sky God has eyes and ears.'

Inside the taxi on her way home, Maria tore open the
envelope and expected more reproach from a world that she
was not at all helping in its distress. Maggie had accused her of
heartlessness; would V.K. Pandy denounce her for cowardice?
Would he ask why she had stayed in fearful hiding instead of

coming out to support Big Bird and why she vanished from the scene as soon as the police arrived?

The message, written in neat, old-fashioned handwriting on old-fashioned blue letter paper, said, 'Dear Miss Seetoh, from what I can see, you are a good, intelligent, kind person. I would appreciate it very much if you could join me for lunch at Raphael's Place on Junie Street (just behind Middleton Square). I have important things which I want to talk to you about, because I trust you.' Trust. She had begun to distrust that word about herself, because a student had repeatedly thrown it back at her.

The day of the lunch would be a Saturday; V.K. Pandy must have inferred she was a teacher and would not be free for lunches on weekdays. Another concession must have been the written form of the invitation instead of a verbal one that would have attracted attention. V.K. Pandy could not have been unmindful of the very brief duration – barely a minute – that she allowed for each encounter with him, as if she, like the others, was aware of the presence of those infamous surveillance cameras that, as it turned out in the end, had been no more than a figment of the fearful imagination. He probably also understood that as a teacher, she came under the strictures enjoined upon the entire civil service against any political activism, meaning any support of the opposition.

Before the end of his first month in St Peter's Secondary School, Mr Ignatius Lim had already circulated three reminding circulars to the staff and singled her out for special attention. As she sat before him in his office, and he poured out coffee and went into a long, smiling preamble on many subjects including the highlights of his career in education, she could not help thinking, 'The man's detestable. How I miss the principal.'

At last he said, 'I understand, Miss Seetoh, that you sometimes buy the pamphlets of the opposition member.' The school had its spies, and she had no idea how thorough they were. 'May I remind you, as your principal, that this is contrary to official regulations.' He fished about busily among a pile of important-looking papers on his desk, pulled out one, and put on his reading glasses. 'Ah, here it is. It says 'No civil servant should –' '

Maria, all outward calm, was all roiling irritation inside. She had to grip the sides of her chair to prevent the contempt from pouring out: 'May I remind you, Mr Ignatius Lim, that you are the best example of the civil servant becoming less civil and more servant by the day.' She had shared the scathing pun with Dr Phang who had reacted with a self-deprecating roar of laughter that Mr Ignatius Lim would have been constitutionally incapable of.

It was a rather pricey Italian restaurant and Maria had already planned on how to take over the settling of the bill without embarrassing poor V.K. Pandy who was gratefully receiving donations casually dropped at his side in Middleton Square by compassionate Singaporeans. She had some wild conjectures as to the purpose of the lunch – to get her to help in raising funds to settle his debts and pay for his wife's cancer treatment, to get her help, as a teacher of English, in the writing or editing of his pamphlets, to get her support to draw public attention to the fear gripping an entire society under the great TPK, as Big Bird had done.

What she was not prepared for was his announcement that he was quitting politics for good and returning to India, to the village of his birth and boyhood. Why was he telling her, of all people?

He said he had been touched by her generosity and her kindness. 'Altogether you have bought my pamphlets thirteen times, Miss Seetoh, more than any other Singaporean,' he said. 'I don't think you bother to read them; you probably just throw them away, but that doesn't make your kindness less.'

Some diners at the restaurant easily recognised V.K. Pandy, nudged their companions and began casting curious glances in their direction. Even if Mr Ignatius Lim had made a severe appearance then, she would not have cared. Her heart went out in overwhelming pity to the man who looked very old and defeated. She asked him about his wife. 'A little better, thank you. She's responding quite well to the treatment.' She asked him about his plans. 'I will live a quiet life. There's an ashram near my village that I will go to for peace of mind.'

She struggled to find the correct words for an intention shaping in her mind. 'Mr Pandy, it will make me very happy if you will accept a small donation from me –' She had had less money since her husband's death, having to make a large monthly allowance to her mother, which she suspected went to the useless, gambling adopted son. But she felt that financial assistance, more than kind words, was needed by the unfortunate V.K. Pandy at this critical juncture of his life.

He pushed back the envelop containing her cheque saying, 'No, no thank you. Right now, we're okay.' He leaned towards her and his face was contorted in the vitriol of a gathering rage as he said, 'It's not even the hundreds of thousands I've lost, my house, my business. It's my dignity, my pride! You know what the great man said to me?' His voice rose in its pain, and the diners at the nearby tables looked down and concentrated on their food. 'He said to me, 'You are nothing but vermin! You will come crawling to me, and then I will grind you under my feet!'

Maria felt anger rising on his behalf. Tua Peh Kong who sat on a throne with a mass of writhing worms under his feet was alive and well in Singapore. V.K. Pandy was by now gesturing angrily with both hands and raising his voice. 'I am a man! I am a human being! I am a Singaporean! He has no right to use all kinds of insulting words to me.'

Publicly the great TPK made it clear that political opposition in Singapore was a useless legacy from British colonial rule, creating nothing but disruption and disorder and thus hindering the smooth carrying out of government policy. He said any thorn in the side of the body politic should be yanked out at once, singling out V.K. Pandy for special opprobrium. V.K. Pandy said, 'You know why? I'll tell you why. I had caused him the greatest humiliation of his life. When his party lost that seat to me and he saw Singaporeans wildly cheering me and hissing at his defeated candidate, that must have been the moment when he swore, 'That man will come crawling to me, and I will grind him into the ground!' Well, TPK, I will show you! I will show who comes crawling to whom.' Aware of the sheer impossibility of that absurd self-promise, V.K. Pandy's eyes flashed with angry, hot tears and his hands trembled.

She had to do something to calm him down. It was not exactly appropriate, but it might work. Taking out a folded piece of paper from her handbag, she passed it to him and said with a smile, 'Here, read it. It's a poem on the great TPK, which I was inspired to write after a friend gave me an idea. We had a good chuckle over it.'

Dr Phang had made a bet with her. 'If you can get *The Singapore Tribune* to publish it, you win one hundred dollars.' She had said incredulously, '*The Singapore Tribune?* Are you crazy? Well, you've already won your bet, but I'm not paying you one hundred dollars.'

V.K. Pandy read the poem. A small twisted smile appeared on his face. 'I like it,' he said, 'especially the comparison of Tua Peh Kong's thunderbolts to TPK's crippling defamation suits. I like the ending:

Even Tua Peh Kong must bow before a greater,
Who has no thunderbolts, no warrior suit, no throne, no spears
Who has no name
Because simple humanity needs no name.

'I like it very much. May I have it?'

'Of course,' said Maria, and was glad that the man's fury had abated enough for him to start eating his pasta. There was a whiff of alcohol about him that added to the overall appearance of defeat and despair.

He said, as they shook hands before leaving the restaurant, 'You will not see me again in Middleton Square or anywhere in Singapore. I leave for India in a week's time.'

'Goodbye, Mr Pandy, and good luck. Do take care.' The newspapers carried a very brief report of his departure; almost immediately there were rumours circulating about how the man had gone back to India to die in his native village, for, unknown to anyone, he had a serious illness that he had kept secret for years. Then for months afterwards, all thought of V.K. Pandy vanished as if he had never existed.

'Oh no,' thought Maria when she reached home and her mother handed her a note, saying, 'It's from Heng. It's urgent, he says.' Why were people coming to her with their problems in writing, as if to use hard documentary evidence against her, if necessary, in the future? I've got a headache and a paranoia coming, she sighed. I want nothing more to do with the world! She slumped into a chair.

'What's his problem now? Why can't he just tell me? Or why don't you tell me, Mother? He must have told you about it.'

'Read it,' said Anna Seetoh miserably.

It was a long, type-written letter which, even at a glance, looked too tedious to be read, for it was peppered with figures and even diagrams. The innocuous technicalities were a cover for the desperate message. Heng was making a request: could she buy over his half of the flat that would go to them jointly after their mother's death? He proposed a sum which he said was much less than the market value; indeed, in a few years, she would be able to sell the flat for a good profit if she wanted, as the accompanying figures and diagrams proved. He did not mention the debts that were behind the urgency of the letter, but as a softening touch, he referred to his decision to send his autistic son to a good but rather expensive school for children with special needs.

'What on earth –' cried Maria angrily. 'How dare he talk of claiming his share, Mother, while you are still alive?'

Anna Seetoh said, looking so wretched that Maria's anger against her brother rose to match the pity for her mother, 'It's okay, since I can continue living here with you. It makes no difference to me.'

Maria got up and walked straight into her bedroom, rubbing the sides of her head to reduce the turbulence of the thoughts screaming inside.

'Well, what shall I tell Heng?' said her mother, standing at the doorway.

'Tell him to come and see me tomorrow,' said Maria wearily. 'I want to hear exactly what is in his mind.' She threw the letter into the wastebasket.

It was the same each time – her mother's pleading on his behalf, her remonstrances, then the buckling on account of the poor wife and son. When Heng sat in a chair before her, looking up only occasionally, she realised, with a little shudder of horror, that the standard image of the addict she had only seen on TV programmes, with the haunted eyes, the look of desperation mixed with a burning intensity of excited expectation of the next fix, was right before her eyes. She had meant, on behalf of the rest of the family who seemed helpless before him, to give him a sound lecture about his unconscionable neglect of his family and to extract a promise to do something about his addiction. But the sheer thought of its futility drained her of all purpose and energy; she knew that of all persons, she would be the last from whom he would accept advice, much less rebuke.

In the end, a single thought prevailed: she wanted nothing more to do with him, and the disbursement of the sum would be a final severance. She might even come to see it as a disguised blessing. It would deplete her savings alarmingly; she had always meant to save steadily towards some vague dream of buying a small studio apartment in a new condominium and living entirely on her own – no mother, no Por Por, no maid. Solitary, single, alone – the word, whatever its connotations for women like Meeta or Winnie, had, for her, its own special meanings of peace, freedom and self-fulfilment.

'Thanks,' her brother said briefly, both to her agreement to his proposal and a gift of some clothes for his wife and toys for his son, which she had in two large paper bags. She could never have trusted him to take back any cash gift for them; he would have made straight for the 4-D betting booth or the jackpot machine in the Manis Club. Anna Seetoh had watched him once at the machine, completely mesmerised by its flashing lights, its idiotic pictures of rows of fruit, lightning zigzags, clown's faces and the seductive ringing sounds of coins pouring out on to a waiting metal furrow. He would not leave, said Anna Seetoh shaking her head, because he was bent on hitting the jackpot which had snowballed to ten thousand dollars. In the end, she had to forcibly drag him out of the gambling room.

Out of Maria's hearing, in the kitchen with his mother, Heng's posture of defeat vanished in a new flare of outraged pride. 'Who does she think she is, talking to me like that?' His dream of winning the million-dollar first prize in the national lottery fired him with the savage triumph of the ultimate revenge, 'As soon as I collect my prize, I will say to her, 'Tell me how much I owe you, plus interest, down to the last cent,' and then I will throw the money upon the floor for her to pick up. But not before wiping my backside with it!' He let out a sharp, hysterical laugh.

His mother said, 'Please, not so loud.' In her early morning visits to the Church of Eternal Mercy, she would double her prayers for her and make a special petition to St Anthony, the saint for hopeless cases.

'My turn to write a note,' Maria thought grimly and she sat down and wrote her brother a note, or rather a warning that he could expect no more financial help from her. The ending words should be seared into his brain if he had any pride at all: 'You are an irresponsible husband and father and should be ashamed of yourself.'

Only *he*, she thought with a return of tender feelings as she prepared for bed that night, would be able to restore her trust in notes. He had never written her one. Even an unsigned one, making oblique reference to a happy moment shared, a joke laughed over together in the parked car outside the Botanic Gardens, or over lunch in the Bon Vivant Café would have brought her so much joy. In a week's time, he would be leaving for Europe; in a week's time, they would be meeting for that climactic moment, even if there were no silken bed in their hotel room. While he had waited with cheerful patience, she had been deliberating about it for more than a year, before succumbing to that irresistible 'Well?' The perfect, one-word proposition.

She was tempted to send him a note that was sure to make him laugh, summarising his romantic quest and its success in a cartoon depiction of a large question mark of hope suddenly straightened out into the exclamation mark of triumph. She had actually done the drawing, in bright red, but thrown it away, because he encouraged neither letters nor calls from her, never once mentioning Olivia's powers of detection which ranged far and wide. Olivia Phang had befriended one of the clerks in her husband's office, a very friendly, talkative girl, who, while thanking Mrs Phang for the occasional presents of perfume and costume jewellery, had no idea she was divulging much valuable information about her husband.

If not a meeting, then a note, if not a note then a call: a yearning woman sadly whittled down her hopes. If, in the midst of his hectic programmes, he had managed to give her a brief call, a very brief one lasting no more than a minute, how happy that would have made her! A woman in love grew hungry for small assurances, and if deprived of them, would pine and wilt.

Meeta and Winnie were far from wilting; both had suddenly found themselves in circumstances that, like a shower after a long drought, revived parched flowers and made them bloom and smile again. Byron was meeting Meeta for lunches and drinks at the Polo Club because he happened to be experiencing his own romantic dry season when one female companion had left with no replacement in sight, and the ever available Meeta Nair, large, overbearing, loud, might do for temporary companionship. He had never initiated any of their meetings, so it was with special delight that Meeta accepted his invitation to be his partner at the coming gala ball in the Polo Club. She understood that his insistence on her finding another couple or two to join them to form a large table at the ball was born of a general unease at being alone with her, a fact she was not too embarrassed to mention to Winnie or Maria before satisfying herself with the sneering proclamation, 'The bastard should realise I'm playing the same game too! One of these days, when I find my Mr Right, I'm going to chuck my for-the-time-being beau!'

Winnie was in the happy position of being free from all doubts and misgivings; in fact she hinted that she would soon be engaged to a man she had met through a friend's introduction, a Chinese-American who did secret work all over the world for the US navy.

Meeta had whispered to Maria, '*Introduction*, my foot! She found his name in some dating column in some newspaper,' and again, '*Secret work in the US navy*, my other foot! He's another of those sweet-talking con men that our poor Winnie's always picking up, who will run away as soon as he's fleeced her enough.'

Winnie seemed to have an interminable source of old money from parents and grandparents who were among the most established families in the historical state of Malacca in

Malaysia. Endless rubber, coconut and oil plantations from the time of British colonisation continued to feed Winnie's bottomless bank account which, like the magic purse in fairy tales, was refilled with gold coins, as soon as the last one was spent. Meeta said that men could smell Winnie's money from countries far away, which was why a Frenchman and now a Chinese-American had come a-wooing.

Maria said, 'Why, Winnie, you look years younger!' Indeed, Winnie looked prettier, her normally sallow skin suddenly irradiated by love's glow.

She said simpering, 'Wilbur makes me feel so happy.' Like a child eager to share happy secrets, she told Maria about her many happy dates. 'We're planning a short holiday to Langkawi,' she confided with the unmistakable coyness about a holiday, at last, with a man. 'I bought some suitable nightwear from Robinson's,' she confided further, blushing deeply.

Maria thought, 'Poor Meeta.' As Winnie's housemate, she must have heard about the planned Langkawi holiday and the bought lingerie a dozen times.

Wilbur, a very happy-looking individual who talked and laughed endlessly, was all for making others happy too. 'My philosophy?' he said. 'Nobody comes to Wilbur for a favour and goes away disappointed! You can back me up on this, eh, Winnie girl?' He put his arm around her shoulder and she giggled. 'Not exactly a useful quality for my kind of work, eh, Winnie sweetheart?' And he winked at her.

Maria had never seen Winnie look so happy. 'What, your friend Maria has no partner for the ball?' he said to Meeta. 'Why didn't you tell me earlier? I'll call Freddie at once. His wife's away, and won't mind him going out and having a good time now and then. Freddie's a great guy!'

'Now, Maria, you can't say no to joining us,' said Meeta severely, 'because Winnie's Wilbur has gone to all the trouble of finding you a partner. We're all going to have a ball!'

Winnie said sympathetically, 'What a pity your Dr Phang is married. Otherwise, he can come as your partner. I'm sure he and Wilbur will get along fine. Both of them are so handsome and distinguished-looking!'

Twenty-Seven

'Mother, for goodness' sake, what are you doing?' cried Maria and wrested the cane from her mother's hand.

'I was only threatening her,' said Anna Seetoh. She complained that Por Por was behaving like a naughty child and had to be treated like one. Rosiah, the maid, whispered to Maria that her mother had three canes in different parts of the house, for instant punishment of an old parent irremediably cast back into an unmanageable second childhood. The extreme state of poor Por Por's dementia, while it provided relief in making her too timid to venture out on her own, pushed her back into a hopelessly infantile state, making her throw her food about, soil herself, sit in her own puddle, break things. The much harassed Rosiah said she could not manage the old woman single-handed and hinted about going back home to Indonesia.

Por Por looked with frightened eyes at Anna Seetoh with the raised cane, as the latter, so long ago, must have looked at her, in the cruel role reversals of old age.

Maria thought, as she put away the cane and bent to comfort the old woman, 'God, if you're still there and not averse to doing favours even for prodigal daughters, could you take me away before I reach Por Por's pathetic stage?' At the back of her mind was one thought, not fully articulated: 'She will have to go to a home. If Rosiah leaves, I have no choice.' Her world could not bear to include the stench and stains of old age left on the floor, the furniture, in the very air itself.

A feeling of guilt tugged at her, and she dismissed it, thinking, 'No, I must be fair to myself. I couldn't take on the burden of caring for Por Por for the rest of her life.' Her mother was already talking about going to live with Heng's family in Malaysia, to save them from ruin, as God had made clear to her. Her school work was demanding, and when she returned home from school, she wanted to lock herself in her room, away from her mother's querulous complaints about her brother, Rosiah's complaints about her grandmother, her grandmother's helplessness against the devastations of old age.

She said to her grandmother, adopting the firmness of voice one used for a particularly difficult child, 'If you don't behave, Por Por, and do as you're told, no more this,' she held up a cheap imitation jade ring, 'nor this,' she held up an *ang pow* opened to show part of a dollar note. The old woman, probably remembering a biscuit tin filled with her *ang pow* money, had accused Rosiah of stealing it, and could only be pacified with another biscuit tin containing a generous scattering of the red gift packets. In a moment her restiveness vanished, as she decked herself with trinkets and counted the money in the biscuit tin. Her childish regressions were far less perturbing than her occasional recollection of an action involving Bernard. One morning she had suddenly gone into the kitchen scolding Rosiah for not helping her get ready the rice porridge and pickled vegetables for Ah Siong's breakfast. On another occasion, she had suddenly stopped in the middle of a shopping trip in a mall and begun to insist on going back into a shop to get something which Ah Siong had requested her to get for him. It would always reflect well on her dead husband and badly on her, thought Maria sadly, that while he had gone from her thoughts, he remained affectionately lodged in an old woman's memory.

A heaviness of heart, of the unfocussed kind related to the overall sadness of the human condition, descended on Maria as she went into Por Por's room that evening to see if she was well covered against the chill of a coming storm; like a petulant child, Por Por sometimes kicked off her blanket or threw her pillows on the floor. The room smelt of the stale smells of sad decrepitude. The old woman was sleeping peacefully. Every woman on the face of this earth, thought Maria, no matter how wretched her life, should have at least a single day, even a part of a day, of joy and triumph, when she could look into the mirror and say, 'I'm so happy! I'll never be that happy again.' What was that supreme moment for her mother? Perhaps having nothing to do with men, it had everything to do with love of the non-carnal, religious kind, and lay not in her past but somewhere in her future with the conversion of her errant children through her prayers and sacrifices, when she could at last rise from her knees in church and celebrate God's love with her arms lifted high in an ecstatic hallelujah.

'I live for my children,' Anna Seetoh had said dolefully, and her daughter had callously retorted, 'Let us do our own living, Mother. And for goodness' sake, be happy, for no one can do that for you!'

What was Por Por's one single unmitigated joy? It surely had to do with the secret lover. Who had initiated that act of love in the warm hiding place provided by the temple? When Por Por stood before the mirror, laughing and smiling at herself in those gaudy trinkets, was she seeing a pretty young girl with her hair in plaits wearing the cheap plastic earrings that had been a secret gift from her lover? The costume that young village girls wore in those days, comprising cloth trousers tied at the waist with string and a cloth jacket with a row of tight frog buttons, was surely a challenge to the lover's trembling fingers, impatient to touch the pure, white young body inside. Between Por Por's moment of sweet daring in the distant past and her own, to be experienced in the very near future in a hotel room in Europe, lay her mother's long blameless, joyless womanhood. Had her imagination, incurably romantic, invested Por Por's experience with a false radiance when it had only been the squalid ground of a rundown temple, full of muddy patches and chicken droppings, followed by the greater squalor of a faithless love, ruthless parents and a ruined life?

One day, she thought, she would write a story about her grandmother's life. It would be a very short story: *She was born, was brought up in a poor village in China, was taught to be obedient, was threatened with punishment if she dared to disobey and be different from the other girls in the village. Then one day, she dared to disobey and be different – she secretly met the man she loved in a temple and experienced the happiest moment of her life. But it was exactly that – a moment only. Soon she was brought back in disgrace, punished by her parents, married off to an opium addict, bullied by all her in-laws in the household, brought to Singapore, despised by everyone including her own daughter as being stupid and incompetent and burdensome, and was finally devastated by the madness of old age.*

The whole of Por Por's life could be written in the passive voice, since she was lived, not living, except for that one moment of glory, one third way through the story, when the active voice proudly proclaimed that she rose in rebellion, dared to defy society and secretly went to meet the man she loved.

Por Por could not take her eyes off her grand-daughter, the bright red silk dress she was wearing, nor the pearl earrings, the pearl necklace, the beaded handbag, the high-heeled shoes. She touched each item reverently with her hands, her eyes wide with wonder. Then she looked at Maria's carefully made-up face and gently pressed two fingers on her bright pink lips.

Rosiah laughed and said, 'Miss Maria, Por Por wants to go to the party with you!' Even Anna Seetoh smiled in amusement, without losing the usual frown of worry and despondency.

Maria said, 'Por Por, if you behave and eat up your dinner, I will take you to the party.'

She had the idea to amuse the old one the next morning by letting her wear the pearl earrings and necklace and carry the beaded purse. Even small indulgences could add up to a happy life for the old one in her few remaining years.

Prepared for an evening of mild diversion at the Polo Club Ball, she had no idea of the shock that awaited her. It should have been no shock that Dr Phang was there, for the ball was a grand public event and he was known to be a much desired presence at many glittering functions, having once casually remarked to her that he and Olivia had more invitations than they could accept.

Meeta, suddenly noticing him, whispered to her, 'Hey, look, there's your beau over there.'

Winnie turned to look and whispered, 'He's with his wife and other couples, but I'm sure he'll come up and ask you for a dance, just to have the chance of holding you! Let us know!'

She turned to say to Freddie who, Maria had concluded within five minutes of meeting him, was unbearably boring:

'You mustn't get jealous when a handsome man comes up and asks Maria for a dance!' Then both Meeta and Winnie, lost in the pleasurable company of their respective partners, forgot about everyone else.

A jealous woman, it was said, had multiple, all-seeing eyes, so that even if she sat still and never moved once, she could see every small action of her man in every part of the room. A woman's jealousy was always born of a deep sense of personal outrage: the man who ought to be paying attention to her was ignoring her and attending to another woman. Jealousy turned its sharpest focus on the rival, noting her every small response, every small look and gesture, to assess the seriousness of the rivalry. A jealous woman was the most tormented woman, her body sprouting a hundred quivering antennae to catch the warning signals to respond to the humiliation of being completely ignored, even of being ridiculed by the laughing, flirting, cavorting pair.

Suddenly aware of this most unmanageable of emotions swelling dangerously inside her, Maria struggled to maintain a calm outward presence, trying to listen politely to Freddie who was talking endlessly about his two teenaged children and their school activities. They were at present on holiday with their mother, and he would join them as soon as his work commitments allowed him.

'I'm going to make a call to them,' he said looking at his watch and rising from the table. 'This is about the right time. They shouldn't be in bed yet.' Maria wished that his phone call would last the entire evening, so that she could concentrate on dealing with this new feeling that was threatening to overwhelm her. It filled her with rage and shame, with hatred directed outwards toward the whole world, and inwards toward herself. Never in her life had she been in such a maelstrom of conflicting thoughts and feelings, which was threatening to toss her around like a small helpless creature in a whirlwind, and then smash her to the ground.

She had no right to be jealous of Olivia Phang. Indeed, how could she, how dared she? The head could only whisper its reproaches which were instantly drowned out in the roar of the heart's anguish. It was the anguish of something even more primitive, because more sexual, felt in one's very groins, linked to the deepest core of one's very survival and sense of being. If all life forms were born competitive, surely Nature designed jealousy as the most effective tool against the competitor?

She watched, without appearing to be watching as she desultorily took sips of wine and fanned herself, Dr Phang looking affectionately into his wife's laughing face during the dancing, twirling her, pressing his cheek against hers, at one stage pressing her body to his with both arms so that, with eyes closed, they seemed to have drifted into some intimate dream-sleep together while swaying sensuously to the music.

As she watched, she experienced sharp pangs of a feeling hitherto alien to her. She had seen it in her own husband as he lay on his deathbed and hurled wild accusations at her, and had dismissed it as pure hallucination. She had seen it in Meeta when Byron paid gallant attention to the pretty women in the Polo Club dining room, and had dismissed it as childish nonsense. Now jealousy, provoked by a man dancing with his own wife with the loving intimacy expected of happily married couples, was unaccountably gripping her like a vise and causing sharp pangs that would be relived again and again in painful solitude. No pain was greater than when a woman reproached herself for it.

Mixed with the jealousy was a growing anger. While she was on the dance floor with Freddie, he had waved to her, and that was all the recognition of her presence for the entire evening. He did not even have the courtesy to come up to their table to greet her, much less ask her for a dance. 'Hey, maybe he doesn't like your new look,' giggled Winnie. 'Next time, change your look. Those pearl earrings make you look older.' Meeta returned to the table with Byron, panting, fanning herself and laughing after their wild gyrations to rock music, and was immediately pulled up by him to return to the dance floor once more. She whispered into Maria's ears as she rose from her seat, holding Byron's hand, 'Just watch your beau with that beauty. No wonder he's not paying any attention to you!'

The beauty was not Olivia but a woman friend from his table who had come with her own partner, a portly, moustached Caucasian. The jealousy she had felt towards Olivia was suddenly transferred to this woman and surged with every moment of watching her as she danced with the man who had whispered into her ear, in the parked car only a week ago, 'I'm looking forward. You have no idea!' Outwardly she was holding a conversation with the dull Freddie by simply timing her nods and smiles to the pauses in his interminable boasting about his accomplished children, but her gaze never left the boisterously happy dancing pair. She detected a special quality in his attentiveness to this woman that she had not seen in his behaviour towards his wife. The woman looked in her forties and was extremely attractive. Perhaps it was her imagination, now in full speculative mode, that saw a secret mutual delight lighting up their faces as they danced, laughed, clapped and hugged each other, as if flaunting a secret liaison in a public place, right under the noses of his unsuspecting wife and the Caucasian partner. Olivia was herself dancing with merry abandon with different dance partners, and for the time being, was too busy enjoying herself to be bothered with the usual vigilance.

She was almost certain that Dr Phang and the woman he was taking repeatedly to the dance floor were having or were about to have an affair. Here was a man who, while planning to meet up with her secretly in Europe in a week's time, was bestowing undue attention on other women, reducing her to one more casualty along his trail of selfish pleasure. In a single moment, the fires of enraged jealousy had reduced all the happiness of the past few months to dust and ashes in her mouth. They could have been instead the sweet spring waters of deep contentment increasing her eagerness for that secret meeting in Europe. If, in the midst of all that open intimacy with Olivia, all that flamboyance with the attractive woman, he had managed to slip to her table for a moment, to touch her hand furtively, to say a word or two from their shared stock of code words, such as 'silken bed' and 'Sheherazade', and then quickly gone back to his carousing with his wife and other women, she would have felt truly happy. Her sense of self would not only have been intact, but strengthened, their understanding of each other richly deepened. As it was, she rose from a scene of such devastation that she surprised herself by her calm, matter-of-fact voice as she gathered up her shawl and handbag and said to Freddie, 'I'm not feeling too well, and would like to go back.' Freddie rose too with a look of concern, but she stopped him saying with a smile, 'It's alright, Freddie. Just a headache. Meeta and Winnie know I get it often. Don't let me spoil your fun. I can easily get a cab back,' and she was gone. Inside the taxi, she thought angrily, 'He will not even notice my absence.'

The pain of jealousy cried out for a salve which would be denied. Tossing about on her bed, she thought of what must at the same time be taking place in the fun-filled Polo Club with its music and merry-makers, its myriad gold and silver balloons decorating the ceiling, that, at the end of the ball, would be pulled down by the men to give to their ladies or playfully burst against their glittering dresses, bejewelled fingers, stiletto heels. Meeta and Winnie would already have been told by Freddie about her sudden departure; they might have looked meaningfully at each other, and then forgotten her completely in the resumption of happy dancing, drinking and laughing with their partners.

Had *he* noticed her absence? The situation might have been saved even then. If he had excused himself from his table and gone to make a quick secret call – 'Hi, Maria, why did you leave? I was going up to claim a dance from you!' – the darkness stifling her heart would have lifted, and she would have turned off the lights and gone to sleep peacefully. As it was, she lay awake listening to the relentless ticking of the clock by her bed. She must have drifted into a deeply troubled sleep, for when she woke up suddenly and looked at the clock, it was already 3 AM, two hours past the official closing time of the ball. He would have gone off home with Olivia; could he already have made plans with the attractive woman to meet for a quick tryst before his trip to Europe, and if he had, could he already be planning, with ease and flair, to make her his new, proud conquest?

Sexual jealousy was more destructive than a simple green-eyed monster that could be searched out and destroyed; it was a flame that consumed from within.

'Well?' he called to ask, a few days before he left for Europe. 'So are we all set for the great adventure?'

She could hear his shock when she said, 'I think not.'

'What?'

'I'm not going after all.' There was a brief silence when the man must have wondered what was the next best thing to say without initiating the argument or confrontation he had always avoided. His quick thinking mind could have grasped the reason for her sudden change of mind, for in his time, he must have had much experience of women's jealousies. If it did, his cheerful nonchalance would have dismissed it as just so much inconsequential behaviour expected of females. In any case, the few minutes allowed for the surreptitious call from his office when the spying clerk had left the room for something permitted only the usual hurried exchange.

'Well, as you wish. May I call you when I come back?'

'As you wish.'

Twenty-Eight

She had a thought to do something which, in her entire career of nearly twenty years as school teacher she had never done: call in sick for a sickness not legitimated by the strict procedures governing civil service behaviour. Medical leave was allowed for teachers who had flu, stomach disorders, pneumonia, morning sickness; the misery of sleeplessness and lack of appetite owing to the devastating effects of jealousy was not a certifiable ailment and had to be borne in silence. The thought of dragging herself out of bed and facing her students and colleagues when she would have preferred to lie under a warm coverlet, in a quiet, darkened room, alone with her thoughts, made her first reach out for the telephone to put a call to the school clerk, then to put it down again. No, the alternative would have been worse: explanations and more explanations to her mother and the maid for a school day spent at home and later, upon her return to school, to concerned, inquiring students and colleagues. The explanations would involve the tedium of pretence and falsehood that would weigh her down.

Mrs Neo would have been the first to make an inquiry, for the simple reason that only the two of them held a perfect record of school attendance. Mrs Neo, who was not particularly friendly towards her, had once put an arm around her to announce to no one in particular, 'Maria Seetoh and I have never once been absent from school; we each ought to be given a gold medal!' Madam Khoo who was on medical leave at least once a month, and, rather suspiciously, on a day that coincided with the eve of a public holiday or a weekend, thereby enabling her to enjoy a nice stretch of days, happened to be present and immediately congratulated Mrs Neo, in a loud voice, for being blessed with the extraordinary good health not enjoyed by many.

Jealousy gouged out holes in a woman's sense of self-worth that could only be filled by proportionate contrition and amendment on the part of the man who had started it all. Surely Dr Phang, however hectic his schedule during the one week he was in Europe, could have called? Anna Seetoh and the maid noticed the eagerness with which Maria, upon returning home from school, rushed to the phone to check for voice messages and again rushed to pick it up even in the midst of a shower or meal. 'I miss you.' 'How I wish you were here with me right now.' 'Last night I dreamt about you.' The lover's banalities, once laughed at and dismissed, were now hankered after, like so much soothing balm for those terrible gaping wounds of hurt pride. A jealous woman's raw nerves tingled to the sound of even the remotest promise of a message – a car engine, the doorbell's ring, a knock on the door.

In one of her many troubling dreams at night, a call had come from him, but she could not hear what he was saying. 'What? What?' she screamed, as the voice became more muffled and was lost in a chaos of background noises. In the end, in great frustration, she put down the phone. In another dream, she was with him in a hotel room; it looked shabby, unlike the plush one she had expected in a plush European hotel. She was wearing a black negligee and lying on the bed. He approached her, saying, 'My, what a beautiful body you have!' and made to touch her breasts. She pushed his hands away and said angrily, 'No, go back to that woman. I know she's here somewhere in this hotel, waiting for you. I saw her just now, but she hid behind some plants when she saw me.' He said, 'Do be reasonable. There's no one. Now, my dearest –', but she pushed him off the bed, screaming, 'Have you any idea how much pain you're causing me?' 'Alright, as you wish,' he said, and left the room. When she woke up, she saw that her pillow was wet with tears.

Thankfully, her mother and the maid never asked questions, though she was sure they were observing her closely, and also thankfully, neither did Meeta and Winnie who were currently engrossed in their respective affairs. Winnie must be the only winner in the hideous game of love and romance being played by them all, for she called to tell Maria, in a voice trembling with excitement, that she and Wilbur had got engaged and would be married soon, after which she was likely to leave Singapore and settle down with him in Washington.

Meeta called once to give the same news dressed up with her usual scepticism. 'She's wearing a big diamond engagement ring. Bought with her own money. That Asian-American by now must have found out how much of family property remains in Malacca and is busy doing his sums. They're buying an apartment in Washington. Also with her money.'

Maria refrained from asking about Byron because Meeta's total silence about him could only mean one thing: her hopes had fizzled out, like the balloons he had playfully tied to the back of her chair on the night of the ball, with the appearance of a new girlfriend on his horizon or the reappearance of an old one. Maria thought bitterly: every woman eventually gets burnt in a game whose rules favour the men. Right now, the flames consuming her had by no means run their course. She was a fool to have got into the game in the first place.

She remembered something her mother had once told her about a woman, a distant relative of Por Por, who was so jealous of the new wife whom her husband had brought into the household that she poisoned the other two wives against her, until the poor girl, who was only sixteen years-old, one morning tied a rope round a staircase railing and hanged herself. By no means abated, the woman's jealousy then turned to target the two wives, particularly the younger and prettier one who was summoned to the man's bed more frequently than the rest. Sexual jealousy often had recourse to supernatural help in the form of secret potions to be put in the man's food or drink for immediate re-direction of his passion and lust.

The modern educated woman was not above making secret trips to fortune-tellers and witch doctors to dispose of her rival: Venerable Mother of the White Heaven Temple, despite her claims to harm no one, was said to have dispensed amulets and other charms that purportedly harmed only those truly evil women who broke up homes, destroyed marriages and caused other women to commit suicide. In the old days, the man, by virtue of his traditional standing as the lord and master in the household, was spared the messiness of a woman's jealousy. If the jealousy happened to be his, he had no need for furtive visits to fortune-tellers and shamans, for he had all the backing of tradition to simply, openly get rid of her. There was a woman who her husband suspected of having an affair with the grocer and thought of setting a trap. But that was too much bother, so he simply gave her a beating and then told her to pack her belongings and return to her parents' house.

His modern counterpart was less fortunate, and indeed could bear the full brunt of his partner's jealousy. Emily told endless stories, with much relish, about how a highly educated woman, enraged at discovering secret love letters hidden in secret places in her husband's office, stormed into it, scattering files, sweeping things off his desks, breaking whatever could be broken. Then, to make her revenge commensurate with the enormous pain she was suffering, she marched into his boss's office and revealed that her husband had been complicit in some nefarious scheme years ago that had cost the company millions of dollars. Sometimes hard evidence was not necessary for a woman to fly into a jealous rage: a woman who saw a pretty waitress talking to her husband while serving him soup during dinner in a restaurant instantly stood up, slapped the waitress and then demanded to see the manager to have her sacked.

Maria thought, in a confusion of thinking that invariably ended with painful self-misgivings: I have no right to be jealous. *I have not even slept with him.* Jealousy claimed prospective rights: she *was* going to sleep with him. It was simple reasoning to which the heart must eventually submit: if you are so tormented with jealousy now, how much more when you have crossed the line and staked your territory? The flames will become an inferno, the flood a deluge. You will be utterly destroyed. Amazed at how little control she had over an emotion so primitive yet so enduring, she thought desperately, No, I can't go through with it.

She thought of the sheer absurdity of being continually tormented at the thought of him celebrating Valentine's Day with his wife, celebrating her birthday, their wedding anniversary, sleeping on the same bed as her every night. Betty told her about a girlfriend, the mistress of a highly successful corporate lawyer, who could not even bear the thought of his wife's picture in his wallet and made him remove it. Imagine the greater torment of a hundred suspicious thoughts each time he went outside marital territory to speak amiably to more attractive, younger women. There would always be countless such women in his orbit. Jealousy, suspicion, anger, humiliation – she could not survive their combined power. Jealousy was part of love's package which she was a fool to think she could approach with a fine selectivity: select in the passion and laughter and pleasure, select out the jealousy and the ugly, painful realities. No woman had ever managed to do that.

She had made up her mind. In the end, in the pursuit of a happy, peaceful, good life, mind was to be more trusted than the passions and urges of the heart. Like a willful, unruly child, the heart wandered dangerously close to the edge, and the head had to pull it back. She was a survivor.

Mr Ignatius Lim called her into his office. 'Green tea? It's the best for health,' he said, pouring out a cup for her. Then he put on his glasses and looked through a very impressive-looking black leather folder. 'Ah, here it is!' He wanted to consult her, he said, on a very important matter that was connected with the current national campaign for greater productivity. The great TPK and his ministers had decided that for Singapore to stay ahead in an increasingly competitive world, there had to be greater productivity in the country's industries, a greater effort put in by the people in all domains of activity. 'Here's where we come in,' said Mr Ignatius Lim enthusiastically. 'Education. We must prove that we too can contribute towards national productivity. And how do we do that? By making a more efficient use of our resources, by re-ordering our priorities.' He loved the jargon of official talk – 'resources', 'efficient', 'priorities' –

which rolled with ease upon his tongue. Miss Seetoh's creative writing class, he explained politely, could not be a priority compared to other more urgent needs. He was consulting her about how best to put his idea into operation: converting it into a Language Remedial Teaching class that would focus on the needs of students who were always failing their exams because of their poor grammar. In an offhand way, he hinted that the results of last year's English language exams were not as good as they should be. 'Miss Seetoh,' he said earnestly. 'Don't misunderstand me. I don't mean that short-story writing, play writing, poetry, all that stuff, isn't important. I did literature in school and enjoyed it. *Friends, Romans, countrymen, lend me your ears!* Even acted in a school play once. But it's a luxury. Bread and butter first, I say, before we can go on to cake and sweets!' He laughed heartily. 'What do you say, Miss Seetoh?'

He did not like her obduracy; after a while, his smiles faded away and he said, 'Alright, Miss Seetoh. You will please put up a position paper to justify the continuance of your creative writing class.'

Maria said coldly, 'There's no need for any position paper, sir. I can't stop you if you want to shut down the class. But let me tell you this: it will be a sad day for the school if by priority you mean only the passing of exams.' 'That will be all, Miss Seetoh,' he said brusquely, and from that moment the battle lines were drawn. He liked to quote the great TPK: 'Those who are not for me are against me,' and Miss Maria Seetoh had decidedly placed herself on the other side.

'Brother Phil, I need to talk to you,' she said to him later that day.

'I know,' he said. 'I know all about this productivity campaign.'

'No, it's not that,' said Maria, 'it doesn't bother me one jot.'

'Is it about Maggie?' asked Brother Philip warily and Maria replied, 'No, it's much worse. It's about me.'

'Alright, we'll have to make it tomorrow. Same café? I'll be wearing the shirt and trousers again to remain incognito.' He had worn the frightfully gaudy batik shirt given by someone who had bought it at a beach resort in Bali when they had gone looking for Maggie.

Maria smiled and said, 'There! You've made me feel better already.'

It was almost on impulse that she had decided to confide in Brother Philip the secret she had been at pains to keep from him. The burden of the secret had become too great not to seek discharge; no real unburdening, only a superficial sharing could take place with the longtime friends Meeta and Winnie. She had previously avoided talking to Brother Philip, a religious man with limited experience and permanently sworn to celibacy. Now for precisely these reasons, she was seeking him out. Perhaps it was the kindness in his eyes or the simple honesty written all over his person.

She had worried about the sheer embarrassment of telling the Moral Education teacher of St Peter's about her plans for a secret rendezvous in a European hotel with a married man, but the telling was surprisingly easy. They were sitting in a coffee-house, and while she poured out her heart, for the first time, to any living being, he sipped his coffee calmly, now and again pausing to look at her. She told him about the unspeakable agonies of a jealousy that was even then troubling her dreams at night and filling her mind with angry thoughts of revenge by day. 'I am not myself,' she ended dispiritedly. 'Please advise me.'

'You go on doing what you've been doing, Maria.'

'What on earth do you mean?'

'Exactly that. I've never come across anyone who thinks and feels as much, as deeply, as agonisingly as you do. Nor anyone who asks for advice she has no intention of following.'

'That's not fair, Brother Phil!' 'That's the truth, Maria. You're okay.' 'Right now, I feel rotten.' 'That's okay too.' 'You're no help at all, Brother Phil!'

'I never intended to be. Now let's go for a proper meal. The stuff in his café is inedible. Let me pay this time. I can afford it.'

'Hey, Brother Phil, I feel so much better already. If it were not for your awful robe of innocence, I think I could give you a kiss.'

'And if it were not for awful gossipers like Mrs Neo, I would return it.'

She thought, 'Dear, dear Brother Phil. Of all the men in my life, I like him best of all.' Loving a man, falling in love with a man, liking him. Women like her had best stick to the last.

He had some serious advice for her, which he said he dispensed to everyone who came to him, regardless of the nature of their problem: get outside yourself, step out of your skin and into another's. It works every time.

Maria did not enjoy getting under her mother's skin, layered over with years of anxious pleasing of her god by saving souls for him, like catching fish in a net or gathering grain in fields white with harvest, now that her own was assured of a place in heaven.

Anna Seetoh said, 'Heng has agreed to take instructions in the faith. Father Rozario has arranged for his assistant Father Dominic to give him the instructions every week.'

With Heng's conversion would come his renunciation of the deadly sin of greed, surely the cause of all his problems. At the back of Anna Seetoh's mind was the eventual conversion of his wife, now still worshipping temple deities, the devil's very own, and of course, the poor son who, for all they knew, was a victim of Satanic powers. She had given Heng a bottle of blessed water she had brought back from her pilgrimage to Lourdes, to sprinkle on his bed every night. Maria thought, poor, poor Mother. It would be impossible to get under her skin to understand how she was allowing the unscrupulous Heng to exploit her religiosity. In the same breath that she had told Maria about his responding well to Father Dominic, she confided, with a sad shake of her head, that he had gone back to the 4-D lottery.

Maria said severely, 'Mother, that large sum of money he's got from me for his share of the flat – why don't you keep it for him in your bank account? He's going to blow it all up, let me warn you.'

Anna Seetoh always ended any heated argument about her reprobate son with words of unshakeable trust, her eyes lifted heavenwards: 'The good God will never let me down,' citing cases of sinners brought back, the sick healed, the fallen raised. Her greatest triumph would be the return of the blackest sheep of the Church of Eternal Mercy in her own daughter, 'You mark my words, Maria. You talk big now, but one day, you will come crawling back to our Lord and His Blessed Mother and they will receive you with open arms.'

Maria hated the picture of the ultimate humiliation the word conjured: herself on abject hands and knees before God and his pantheon of saints including her dead husband, V.K. Pandy in similar locomotion of forced humility before the great TPK, a whole society in humble obeisance to what was being described as the most powerful deity in Singapore, the acronymic god of the material five Cs of Cash, Car, Condominium, Credit Card and Country Club Membership.

Her moral report card from dear, wise, kind Brother Philip would show, alas, the red marks of failure for her behaviour to her own family. It would fare a little better regarding Mark and Yen Ping. It surprised her that despite the tight net of vigilance thrown around them by Mark's mother, they managed sometimes to wriggle through the tiny interstices, like small desperate fish, to meet and exchange love notes and poems. But the net was getting tighter and crueller, and they racked their brains to outwit it.

Yen Ping said, one afternoon, after the creative writing class, 'Miss Seetoh, Mark and I need your help.' Their plan seemed a simple one: once a week in the evening, Mark would be chauffeured to and back from his maths tutor's home; on the way back, could he occasionally drop by at Miss Seetoh's house to pick up notes from Yen Ping and leave his for her? It would take seconds, if Miss Seetoh would allow the maid to be the messenger; Mark would be all the while in the car, never out of sight of the watchful chauffeur. Mark would of course have told his mother beforehand that kind Miss Seetoh was helping him with some useful points for English grammar or creative writing, and if she insisted on taking a look, he would have enough material as proof.

Maria, astonished at the vast scheme of deception of the young lovers who continued to look as innocent and pure as children, could only marvel at their strength of purpose. She had never seen them together since Mark was taken out of St Peter's by his mother, so it came as a shock when, one afternoon, instead of the usual routine of Rosiah going up to the waiting car with the putative teaching notes from Miss Seetoh, she saw them both together, standing at the foot of a flight of stairs leading to her flat, well out of sight of the waiting chauffeur. 'Miss Seetoh, I'll explain later,' whispered Yen Ping, and the lovers spent the few stolen minutes talking in low voices to each other, their foreheads almost touching, their hands inside each other's. Yen Ping demurred about how they had arranged the meeting, keeping even the trusted Miss Seetoh out of love's secret daredevilry, but showed her, with tears sparkling in her eyes, a poem she had written for Mark entitled 'Dear Heart' and his response entitled 'Soulmate.'

Brother Philip said, 'Maria, if I were you, I would be more careful about being part of those kids' secret meetings.'

'Poor kids, I feel happy for them,' sighed Maria. 'I think I understand them perfectly, for I not only got into their skin but was able to crawl around!'

The date of Dr Phang's return from Europe was not marked on her calendar, but it stood out as if circled by a huge red reminder of both threat and promise. He called at last on the third day of his return. 'Well?' He was inviting her to lunch, clearly having decided to go back to square one and start all over again. In the jargon, there was nothing to lose. She had meanwhile lost much, mainly her peace of mind. Honesty – she had always prided herself on that and there had been little of it in her erstwhile foray into the perilous world of secret passion. The greatest peril, jealousy, once it reared its head, went on a rampage of destruction, sparing nothing, not even the basic sense of truth and fairness, for women, enraged at the sight of cheating men, forgot that they were in the cheating game themselves. If she were ever to be destroyed by any emotion, it would be jealousy. She never wanted to encounter that monster again.

'Well?'

'I think not.'

'But what do you *feel*?'

'I feel not too.'

'Well, don't think or feel then. Come and just tell me your stories. I miss my Sheherazade!'

Twenty-Nine

The news circulated far more effectively in the underground grapevine of the coffee shops and private homes than it could ever have had through the official media. In fact, it was not mentioned at all in any of the newspapers, the radio news bulletins or on TV, not even as an unverifiable rumour best dismissed. Singaporeans were whispering to one another, 'Have you heard? V.K. Pandy's dead.' Nobody could trace the source of the news, but it was said to be a very reliable one, a nephew from India who had made known that his uncle had died in the ancestral village that he had returned to shortly after his departure from Singapore. How did he die? Even the nephew was not sure. Probably a broken heart. He had died a sad, disillusioned man and on his deathbed had expressed the wish to return to Singapore which he said he would never forget, for it had been a beloved home for so many years.

If death softened the image even of the authoritarian leader or the corrupt politician, it invested the much-battered political opponent with an aura of sanctity and martyrdom. Suddenly from the depths of his humiliation, he rose to new, awed recognition. Suddenly, everyone felt profound admiration for the dead V.K. Pandy, mixed with an overwhelming pity for the remembered V.K. Pandy whose sufferings at the hands of a ruthless government had surely been a living hell. The image of the man, solitary in the vast space in Middleton Square, reduced to a position of beggary through no fault of his own came back to seize the imagination and tug at the heart. While Singaporeans had gone about their business of making money and fattening their 5 Cs on an already overladen table of plenty, the poor man had stuck to his principles and in the process lost everything – his business, his house, his health. While they walked by quickly, their heads lowered in fear of being seen, he had been the solitary, unafraid voice in the wilderness until struck down.

Nobody could remember what ideology he preached but everybody recalled the pathetic sight of the man when he called to a heedless crowd hurrying past, waving his pamphlets at them as he sat on a stool in the sun in his shabby, sweat-soaked shirt and tie, and thanked the small children and maids sent to put donations in his hands, while the furtive donors looked on from a discreet distance. It was never verified that when he lost his seat in parliament, he squatted on the ground and cried like a child, but that image too was conjured up in uneasy collective memory.

Guilt came quickly on the heels of pity, and some Singaporeans began asking, at least in the private tribunal of the conscience: had a whole society been unfair to V.K. Pandy? Beside the wretched man, now dead and his ashes cast into the waters of the holy Ganges, the great TPK, still very much alive with the thrusting jaw and jabbing forefinger, looked a much diminished human being. His huge juggernaut of control and punishment, like the iconic giant tank about to mow down the little man standing in front of it and calmly blocking its way, was now an enduring symbol of oppression of all and sundry who dared to oppose him. The indomitability of the human spirit, courage, strength of will, sanctity of purpose, all hitherto only vague abstractions with little relevance in a society committed to getting and spending, suddenly became palpable realities deserving serious thought and discussion.

Maria, quite by accident, watched the beginning of a scene that she would remember for the rest of her life. It was Saturday morning, and she was as usual in the dispensary at Middleton Square, looking idly upon the spot vacated by the poor V.K. Pandy, now a spirit hovering somewhere over the vast Ganges, when she suddenly noticed a small object on the ground close to the spot where the opposition member often placed his wooden stool. She looked more closely: it was a small bunch of yellow flowers wrapped in white plastic, tied with a white ribbon. Somebody had placed a memorial bouquet for the dead man. Then she saw a woman approaching, holding the hand of a little boy who held a bunch of red and white carnations, tied with a large white bow. The woman whispered something to the child, and he placed the flowers close to the first bouquet. The woman then stood, with her head bowed for a few seconds, before hurrying away with the child: was she saying prayers for the repose of V.K. Pandy's soul, or saying sorry for the time when her little boy broke from her to smile at the outcast and she rushed to pull him away, terrified of those surveillance cameras?

Maria decided that as soon as she had delivered the asthma medicine to her mother, she would return to watch what promised to be a most unusual happening in Singapore.

'This is unbelievable,' she gasped, as she looked upon the floral tributes now occupying a large stretch of ground.

In the half hour that she had taken to return to the scene, the offerings had multiplied. There were elaborate bouquets as well as simple single stalks, some carefully wrapped in transparent gift wrapping paper, all neatly laid side by side, with the merest overlapping, each visitor claiming space for the full display of his or her offering of respect and regard, while being mindful of the claims of others. And still they came. Each bent to place the tribute, then withdrew to make way for others, staying on to join the crowd that had gathered to watch. The flowers on the ground were building up to an immense carpet of richest hues, and still they grew. Nobody made the slightest sound, as if the silence of profound awe were better than any rhetorical tribute. In the distance, the sounds of moving traffic could be heard, but in the square itself, perfect silence reigned.

Who were these Singaporeans? As far as Maria could tell, they were the ordinary men and women who daily walked the busy streets and frequented the bustling shopping malls and open eating places of the clean, bright city. They represented the widest possible spectrum of Singapore society, coming from plush offices in the city's busiest business district and the most rundown of old shophouses tucked inside Chinatown. She saw a woman in her thirties, dressed in a smart black business suit and carrying a leather briefcase, walk up, place a spray of purple orchids, then return to her waiting Mercedes. She watched a middle-aged man – was he the same man who had vigorously declined to take pictures of Big Bird that day? – arrive with a woman who was probably his wife; she carried a small bunch of lilies that looked like a delicate bridal bouquet and placed it gently beside the business woman's orchids. A group of three women who looked like school teachers had a joint offering of a large bunch of white roses which one of

them placed reverently on the ground while the other two
looked on. There was a small transparent jar filled with water,
carrying a single stalk of some unidentifiable orange flower
that would outlast all the other offerings in the late morning
heat. A little girl of about six, holding several stalks of gladioli,
opened her mouth to say something to her mother but closed
it again when she saw the silencing maternal forefinger raised
and placed against the lips. A man profusely sweating in a
dirty shirt and shoes must have taken time off from his work
at a construction site or some road repair works, holding in
his hand a little bunch of dahlias that had probably cost him
his lunch. Another man who looked like a cook, wearing a
white singlet still carrying stains from his kitchen, came with
a woman who must have hurriedly changed into neat skirt
and blouse; she placed a small basket packed with tiny golden
showers and ferns and then bowed her head reverently. An old
woman in a wheelchair, and an elderly man with a walking
stick – V.K. Pandy was also attracting the sick and disabled
who had come, not to seek healing but to pay their respects to
one whom society had injured beyond healing.

There were envelopes with cards inside, lying among the
flowers, with the name of V.K. Pandy written on some of them,
mostly in the awkward block letters of a childish or an unsure
hand. What did they say? What messages did Singaporeans
have for the poor dead opposition member? They could only be
words of praise, condolence, consolation, respect, compassion,
but most of all, praise. The sheer temerity was staggering. Were
not the writers afraid that the anonymity of the messages was
no protection against the cards being traced to them and used
against them at a later date, when it came to getting a job,
getting a promotion, getting a study grant, a business licence?

If there were the dreaded surveillance cameras around, for one single moment in the life of the society, Singaporeans dismissed them and said, We are not afraid. Let us do what ought to be done. For one single moment in the life of a society, a bond of fellow-feeling united Singaporeans, more powerfully than the camaraderie of cheering for the national team in the football stadium, even than of standing together, hand on heart, to sing the national anthem on National Day, because it was unrehearsed and came from the depths of a consciousness too difficult to articulate except through the public act of simple, silent tribute.

It was weird, this spontaneous coming together of Singaporeans who otherwise lived their separate lives and went their separate ways, as if their common purpose had taken a life of its own, moving to its own momentum, growing, swelling, like a huge organism sometimes seen creeping along on forest floors, far bigger than the sum of the millions of tiny creatures that were its component parts which now had no choice but to act in accordance with its will. Nothing of the kind had ever been seen in Singapore.

Maria thought, I have to be part of it, before it disappears. Such an organism had but a short life cycle; soon it would reach its peak, then rapidly decline and vanish into its myriad component parts, each once again helpless on its own. Soon Singaporeans would go their separate ways again and forget they had ever come together that astonishing day to pay their respects to the most denigrated man in their midst.

Remembering a small florist shop behind Middleton Square, Maria dashed to it and was told by the owner that all her flowers had been sold; she had never had such good business. She had some artificial sunflowers, though, that looked like the real thing. 'Quick, give them to me,' cried Maria and was back in

Middleton Square in an instant. She scribbled a short message, 'Dear V.K. Pandy, I do miss you. Maria', and laid it on the artificial sunflowers.

She could not bear to tear herself away from the strange sight, her eyes roaming from the immense carpet of bright blooms to the sombre faces around. She saw a few balloons floating among the flowers and a small teddy bear, as if something connoting joy and celebration and innocence were needed as a counterweight to the sadness of the occasion. Then something caught her eye. It was a blue folder of cuttings of newspaper reports of V.K. Pandy over the years, opened at precisely the page to show him at his moment of greatest triumph, years back, when he unseated a member of the great TPK's party at the general elections; he had a stack of garlands around his neck that came right up to his ears and was waving jubilantly from his perch on the shoulders of cheering supporters with their fists raised in the air. Who was that follower who had loyally kept a record of the vicissitudes of the man's long political career before he returned to die in his ancestral country? Could he have been Big Bird whose loyalty had taken a big risk that day?

A large greyish bird circled overhead, its squawks being the only sound heard in the whole square. Some from the crowd looked up; already in their minds a story was shaping about V.K. Pandy's spirit in the form of a bird, returning to see how Singaporeans were reacting to his death. The story would accrete absurd details as it was passed on: the bird circled a number of times over the crowds; it was an owl and it alighted on one of the bouquets; it was a strange-looking bird that nobody had ever seen before and it alighted on precisely the newspaper cutting showing V.K. Pandy's moment of triumph, staying for a few seconds before flying off again.

A group of tourists in shorts, T-shirts and hats stopped to watch. Curious to know what was happening, they got only apologetic smiles from the locals who moved away. There was enough danger for the day; nobody wanted to take the additional risk of providing information about the political opponent to foreign journalists, especially one from the blacklisted *International Courier*, even if anonymity was guaranteed. A man in his forties whispered something very quickly to a young woman who was scribbling in a reporter's pad, mouthing an urgent condition: 'Don't quote me.'

Maria was sure that a face looking out of a parked car some distance away was that of Dr Phang, but when she moved to have a closer look, the face turned and the car moved off. Was the man there in the capacity of a government spy, since he was a senior officer in the Ministry of Defence? What manner of man was he that while one part was claimed by loyal service to the great TPK, which included the maligning of the great one's adversaries, another part rebelled against the subjection to the point of making secret donations to the arch enemy? She was almost certain that it was through his intervention that the Big Bird incident had not resulted in more fines for V.K. Pandy and his supporters. And what manner of woman was she that while she was now paying tribute to V.K. Pandy, she had actually helped her husband in the crafting of his vicious letters against the poor man to *The Singapore Tribune*? She remembered the rare occasions when she and Bernard had laughed and joked with each other over the letters. Like everyone else, she had been complicit in the tragedy of V.K. Pandy.

She suddenly had the idea to write a letter begging his forgiveness, undeterred by the sheer futility of opening up one's heart to the dead, as she had done once, when she wrote a long letter to Bernard and placed it inside his coffin. Letters to the dead were free of all falsehood, and were useful to the living in bringing relief to an over-charged heart. She would tell him she was so sorry for providing her husband with all those scathing epithets that must have been so hurtful, and would he forgive her?

Very early the next morning, when she went to Middleton Square to lay her letter among the flowers, she found that everything was gone. Overnight, the square had been cleared, and all that remained was a faint scattering of remnants of leaves, ferns and flower petals. She wondered about the fate, in particular, of that file of newspaper cuttings: by now the efficient machinery of surveillance and control would have traced the owner. She looked up, and saw one of the balloons with its long string entangled on a TV aerial sticking out of a building. Then she looked down again and caught sight of a burnt-out stub of a red candle on the ground, half hidden under a scrap of newspaper. Had someone been praying to V.K. Pandy? Obviously, an inveterate Singaporean punter ever on the lookout for the lingering presence of the dead, whether in accident sites or funeral parlours, since they were the most reliable source of winning lottery numbers, had made an unobtrusive appearance in Middleton Square.

Thirty

Winnie's wedding was the only bright spot in a vast desolation of broken, bleeding hearts.

Having made up her mind never to see Dr Phang again, Maria yet waited eagerly for his call for their next meeting. Women were ever Marys who were quite contrary, running away from men, running to them. The last meeting would have to have something of closure and finality about it. She was determined for it to be in the public setting of the Bon Vivant Café or a restaurant, not the dark isolated area of parked cars outside the Botanic Gardens, where, under the combined influence of a beguiling ambience and the man's unfailing charm, she might succumb once more and agree to a love tryst in a hotel room. Their last meeting, after which they would never see each other again, should leave her pride intact, her good spirits restored, her peace of mind assured. Above all, the honesty she never wanted to lose in herself because she valued it so much in others should remain protected. She had been carried away by whatever romantic follies that sometimes overpowered common sense and decency in even the most sensible woman, but had been saved in time, ironically, by that most toxic of all human emotions: jealousy. One day, she thought, she might even say to the fearsome monster acknowledged in song and literature, thank you, you saved me. Right now, she could only cry out, enough, enough of the pain and anger.

Rehearsed speeches, in her experience with Bernard, had been a dismal failure, but she felt they would succeed with the amiable Dr Phang who would listen without the slightest frown on his handsome, open face. She had actually written down the last speech for the last meeting to make sure she got her message across clearly, firmly, truthfully. Until she did that, the waiting would be unbearable, requiring enormous effort to hide her nervous tension while standing in front of her class and teaching them the strategies of avoiding the most common grammar mistakes in the exams.

'Yen Ping, you're crying. What's the matter?' she asked as the girl struggled to hold back her tears. They were sitting at a table in a quiet corner of the canteen where they were not likely to be heard. Mark's mother was abroad on one of her business trips, and she had got her younger sister to stay in the house for the entire duration of the trip to keep an eye on Mark. The sister who took her responsibility very seriously sometimes accompanied him to and from school in the chauffeured car. She had on one occasion done a secret search of Mark's room, and discovered some of the poems that Yen Ping had written to him and also a small teddy bear with their initials sewn into its collar.

'Miss Seetoh, I don't know how long we can go on like this,' said Yen Ping tearfully. She revealed that they had only managed to meet once that week, and only for a few brief minutes, and he had managed to speak to her twice on the phone, also for only a very brief while. They had devised a system of codes for their phone contact. She said, 'Miss Seetoh, next week on Friday,

Mark's auntie won't be able to accompany him to his maths tutor's house; can we meet at your place on his way back?'

The young couple had apparently managed to work out some plan by which the chauffeur would be told that Mark would have to consult Miss Seetoh for half an hour on an important school project, during which time the man would be sent on an errand to town that would take a convenient forty minutes.

Maria said, 'You know, Yen Ping, I don't feel comfortable about all this deceit. I suppose your parents don't know either?'

The girl had already told her parents she had broken up with Mark.

The enormity of their love carved out its own path of explanation and justification; if they told lies, those lies could only be the whitest of white, reflecting the purity of their purpose.

'Yen Ping, let me ask you this,' said Maria hesitantly. 'Do you and Mark feel uncomfortable about all these lies, I mean, I can't imagine either of you deceiving others like this?'

Apparently the pair, still looking like lost babes in the woods, had thought out every move to thwart parental suspicion. Without their being aware of it, they were following to perfection the wise biblical advice to be both dove and serpent. The time of dove was over, and serpent had to take charge to survive the pitilessness of parents.

Yen Ping said, her lips trembling, 'Oh Miss Seetoh, I don't know what we can do without you.'

'Yen Ping,' said Maria looking at her with frowning seriousness, 'I hope you and Mark won't do anything stupid – you know what I mean?'

There had been a dream in which Yen Ping's mother dragged her by the arm to the kitchen, to watch the girl, pale and crying, bent over the sink, retching dreadfully. 'See!' screamed the woman. 'My daughter's pregnant, and it's all your fault. You let them use your bedroom for their secret meetings. You, their teacher! Shame on you!'

Yen Ping tried to hide her shock at Miss Seetoh's unseemly suggestion. 'We promised ourselves that we would remain pure for each other till our marriage, Miss Seetoh.' Neither Mark's Christianity nor her Taoism made any such demand, she explained, but their special love did. 'I'm going to tell you something we've never told anybody,' she said, her eyes shining through her tears. 'We made our promise in blood.'

They had made small incisions in their wrists, mixed their drops of blood and written their initials with it. 'We each have a copy of the promise,' she said, 'and I keep it close to my heart. See?' She pulled out a small silver locket from under her shirt, and opened it to reveal a roll of paper inside. Young love was transcendental, awe-inspiring.

Beside its pure sheen, Meeta's and Byron's affair was all dross. Since the evening of the Polo Club ball, they had been dating, mainly on Meeta's initiative. As he grew more anxious to get out of what was an increasingly tedious affair, she grew more demanding, assuming the rights of the officially acknowledged partner who in the past would have been able to sue for breach of promise and compel the man to marry her.

'I never slept with her,' Byron confided in friends. 'I tried once. Couldn't. That woman's *off-putting*.'

For a while, Meeta tried what she had in the past disdainfully called 'the Winnie exercise in futility'. Thus had she overwhelmed Byron with gifts and favours, such as expensive soup dishes of healthful black chicken and ginseng which she had got the maid to brew for hours, ordering books he had expressed an interest in, that were not available in Singapore's book-stores, looking all over town for a special table lamp he wanted. Byron fled before the avalanche of gifts, sometimes pretending not to be at home when the doorbell rang and he peeped out to see Meeta's formidable person outside, all garbed in bright sari and jewellery, carrying something in her hand.

'Do you think she could be slightly – this?' Byron asked a confidante, twirling a finger against the side of his head to indicate the beginnings of lunacy.

The confidante told him about a woman he once knew who became so unhinged by unrequited love that she stalked the poor man in his office, his home, his favourite hawker centre, and once called him twenty times in one hour, until he had to change his phone number and also the locks in his apartment.

A man by nature too indolent to upset the weaker sex and risk a confrontation, he made all sorts of excuses when Meeta phoned him, until he ran out of them and one evening forced himself to say firmly but very kindly, 'It's no use, Meeta. It's not working. You're a very nice, attractive person, but it isn't working.' At that advanced stage in her infatuation, Meeta was prepared to cling to any shred of hope; the absence of outright hostility was all that it needed to sustain itself. Desperate hope could be pathetic, and the intelligent, perceptive part of Meeta must have occasionally recognised the depths to which it could sink in each desperate excuse to rationalise away his remissness: 'Well, he tends to oversleep when there's a storm. Also, you know how dangerous the roads are when it rains like that.' 'His sister-in-law was on a visit with her children. She's very demanding and requires him to be them all the time.' 'He's confused by his feelings. This is the first time that he's taken a woman seriously. I'll have to be patient.'

It was now Winnie's turn to say, 'Meeta, you're wasting your time; he's simply not interested.'

Safe in Wilbur's love and devotion and happily preparing for her wedding, Winnie was unaware that her advice, confidently and cheerfully given, could only hurt by the sheer contrast in their present positions, a contrast that would be even more pronounced in the future after she left the house they had been sharing for so many years for her new home in Washington.

As soon as the wedding cards were sent out, Meeta's habitual caustic remarks ended. She submitted sullenly to the reality that Winnie now had a man in her life, whereas she had lost all prospect of one. She wanted to have no part in the wedding preparations, saying stiffly, 'I'll attend the wedding dinner, that's all. I can't stand all that noise and fuss from her. She thinks she's the only one in the world who's getting married!'

Her pride recoiled from the thought that friends could be whispering to each other about how Meeta Nair was behaving towards Winnie because of jealousy.

'Me, Meeta Nair, jealous of Winnie Poon? Don't make me laugh!' she said to Maria, and there and then decided to dispel all such notions: she would give her housemate the most expensive wedding present of all, a pair of sapphire earrings that Winnie had once seen in a jeweller's shop and liked very much.

Winnie had whispered to Maria, 'Meeta's behaving strangely, but I understand. I told her not to be serious about Byron. He's been avoiding her.' It fell to Winnie to do something which she said was the most difficult thing in her life. Byron had called her with a message: 'Please tell your friend and housemate Meeta to stop harassing me! I'm fed up with her. Tell her in exactly these words.' Winnie recruited the help of Maria.

'I'm too nervous,' she said in a hushed voice. 'You don't have to say anything, Maria. Just be with me, to give me support.'

To their surprise and relief, Meeta received the message calmly. 'Oh, life goes on!' she said breezily. 'The bastard thinks that he's God's gift to women! Tell that cock to stop thinking the sun rises every morning to hear him crow! Hee, hee!'

At Winnie's wedding reception which was held in a hotel, Meeta was silent and surly-looking throughout, curling a disdainful lip or rolling sceptical eyes each time the much enamoured bridegroom professed his love for his bride in his speech.

'Listen to him,' she muttered, 'All that drivel about eternal love and everlasting devotion. Why can't he be more original? Gives me the goose pimples.'

At one point she turned to whisper to Maria who was sitting beside her, 'Let's see how long all this cooing of the love birds will last. Until her money runs out.'

Maria said, 'Hey, Meeta, come off it! Today's Winnie's big day. Why don't we do this – think all the nice things about Winnie and Wilbur, and all the nasty things about the men who have left us in the lurch. Then we go out and get drunk together!'

Humour could not save the situation for poor Meeta, unable to cope with the sudden good fortune of the housemate who she presumed would go through life depending on her for advice and guidance in matters regarding men. She left the party very soon after, complaining of a headache. Winnie never looked happier or prettier; the services of a professional make-up artist and dress designer had transformed her beyond recognition. Part of her happiness must have lain in the triumphant thought: 'It's Winnie the Blue, Winnie the Blur who's got her man after all, not you two clever, smart-talking women!'

They were, for the third time, in a parked car in the lovers' haunt outside the Botanic Gardens.

'I missed you, Maria,' he said, and would have attempted to pull her towards him except that he sensed a new mood and purpose. 'What is it?' he said gently.

He could accommodate any female mood, humour any female whim. The rehearsed words remained locked in her throat.

She could have begun, 'I can't take it. The jealousy will destroy me,' and he would have simply swept her into his arms with his usual easy smile and laugh of dismissal; she would have aborted the rest of the prepared speech and lain contented against this warm, reassuring, handsome, smooth-talking, very dangerous man.

'Hey, you're crying,' he said and wiped her eyes. He would of course not risk asking her the reason for her tears. Silence was golden, a rich lode he could continually mine to manage women.

They were silent for a while. 'Tell me a story, my Sheherazade. You have so many stories to tell.'

With his other women, he could have said, with the same gentle, reassuring voice, 'Tell me about your Bangkok trip.' 'Tell me about your plans to move to a new apartment.' 'Tell me about your new Persian cat.' *Tell me anything so long as we don't start those tedious explanations and arguments.*

She said, 'Alright,' and felt a surge of new purpose strengthening her for the last story she would ever tell him:

There was a woman called Sheherazade, actually only a pet name given to her by her lover. She lived in Singapore in a small apartment in Ang Mo Kio, which he visited whenever he could get away from his wife or business associates. He loved her because he enjoyed listening to her stories, to the melodiousness of her voice, her habit of gesturing with her small pretty hands as she told the stories. Like her namesake, she postponed the telling of the ending of each story, causing her lover to be in a frenzy of curiosity.

'Please, please, please,' he begged like a wide-eyed child wanting to know what happened next, and next and next. 'Tell me what happens in the end.'

'No, I will only tell you on your next visit,' she said, thus cleverly making sure he would never leave her. Like Sheherazade's enthralled story listener, the wicked sultan who kept postponing her execution to hear the ending of each story, he came again and again to see her in her Ang Mo Kio flat, without of course, his wife's knowledge. But there was one story whose ending *she* wanted so much to know – *their* story. How would it end? Would he leave her? Would he divorce his wife, as he sometimes hinted, and marry her?

One day he told her, rather awkwardly, because he knew she would be very upset: 'This is my last visit. I'm leaving you. I've found another woman.' She was aghast.

'No, no,' she said. 'Another woman? Does your wife know?'

'That's beside the point,' he said, 'For she'll never find out. Besides, I love this woman very much. I've given her a special name – Pearl. In fact, I think I can't live without my Pearl.' She began to cry, and he tried to comfort her.

'These things happen,' he said. 'But we can still be friends, can't we? I may still come to my Sheherazade to hear her wonderful stories, who knows? But for the time being, this is absolutely my last visit.'

She said, her face by now all splattered with tears, 'Please come one more time. I will prepare a special dinner for you. Our last supper, a last story, then a last goodbye.'

'Alright,' he said. So he came for his last meal with her. It was such a delicious meal, of his favourite abalone and mushroom soup, beef noodles, deep fried prawns and the most succulent vegetables, that he felt drowsy afterwards and fell asleep in his chair before he could ask her for her story. A tantalising little thought had occurred to him, just before he fell asleep: 'She will withhold the ending, to make me come again, the clever little thing. But no, this will positively be my last visit!'

As he lay sleeping in his chair, emitting the gentle snores of deep, comfortable sleep, she went into the kitchen and brought out a large knife which she pressed deep into his heart, killing him instantly. As he slumped in the chair, his blood coming out in large pools and spreading rapidly on his shirt, down his trousers and on to the space around his chair, she knelt down beside him, looked at him and said sadly, 'You had no idea, my dearest, how our story would end, had you?'

There was a short silence as Dr Phang, startled by the story as by the earnest, urgent manner of its narration, cast about in his mind for a suitable response without losing his equanimity. His first thought was, 'She is not her usual self. I must be careful.' It was a situation he had never found himself in, but he would not be caught unawares. He would not ask any questions as that would only provoke the impossible questions of hysterical women; he would not make light of the story as its strangeness seemed to demand a serious response. In a few seconds, he had decided on having recourse, once again, to his usual reaction to an angry, accusing woman – a two-fold strategy of deflecting the accusation and pacifying the accuser. Through the marshalling of all his resources of mild persuasion and tender caressing, he would draw her back into a state of calm, smiling mutuality. Looking at the pale taut face beside him and grasping her hands, Dr Phang said with all the gentleness he could muster,

'Dear, don't get upset. Come here.'

Maria broke free from his arms. She said, 'I never want to see you again because we can't go on like this. If I have an affair with you, we'll just end up hating each other.'

That was as close as she could get to verbalising the brutal truth that she had earlier set out at great length in writing. *Affair*. They had always avoided the word with its messy connotations. He made one last attempt.

'Dearest, we love being with each other – that's all that matters.' The word having been uttered, its repetition came more easily.

'If I had an affair with you,' she said earnestly, 'it would always have to be shrouded in secrecy and remorse and guilt. Don't you see?'

He had no answer, so he made certain non-committal sounds and continued to try to take her into his arms.

There had to come a point, even for this supremely self-confident man, when the truth would sink in and he would understand that the game was over. He withdrew, no longer smiling, and sat still in his seat, looking out of the window into the darkness.

'I had no idea,' was all he could say. It was not in his nature to resort to the crude peevishness of the rejected male's parting shot, 'When you grow into an old woman and lose all your attraction for men, you will look back with regret upon this day of missed opportunity.' But he felt the urge to regain a little of the wounded pride by saying drily, 'That was the most spiteful story I'd ever heard. Spitefulness doesn't become you at all, my dear.' Then he started the car engine, and drove her home without a word. When she got out, he said, with a return of the affable smile. 'Well, goodbye, Maria.'

'Goodbye, Benjamin.'

It might have comforted her to know that throughout the rest of his drive back, he gripped the steering wheel so hard that his knuckles stood out like hard, white stones, and that he muttered 'Damn' a few times under his breath. And it might have comforted him to know that as soon as she entered her bedroom and locked the door, she threw herself on the bed, covered her face with a pillow and sobbed silently.

She did not even want to read the daily papers because occasionally there was something about him, usually about his work in the Ministry and the conferences abroad. But about three months later, as she was watching TV and listening to the news presenter, she learnt that he had been sent to Germany on a posting as Singapore's ambassador.

Thirty-One

When she was a little girl of about seven, a neighbour's child one day came over to play with her, attracted by her several dolls, boxes of beads and a plastic tea-set. Later that afternoon, she went to her mother crying, 'My Snow-White's gone! Mee Mee's stolen it!' The neighbour's child must have hidden the doll under her dress and gone home with it.

Anna Seetoh was at that time in the fervid stage of preparing for her conversion to Christianity, when its doctrines and tenets had never been more appealing, ready to flush out every vestige of the old religion and sweep her into a new bright world of hope, purpose and meaning.

'What?' she said to the crying child standing before her holding a large basket containing three dolls and a space where the fourth should be.

Maria again howled, 'Mee Mee's stolen my Snow-White!'

Anna Seetoh said, 'We're going to Mee Mee's house right now.' To the child's puzzlement, she said, pointing to the remaining three dolls in the basket, 'Pick one. We're bringing her along.'

Maria chose her favourite, a cloth doll called Sayang, with a large head and black wool for hair; in the privacy of her little secret space under a table or behind a door, she would often whisper to Sayang her dreams of becoming rich and happy one day, with a room of her own.

'Alright,' said Anna Seetoh, as she and Maria stood before Mee Mee's mother who was wondering about her daughter's frantic efforts to hide behind her back. With the formality of tone required in a religious ritual, Anna Seetoh commanded her daughter, 'Now give that doll to Mee Mee.' Maria stared at her mother. Then all was pandemonium as the full injustice of the command sank in: she had not only lost Snow-White but was about to lose her favourite Sayang to the thieving Mee Mee.

She screamed and made a rush at the frightened girl still hiding behind her mother, shouting, 'Give her back! Give my Snow-White back!' Anna Seetoh managed to pull the beloved Sayang out of her arms and hand it to the thief who was too frightened to take it and continued clinging to her mother who could only say, 'What – what –' in great bewilderment. In the end, looking both confused and worried, she held the cloth doll in a limp hand and watched Anna Seetoh stride out of the house dragging the crying Maria with her. Out on the road, her mother said soothingly, 'One day Jesus will reward you. He sees everything.'

It would be years later that she understood the reason for her mother's strange behaviour that day. Anna Seetoh had taken to heart the biblical message of unlimited magnanimity that God enjoined on all the faithful: you give your neighbour not only your spare cloak but the very one off your back. For a while after her conversion, she gave the message literal application – giving a neighbour two bowls of rice flour when she had come to borrow only one, giving a beggar standing outside the church a dollar and then turning back to drop *another* into his begging bowl.

The breath-taking scope of the charity of the new religion was new for Anna Seetoh; its call for patience and endurance in suffering was not, being simply an extension of the traditional stoicism that she had inherited from an elderly relative who used to talk to her very seriously, even as a child.

'I never learnt anything from your mad Por Por; it was God's mercy that I had your Second Grand-aunt to teach me to be a good person.'

The aunt had instilled in her habits of quiet endurance under the greatest privations, because, she explained, it was a woman's lot in life. Women were born to endure. 'But Sky God hears and sees everything,' she would say, pointing a serene finger to the sky. Sky God's handmaiden, Kuan Yin, the Goddess of Mercy, would never ignore women's cries.

When Anna Seetoh converted to Christianity, it was a simple switch of alliance from the merciful goddess to the gentle Virgin Mary.

Maria had often marvelled at her mother's strength in coping with the many adversities in her life's journey, and concluded that but for her religious faith, she would have been utterly crushed half way through that dolorous vale of tears called other names by her ancestors. But the relentlessness of her god in testing her was not done yet, even in her ageing years. In obedience to his wish, she was making preparations for a new life that would surely call for greater sacrifices; she said she was going to live with Heng and his family in Malaysia and take care of them. They would be in a small town with a church called, very significantly for Anna Seetoh, the Church of the Mother of Mercy. For she had had a dream in which the Holy Virgin had appeared to her and assured that all would be well; Heng would be converted, become a good Catholic, live a good life, and by his example lead his wife to the church too. In the dream she saw the little autistic grandson cured and kneeling, bright-faced, at the altar with all of them and even receiving Holy Communion.

'Then my life's work will be done,' said Anna Seetoh with tears in her eyes, 'and I will die in peace.'

If she had failed in bringing her daughter back to the church while alive, she would succeed in her new role as heavenly intercessor. In her saddest thoughts about her impossible daughter, she had clung to the brightest hopes. Por Por, being too old and beyond anyone's capacity to change, was beyond the pale of her help.

There was something that happened years ago which had made her give up hope of converting her mother. It was a small enough incident: Por Por refusing to throw away a small, chipped porcelain dragon that Anna Seetoh's prayer group had identified as a Satanic object, emanating evil that was spreading in the house. When Maria came to Por Por's defence and actually took over the ornament for safekeeping for her, the two were permanently ranged with the arch-enemy himself beyond the power of earthly help. There was enough filial piety in Anna Seetoh to pray for at least a peaceful death for her mother: who knew what miracle the Merciful Mother of God might work even at the deathbed of an old difficult woman past all hope?

Anna Seetoh said, 'Maria, there's something I've got to ask of you,' and she knew it had to do with the hard realities of financial contingencies, which even her mother, lost in heavenly schemes, would be forced to face at some time.

Apparently, it was a request that Heng had coached her to present very carefully, argument by reasonable argument: since she would no longer be living with her, Anna explained slowly,

Maria would be saving on both the cost of maintenance as well as the monthly allowance. Would she then be so kind as to disburse a sum, a once-and-for-all payment, to enable her mother to begin her new life in Malaysia?

The wily deviousness of her brother once again stung her into a sharp reply, 'Of course you will continue to have your allowance, Mother, as long as I have a job. How can you think otherwise?' She added reproachfully, 'And of course I'll give you whatever you need for your new life in Malaysia.' In her mind, she was working out some quick sums: would she have enough in her bank account to sign a cheque for exactly the amount she had paid out to her brother for his half of the flat? In her mind, she was already making the washing-hands gesture of final severance; any remnant of unease still attached to the inheritance would be cleared away, like a piece of dirt, a stain.

Anna Seetoh said, 'I'll have to get some new furniture, a new fridge, as the old one's broken down, everything's just so pitiful there – ' Maria thought, 'There goes my dream', and the little apartment she had dreamt of, a pretty studio apartment that she had seen advertised in the papers where she would live all by herself, rapidly retreated into the distance and vanished. She wished she had more money. It could buy dreams and vanquish nightmares, including the most horrible ones created by one's own family. Money, even if the filthiest of lucre, could help save family relationships.

It could also save friendships or destroy them. Winnie had told her, with much agitation, that Meeta's very expensive wedding present of the sapphire earrings had been more poison than gift. She had sent it through the maid who arrived, looking very embarrassed, at the hotel where she and Wilbur were temporarily staying before leaving for Washington.

Philomena had said very briefly, 'Ma'am said to give you this,' then left abruptly. There had been no card carrying the felicitations demanded by the occasion.

'I was going to return the gift,' Winnie had confided angrily in Maria, 'but Wilbur said, 'Never mind, honey, don't upset yourself. Just take the gift and forget all about it.' Wilbur's so right. You know what? I'm going to sell it and give the proceeds to charity!' The twenty-year-old friendship had come to an end.

Maria thought with some envy that Winnie was the only one carried along on life's friendly, placid stream, while all around, everyone was tossed about in the dark churning currents of disappointment, disillusionment, fear, anger, greed, lust, jealousy, hate – herself, her mother, Heng's wife, Meeta, Maggie, Yen Ping and Mark. Also poor V.K. Pandy, now freed by death, but not Mrs Pandy who was said to be in India, still struggling with her cancer. And the great TPK's wife who was lingering on in her illness, beyond the power of even the most advanced medical skills. All, all in this tumultous vale of tears, humanity's unavoidable passage in its long journey.

There was another, of course, besides happy, smiling Winnie, being borne along serenely on untroubled waters. Until she subdued the turbulence of feelings inside, she could not even bear to mention his name, although she thought of him often, wondering how he was faring in his ambassador's post in Germany. There had been a dream, a very brief one, in which he was speaking at some glittering diplomatic function, with Olivia sitting beside him. At one point he looked up from his speech and saw her as she stood observing him from behind some tall plants. He waved cheerfully to her, until rebuked by Olivia who turned to her and said angrily, 'Leave my Benjy alone!'

She practised what she had preached to indolent, careless students: don't just make a resolution to work harder, write it down, paste it on the mirror and stare at it every day. Her resolution stared back at her every morning before she left for school: no looking back, only looking forward. She would pull herself out of the quagmire, sluice herself clean with pure water and start working towards a new life.

'Hey, God,' she said, glad that her old irreverence was coming back, a promising sign of the restoration of spirits, 'are you still there? You take care of Mother and Heng first, and then, if there's anything left of your largesse you can throw it at me!'

Her mother's all-out storming of heaven through a series of novenas in church, during which she was half the time on her knees, could only be matched by Meeta's massive plan to go on a pilgrimage to India to personally meet with the holy god-man Sai Baba and return with his blessing. The plan had nothing to do with winning back Byron who she realised was just a useless bum not worth having, but everything to do with regaining her precious health and peace of mind. She would make a request for something rarely conferred, that is, a personal meeting with His Holiness. But even if that request was not granted, she would return to Singapore a happy woman, for the saint was known to see into the hearts of grieving women and relieve them of their torments.

'Oh Meeta,' Maria said, grasping her hands for the sight of the defeated-looking woman who had lost much weight, pained her. 'I hope everything works for you, and you'll be happy.'

It consoled Meeta somewhat to have company in suffering. 'Just forget him, Maria. He's a cad, like the rest. I can see you're taking it all badly, despite your brave attempts.'

She invited Maria to join her on her pilgrimage to India. Maria said, 'I wish I had your faith, Meeta. Or my mother's. That might make things less complicated for me.' Too much cerebra, too little viscera, he had said jokingly to her, tweaking her nose in the endearing way she would always remember. Neither had worked for her, either on its own or in combination. You think too much, he had said. You should feel more. She thought, Maybe I think too much *and* feel too much. That was why her tunnel had become twisted, darker and more difficult to negotiate, with the light at the end always eluding her.

'I am making a visit to the principal,' said Brother Philip. 'Would you like to come along? I think he's not averse to visitors now, and might welcome our presence.' Almost a year after his departure in disgrace from St Peter's Secondary school, his teachers and students were still referring to him as 'the principal', as if in subconscious rejection of the new head. Even at that stage, nobody knew the exact nature of his offence and his fall from grace; the story was still of the improper awarding of the building contract to his brother-in-law. It was a reflection of the general goodwill towards him that nobody cared to find out the truth but stuck to the belief that he had been manipulated by an unscrupulous relative, and had not profited by a cent in the whole sordid affair.

Money, money, money. Was it an even stronger force than love? Did it create jealousies among women that were even more corrosive than sexual jealousy? Betty told the story of a grand-uncle who put an end to the jealousies of his three wives, not by giving them equal time on his bed, but equal allowances from his coffers. Did men become corrupt because money could bring them love, and not the other way around?

The principal was glad to see them. Maria had brought a

gift of fruit for him. He had lost a great deal of weight and his hair had become thin and grey. But as soon as he talked to them about a hobby he had just acquired, his face lit up with deep satisfaction and joy. He called it a hobby but it was a mission of mercy, a vocation to imbue his new life with purpose and meaning. For he was now doing charitable work in a community that his member of parliament, a kindly person who had kept in touch with him during the months of suspension from school, had arranged for him.

'I visit the homes of the aged, the poor, the destitute,' said the principal smiling. 'I talk to them, read to them, bring them simple gifts of food and groceries. They show such deep appreciation!'

There could have been the merest tinge of disillusionment with the world of power and influence that had not shown appreciation for the support he had given them through the years; he reminded Maria, in a voice filled with regret, of the many times that he had got her help for crafting papers to help the Minister of Education make decisions on a variety of educational issues. In the depths of despair when he was first suspended, he had written a pleading letter to the minister, but had got no reply. She tried to remember his real name and had to ask Brother Philip on their way back. Augustine Tan Chee Kuan. No, she would always refer to him, and remember him, with affection, as 'the principal'. Exactly a year later, she would be shocked to read in the Obituary pages of *The Straits Tribune* that Augustine Tan Chee Kuan, aged sixty-two, had passed away. She would have gone to the funeral with Brother Philip except that by that time Brother had gone back to his native Ireland, and too many distressing things were happening to make it the darkest period of her life.

'Brother Phil,' she asked after waving goodbye to the principal who had walked with them to the gate of his modest one-storey terrace house, 'have you ever gone through a time in your life when you were tormented by doubts and misgivings, when you actually hated yourself a little?'

'I don't know about the hate,' he replied smiling, 'but yes about the doubts and misgivings. All the time.'

She needed the fresh air of the Botanic Gardens to clear her mind and her heart. The place could not hold very happy memories for her, with the two rings of unhappy association with her husband lying at the bottom of its fish pond, and the wooded area deserted at night, not far from its gates, holding the most painful recollections of her erstwhile lover. But she continued to love the place and to be drawn to it as a living, breathing entity that had become bound up with her very existence. She looked at her favourite tree, a very old gnarled and fascinating structure of trunk, branches and roots so closely, densely intertwined that you could not tell them apart anymore. During the brief period when its pale pink flowers burst into bloom and drifted down with the slightest touch of breeze, she liked to sit under it and turn her face to receive the falling showers. She thought, how nice, when I die, to have my ashes scattered among its roots and washed into the ground by the rain.

Romantic notions always had a softening effect on the mind and heart, no matter how burdened with pain, confusion, regret. Everybody, when faced with pain, summoned their coping strategies, whether of religious faith, like her mother and Meeta, or humanitarian instincts, like the principal, of sheer serpent's wile, like Heng, Maggie, Mark and Yen Ping. Perhaps even V.K. Pandy's dull-eyed despair, ending with death, was a kind of coping mechanism.

She still had to work out hers, and right now, as she sat under her favourite tree, she was contented with simply enjoying the beauties of her favourite spot in Singapore. She saw a jogger approaching her and recognised him instantly, the one who had first seen her with her Jane Austen novel some years back. He was waving and smiling broadly, and as she expected, immediately sat down beside her, wiping his handsome face with the towel round his neck and peppering her with questions; how she had been, when they had last seen each other, did she remember playing like a child in the fountain playground. She had her own questions which she had never been able to ask other men – her husband, her near-lover, her best friend at St Peter's – but which she was going to throw at him now, systematically, one by one, in the manner of the serious investigator and inquisitor. She only needed the opening gambit, which came very soon. As they talked about a whole range of inconsequential things, she noted, as she had indeed expected, that he was making a conscious effort to turn the conversation towards the subject of sex, all the time watching her reaction. That was assuredly a man's way of assessing his chances with a woman pretty and friendly enough to mark out as a potential. If she smiled, that was encouragement; if she frowned or looked down in embarrassment, that was the end of the move which could be wrapped up and saved for another day.

Maria smiled throughout as the jogger, by now cool and rested, talked extensively about an encounter, not too long ago, with an American lady jogger who happened to be jogging at the same time in the Botanic Gardens. She was on a month-long visit to Singapore, on some assignment from her company based in New York, and had taken a service apartment very near the Gardens.

'She invited me for a beer in her apartment,' he said casually, and added, casting a sly glance at Maria, 'It was the most wonderful experience – for both of us.'

Maria said, also very casually, 'But you told me you're married!'

He said, 'Aw', dismissively, as if the question had no relevance. But her blood was fired up. There was no stopping her questions now.

She said, 'You've got to tell me this: just how do you reconcile these two things?'

'What two things?'

'The fact that you're happily married, with three children, and your having an affair with this woman.'

He did not like her question, but answered it with much bravado, 'Hey, it doesn't mean I don't love my wife!' And he went on to protest that it didn't mean either that the lady jogger – he even revealed her name, Bonnie – didn't love her husband.

She had been married six years, with two lovely kids. She had shown him their pictures, which she carried around in her travels. The jogger added, 'It's just an affair, that's all. Everybody's in the game,' adding with a wink, 'those who aren't, can't.' And still she wanted to ask him questions about men and what they wanted of women, whether they were capable of loving more than one woman. And like the rest of men, he did not like questions and evaded them. Soon he grew tired of the subject, turned to her and said, 'You're very attractive, you know. Care to have a drink sometime?'

She was out of the game because she could not cope with its complexities. Right now, she was still coping with the painful doubts and misgivings arising from those complexities. There was only one thing to do because of its certain rehabilitative power. She would adopt the principal's exemplary coping strategy, which in fact dear Brother Philip had already articulated for her: get outside yourself, get outside your skin, get into another's.

And the skin that needed getting into was Meeta's. Winnie had called to say that she was delaying her trip to Washington to help Meeta through a crisis: the poor woman had gone into deep depression and was in fact on medical leave at home, being attended by a younger sister who had flown in from New Delhi. The pilgrimage to India had not been made after all. Perhaps Meeta had never been serious about it.

A student from her class in Palm Secondary School had one morning run into the office of the principal and said breathlessly, 'Please, Madam, Miss Nair has collapsed. She was teaching us when she suddenly collapsed to the floor, and now she's crying, pulling her hair and beating her chest, and nobody knows what to do!'

One of the teachers who happened to meet Winnie on one of her last-minute shopping trips relayed the bad news and Winnie immediately called Maria.

Thirty-Two

The complete story of poor Meeta Nair's sudden personal tragedy took some time to assemble from a variety of sources, mostly reliable. For while Meeta was noted for her loud voice, loquacity, sense of fun and love of attention, she kept much of her private life hidden, even from her close friends, carefully selecting for release only those bits that confirmed a self-image she wanted others to share – that of a supremely confident, contented woman at ease with the rest of the world. In particular she wanted the world to know that when it came to men, she was as far removed as was possible from her silly housemate Winnie and that group of nervous, eager women in the government's matchmaking programme who were always on tenterhooks about whom they would be matched with. 'I couldn't be bothered, it's beneath me,' she would declare with queenly hauteur, blissfully unaware that at some unconscious level of body language or verbal slippage, she was conveying exactly the opposite impression, especially during her visits to the Polo Club where her avidly searching eyes had given her the nickname, among the more spiteful female club members, of 'Meeta the Manhunter'. She had amassed an immense stock of popular gender jokes, some quite gross, which she readily shared with girlfriends, provoking hysterical laughter.

While she had liberally divulged the secret of her liaison with the maharajah's cousin, (the truth of which her sister, looking very puzzled, could not confirm) she had kept concealed a little affair when she was eighteen (which her sister could confirm). There was a man, a technician, shy but sincere who had courted her and applied for her hand in marriage. Because he was a Sri Lankan, her father who was a very conservative and authoritative figure turned him down and forbade her to see him again. He later married someone else, and was apparently happy in his marriage and successful in a business he had started soon after. According to Meeta's sister, she kept his letters and small gifts, but burnt them all when he got married.

This sad little episode in Meeta's life so many years ago, which must have lain somewhere in the obscure depths of tender memory, had suddenly surged to the surface in the most fearsome way on the day of her nervous breakdown while conducting a lesson for her students in Palm Secondary School. Reports from various sources had pieced together a story as sad as any about the forsaken, mad woman in popular literature. When Meeta finally realised the futility of pursuing Byron – he took leave from his work and fled to a little known beach resort in Thailand for a week – she went into a despondency that was noticed by her colleagues at Palm Secondary, and would have been noticed by Winnie if she had been around. The maid Philomena had made an urgent call to Winnie in her hotel to say that Ma'am Meeta would sit by herself for hours in the dark, sometimes sobbing quietly.

Meeta agreed to take medical leave to rest at home, but on the last morning before the one-week leave, she went into class for the usual English language lesson with such a strange look in her eyes that her students looked at each other uneasily ('Like she is possessed by devil, like in trance or something,' said one of the students in an awe-stricken voice).

She faced the students with her blazing eyes and said in a voice shrill with urgent purpose, 'Today, boys and girls, I'm going to teach you the Conditional Mood. You know what that is? 'If only.' 'If I could –' 'If I hadn't done that –' If, if, if. The mood that tells about wishes, hopes, dreams.' She began to scribble sentences on the chalkboard, reading out each word as she wrote it: 'If only I had listened to my heart!' 'If only I had stood my ground with Father!' 'I wish that I had never been born to such a selfish, mean, heartless, domineering old bastard!' 'What's wrong with Sri Lankans? That man would have made me happy.' 'If I could make that bastard Byron come crawling to me –' She stood majestically before her students, the bun of hair at the back of her head coming undone and falling in loose strands upon her back, and flung out her arms in a final dramatic gesture, 'So now I have taught you the Conditional Mood. I hope you need never use it, boys and girls, because it's the saddest mood in the English language. It's the language of loss and missed opportunity and dreams dashed to the ground. And you know what, boys and girls? My whole life is the Conditional Mood!' It was at this point that she collapsed to the floor, weeping, and her students sprang up from their seats and rushed to her aid.

It would always be a reflection of loyal and unstinting friendship that Winnie actually delayed her honeymoon in Europe by some days to be with her poor housemate in the hour of need, though it did not help that while busying herself with this or that to make Meeta comfortable, she was sharing her new happiness in an incessant stream of chirpy talk.

'Ah, here are the pills. Meeta, you're to take them every three hours. My darling Wilbur's aunt went into depression too some years ago, and he got her exactly these pills.' 'Meeta dear, try to look happy. Sometimes just trying helps. Tell us some of your jokes. Dear Wilbur is full of jokes. He makes me laugh all the time!' 'Maria, are you going to be with Meeta for the rest of the evening? Can I go back to the hotel now? Wilbur's waiting. He's taking me out for a romantic candlelit dinner this evening!'

Meeta, coming out briefly from her despondency, said in a low voice to Maria, 'Look, I can't stand it anymore. Can't you stop all that nattering?'

Winnie left for Europe at last – 'My Wilbur says he can't wait any longer for our honeymoon to begin!' – hugging Meeta warmly as she said, 'Goodbye, my dear Meeta, take care. I'll call you when we're back home in Washington!'

Meeta muttered, 'Thank goodness.'

The brief periods of lucidity were enough for her to remind her sister and Maria that Winnie's kindness to her now exactly matched hers, many years ago, when Winnie was hospitalised for a serious illness and depended on her, rather than her own sisters, to help her through the recuperation. My favour cancelling out yours. Now we're quits. It was the dove's equivalent of the serpent's an eye for an eye. Pride, revenge, kindness, gratitude, resentment – they were all inextricably tied together, as were love and hate, attraction and revulsion, sense and folly, all horribly smeared together in the complex human psyche desperately seeking a balance to stay whole.

Maria thought, with some wonder, how many friends, lovers, married couples were in perpetual Conditional Mood, staying together by default, in harmony on the surface, in silent resentment underneath, waiting for the moment to break free. *If only I had the financial means to be on my own. If only the children were old enough. If only the old one would go off mercifully; the hospital bills are mounting by the day.*

She could imagine Winnie, cuddled up against her Wilbur, saying, 'Darling, you can have no idea how I longed to be free of Meeta,' telling him about all the times Meeta had made fun of her, discharging years of resentment that must have built up even as she was telling others in her nervous, little-girl voice, 'You know, I wouldn't know what to do without Meeta. She advises me, counsels me, scolds me, checks my accounts for me…'

Maria thought, I could write short stories about the sad lives of women, using only the rich resources of English grammar. Thus: the Passive Voice for subjugated women like Por Por who were *lived*, not living; the Conditional Mood for hopelessly yearning women like herself and Meeta, with its brutal ifs upon which to hang their shredded dreams. The Perfect Tense? It was a frightful misnomer because it could only be used to describe an imperfect world.

Right now, it was also a laughing mockery of two women keeping each other doleful company, looking back upon their painful experiences in the past that the special grammatical form made clear were still impinging upon their present: 'I have made such a terrible mistake.' 'He has broken my heart.' 'We have made such fools of ourselves.'

That evening, on a whim, she decided to go to a part of the city she had only once glanced at from her taxi window. It was one of those derelicted parts, away from the gleam and gloss, that the government, particularly before an election, promised to clean up, put in more roads, more street lamps, tear down the dilapidated buildings and put up new ones worthy of the name of the cleanest, greenest, most progressive city in Asia. She took a walk along a small, broken road covered with puddles from the last downpour, and watched its occupants going about their business, or simply sitting idly on chairs and stools by the roadside since there was no business to go about. Two old men were sitting at a low table playing Chinese chess. Another old man was feeding a bird hopping about in a cage strung up on a wooden pole. A middle-aged woman at the doorway of a rundown shophouse was preparing to send two small children, probably her grandchildren, to school, both of them in clean, green-and-white school uniforms. As they walked out into the sunshine, the woman, with a little warning cry, pushed the children out of the downward path of water dripping from clothes strung out to dry on a row of bamboo poles from upstairs windows. She raised an angry fist to one of the windows, after something dropped to the ground at her feet, a styrofoam box falling apart and scattering the remnants of someone's lunch. A young woman was crossing the road with a little girl in a red Mickey Mouse T-shirt, and green pants, her fringe of hair reaching down to her small bright eyes. A very old, very bent woman was rummaging about in a garbage bin, a trolley beside her, half filled with empty beer cans and cardboard boxes. She was ignoring a young man watching her and making little gurgling noises; he had all the marks of the village idiot – large bulging eyes, slack, drooling mouth, stiff movements, shabby clothes. An old man was sitting at a table, drinking some milky tea from a large glass; he could have been the same man that her taxi driver had once pointed out to her, the sad victim of a greedy young woman from China who cleaned out every cent of his pension money.

They were all living the Conditional Mood of regret and yearning. If, if, if only.

Maria then decided to go to Middleton Square, not in respectful remembrance of its most notable occupant whose death now seemed only a faint memory, but simply to watch the Singaporeans there, well-dressed and prosperous-looking and therefore in no need of the Conditional Mood. A young man in smart shirt and tie was walking rapidly beside two Caucasians in smart business suits and carrying briefcases; he was talking animatedly to them and could be steering them towards a big business deal over drinks in a posh pub. Two young women with long straight hair, wearing bright T-shirts and jeans were giggling over some shared secret; they were carrying large fashionable tote-bags, one wearing impossibly high heels, the other dark green sandals showing off her toenails varnished a brownish red. A maid was on a shopping trip with her *tai tai* mistress, her arms straining under the weight of shopping bags bearing designer labels.

All would have appeared, at some time or other, in the glossy tourist posters and advertisements proclaiming the city's success. The brightness of their appearance and vigour of their movements would still have warranted the use of the Passive Voice: *We are told to keep our city clean and green and attractive. We are prohibited from chewing gum and spitting and littering. We have been warned against offending our government. We have been promised a Utopia. We have been bought.*

But the Passive Voice could have been easily shouted down by the Active: *They give us clean, crime-free streets. They subsidise our flats. They give scholarships to our children. They put money in our pockets. They give us not only the five Cs but newer, better versions of the five Cs!*

One of Singapore's most prestigious hotels, The Summit, employed humour to enable Singaporeans as well as tourists to get rid of whatever irritation they might experience about the harsh anti-littering laws: it provided a special bar where unshelled peanuts lay waiting in small attractive baskets for patrons to pick up, pop the tasty kernels into their mouths and then throw the shells, not into the mandatory waiting bins, but upon the gleaming polished floor itself, thus celebrating the Active Voice with joyous abandon: *I am littering. I littered. I have littered. I can litter as much as I want!*

Meeta's recovery was slow, but she made steady progress under the devoted care of her sister from New Delhi who made arrangements for a cousin to take over when she had to return home. Her sister Saroja had made a firm offer: 'Leave Singapore, come and live with me, my husband and our four children who adore their aunt Meeta. You will have a maid to yourself. You will have nothing to do but enjoy yourself.'

Meeta had confided in Maria, 'No thank you. Saroja's the sweetest, most generous sister you'll ever find, but I want a life of my own. Like you.'

Her mirror moment of truth, like Maria's, was of the literal kind, coming as she looked steadily at her reflection, staring at the changed lineaments on her face, the dullness in the once bright eyes, the limpness of hair once in bright coils enhanced by sparkling hair clips, the lusterlessness of a life once an inspiration to others.

And in that one moment, Meeta's pride asserted itself as it never had before, vanquishing depression and launching her on the road to full restoration. Her volatility, having plunged her into desperation, now pulled her up, with the same ferocity for the immediate task of self-rescue. She called loudly for the maid who came running and ordered her to get her bath water ready, with her favourite jasmine-scented bath soap, also her blue and green sari, nail polish, pearl hairclip, black-and-silver sandals. Then she took a last look at herself in the mirror and said with a smile, 'That's the last I'll see of the old, stupid Meeta Nair who was stupid enough to fall for a bum, a man not fit to kiss the sandals on her feet. The next time I stand before you, Mirror, it will be a brand new Meeta, more beautiful and carefree than ever! I'll show him!'

Mirror, mirror on the wall. Women cared less about being the fairest of them all than about coming out of a crisis with their dignity intact.

Meeta, through sheer pride, never asked exactly what happened that day in the classroom; the incomplete recollection was enough to tell her she had behaved in the most embarrassing way, badly damaging her image with her students and colleagues at Palm Secondary School who were probably now all whispering to each other about her. She never returned to the school, after her extended medical leave, and chose instead to continue her teaching career in a private school. Her meetings with friends grew fewer, and one day, some months after her breakdown, she called Maria to say that she had resigned from her job and had accepted her sister's invitation to live in New Delhi. Her plan to do a pilgrimage to meet the holy Sai Baba was revived with a dream, almost a vision, that she had had of him, in which he appeared in a thick mist and blessed her.

'I'll visit his ashram, then go on to New Delhi,' she said cheerfully. She spoke at length about how she would devote herself to Saroja's children and give them the time that their busy parents could not afford.

'Have I told you,' she said, 'Saroja's house is a mansion, with that kind of garden you'll never find in our land-hungry, little Singapore. It has at least a dozen varieties of mango alone. And Saroja's friends include the arty-farty kind who will take me to the theatre. I don't know how I will find the time to do everything!'

Meeta said that she practised what she had taught her students to do in times of indecisiveness: take out a piece of paper, draw a line down the middle and call the two columns 'Pros' and 'Cons', to list out all the reasons for or against a decision. Writing down one's thoughts clarified them marvellously. She showed her pros and cons list for leaving Singapore to live with her sister, the top reason for vamoosing, she chuckled, being lack of political freedom. 'But you've never shown any interest in politics,' said Maria. 'Aw, everybody knows we don't have any freedom! Look at poor V.K. Pandy.' It was the first time that Maria remembered she had mentioned the opposition member.

Meeta confided hearing from a reliable source that at long last she might get an invitation from the Ministry of National Affairs to be a member of the Council for Religious Harmony.

'High time,' she said loftily, and toyed with the idea inspired by that tale about a genie in a bottle that waited a hundred years to be rescued, getting more impatient by the day. He was so fed up with waiting that he swore that the person who rescued him, instead of being rewarded, would bear the brunt of his annoyance.

'When I get the letter,' declared Meeta, 'I'll write and say, 'Too late! No thank you'.'

The letter never came. Maria one afternoon found her playing with the dog Singapore.

She said, hugging the dog to her chest, 'This is the only Singapore I will trust!' She was deep in thought for a while and then asked, 'Hey, do you think I should write a book? About my life. There's so much to tell.'

Maria thought, 'Poor Meeta. She's still looking for a workable coping strategy. But aren't we all.'

Winnie called a few times from her new home in Washington. The celebratory joyousness of voice in the early days of her marriage could not be sustained indefinitely. There was a call when she said, in rather subdued tones, that she missed her old life in Singapore. Winnie was never one to impart anything clearly and coherently, either when asking questions or giving answers, and it was some time before Maria understood that she was talking about some problems related to Wilbur's drinking and his odd habit of disappearing for days, which he said, had to do with his secret work with the US navy.

She said bravely, 'He says he loves me very much and will always take good care of me. So I should not complain about anything!' adding, 'Every morning, he brings me breakfast in bed.'

About what was going on in Maria's life, she showed little interest, about Meeta's, even less. It would only be a matter of time before the three friends whom Meeta once called 'The Terrible Trio', 'The Golden Girls', 'The Three Misses Who Missed', ended all communicaton with each other and disappeared into the darkest corners of memory.

Maria called her mother a few times in her new home in Malaysia. 'We're all doing well, praise be to the Lord and His Holy Mother,' said Anna Seetoh. 'Heng will be baptised next month. His new name will be Vincent, after St. Vincent de Paul. His godma will be Francesca Low. I must have told you about her, a truly pious lady who's been to Lourdes three times. Heng's a completely different person now.'

Anna was anxious to know about Por Por who was getting to be more unmanageable, refusing to eat or have her bath. A few times she had grabbed Rosiah's hand and bitten it. Maria had bad news. 'Rosiah's leaving in six weeks' time. She says she's getting married, but I suspect it's an excuse. I don't blame her. She's no longer able to manage Por Por and can't wait for me to come home everyday to take over.' 'What are you going to do?' asked Anna anxiously and Maria said sadly, 'I'm going to put Por Por in the Sunshine Home.' She wished it could have been the Silver Valley Home which had better facilities and round-the-clock medical care, but it was too expensive. She wished, with all her heart, that she had more money.

Thirty-Three

'Oh no, you can't do this to me,' gasped Maria when Brother Philip told her the bad news: he was going on long leave to Ireland after which his superiors there would decide on his next posting which would likely not be Singapore again. 'Oh no, dear Brother Phil, you can't leave me when I need you most. You know that I need you, don't you?'

'Of course, Maria. I know that.'

'Then why are you leaving me?'

'I have no choice, Maria.'

'This is nonsense, Brother Phil. Of course you have a choice. Don't you love me at all?'

'Of course I do, Maria. Now stop behaving like a spoilt child.'

'No, you can't love me if you're abandoning me like this!'

It was strange that they were using the language of lovers when they were not, nor could ever be. If it was true that real, lasting love between a man and a woman went through a number of stages, beginning with the heat of passion, then a tumultous power struggle to see who would be in control, followed by a period of painful accommodation and finally, the ultimate reward of perfect soulmateship, then she and her colleague in

St Peter's Secondary School, worlds apart in temperament and chosen way of life, had co-opted the entire process and made it their own; they had dispensed with all the burdensome stages of the journey and leapt directly to the golden reward at the end. They had managed this magical flight, like two winged creatures, precisely because they carried no lovers' baggage.

After she had fully opened up her heart to him about the painful dilemmas of a near love affair, she had learnt to trust him completely and relish the pleasure of his wise, witty company; it did not matter if the gossips in the school were wondering why Maria Seetoh and Brother Philip were seen so often together. Once she had asked him, 'There's a rumour going on about us. Does it bother you?' and he had said, 'Only if it's true.' She had thought, 'Dear, dear Brother Phil. He makes me feel what no man has ever made me feel – *comfortable.*'

She made him promise that he would write to her from Ireland and let her know what was going on in his new life.

'Nothing much happens. Long hours of study, prayers, walks in my favourite fields and downs. Maybe an occasional visit to a pub for beer and Irish music.'

'I wouldn't mind that kind of peaceful, uncomplicated existence! But no, dear Brother Phil, you must still write, I want to know.'

As a parting gift, she gave him a pen with his name inscribed. 'Remember you had once wanted to collaborate with me in the writing of a play?' she asked. 'Maybe one of these days, should you get a re-posting to Singapore, we could still do it.'

'Maybe,' said Brother Philip, looking at her very affectionately. She had wanted to give him a hug then, but desisted. There was only one time he had held her, but that was because she was crying over her failure to reach Maggie and he wanted to console her. Here was a life that was undamaged and happy, and she, with a life still to recover from damage, a happiness still to be found, had no right to come knocking on the gates of his Eden.

The school gave him a farewell dinner in a restaurant. That evening, she tossed about in fretful sleeplessness, drifting into a troubled sleep at dawn, heavy-hearted at the thought that only his vacated desk in the staff common room would greet her every morning. The true test of a woman's feelings for a man, it was said, lay in how much he was missed. By that reckoning, she must have loved Dr Phang a little, and her husband not at all. Brother Philip's departure hollowed out a huge part of her inner self, leaving an emptiness shockingly alien to her sense of independence and love of solitude. It frightened her. Perhaps she was confusing need with love, only this time it was not the need for the warmth of a man's body in a parked car or on a silken bed, but of something superior and subtler – his unconditional friendship. If she was now confusing love with friendship, it was no bad thing, for indeed, at their best, they were one. Was love an ersatz friendship, or was it the other way round? The need to hear from him grew sharp and insistent with each day of his absence, making her wait for a letter that she had told him there was no need to write, for a call that would never be made as he could not afford expensive overseas calls and she had been too embarrassed to tell him, 'make it a collect call.'

A card showing a church in the lovely Irish countryside arrived nearly two weeks after his departure. 'To my dear Maria,' it said and was signed, 'With love, Philip.' Yearning women, holding a gift or card or letter, did a thorough search for signs of love, looking up and down, around and through, inside and out, so that no sign of the love whether already lost or still unclaimed, would be missed. Sometimes yearning embellished truth, turning morsels into a feast to feed the hunger. Maria was ready to believe that the little postcard with the usual inquiries about her health, family, schoolwork, etc was some kind of love note, emboldend by distance and absence, until she realised that it was the exact reciprocation of her own endearments in a card she had written to accompany the gift of the pen. It would be the first of many cards, cheering her, also filling her with deep melancholy.

As soon as she entered Mr Ignatius Lim's office, the woman who had been talking to him, swung round in her chair to face her. She was Mark's mother; in front of her, laid on Mr Lim's table were a number of sheets of paper which Maria instantly recognised to be the pale blue paper that Mark and Yen Ping favoured for their poems to each other. The woman had a look of intense hostility which was accentuated by her heavy make-up and the long jade earrings swinging from her ear lobes.

Mr Lim said, 'Miss Seetoh, this is Mrs Gloria Wong, the mother of Mark Wong.'

Preparing for a confrontation between the silently fuming visitor and the difficult maverick teacher, he assumed the look of the consummate peacemaker and mediator, and said with slow deliberation, 'Miss Seetoh, Mrs Wong has drawn my attention to a certain – ahem – issue, problem which I have no doubt we can all solve peacefully together.' The principal then showed her the love poems and notes that Yen Ping had been writing for Mark, apparently during her creative writing classes; indeed one of them referred to a time when they were together, sitting side by side in the class.

Impatient with the principal's slow dilatory way of communicating her complaint, Mrs Wong took over, saying in a voice shrill with anger, 'Miss Seetoh, I must protest! I had understood that the staff of St Peter's had the responsibility of making sure their students behaved properly, and yet you have allowed this girl to write love poems to my son! Luckily, my sister found them in his room.' She launched into a bitter tirade against school laxity allowing young boys and girls to indulge in nonsensical behaviour when they should be studying hard and making their parents proud of them. 'Miss Seetoh,' she said standing up and holding up a warning forefinger. 'I want you to promise me that in future you will not allow this girl to write love poems to my son! I don't know how she manages to smuggle them to him because he's on twenty-four hour surveillance!'

'I make no such promise,' said Maria coldly, and made to leave.

'What – what, how dare you –' she turned to the principal who, realising that a noisy quarrel between two women was the last thing he wanted in his office, began to pacify her.

The last words that Maria heard as she strode out were those of earnest assurance which rose above the woman's noisy protestations, 'Yes, yes, I'll make sure it doesn't happen again.'

How she wished Brother Philip were around for her to share the angriest thoughts and feelings she had ever experienced: 'The detestable man is closing down the creative writing class, with immediate effect, as his letter says. It doesn't mention Mrs Wong at all, only the need to cooperate with the National Productivity Campaign.' More fervently than ever did Maria utter an increasingly felt need: how I wish I had more money. Into her mind came the deeply gratifying image of herself sweeping into Mr Ignatius Lim's office, laying a letter on his table, saying nonchalantly, 'Mr Lim, I resign, as of now,' and then sweeping out.

She had done some quick sums, which only cast a pall of gloom. Even if she gave up her dream of buying that studio apartment, she would not have enough money, without her monthly salary, to continue with her mother's monthly allowance and the cost of keeping Por Por in the Sunshine Home. Resignation from her job was not an option.

'Hey God,' she said, feeling that humour was necessary to dispel the growing gloom, 'if you're still there, and itching to work a real miracle, I have a suggestion. Tomorrow, when I pass that newsstand that sells the National Jackpot lottery tickets, could you guide my hand to pick the winning one? The first prize, nothing less, God, that will enable me to buy my dream apartment and pay Mother her monthly allowances *and* transfer Por Por to the Silver Valley Home.'

It was said that there was a one in a million chance of winning that jackpot in the National Lottery, a one in a five or even ten million chance of winning the mega millions in those amazing super lotteries in the US and the UK. That meant that God only answered one out of the millions of beseeching, bombarding prayers from hopeful punters. It was as good as saying that God was merely following the laws of probability by which there would always be someone, somewhere who would hold the winning ticket. 'Well, God, may I call you Chance, or Randomness, or Luck or Probability, whichever is the truest,' said Maria, 'and if you are so kind as not to mind this rude reduction of your name to the mean calculations of science, then you could still listen to my prayer!'

The jesting put her in a light mood that lasted long enough for a single, smiling thought, one of these days I could write a humorous book and call it 'God and Me (Not our Real Names)'. She would invite Brother Philip to contribute some witty limericks that would still be in keeping with his vocation; the irreverent humour would be all from her side. She imagined Brother Philip in Ireland reading a copy of her book, rolling on the floor with laughter, and then writing her a reply: 'You prodigal daughter, you,' ending with 'Still praying for you, Love, Philip.'

About a month later, Yen Ping waited for her at the school gates after school to say, almost choking with tears, 'Miss Seetoh, Mark will be gone. In two days' time.'

'What do you mean?' said Maria.

'His mother has arranged for him to study in London. His air ticket's bought, he's all packed. She will go with him.'

'How do you know, Yen Ping?'

'He told me yesterday. He managed to make a quick call when his mother was upstairs.'

Mrs Gloria Wong had stopped the maths tuition, suspecting that her son had been making use of the trips to and from the tutor's home for his secret meetings and exchange of love notes and poems.

Yen Ping was inconsolable. Maria could only remind her of the promise she had made to herself some time ago, and turn it into both advice and consolation.

'Yen Ping, you told me once that you and Mark would study hard and prove yourselves. Once Mark's mother and your parents realise how serious you are about each other, how responsible you are, they will cease their objections. It has happened before.'

And Maria told some stories of young, thwarted lovers that had happy endings, creating one or two of her own.

Yen Ping wiped her tears and said, 'Thank you, Miss Seetoh. I will do as you say,' adding in such a wistful voice that Maria felt a little catch in the throat, 'he leaves so soon, and I can't even say goodbye to him.'

Thirty-Four

It was Sunday, her day to luxuriate in bed with the perverse intent not to rise until the hour of noon that officially marked the end of the morning to compensate for the previous six days' tyranny of the alarm clock.

At about six in the morning, when it was still dark, the phone rang shrilly. It was Maggie. She said, 'Miss Seetoh, did you read your newspaper yet? Look at page six of *The Singapore Tribune*. Also the Chinese newspaper. They even show picture.'

It took Maria a few seconds to shake off the languor of sleep and ask, 'Maggie, what on earth are you talking about?'

The girl, wherever she was, whatever she was doing in her new life, had not left off her old love of positioning herself with new knowledge that others would have to come begging for, exerting new power that would require others to come pleading for forgiveness. Maria would never forget that day in the café when Maggie had gone all out to humiliate her.

But the girl's voice had none of the remembered defiance or malice. She repeated matter-of-factly, 'Miss Seetoh, I just told you. Look in newspaper. Better the Chinese newspaper. More news.'

'But, but – Maggie, wait!' The girl had already hung up. Maria was sure, as she got up quickly, that it would not be the last of Maggie's calls.

She wished that her former student, hard, bitter, relentless, were completely out of her life. Somebody had told her that Maggie had been seen in lounges and bars with hard-drinking men, almost unrecognisable in the full unabashed trappings of the playgirl companion: heavy make-up, tight-fitting clothes with plunging necklines, black stockings, high-heeled shoes, the defiant cigarette in the pouty red mouth. She wondered what was happening to her sister Angel.

The Singapore Tribune ignored suicides unless committed in unusual circumstances that made for newsworthiness over at least a successive week's reporting. It carried a brief report only of the suicides of Mark Wong and Loo Yen Ping but the details in the report were tantalising enough to promise follow-up reports: both were wearing the blue-and-white uniforms of St Peter's Secondary School, a mixed Catholic school, when they plunged from the twelfth storey of a block of flats in the vicinity of the school, probably in the early hours of Saturday morning; both carried farewell letters to various people in their pockets; both had died on the spot. Probably the most tantalising detail was the fact that they had jumped side by side, their wrists bound together by a red silk scarf.

The Chinese newspaper carried a picture of the dead couple, under a large white plastic sheet, with the right foot of the boy peeping out, as well as of a hysterical Mrs Gloria Wong kneeling beside the bodies, supported by two relatives or friends. The report was very detailed. Mrs Wong was screaming again and again, 'I curse the day that you were born!'; she could have been directing the curse at the girl who had caused her son's death, or even at her son who had brought her so much suffering despite all her efforts to give him a good future. The newspaper reporter, looking to flesh out his report, quickly concluded that parental objection had been the cause of the suicide pact. He did some quick, skilful investigation and interviewing of those relatives who were prepared to talk. He made much of the fact that the pair had been classmates in St Peter's Secondary School, and that the boy had chosen, in death, to wear his old school uniform. How had he got the information that the silk handkerchief of intimate union in death bore the couple's initials? There was reference to a small teddy found on the scene. Maria remembered that Yen Ping had told her of her having embroidered their initials on its collar.

Mrs Wong had been too distraught to say anything after the cursing; she had fainted several times, and had to be carried into a car and taken home. There was no mention of the parents or relatives of Yen Ping arriving at the scene of the tragedy. The Chinese newspaper reported, accurately, that the boy was preparing to go to the United Kingdom for further studies, and, inaccurately, that the girl was preparing to join him there. In the following days, journalistic enthusiasm overreached itself, and managed to secure some pictures of the couple in happier times, which were splashed in the newspaper. One showed Mark and Yen Ping at some school outing, dressed in their blue-and-white school uniforms, another in an unidentified place with trees in the background, standing very close to each other, but not touching. *The Straits Tribune* did not have any follow-up report on the request of the Deputy Minister of Trade and Business who was related to Mrs Gloria Wong.

'Oh my God, oh my God,' gasped Maria, and rushed to the bathroom to be sick. The school would be full of the terrible news the next morning, but meanwhile, she found herself being propelled along, pale and hollow-eyed, in a thick, dark fog that seeped into her mind and clogged it, preventing her from thinking clearly, and into her heart, suspending all feelings except shock. In the numbed state two thoughts occurred but were soon absorbed back into the dark, chill numbness: should she put a call to Brother Philip in Ireland to let him know, since she had been confiding the story of poor Mark and Yen Ping to him? And should she go to the mortuary to take a look at the two broken bodies, as they really looked in the tragic culmination of their love, bearing the marks of their violent death, before the embalmer came to do his work of erasing the brutal truth with his powder and paint? Maria had seen few corpses in her life, and they all looked peaceful and serene as they lay in their coffins, the lines of anxiety or pain on their faces smoothed out, their hands placed gently by their sides or folded upon their chests. Sister Elizabeth, despite the ravages of her cancer, actually looked beautiful, as if she were in calm, undisturbed sleep.

No, there was no point calling Brother Philip; she would only sound incoherent in her distress, and be unable to answer the questions that he was sure to ask. No point distressing him when he was so far away, unable to do anything. And no, she shouldn't go to the mortuary not only because there might be regulations about admission for only family members, but also because she feared that each time she wanted to remember the much loved students, memory would conjure up only an image of two blood-encrusted bodies lying on cold stone slabs in the mortuary. She thought of the time she saw them sitting on the stairs of a school staircase, Mark helping Yen Ping neaten her plaits, combing out her long hair and watching with a waiting clip in his hands as her fingers expertly did the plaiting.

In her album of memories of the dead, the images would be carefully selected for their special pleasant associations. But it had a dark ugly twin that forced itself into memory and night dreams. It bore only fearsome images – of impenetrable forests and murky ponds, bodies and rings lying at the bottom of the ponds, owls hooting, children in flight – and she knew that it now included that newspaper picture of the crumpled bodies of Mark and Yen Ping lying under a large white sheet, with Mark's right foot, bereft of its shoe, protruding.

The shock of an event could actually elicit hope; something so shocking could not have happened, so it could only be a nightmare. She had heard of a bereaved mother who covered her ears against the news of her son's fatal fall from a cliff during a school camping expedition, screaming: 'No, no, no, go away! This is a bad dream, and I'll wake up tomorrow and find Barry coming downstairs for breakfast!'

At no time did Maria surrender to the sense of surreality that gripped her and say, 'It's not true, there must be a mistake somewhere,' so that her faculties, instead of being mobilised for denial, were readying themselves to accept and cope with the brute truth of an unspeakable tragedy – Mark Wong and Yen Ping were truly dead and gone, in a suicide pact, oblivious to the messy aftermath of police investigations, parental grief, a whole school in shock.

Maria paced the floor by the phone table, wishing Maggie would call again; Maggie, the inveterate seeker of information bent on ferreting out every tantalising detail, might by now have more to share. What was in the letters addressed to the parents? The Chinese newspaper had reported several letters now in police hands; could one of them have been addressed to her, the teacher they had trusted with their innermost secrets?

She would keep the letter in tender, anguished memory for the rest of her life. She suddenly remembered their pledge of eternal love written in blood, which Yen Ping had shown her, worn in a little silver locket round her neck. Mark's token must have been hidden in some secret place; had he taken it out and worn it too, just before their plunge from the high-rise block of flats? The meticulousness of the young couple, seen in the care they had taken over their various class assignments could be extrapolated to the planning of the pact – the choice of day, time and place, the choice of clothes, the selection of the binding scarf.

In her mind, Maria had a vivid picture of the couple, huddled together in the dawn darkness on the twelfth floor of the building, speaking in low voices, checking, for the last time, that everything was in order and as planned, going through the various items they wanted to take with them in their final, loving journey together.

Why had they chosen that spot? Did it have some sentimental value for them, having been one of their trysting places? Maria suddenly remembered that in one of her stories for the creative writing class, Yen Ping had described a suicide pact between two young lovers; they had not plunged from a tall building, but waded into the ocean together, and there was mention of a *silk scarf tying their wrists together*. Had the young lovers, even as they were telling her of their plans to study hard and prove themselves worthy of their respective families' trust, already decided to die together? Maria cried out in her anguish, 'Oh Mark, oh Yen Ping.'

All morning, she waited by the phone, longing for a call from Maggie, from a colleague who might have happened to get the news early, from a student in the creative writing class who might have hurried to the scene, from Mr Ignatius Lim, from anyone at all. On impulse, in the late afternoon, she went to the scene of the tragedy; it had been cordoned off by the police. She stood looking at the spot where they had fallen together, now cleaned of the blood that must have gushed out simultaneously from their bodies as they hit the ground together. What were their last words to each other? These could have come from any of the poems written on the favourite pale blue paper, which, if they had not been so profoundly felt, would have been dismissed as worthless cliché in the creative writing class: 'Our bodies may breathe their last, but our love breathes on in the silent wind and stars,' 'We will meet on love's eternal shore where no more tears will flow, where love can only grow.'

On the other hand, the last words could be the unuttered ones of sheer panic, as they looked at the hard ground rushing up to meet them, and suddenly saw, in a flash, that perhaps after all, they had a mistake too late to undo. Did they see the years of arduous study in college, and patient waiting, culminating in a marriage and a happy family life, all wiped out by a mistake which carried its own fearful momentum, ending only when their bodies and the hard ground were brought together in one blinding, pitiless second? Perhaps they saw themselves falling through the air together in slow motion, like a giant soft toy thrown out of the window by an angry child, sailing slowly downwards, its limbs flopping about gently, ending in a black void of nothingness, while friends, family and schoolmates went about their usual business in the world.

Mr Ignatius Lim held an urgent meeting with his staff. His face taut with anxiety, he told them there would be police investigations including interviews with Yen Ping's teachers; this was the special demand made by Mrs Gloria Wong who had already informed him that nobody from St Peter's Secondary

School would be allowed to attend Mark's wake or funeral. She had placed an obituary notice the day after his death, with a recent photograph of him in coat and tie; it had said simply that Mark Wong Lam Yoong, aged seventeen, had passed away peacefully, leaving behind his beloved mother Mrs Gloria Anne Wong and ended with the terse request: 'No wreaths please.' Mr Ignatius Lim said, his brow knit with worry, 'It is most unfortunate that St Peter's has been implicated, most unfortunate indeed. Our good name will be gone. The Ministry will want to conduct its own investigation.' He shifted about in his chair and continued, 'And all because of some poems that the deceased had written to each other in the Creative Writing Class, which, as you all know, has been converted into the Remedial Language Lab.' He avoided looking at Maria, as did everyone else at the sombre meeting.

She thought, the bastard. He only cares about the reputation to his school, and rose to say, in an even voice, 'I'm sorry about this unfortunate incident, and take responsibility for the poems which Mr Lim just now mentioned, because I had encouraged my students to express their thoughts and feelings freely. I would like now to give notice of my resignation.'

Then she walked out of the staffroom. She would have liked an immediate resignation, but the twenty-four-hour notice entailed financial costs she could not afford. Besides, she needed time to be with her students, to explain things as best as she could, to give closure to her life at St Peter's Secondary School. It was the practice of the school to give a farewell dinner to a departing teacher; she would remember to write a brief note of polite refusal to Mr Lim.

Outside, at the gates of the school, she did not turn back to have a look, nor wipe the tears from her face. They were not for poor Mark or Yen Ping, but for herself, for she had failed them, as she had failed Maggie. As soon as she reached home, she would consign that plaque of merit, awarded to her on Teachers' Day, to the dustheap of memory's shame.

Thirty-Five

Maggie was among the visitors at Yen Ping's wake, held on the ground level of the housing estate where the dead girl had lived with her family in a three-room flat on the sixth floor. From where she stood at the far end of the area used for the wake, Maria saw Maggie go up to Yen Ping's mother who was receiving visitors and weeping noisily, and give her a white envelope containing the condolence money. Among the appropriate blacks, blues and greys of mourning, Maggie's light purple blouse and dark purple pants, together with her vivid make-up and abundance of curls cascading down her back, stood out and invited curious side glances.

Maria thought, 'How magnanimous of her,' remembering her open hostility to Yen Ping during the creative writing classes, and the occasion when she had viciously spat at the girl as they met along a corridor. 'I've got to talk to her,' she thought.

But Maggie was gone in a flash. She had seen Maria approaching, smiled to herself, then broke into a run, in her high heels, to a red car parked in the large carpark of the housing estate. There was a man wearing dark sunglasses waiting at the wheel, and as soon as Maggie got in, they drove off.

'That's Maggie all over,' sighed Maria. 'She would have wanted me to run after her, calling her name.'

It was a staged magnanimity; the girl must been waiting for her arrival to bear witness to the deed before doing one of her tantalising disappearing acts.

She saw a large number of Yen Ping's classmates, dressed in their school uniforms, and some of her teachers, including Mrs Neo and Teresa Pang. They all went up, one by one, to Yen Ping's mother to offer their condolences in low voices, while she wept, shook their hand and drummed her fists on her chest, as if a lesser demonstration would have been inadequate to tell the gods up there how unkind they had been to her who had served them so well. Yen Ping's father had taken the news so badly that he had collapsed repeatedly and had to be sedated. Yen Ping's brother and three sisters, all dressed in white T-shirts and black pants, moved quietly among the visitors, offering drinks in small packets with drinking straws. In a corner talking quietly to each other were the old and new principals of St Peter's. Maria walked up to them, mainly to talk to the old principal who looked thinner and greyer; she was tempted to snub Mr Ignatius Lim by disregarding his presence, but relented when he initiated friendly overtures and said, sincerely enough, that the whole school was going to miss her.

There had been talk that Yen Ping and Mark had requested, in a note found on the floor from which they had jumped, to be cremated and for their ashes to be mixed together and scattered in the sea. In Maria's mind flashed a picture of the young pair, their heads almost touching as they discussed this last request for the perfect union, perhaps even quietly arguing about whether their final resting place should be the sea or simply a quiet niche in a columbarium bearing inscriptions of their favourite nicknames for each other. Yen Ping was a Taoist, Mark a Christian; their eternal resting place, as decided by their romantic imagination, was a universal nameless one, existing for all time, everywhere and nowhere, a distant shore, a land of gentle mists where love reigned supreme. In an illustration for one of her poems, Yen Ping, who showed artistic talent as well, had done a water colour illustration, in soft pastel shades, of the paradise which lovers had been denied on earth.

It seemed that when Mrs Gloria Wong learnt of the young couple's wish, she went into another bout of hysterics and could only scream, 'Never, never, never!' For the rest of her life, she would put the blame for the tragedy entirely on the girl – she could not even bear to pronounce her name, referring to her only as 'that girl' and her parents as 'those hawkers' – and by extension, on her school. Mrs Wong habitually expressed regret in the theatrics of cursing: I curse the day I sent my son to St Peter's Secondary School, I curse myself for donating so much to their school building fund. There was talk that she was planning to sue St Peter's Secondary School for millions of dollars for her suffering.

The young couple's note had said, 'Please grant us our last wish. It is to be one, in our bodily remains, as we have been one in spirit.' They had been as close to being one in body as their sense of morality would allow, stamping an invisible ownership sign on their seats in the back row of the creative writing class, tying an invisible scarf of exclusiveness on their wrists that carved out their own space in the school, which was always carefully avoided by the other students.

Despite their plea, their bodies lay in separate places of repose, in different parts of the city, subjected to the different rituals demanded by their respective faiths. Maria who wished so much to have been allowed to pay Mark a last visit, pictured his body lying in one of the funeral parlours of Peace Casket, Singapore's most established funeral company, surrounded by white lilies and candles, a large, flower-bedecked cross at the head of his coffin, and his photograph, in a large frame of white and yellow chrysanthemums, at the foot. A priest was in attendance saying prayers from a book, joined by a group of visitors sitting in white plastic chairs arranged neatly in rows. Mrs Gloria Wong was a woman of strong determination and would have come out of her fainting fits to receive guests, make sure everything was in order, and sob out her story.

Contrasted with the organised neatness of Mark's wake in a funeral parlour was the disorderliness of Yen Ping's in the open space of a housing estate, where unruly children from the nearby flats could be seen running around and occasionally stopping to watch the visitors coming in, the bereaved family members speaking in low voices to each other, a monk in a bright saffron robe chanting prayers with a bell in a haze of incense smoke. Yen Ping's photograph, showing a pretty smiling girl, was framed with multi-coloured flowers; it was set upon a large table, covered with a red silk embroidered tablecloth, holding small golden statuettes and effigies of temple deities, urns of joss-sticks, as well as food offerings of oranges, biscuits, noodles, peanuts and cups of tea.

The girl looked peaceful, her hair combed back, her face lightly made up. There was a gash on her forehead that defied the brave efforts of the mortician, and showed up distinctly under the make-up. She was dressed in her school uniform and covered up to the shoulders by a pale blue cotton sheet, as if her arms and legs were too badly smashed for public viewing. Where was the silver locket containing that promise written in blood?

Maria had to ask one of her sisters. The girl whose name was Yen Ling shook her head. Nobody knew about that locket; perhaps it had been flung out during the fall and was now lying in a drain or a clump of grass, irrecoverably lost. Yen Ling said that she would make a search for it as soon as she could. Maria had a sudden thought which produced a little tremor: it would not have been beyond the romantic intensity of the pair to decide for each to swallow the other's small scrolled promise before the plunge. She had an image of them facing each other, of Yen Ping counting to three to ensure a perfect simultaneity for the acts of loving ingestion. Then there was the counting again, one, two, three, perhaps by Mark, for the leap over the wall of the twelfth floor of the building.

A white pearl had been placed in Yen Ping's mouth, partly showing on her underlip; it had to do with some tradition about lighting the way for the dead one in the journey to the beyond. In one of the stories that Maria had read to her class, a woman had died and was making this journey, a very long one through heat and dust, when she finally reached the gates of the abode for the dead. But the gatekeeper there stopped her, saying, 'Open your mouth.' She did not have the requisite pearl, claiming that her family had forgotten about it. 'But see, I have still managed to arrive!' she argued. 'No, you can't enter,' said the gatekeeper firmly. The woman wept and said, 'I can't go back. Nobody wants me. I died in the first place because nobody wanted me.' 'Then,' said the gatekeeper, 'you will be condemned to wander the face of the earth for one hundred years.' Yen Ping's mother would make every provision to ensure that her beloved daughter would never be an aimless wandering spirit.

What was the beyond for this pair of young lovers? Maria had exactly the same thought as when she was looking upon the body of her dead husband in his coffin: could Mark and Yen Ping, now pure spirits, be hovering about somewhere, looking upon their own dead bodies, their grieving parents, the quietly composed visitors, the instruments of bell and book calling upon the bereaved to pray for the departed souls, and seeing everything, at last, with the eyes of truth? What was their truth like?

'Miss Seetoh, my mother wants to speak to you,' said Yen Ling. The woman, haggard from lack of sleep, dressed in a light blue blouse and grey pants, came up to Maria and clasped her hands. She spoke in a dialect that Maria could not understand, and Yen Ling did the translation. 'Tell Miss Seetoh that Yen Ping often spoke about her with great affection. She was Yen Ping's favourite teacher.' And it was at this point that the tears that had been held back with difficulty burst forth. Maria could not stop her sobs. Yen Ping's mother put a soothing hand on her arm. 'It's alright,' said the brave woman. 'Yen Ping will have her wish, and you will be a witness. We will call you when we're ready.' She got her daughter to take down Maria's phone number.

Yen Ling called exactly a fortnight after the funeral to give news of an event that had brought some cheer to her parents. Yen Ping had come back, as invited, which meant that her spirit was still in loving contact with her family.

'How do you know?' said Maria who had taken a liking to this sister, two years younger, and very bright, mature and confident.

There were all the signs, said Yen Ling. The room that she had shared with her three sisters had been vacated by all of them to prepare for her return – the bed had been properly made, the blanket placed neatly on the bedsheet, the pillow, with a new white pillow case, well fluffed up. Beside the bed on the table, was a glass of tea. Then the windows and the door of the room were locked. In the middle of the night, the family heard the faint howl of a dog, a sign that it had sighted a spirit not visible to human eyes, and in the morning, they opened the bedroom door and saw that the bed had been slept in – the sheet and blanket were slightly displaced and crumpled, and there was a distinct hollow in the pillow where the head must have been. But the most persuasive sign from Yen Ping was related to the glass of tea – the level of the tea was clearly much lower.

Yen Ling said, 'We were all happy to see that her spirit had come back on the fourteenth day.'

Maria asked, 'Will you be inviting her spirit to come back again?' and Yen Ling said, 'Oh no, my mother wants to make sure she won't. She's already making preparations for that. You will be invited as a witness to the ceremony, as you were my sister's favourite teacher.'

Thirty-Six

Rosiah the maid insisted on paying Por Por a visit in the Sunshine Home before she left for home to get married.

'Tell me about the man you're marrying,' said Maria pointedly.

She did not want to associate the maid, after years of faithful service, with a lie both unnecessary and uncharacteristic of the simple village girl from Indonesia who had served the family loyally for years. She said, 'Rosiah, you're not telling me the truth. You're not getting married at all.'

Rosiah said awkwardly, not looking at her, that it was not herself who was getting married, but her sister: Ma'am must have heard wrongly.

'But all your sisters are married; you'd already told us that.'

Rosiah needed to be rescued from the lie that she was floundering deeper into.

'It's alright, Rosiah. You can't manage Por Por anymore. No one can manage Por Por anymore; that's why I've put her in a home.'

Greatly relieved, Rosiah had more stories to tell of how difficult the old woman had become in the past six months – she soiled herself, refused to get out of her soiled clothes, threw food into Rosiah's face and on several occasions threatened to kill her with a knife, a pair of scissors, a long bamboo pole. And she screamed curses at her in an unintelligible dialect, but which Rosiah knew to be filled with the worst obscenities. Dear gentle Por Por – what demons of frustration and resentment had been lying dormant inside her confused mind and heart all these years, to break out with such savagery?

Maria had said to Rosiah, 'I wish you could continue to work for me, but I can't afford you now.'

The loyal girl had said, 'Oh Ma'am, you can cut my pay, I don't mind,' and it was at that point that Maria started crying again. The tears flowed readily those days, a time when she would remember as the darkest in her life.

The only thing that seemed to calm and comfort Por Por in the home was the sight of the small porcelain dragon ornament, probably from some temple or shrine, that must have been in her possession for more than half a century. Maria had put it in a cloth-lined box which the old woman carried everywhere with her in the home, afraid to let it out of her sight. The ornament had had the opposite effect on Anna Seetoh who was convinced it was a Satanic object and had recoiled in horror from it. She wanted it thrown out of the house. Surely there was no greater generational estrangement than theirs: an old woman, still clinging to the traditional beliefs of her childhood, and her daughter, secure in the Christian religion of her conversion, convinced that ties of blood mattered much less than ties of faith. Maria Seetoh had taken her grandmother's side in a noisy quarrel over the dragon ornament, and had insisted that it not only remain in the house but have a place of honour in Por Por's room, as the old one wanted.

It was Anna Seetoh's belief, never openly uttered, that the evil object had been partly responsible for her son-in-law's death, since its presence had invalidated the prayers of the church group that had come to pray for him. It was the cause of persistent estrangement, for Anna made it clear that as long as Por Por revered the object (in a dream she had seen the dragon, covered with pitch black scales, crawling out of a swamp) she could never pay her a visit in the home, much as filial duty dictated.

'What when Por Por dies?' Maria had asked angrily. 'Will you even come for the funeral?' It would be a funeral with the Taoist rites that Por Por would have wanted.

Anna Seetoh had replied sadly, 'I will pray for her,' adding, 'as I am praying for you, Maria,' for she believed that even non-believers would be eventually saved by the persevering prayers of their loved ones, through God's merciful establishment of a place called Limbo, a kind of holding station for the unbaptised or those who had renounced their baptism whose fates had yet to be decided.

Rosiah had brought gifts for Por Por – her favourite coconut pudding, a bead bracelet and a new cotton blouse. The old woman stared uncomprehendingly at her and her own grand-daughter, and let the gifts drop from her hands on to her lap, then to the floor. In the brief time that she had been at the home, her mental condition had deteriorated alarmingly, as if she had lost all will to live. The large staring eyes carried a reproach: you have abandoned me. Maria sat numbly beside her throughout the visit, her heart too heavy for words, while Rosiah chatted brightly and at one stage, took out a comb, to comb Por Por's long, untidy strands into a neat bun at the back of her head.

If at Yen Ping's wake she had reflected on the tragedy of a young life cut short, here in the Sunshine Home she saw the dereliction of old lives waiting for death that was too long in coming. A very old woman, probably in her nineties and sitting in a wheelchair, looked around with the terrified look of a small child lost in a crowd. Another, equally old, sat in a large chair, carrying in her arms a life-size plastic doll dressed in a pink dress and rocking it to sleep; the doll must have been given to soothe the pain of the revived memory of a dead infant so very long ago. A nurse in blue was attending to a woman in a wheelchair specially constructed to accommodate her massive obesity which oozed out at the sides, like some giant, boneless monster from the depths of the ocean floor. There was a woman who looked too young to be in a home, being in her sixties at the most, dressed in a floral print blouse and black pants. She could be taken for a visitor except that she was being attended by one, a young woman, probably her daughter, who had brought her a box of biscuits and a plastic bag of grapes, and was speaking to her in the cajoling tones one used for a recalcitrant child. Was the woman suffering from early dementia, like Por Por had, years earlier, and had the daughter put her in a home for the same reason – it was no longer possible to cope even with a loved one?

The term invariably appeared in obituary and memorial notices, whether the deceased one was loved or not, whether indeed, he or she, in the last stages of disease or dementia, had become so unmanageable as to become unloveable.

A faint smell of dried urine and disinfectant filled the air, despite the presence of pots of green plants to sweeten the decrepitude of old age. Somewhere from one of the nearby rooms a thin wail followed by incoherent mumbling, like someone having a bad dream in the midst of day, floated out to add to the desolation. Maria and Rosiah sat two hours with Por Por who ended up petulantly stamping on their gifts and making shrill noises of protest. Rosiah would not be coming again, and Maria sighed at the thought of the next week's visit.

It was money that filled her mind again, although this time, the thoughts took a different colouring: even if Por Por were in the Silver Valley Home well-known for its beautiful surroundings and up-to-date medical facilities, she would still be staring at her with those eyes of deep despair. A loved one beyond loving and being loved. But no, Por Por had earned her love which would always rise above the petty disappointments and distress of each visit.

Maria would always be grateful for the last conscious act of a hopelessly demented woman. It was as if Por Por, aware of her approaching end, managed to wrest one moment of lucidity from the rapidly descending darkness and asked for her. She had actually mentioned her granddaughter's name. Maria would keep in fond memory the small details of the message that the home superintendent told her; the old woman, to make sure that they would send for the right person, had indicated Maria's ponytail by tugging at the bun at the back of her head, and her pretty face by circular hand motions around her own face, followed by a perky thumbs up.

Maria had visited only the day before and noticed there was no change of mood or condition in her grandmother. But the next morning, to her surprise, the home superintendent called and said the old woman wanted to see her, and could she come quickly. Por Por had refused to get up from bed and seemed very agitated. Maria arrived in time to say goodbye. She was at her grandmother's side, holding her hand, whispering into her ears, until she heard a tiny gasp and saw that her Por Por was gone. The only memento she wanted of her grandmother was the dragon ornament, still in its cloth-lined box, but for years, just looking at it brought tears. It was part of her closure that she had put in the box a note from Rosiah that she had received two weeks after Por Por's death.

Rosiah had got someone to write it in English for her: 'I am very sad for death of Por Por. She is good kind person. She bite and scold only because old and sick. I pray Allah Por Por now well and happy.'

Thirty-Seven

Brother Philip's letter fom Ireland was half solicitous and half reproachful. How was she? Why had she not replied to his cards? Why had she not told him about the deaths of Mark and Yen Ping, of her grandmother? Of the principal? Why had she not told him she had resigned from St Peter's? How was she coping, etc., etc. The letter bristled with a hundred question marks of caring; Maria could imagine the creases of anxiety on Brother's calm forehead as he wrote. There was no direct mention of Dr Phang; instead, a skein of veiled hints, some rather clumsy, indicated how curious he was to know about that part of her private life.

Distance had, at the beginning, sharpened need; then as the months went by, had actually blunted it, so that she no longer felt the urge to write that long anguished letter in which she would pour out her heart and soul to him. The urge to pick up the phone and put in a long distance call to Ireland had long subsided. If her heart had been broken at his departure, the tumultous events that followed had simply shaken it back into full operation to continue to bear yet more of life's disappointments. To Maria Seetoh, they seemed to be saying, borrowing the words of Brother Philip: get out of your skin! You are in the real world, and there's no escaping from it. They also said, Maria Seetoh, your story's not over; it's still unfolding.

So she wrote only a brief, quick reply to all the anxious notes. 'My dear Brother Phil,' it said, 'At this stage, I can only give you a factual account of each of the events you referred to, and a factual account is the least useful thing at the moment. In any case, I am just too tired to do it. I don't care for the facts any more, only the meaning, and if you were here with me, my ever dear, kind, wise Brother Phil, you would help me extract a little of that. In any case, my story's still unfolding, and I'm not sure what's going to happen in the future. I can only write these dark, dreary, depressed little notes to you, which you're better off without. Love, Maria.'

It was the second phone call from Yen Ling, more than three months after her sister's tragic death. 'We found the silver locket you told us about,' she said excitedly. 'It was stuck in a hole in a drain, and we could get it out only by knocking off some of the cement.It was all dirty and rusty.'

She went on to say that the locket, containing the pledge of love, would be used in the coming marriage ceremony which of course Maria, the favourite teacher, must attend.

The ceremony was conducted, as the wake had been, in the same ground level area of the housing estate, but needing only a small part of the space, as only a few people would be present. There was a monk from a nearby temple in attendance, dressed in a long brown robe, wearing a long strand of brown beads round his neck, chanting prayers to unite the deceased couple in a marriage that had been denied them on earth. They were just two large paper effigies, crude cut-outs only, both wearing red paper mandarin robes with the frog buttons drawn in. They were placed side by side on a table covered with a richly embroidered red tablecloth that must have been borrowed for the occasion. No likeness was necessary, only distinct marks of their respective genders, so that one could tell which one was groom, and which bride. Thus Mark's effigy had short hair and wore a skull-cap, and Yen Ping's had long pigtails and circular red dots on her cheeks. Both had the large staring eyes of dolls, with unnaturally long lashes. Maria looked to see where Yen Ping's silver locket with the pledge of love was placed, and noticed that it lay in a little space where the effigy hands overlapped.

The monk chanted prayers to unite them in marriage for all eternity. He swung a censer of fragrant incense ash over the bridal couple, before placing them in a miniature funeral pyre and setting them on fire, imploring them to be on their own now and not to be bothered by the living anymore, a gentle, indirect way of saying: Please don't return to earth anymore. For the living too needed their peace to go on making their living in a hard world. Yen Ping's parents had already resumed working at their drinks stall in the market, their attention now concentrated on their other children.

There was the story, reported years ago in the Chinese newspapers, of a young couple similarly frustrated by parental objection to their relationship, who decided to end it all one dark night, inside a locked car, setting themselves on fire. By the time they were discovered, their bodies were just a charred heap. Their respective parents decided to put aside their hostility in order to meet and conduct a ghost marriage for their children, who had appeared to them in their dreams, expressing such a wish. The effigy wedding was not the end of the matter, for about a year after the event, the girl's parents found an abandoned baby at their doorstep who they instantly concluded was a ghost child despite its human appearance.

They took it in as a much loved grandchild. For a while the papers were full of the rumours that the baby indeed was a ghost child, for it had no shadow and could give winning lottery numbers.

Yen Ping's mother had no need for any such dramatic, elaborate aftermath of dealings with the other world, even if it brought gain, being too down-to-earth and needing only the necessary closure provided by the wedding ceremony to pick life up again and earn money for her remaining children's education. As soon as the effigies were reduced to a little heap of ashes, she invited the wedding guests comprising only Maria and two relatives to partake of the wedding feast set out on a small table, comprising some pink buns, biscuits, candied peanuts, pomelo and packet drinks. Then she bade them goodbye, thanking them warmly for their attendance.

For Maria she had the kindest words, saying again and again, 'My Yen Ping was always talking about you.' As soon as she had given the monk a donation for his temple and cleared the place of every vestige of the ceremony, she assumed a look that said, 'It's all over. I have done my duty to my daughter.'

The good woman would now devote herself to caring for her husband who had never recovered from the pain of his daughter's death, and to her business of selling soft drinks at the market, which had suffered a considerable loss of takings since the tragedy.

Up till the end, Maria was still hoping that of the several letters that the police had returned to the dead girl's family, one would be for her. But Yen Ling who would have been put in charge of such matters never mentioned such a letter. Her last words to Maria were the same as her mother's, 'Thank you very much for being such a kind teacher to Yen Ping.' Maria never heard from her again.

Out in the bright sunshine, standing by the roadside to hail a taxi, she said to herself, 'Oh no, am I never to be free from her?'

For the driver of the red Volvo that had screeched to a halt in front of her was none other than Maggie, as if she had lain in wait all through the ghost wedding, watching somewhere from her parked car.

She was smiling and said brightly, 'Hi, Miss Seetoh, get in. I'll give you a lift to wherever you want to go!' Beside her was a young, very pretty-looking girl who was also smiling amiably.

Maria's immediate impulse was to say, 'Thanks, Maggie, but it's okay. I can get a taxi easily.' Clearly it was part of Maggie's plan, whatever it was, whether then taking shape or already fully formed in the girl's permanently active, scheming mind, to get Miss Seetoh into her car for the useful duration of at least half an hour to put the plan into operation.

'Miss Seetoh, get in, quick! There's a car behind honking. Okay, you impatient idiot!' She turned around to make a rude sign, ordered her young passenger to open the back door, and in a second, Maria, as if against her will, was swept into the back seat. 'Miss Seetoh, this is Angel, my little sister. You recognise or not?' said Maggie laughing shrilly. 'She grow into big girl now. Very pretty, but very naughty girl. Angel, say good afternoon to Miss Seetoh!'

The alarm bells in her head never rang more insistently. The red Volvo reeking of the smell of new leather, probably a gift from one of the hard-drinking companions in the bars and lounges, possibly the man with dark glasses she had seen waiting for Maggie at Yen Ping's wake, the whiff of the bars and lounges clinging to Maggie's extravagant hairdo, clothes, perfume, high heels, make-up, nail varnish and multitude of jangling jewellery, the new sly smile of the young Angel signifying an innocence already lost or about to be lost in the older sister's plans for her – oh no, the world of Maggie spelt danger of the worst kind that should never be allowed to even remotely touch hers.

Maggie said, as she drove along and Maria tried to work out the motive for the new mood of expansive affability, 'Angel and I going to the Hotel Premier for high tea. Their high tea really high class, I tell you! Come and join us, Miss Seetoh.'

Maria declined firmly. 'No, I hope you don't mind, Maggie, but I really have to be home now.'

The girl now turned on her a look of deep distress, apparently part of an ongoing scheme of enticement, 'Miss Seetoh, something very important. About my sister Angel, I need your advice. You are only one I trust for advice, Miss Seetoh. I really trust you, Miss Seetoh.' Maggie could use that word to serve any mood or purpose. There was no relenting in Maria.

'Maggie, I've already told you. Our days as teacher and student are over. Too much has happened. It's best that we don't see each other again.'

Maggie's eyes suddenly filled with tears. They were not the tears of defiance and anger that Maria had seen that awful day when she rushed out of the creative writing class, but the artful tears of manipulation, causing the alarm bells to ring shrilly. The girl turned to say something to Angel who responded sharply. They were speaking in a dialect that was totally unintelligible to Maria except in the strident tones of accusation, for Maria was convinced Maggie was blaming her sister for what was happening. Soon the sisters were shouting at each other, and Angel started crying.

'For goodness' sake, stop all that,' said Maria severely. 'What on earth's going on?'

'We both in trouble, Miss Seetoh,' said Maggie blowing her nose on a piece of tissue paper, 'and only you can advise us. Please, Miss Seetoh, don't say no.'

Over high tea at the Hotel Premier, Maria thought, as she listened to the indefatigable Maggie, now all dry-eyed and cheerful, I must never let down my guard with this girl. It turned out that the big problem Maggie had intimated was none at all; it had to do with Angel who was not paying enough attention to her studies, and too much to her boyfriend, someone called Eddie who worked as a deejay.

Maggie who had settled on certain awkward euphemisms (where on earth had she got them, Maria wondered) to describe her work – 'I am in the social entertainment enhancement industry, Miss Seetoh,' 'I provide professional services to select clientele of certain social standing, Miss Seetoh' – said disdainfully, 'A deejay! I said to Angel, 'Why you so stupid? What future you got with deejay? Your sister work hard for you to go to university and you want to go with deejay'?'

Maria now understood what the noisy quarrel in the car had been about, for Angel screamed back, 'You leave me alone! You don't boss me around. I can go with whoever I like!'

Maggie ignored her, as if she were a recalcitrant child, turned to Maria and said with a very serious face, 'Miss Seetoh, I know you already leave St Peter's. Now no job, no income. How about you give private tuition to Angel, prepare her for the English language G.C.E. O Level paper? I can pay you well, Miss Seetoh, because you excellent teacher. Also, Miss Seetoh, I can find you other students, go to your place for private tuition. You can make lots of money, more than teacher's salary. You know or not, the old Chinese language teacher at St Peter's, Mr Kam, he left and give private tuition, bought big apartment.'

Everything came out in one rushed, breathless effort of persuasion that was too urgent to be interrupted. Maria, now clear about the purpose of Maggie's ambush of her as she was waiting for her taxi, said firmly, 'Right now, Maggie, I have no thought about giving private tuition. I can only think about writing a book, which I've always wanted to do.'

The first statement was a lie, the second the perfect truth: she would have no choice but to work as a private tutor to support her passion of writing which might remain just that – a passion only, with no financial reward.

Her new life was shaping more clearly by the day. With Por Por's death, she could sit down and work out the practicalities that had to be in place before the dream could be invited in. It would be divested of its centerpiece, that lovely little studio apartment that grew lovelier with its unattainability, but it could still be the happy, peaceful world she had long yearned to be in. If it was to maintain its peace, Maggie and anyone connected with her had better not be part of it.

Maggie pushed a little further, commandeering her entire panoply of persuasive skills, including melodrama and clowning. She said, tugging a lock of Angel's hair and making the younger girl scream in protest, 'Miss Seetoh, you know how much I love my little sister, will do anything for her. You know or not, I open bank account for her, to save money for her university education. Because she is very bright girl, with brains and can go to university, not like her stupid sister Maggie!'

Angel made a face and began eating a large plate of ice cream. She said sullenly, 'Always checking on me. Always calling to see whether I am doing my homework.'

In Maria's ever active imagination suddenly flashed the most bizarre picture of Maggie in the black sexy lingerie she had once seen her in a dream, wearing for a triumphant Bernard no longer burdened with cancer; the man in the picture was not her husband but the man with the dark glasses in the car, and Maggie was saying to him, right in the throes of lust, 'Please excuse me, something very urgent, can't wait,' before jumping out of bed and going into another room to make a call to her sister, 'Angel, good, so you at home. Are you doing your homework? When I come home, show me.'

Then she saw Maggie, now divested of the lingerie, climbing back into bed. Maria had to suppress a smile for the situation had lost its lightness, and Maggie was looking at her with the old hardness and resentment. The girl opened her gleaming leather handbag to take out a name-card to give her.

'Here's my phone number, Miss Seetoh. If change mind, want to coach Angel, just call me. I can pay you double the normal tuition fees, no problem.' She placed a hand on the table where Maria could see a sparkling diamond on her middle finger that she was sure had not been there before. A thought occurred to her and froze her: could it be the lost Tiffany ring that was not lost after all? Maggie was a liar, cheat, braggart and thief, all rolled into one. She had not seen the ring long enough to be able to identify it; in any case, she did not care, and as she rose to leave, insisting she would take a taxi back, she never disliked her former student more.

Neither Maggie nor Angel would be allowed anywhere near her new world. She would remember to change her phone number so that she would not be bothered by Maggie's calls again.

Thirty-Eight

The visit from Father Rozario was uncomfortable; she was sure it had to do with her mother and she was right. 'Your mother asks you to forgive her,' said the good priest, and before Maria could ask an astonished 'Why?' he said, 'For not attending your grandmother's funeral.'

There was the dilatory explanation expected of her mother, which the good priest, on her behalf, must have memorised word by word, about needing to act in accordance with one's conscience; Anna Seetoh's conscience had told her it would be wrong to take part in a Taoist ceremony.

'Is it wrong, Father?' asked Maria, and Father Rozario replied, 'I suppose in the end it depends on your conscience.'

In her new life with Heng, Anna was in the midst of a novena of prayers to bring about the conversion of his wife, one more feather in her cap of evangelical zeal, and she did not want to spoil it by attending a pagan ceremony. She wanted priestly support of her stand, and Father Rozario had readily, good-naturedly obliged. 'Pagan?' Maria remonstrated. 'Do you call Por Por 'pagan'?' Father patiently explained that Anna Seetoh had used the word in the purely technical sense of a non-Christian, with no derogatory meaning intended.

'Father, my Por Por was a good, kind person. Do you think she is in heaven now?' Maria's willful streak, already manifested in childhood when she had asked impossible questions of the kindly Sister St Aidan ('Sister, how come if the Garden of Eden was in a dry desert area it had an apple tree?'), was asserting itself now, not to discomfit the priest whom she actually liked for his generosity to all his parishioners, but to hear what God's representatives in a multi-ethnic, mutli-religious society, had learnt to say in response to tricky questions.

Father Rozario said, 'God is our merciful father. He will never condemn a good person.'

He winced slightly when Maria, her willfulness not at an end, asked, 'Can animals go to heaven, Father?'

'I could look it up in the Bible for you if you like,' he said desultorily, and it was then that she administered a stern rebuke to herself: 'Maria, for goodness' sake, stop harassing the poor priest!'

He stayed for coffee and cookies, prudently sticking to innocuous topics of a non-religious nature, such as the weather and the declining health of poor Mrs TPK whom many parishioners were praying for. Then he rose to take his leave, never mentioning once that in the list of people to be prayed for by the church prayer group, it was not Mrs TPK but Maria Seetoh, widow of the good, pious Bernard Tan, who headed the list.

Shortly after, Anna Seetoh paid a visit to her daughter. 'If it makes you happy,' she said, 'I will visit Por Por's niche in the columbarium with you, and say my own prayers for her.'

Maria said, 'Mother, let's sit down. There's something we have to talk about seriously, if we don't want to end up not talking to each other at all.' It was the simplest of modus vivendis: agree to disagree on the matter of beliefs and thereafter steer absolutely clear of any topic that might break the agreement. 'For one thing, Mother,' said Maria, 'I don't want you to threaten me with hellfire. For another, I don't want you, every time you say something to me, to add, 'Praise the Lord', or 'God's will be done', or ' Blessed Mother Mary knows.'

For Maria, the invocations had reached a point of irritation equal to the infliction of tinnitus; each time her mother shared a piece of information, good or bad, made a complaint, issued a warning, paid a compliment, the sheer certainty that the invocations would follow in a precise second, made in exactly the same tone of voice, with exactly the same pious uplift of eyes, would drive her crazy.

'Alright, Mother? And a third thing. No reference to what Heng is saying and doing now that he's a devout Christian. I don't want to hear a word more. Alright?'

'Alright,' said Anna Seetoh curtly. 'You do all the talking. I'll listen.'

'No, Mother, that's not the point,' said the strong-willed daughter. 'You can do as much talking as you like, minus those three irritations. Now, to be fair, I want you tell me what you want me to avoid saying or doing, so as not to irritate you.'

Anna Seetoh said stiffly, 'Nothing. You can do and say anything you like. You are the smart one. I'll just keep quiet and listen.'

It turned out that Anna had something to talk about after all. Maria had noted on previous occasions her mention of a certain Joseph Boey, the sacristan of her church, who she described as an extremely kind and helpful man. He had gone out of his way several times to make her and Heng feel comfortable in their early attendance at the church services. When his name came up for mention a few more times, Maria decided to do a little investigation of her own. Over her mother's favourite minced pork noodles in her favourite restaurant, she pounced on the name as soon as it came up again, watching eagle-eyed for tell-tale signs. Anna Seetoh's mood was a big improvement over the sullen guardedness of the first few days, which made it easier for her to say with teasing gusto, 'Aha, Mother! Who is this Joseph Boey? Don't tell me you've found your heartthrob?'

The sheer novelty of teasing her mother on a subject as alien as it was shocking, and watching the sudden flush on her cheeks and her little cries of protest, provided a special piquancy to a mischievous nature carried over from childhood. She remembered that as a little girl, she had one day put a grasshopper in her mother's hair for the thrill of seeing this most prim and well-mannered parent break out into a frenzy of screaming and hair-searching. Every memory of her mother playing and laughing with her, telling her stories of ancient gods and goddesses, was precious, and its pleasure worth recapturing even in the sober years of their adult lives.

Joseph Boey was one of those elderly, very pious retirees, mainly widows and widowers, who formed a reliable pool of volunteers found in any church, who could always be seen cleaning the altar, dusting or polishing statues and candlesticks, getting ready the prayer books for the next service, arranging the flowers, lighting the candles. As they went about their work in quiet devoted service, often working together, anything more than pious fellowship would be both a scandal and a sacrilege. Joseph Boey provided the perfect opportunity to steer her mother from her dreary, religion-drenched talk to something that might just expose another, unexpected, indeed, refreshing, side of her.

'Ah, Mother, I see you're blushing!' said Maria pursuing the subject with relentless relish. 'It's alright, Mother. It's alright to take a lover, if he makes you happy.'

Anna Seetoh uttered a little cry of protest against the obscene word. 'Maria, how can you say anything like that? You ought to be ashamed of yourself!' She began a flurry of hand gestures of frantic dismissal accompanied by cries of '*Choy! Choy!*', exactly as she had done, years ago, when she wanted to dismiss the evil image of the man who had sat opposite them in a ferry and exposed himself.

Lust, concupiscence, carnal desire. Even married couples could be guilty of these sins. After her conversion to Catholicism, with the presence of a daughter to attest to her fulfillment of holy matrimony's purpose, Anna Seetoh had rejected all her husband's attempts at sex.

Maria watched her mother closely. There was the unmistakable blush, as of a young girl caught unawares. 'You must introduce me to this Joseph Boey one of these days, Mother.' Anna Seetoh, secure in her faith, terrified about what fellow parishioners would think of her, would never have a romance, or even remotely approach one. There would be none of the torturous quandaries that her daughter had experienced, there would be no line to cross, no perilous edge overlooking a chasm to peep into and withdraw from. When Anna Seetoh went down on her knees to pray, it was for others, never for herself, for in her simple, ardent soul there were no inner demons to vanquish. But the blush, the frantically denying hand gestures, the stern prohibition against the subject ever occurring again, her own guardedness in future conversations – all proved that even the thick encrustations of nun-like piety that Anna Seetoh had, over so many years, laid over her consciousness, could be penetrated by every woman's need to be loved, touched, or at the least, singled out for attention by a man.

She had done her mother a disservice. Now poor Anna Seetoh, confused by the new light in which her perverse daughter had made her see her friendship with Joseph Boey, would very likely avoid him like poison. If he as much as tried to hold her hand, she would recoil in horror and flee the occasion for temptation. If she had a dream of them together, she would run to the cleansing power of the confessional the next morning and sob out her guilt: 'Father forgive me, for I have sinned. I had impure thoughts…'

Maria said again, 'Mother, it's okay! You are a widow, Joseph a widower; there can be no sin.' She reminded her mother of the example of two similarly circumstanced parishioners of the Church of Eternal Mercy, both in their sixties, who fell in love and got married.

Anna Seetoh pressed her hands to her ears and said, 'Stop. Stop this instant. You are saying disgusting things. Never talk like that in my presence again.'

She was unusually quiet during a shopping trip after lunch, when Maria, feeling closer to her mother than she had been for a long time, bought gifts, including books and toys for the autistic nephew, to take back to her new home in Malaysia.

Back home by herself, she thought with an amused smile, 'If I write about the love lives of the women in my family, poor Mother's innocence, would lie in the middle, a pure bright pool in stark contrast to the dark, churning waves at each end.' Was any family as strange as hers, where the woman in each generation could truly say, 'My mother and I were so different – like night and day,' and the outside observer could ask, with much astonishment: 'How could someone like you have produced a daughter like her?'

She thought of herself in old age; in her chosen life of solitude would she, even then, find love? Would she be like that lonely elderly widow who sought and found love, whose story was well-known in Singapore? The widow of a fairly successful businessman, she had found a lover eighteen years younger and was happy for the remaining years of her life, baffling all predictions about a faithless fortune-hunting husband.

When she died, he said proudly to his relatives and friends, 'It was not what people thought. It was love of her, not her money. I gave her seven years of happiness,' and made clear it was not just the happiness of gentle companionship during her extensive travels round the world, but the special happiness enjoyed only on the silken bed.

She met the jogger one more time in the Botanic Gardens, and once again, there was the proposition, a bold direct one without the usual preliminaries for testing the water. He had persuaded her, since it was getting dark, to take a lift home in his car; when he reached the car park of her block, he turned to her and said with a smile, 'Won't you ask me in for a cup of tea?'

They were sitting very close together in the growing darkness. She was suddenly gripped by one image that could sum up the amatory quandaries in her life: a parked car, herself and a man in the parked car, the enveloping darkness of evening to assure privacy and intimacy. Each time, it had ended either with a proposal or a proposition. The stark difference between the two would determine a woman's response; she was likely to rejoice at the first and react with anger or embarrassment to the second. She had recoiled at Bernard's proposal and demurred at Benjamin Phang's proposition, finally rejecting it. There was no hesitation at all in the case of the third supplicant. She simply said to the jogger, 'No. Goodnight and thank you for the lift,' and was gone in a second.

In later years she could not even recall his name or appearance, only the startling boast, the first time he had sat down and talked to her in the gardens, that he had bedded an American lady jogger the very first time he met her.

Alone by herself in those first weeks of retirement from her job at St Peter's Secondary School, she surrendered to the luxury of lying in bed for hours and letting her thoughts wander on their own. Like a flock of butterflies, they settled on the sweet allurements of love, lust, romance, sex, each a bright, enticing, fragrant bloom, gloriously indistinguishable from the other.

Maybe they were all one and the same, just different aspects of Nature's single, supreme strategy to propagate life on the face of the earth, so that the mountain goat in musth chasing the coy female across steep rocks was no different from her parents on their wedding night, her father eagerly lifting up her mother's chaste white cotton nightdress, no different from Por Por's and her lover's tentative explorations of each other's nakedness as they lay on some improvised bed of old sacks on the floor of a dark corner in a temple, no different from herself in the parked car where she lay against the warmth of Benjamin Phang's body.

This need of woman for man, of man for woman, must have received Nature's fiat to transcend even the restraining forces of culture, even the sternest strictures of religion and morality. Thou shalt not commit adultery. If you lust after a woman in your mind, you have already committed adultery. In every church there must be men and women, quietly sitting in the pews and listening to sermons about the sanctity of the marriage vows who had already broken them, in thought, word or deed.

The conscience in the end would be the most accommodating organ of the human self, reduced to a tiny voice that said, 'So what. Everyone does it.'

Nature probably never intended for this most primordial of needs to transcend death as well. The mountain goat, the prairie mole, the moth – they went their separate ways to die eventually of old age or as food for others; indeed, after the act of sex, they lost all interest in the partner. But the human being could pay no less homage to love than ascribe to it an eternal existence. In the Christian heaven there was no marriage and no sex, only pure love, but in the myths and legends that had endured from time immemorial across cultures, gods fell in love with goddesses and competed for their sexual favours; gods fell in love with earthly maidens, came down to earth or took them up into heavenly abodes; mortal lovers achieved immortality when they met at long last on an eternal shore; mortal lovers who were cruelly separated on earth could still be united in death by a marriage of their effigies.

Nature probably never intended for this need for love and sex to turn defiant and separate itself from the primary goal of propagation. As soon as they were able, men and women must have learnt to enjoy the pleasure without having to pay its price, delighting in the marvellous workings of Nature's love chemicals, and profiting from Nature's thoughtful provision of ambient moonlight, starlight, flowers in bloom. Nature's gift had become a free for all, satisfying the entire range of needs of the complex human being who liked to think of complexity only in terms of head and heart, forgetting a multitude of other entities, mostly nameless and unnameable, often vaguely referred to as the subconscious, the unconscious, the subliminal, each with its own pressing needs and demands. Thus, in catering to human complexity, love had become an obfuscation, defying definition, eluding scholarly efforts to pin it down to something comprehensible. It had the largest possible clientele – the young, the not-so-young, the brazen old, the poorest and the richest, the most powerful and the humblest, the most beautiful and the ugliest, the most saintly and the most sinful.

Moreover, it allowed a generous bursting of all boundaries, so that all could come together in a gloriously crazy mix: marriages and love affairs galore between young, winsome May and old, hoary December, waitress and multimillionaire banker, king and commoner, president and stripper, Esmeralda and Quasimodo, Lancelot and Guinevere, Lolita and her ageing professor, Abelard and Heloise. Love too claimed its martyrs, for, as frequently reported in newspapers all over the world, a girl from a high caste or a conservative, punitive religion, would run away to get married to her secret lover, and risk being murdered by her own family in a brutality called an honour killing.

Love had become marvellously, exasperatingly multiform, multifaceted, multidimensional, a vast fluid term to accommodate any variant of human need and emotion, so that even Anna Seetoh, experiencing the small girlish stirrings of pleasure in the presence of Joseph Boey, and Maria Seetoh, experiencing an inchoate, vague but still very real pleasure in the recollection of her days in St Peter's Secondary School with Brother Philip, could inhabit its vast hospitable mansions.

To each his own. Live and let live. Life goes on. In the end, life was lived according to the earthy wisdom of banalities and clichés, in accordance with Nature's primary law that said, Survive, be happy. In the end, Nature's brute laws of competition and forced cooperation in the game of survival, prevailed, not the high-sounding pronouncements of religion and morality.

In one of his letters, Brother Philip had described some educational project he had undertaken for the poor children of his parish and mentioned a co-worker named Sister Bridget who taught in the Convent of Mary and the Angels. In subsequent letters, he again referred to Sister Bridget in the warmest tones. Jealousy, which the head denounced as most unreasonable and downright despicable, could still be sustained by the heart's persistent questions: who was she? Was Brother Phil in love with her? Why was he singling her out for special mention in his letters? Was he trying to make his former colleague and close friend in St Peter's jealous? Did that mean that he was in love with her? What did it mean when a man who was committed to chaste service to God fell in love with a woman? Could it mean only love of the pure, non-sensual kind? Had he, in the first place, asked for the posting back to Ireland because he had become afraid of his feelings for her?

Maria decided that the inaction of solitude was bad for her, throwing her into agonies of thinking, that were traceable in the end to pure, useless vanity. In any case, thinking was now a luxury. She had to start planning for a new life, alone in an old, rundown apartment that needed repairs, having little money beyond some modest savings, keeping alive her passion to write when writing guaranteed no income. She stared gloomily at the old ceiling, the cracked cement floor of one of the bathrooms, the scuffed dining room set. Then she stared, even more gloomily, at a clutch of bills in her hands. She would have to think seriously about giving private tuition – coaching students to improve their grammar, pass their G.C.E. O Level English Language paper. The thought alone was dispiriting.

But there was no choice.

Thirty-Nine

Maria had always believed that when she looked back upon her life, in some distant time in the future, and picked out the happiest moment, it would have everything to do with her passion for writing, little to do with men, and still less to do with money.

The anxieties regarding her insecure financial position were increasing by the day, threatening an onslaught of those headaches once brought on by other matters. 'Oh dear,' she thought, looking at the intimidating bills that came in for water, electricity, servicing of the one air-conditioner she allowed herself in the apartment, replacement of some window panes that had cracked, and a new sofa to replace a very old one.

There was an official letter that puzzled her, and when she understood what it was all about, she yelped for joy, and said, 'Oh my God, Oh my God,' for not only would all her money problems be solved, but that long dreamt-of studio apartment in the heart of the city was within reach. Best of all, it would make it no longer necessary for her to earn a living through private tuition. If she, profane as she was, dared to see herself as a pilgrim, she was one moment in that Slough of Despond and the next, looking up at the brightness of a city beckoning from a hill top.

Singaporeans' lives would be changed forever by the new phenomenon called the en bloc fever, by which ordinary, modest home-owners became millionaires overnight. It was truly a fever, with a rash of generous offers from property developers suddenly aware of the value of old developments and the homeowners delirious with excitement. The developers sniffed out the potentially valuable housing estates, even if old and rundown, to buy, then to tear down, and raise in their place gleaming sky-high condominiums attractive to the newly rich and the foreigners coming in droves to work in Singapore. The newspapers for a while were filled with amazing reports of these instant-wealth stories. One ran a story about a couple, a clerk and his wife, who thirty years ago had acquired an apartment in a housing development that was now five times its original value. Maria's apartment was in that breathless category, causing her to say in a voice weak with astonishment, 'Oh my God, that's even better than winning that coveted first prize in the Singapore National Lottery.'

She remembered the time she had prayed to God for that win, and now he was answering her prayer. Or rather, since he had been de-deified and de-anthropomorphised by her, and had melted into any number of abstractions that could be called, variously, Chance, Randomness, Probability, Accident, Happenstance and Luck, it was in the capacity of the last named that he was answering her prayer. And since she could not thank Luck personally, she could at least show her gratitude by spreading it around a little.

She called her mother and Heng in Malaysia to tell them the good news. She told them, for a start, that she would pay for the expensive fees that were being charged by her little nephew's school for special needs children. She also offered to pay for some expensive dental treatment that Heng's wife needed. She thought with some pique: couldn't her mother and brother rejoice with her in her good luck? They had received her news with an uneasy silence. Heng was obviously in deep shock about the sheer bad luck of signing over his share of the apartment to her for a sum of money that was but a fraction of what he would now have got and that he had long dissipated at the gambling table. Her mother was in a different kind of shock: how God could have favoured a prodigal daughter over the returned black sheep, and concluded that even money, that featured so strongly in the Seven Deadly Sins, could be used in Providence's mysterious ways to bring back a sinner. She said, 'Maria, it is God's doing. He has a purpose for you.' There was a moment of returning dislike for her brother when he said he would get his lawyer to look into the terms of the document he had made her sign in the purchase of his half of the flat; so the old greed was still there, and he was hoping some legal loophole would enable him to claim a share of her new fortune.

A new kind of pleasure had been opened up for her by new wealth, starting with the acquisition of the studio apartment. For the first time in her life, she would live in a place that bore the full stamp of her personality, her taste, her every preference. The sense of sole proprietorship was deeply satisfying. 'Oh, how happy I am!' she thought as she looked at her new home, explored every little room, smelt its newness, for she would not have wanted a place that had already been lived in, that bore the marks of another's life story. She was not superstitious but grimaced at tales of the new occupants of a house seeing strange shapes, hearing strange noises that turned out to be the last mournful sounds of the deceased former owner.

A bed, a room, a house, a life of her own – the secret dreams that had begun in childhood and persisted through the years of her marriage, and again through the years with her mother and grandmother, were now all coming together in a grand finale of ownership, fulfillment and supreme happiness. Against the background of a home beautifully appointed to her taste (she could now afford to replace the old ugly furniture, curtains and crockery), in the peace and contentment of a life renewed and energies revived, she could concentrate on the greatest dream in her life: to write a book, and then another, and another. All this was made possible by the huge cheque that Luck had dropped on her lap. She would always remember that thrilling moment when, excited as a child showing off a new, expensive toy, she had taken the cheque to be deposited into her bank account and watched the expression on the face of the bank officer. She was somewhat disappointed that the girl appeared unimpressed, being used to handling fabulous sums in a city where, it was said, ordinary hawkers could walk into a bank in their open shirts and sandals and hand over the counter a large paper bag stuffed with cash. A moneyed city state – for the first time she became part of it, wide-eyed with gratitude and joy.

She took an intense interest in every story she read or heard about, regarding Luck's visitations upon other favoured Singaporeans. A couple who thought they could never afford to retire, finally did, went on a round-the-world cruise and came back to their brand new apartment in a much better locality. A single mother who was carefully saving up to pay for the university education of one of her two sons could now afford to send both to a university in Canada. She was also thinking of buying a small apartment near the university, so that all three could continue living together, and she could cook their favourite Singapore *laksa* and *mee siam* for them.

There were unhappy stories as well. A divorcing couple who had peacefully settled on who was to get which of their two jointly-owned properties, soon quarrelled violently and went to court over the terms of the settlement, for the husband's share was now only a pitiable quarter of the wife's in value. A man who had generously sold his flat to a sibling at a price below market value was suing her for a return of the flat now worth hugely more, arguing that it was not a sale at all, but a temporary gift. In a housing estate that could not go through the en bloc sale because some residents refused to move, there were angry anonymous letters put into their letter-boxes, rubbish left outside their doors and black paint smeared on their parked cars, and vicious rumours about two mysterious suicides in the estate, condemning it to bad luck for years.

Maria thought, in my new world, I want to have nothing to do with the greed, envy, superstition, folly, stupidity in the big world out there. She saw a delightful image of a clean, white bubble in mid ocean, sealed against floating scum. She wanted nothing even of the minor irritations of dealing with unreasonable bosses, mean colleagues, difficult students, that had come with her teaching job. It was a wonderful irony that money had freed her from its own tyranny.

In her new world too, there would be nothing of uncertainty, doubt, guilt, jealousy, wounded pride, since she would no longer have anything to do with love and romance, much less marriage. She had tried and failed miserably. Some of her girl friends, also living on their own, said, 'If it comes, it comes,' meaning that they were still open to a proposal, a proposition.

At age forty-three, she thought, 'That part of my life is over. There is so much living to do! I can hardly wait to begin.'

Goodbye to the old Maria Seetoh. Long live the new!

Happy future plans, once only a remote dream, unfolded like a lovely gleaming silk scroll of promise and enchantment. She could travel, do the exciting cruises she had heard about. Some of her friends had gone on safaris in Africa and desert treks in India; they had camped on snow-clad mountain slopes in Austria and visited remote villages tucked away in the Himalayas. Her own mother had been to France, to the renowned pilgrimage centre of Lourdes. She wanted to do her own pilgrimage, to Greece to see and touch the very places where her favourite philosophers had taught thousands of years ago. Even better, she would go abroad for those summer writing courses she had read about, even do a postgraduate degree in a university in Singapore and abroad. It would not matter if she sat in a class with students half her age. Her student days had been among her happiest; she could reclaim that happiness under even better circumstances. Best of all, she could now get down to the serious job of looking into the huge pile of notes, the raw material for her writing, accumulated over so many years. They were in old shoe boxes, stacked somewhere on high shelves, groaning with the treasures and the debris from the past that would have to be carefully separated.

'My dear Brother Phil,' she wrote. 'This is going to be such a bright, cheerful letter which I never thought I would be able to write to you. No, it has nothing to do with any reversal of the sad things that have happened: Mark and Yen Ping continue to live in sad memory; Maggie and her sister Angel are in a world that I have no wish to even peek at; I am permanently out of St Peter's and permanently unemployed; poor Por Por is dead and gone, her ashes kept in a temple columbarium; my mother is in Malaysia with my brother Heng, and despite her fervent prayers, he has lapses of the gambling habit which she won't tell me about; my little autistic nephew is improving, but very slowly; I occasionally think of poor V.K. Pandy who is now only a very faint memory in Singapore.

But I am happier now than I have ever been. It is not good to talk about money to a man of God who is committed to, among other vows, the vow of poverty. But dear Brother Phil, if I could, I would give this filthy god Mammon a kiss for showering his filthy lucre on me! He has a Chinese counterpart, the Deity of Prosperity who has been around a long time in Singapore, claiming a very honoured place in local temples where devotees show their gratitude after winning lotteries by burning giant joss-sticks and making big donations to the temple. It would be too tedious to go into all the details of this new phenomenon in Singapore that everyone is calling the en bloc madness. It is a kind of collective sale whereby developers are prepared to hand out large sums to homeowners for their properties because of the much larger sums they will get in return from the condominiums they will build on every available inch of land they have acquired. I think you can guess what has happened. I can thank my old apartment for relieving me of every financial worry, the major one being of course finding a job to support myself. I was in fact getting ready to offer private tuition, to spend the rest of my life preparing students for those hateful exams! Can you imagine me, dear Brother Phil, growing grey and furrowed as I struggle to get that dumb student to score at least a credit in his English language paper. Now, thanks again to Mammon/ Deity of Prosperity (whom I hope I never worship but only offer a genuine, profound, once-and-for-all thank you card) I can concentrate on my writing; you, dear Brother Phil, more than anyone, had encouraged me in the pursuit of this passion. How I wish you were here for me to talk to you about it. I'm as excited as a child.

Only the other day I was going through some of the notes I'd been scribbling down for years in notebooks and scraps of paper, and found some that must have been inspired by you or that I must have shown to you. Do you remember that we had actually talked about collaborating on a play in Singlish? I think the idea came from you. Well, dear Brother Phil, if you are not too busy working on that educational project with Sister Bridget (now you must tell me more about her so that I can decide whether or not to be jealous) and if by chance you happen to come to this part of the world, could I invite you to my new home and my new world? By that time I should be able to cook up a decent meal of fried *bee hoon*. I'm thinking, now that I have much more free time, to do a cooking course. Can you imagine me in apron and chef's cap?! Maybe also swimming. And yoga. And computer. And dancing. You could start warning me about those dashing young dance instructors who are able to sniff out new money.

I have at least three stories about Singapore's *tai tais* who fell for their dancing instructors. But no, no flamboyant adventurer, beau, swain, suitor, in my life. I'm out of the game completely. (If you're curious about a certain suitor whom I had told you in confidence about, we'll leave that to a later time when I can look at things even more dispassionately and honestly.)

Come to think of it, you will be the only one admitted into my new world. For you're the only one who has ever made me feel comfortable. For once, I'm going to ignore your advice about getting out of my skin. I'm going to be very happy staying inside it.

Do come visit, dear Brother Phil. For a start, I could show you some memorabilia from St Peter's, (including the 'plague' award that made us laugh so much, remember?) for although I left in unhappy circumstances – I will leave the details to some future letter – I still have fond memories of my home class students, my creative class students, and of you, my best friend in St Peter's. I have saved all your limericks. They still raise a smile.

Much love,

Maria.

PS Could I make a little donation to your educational project? I'd love to.'

Forty

I keep saying I'm happy, thought Maria, but what does it mean? I'm going to examine this happiness, observing it both from the outside with the calm objectivity of the true experimenter, and from the inside with the exuberant subjectivity of my own personal self. For happiness must be both science and art, belonging to the realms of reality and of the imagination in equal parts. She wanted to see how the reality of her new world, in the concrete, tangible, measurable details of day-to-day living, on the one hand, and the inner life of her emotions, on the other, were bearing upon each other.

The unit of a typical day was good for the observation. The self-observing observer. It began with the child's delight of a day free from school, from the tyrannies of alarm clock, rushed breakfast, rushed taxi ride to school, the start of a routine predictable to the last minute accounted for in the class timetable. Routine – that word would acquire new connotations of reassuring familiarity, cosy domesticity. Like a disembodied presence, she saw herself getting out of bed at last, swinging her legs over the edge, going to the front door to pick up the morning newspaper on the doorstep, reading it in bed with a leisureliness so unaccustomed and hence so relished that it could be the very raison d'etre for reading at all. And the two cups of coffee she allowed herself everyday at breakfast: while enjoying the aroma of the first, she was already anticipating the pleasurable indulgence of the second. The gratification of a self-imposed discipline.

She had bought several health books and guides, being suddenly aware of the need to take better care of herself and enjoy her independence to a very ripe, very old age where both mind and body (unlike poor Por Por's) would be in perfectly harmonious working condition. Cooking simple, healthy meals for herself instead of sitting down to a common meal prepared by the maid with a view to pleasing different tastes was a distinct satisfaction; she remembered hating the meat or vegetable dishes that had to be cooked to a paste to allow for poor Por Por's toothlessness. Even greater than the freedom to eat exactly what she liked was the freedom to eat precisely when she liked; her mother and grandmother were used to rigidly fixed mealtimes, whether or not one felt hungry.

One evening, she had fallen asleep over a re-reading of a novel by Conrad that she had read years ago, only because it had been required reading for her literature course in the university. She woke up, thinking, 'Well, time to prepare lunch,' and discovered she had slept through the meal. In the past, her mother or the maid would have awakened her. Mealtimes could be gloriously disregarded, hunger completely untied to any regulating schedule. Sleeping through the hours when she would have been in the classroom standing before the chalkboard or sitting through a dreary staff-meeting gave an even sharper tang to the new liberating sensation.

When she was growing up, her mother had never felt the need to teach her the obligatory female skills of cooking, sewing, housecleaning; Anna Seetoh had always said, 'You study hard, be a good person, that's all I ask of you,' and did everything for her, ironing her school uniforms, cleaning her shoes, even combing and plaiting her hair. In the years of her marriage, her husband never wanted to see her sweep, clean, cook or do any household work, except when it came to personal items like his shoes, preferring her to spend all her free time by his side. She had looked upon housework as a chore that mercifully, she had been spared all her life. But now, in the little apartment of her choice, surrounded by domestic appurtenances that bore the stamp of her approval and taste, down to the last little teaspoon and potted plant, she felt that household work was not only pleasurable but ennobling, a woman's daily affirmation of life and selfhood. She noticed, with a heightened sense of recognition and wonder, that it was always when she was doing the simplest, the most mundane things that certain ideas would come to her mind, lighting it up to illumine stories rapidly taking shape. Such inspirational moments had been experienced before, but now they came with a new energy to match the briskness in her limbs as she went about the daily tasks of dusting, sweeping, washing dishes at the sink, putting clothes in the laundry, taking them out to dry. She even felt an affinity with inanimate objects that submitted to her will and emerged from her hands spotlessly clean, gleaming, radiating with housework's sanctity.

She found herself humming as she worked, then singing aloud, mainly the silly love songs of her girlhood. She thought of a party at which the girls of St Anne's Convent School and the boys of St Stephen's Brothers' School got together for a decorous, chaperoned church event, and recollected that one of the boy organisers had cunningly slipped into the approved selection of boy scout and girl guide songs a love song in which Doris Day sang about wanting to croon love's tune by the light of the silvery moon. The boys and girls erupted in wild cheering, and Sister St Agatha merely smiled stiffly and avoided looking at Brother Aloysius.

Her pleasures in solitude would cover a dazzling range, from the intellectual stimulation of the books she had hidden from her husband to the seductive allurement of girlhood romances.

She remembered, with fondness, the artistic student in her home class at St Peter's who did all the memorable cartoons for her language lessons. If she commissioned a picture captioned 'Where Does the Inspiration Come From?', he would probably draw a cartoon of her, with hair piled up, one stray strand down a sweaty forehead, a clothes' peg in her mouth, hanging up a blouse on a clothesline bristling with items of underwear, while just above her head, hung a lightbulb with a brilliant sunburst of rays.

Her happiness, she realised, was deep and enduring precisely because it comprised the very small, the ordinary, the quotidian. She had yearned to scale the lofty heights of passion and found peace in the rootedness of small things on the ground. She had longed to write on the large canvas of life, recording the sweep of human thought and emotion, and concluded that her talent lay in working on a little square inch of ivory, with reliable, painstaking stylus, as her much loved novelist from childhood, Jane Austen, had recommended.

The small events, the insignificant people of her childhood who now crowded her memory, including the little girl whose death was announced by the cry of an owl, the old woman picking up empty beer cans and cardboard from a rubbish bin to sell for a few cents – they would populate her stories, their littleness radiated by the simplicity and honesty of their lives. Happiness miniaturised, like the tiny dolls she had once seen, with every fineness of detail preserved, with none of its beauty lost.

There was a knock on the door. Surprised, for since moving into her apartment in the new condominium, she had not made a single friend, she got up to look through the peephole, and saw three children all dressed in Halloween costumes. The custom was largely observed by the expatriate community only, but of the three children only one was Caucasian, a blonde child dressed like a witch. The other two were dressed as demons with the unmistakable horns, forked tail and trident. All had paint on their faces to show elaborate frowns, wrinkles, fangs. They must be the children of occupants in the condominium.

'Trick or treat?' they said shyly. She would remember to keep a stock of candy; right now she only had cookies which the children received with a disappointed look before running away.

She made friends with one of the security guards, a cheerful woman named Asma whose heavy make-up and brightly varnished nails contrasted oddly with the drab khaki guard uniform. Asma introduced herself to each of the condominium residents with a joke, 'My name is Asma, spelt A-S-M-A. Without the T-H,' upon which she would simulate an exaggerated attack of wheezing and panting before concluding with a loud chuckle, 'I am your very healthy, very capable security guard!'

'My dear Brother Phil,' she wrote. 'You were rightly amused by all the trivia I had written in my previous letter. Here's more trivia, but in a completely different sense. I've come to notice and love the very small things in existence which I had taken for granted. Now I realise they are the very stuff of existence and meaning. I wanted to know what I was happy about, and at the end of the day listed a dozen things that were all small, ordinary, everyday. The last item of happiness was a TV programme about outrageous pets, which I enjoyed thoroughly, because it made me laugh out loud. You would, if you had seen the little cocker spaniel taking full possession of the house, including the master bedroom. No, the last item was actually a quiet read in bed, before I fell asleep, of quotations from wise men and women that I had picked up over the years. One was a poem, and it made me think of you, because I had copied it out for you – remember the lovely poem by that marvellous Lebanese-American poet Kahlil Gibran about being together, and yet staying apart as individuals, about being like the separate strings of a flute yet quivering to the same music? See, I continue to be the incurable romantic, but the self-contradictory one with head in a swirl of clouds and feet planted firmly on the ground! (I can see you smiling and shaking your head.)

About a week ago, I saw the ghost of my Por Por. Or rather, thought I saw. It was about ten in the evening. She was standing near the writing desk where I had placed the box containing her favourite dragon ornament inside the top drawer, and she appeared to be looking for it. She turned to give me a look and seemed well and happy. And, most oddly, I did not regard her as a supernatural visitant then, but as my flesh-and-blood Por Por who was always looking for this or that thing, searching shelves and drawers, and asking Rosiah or me for help. I said, going up to her, 'Por Por, it's in there, let me take it out for you,' but at that instant she vanished. Now I know why Yen Ping's family insisted that her spirit had come back, as proved by the displaced blanket on the bed, the slept-on pillow, the drunk tea. I looked closely at the table to see if there were displaced objects, and guess what I noticed? The drawer had been slightly pulled open. I am almost positive it was completely shut when I last saw it. There you are – the yearning heart that sees what it wants to see!

Yesterday, three small children in Halloween costumes came to my door. They looked adorable. My mother had actually suggested my adopting a child. Imagine that! I suppose she wants someone to take care of me in my old age. No thank you. I love children and animals, but from a distance away from their mess and noise and crankiness! (I can hear you say, with that tiny, crinkling, cynical smile: 'She likes humanity, not people; she likes God but in the abstract; she loves men but across a chasm.') Do you realise that we are both at that dreadful period of life called the climacteric that heralds decline and decrepitude? Can you imagine us growing old together, old and grey and full of sleep, wearing our trousers rolled? No way! I've got a new hairstyle and a new lipstick to match the precise pink of a new cushion cover. Frivolity, at any age, is a legitimate female indulgence. Which Sister Bridget must be free from. By the way, you still haven't told me about her. When you do, I will use all my writer's skills of forensic detection to scrutinise every noun, adjective, verb and preposition to decide whether jealousy is called for.

Love
Maria.'

In her happiness, she had tamed jealousy, making it a ready tool for wit and self-deprecatory humour. A thought occurred at this point: if she happened to see Benjamin Phang now at the Polo Club, dancing with an attractive woman, holding her close, would the old feelings of shock and hurt return? Would she have another night of fitful sleep? She had read about scientific experiments on jealousy that concluded it to be a purely reflexive, unconscious reaction, so that a woman, while all the time denying it, was actually registering all the physiological telltale signs on the instruments attached to her head, chest and fingertips. She had no doubt she would defy those instruments and pass the test.

There had been a single postcard from him when he was ambassador to Germany, addressed to her at St Peter's and redirected to her old apartment, bearing only the brief salutations and niceties necessitated by an open mode of communication. 'How are you?' he had asked. But it was only a typical opening line, not a genuine question requiring an answer. In the first few days in her new home, while watching TV, she heard the newscaster announce his new posting to Japan and saw his image appear for a few seconds. On both occasions, there had been no reaction from her. She had passed the most crucial test of all, a self-imposed one: there had been no more dreams of him since she moved into her new life.

Happiness could be infectious, reaching across continents and oceans. Meeta wrote a note to say that her sister and brother-in-law were thoroughly spoiling her; she was enjoying a very active social life with the arty crowd in New Delhi. Meeta painted her new happiness in the brightest aphorisms: live life in technicolour, not monochrome; be a glutton at life's smorgasbord! Winnie expressed her joy in more down-to-earth terms: Wilbur was building an extension to their already large house in the countryside to accommodate the increasing number of grandchildren who always came with their parents to celebrate Thanksgiving. God/Providence/Force/Fate/Chance was in his/her/its heaven; all was well with the world!

My little square inch of paradise on earth, thought Maria. How I love my tiny two-room studio apartment. Its description announced its purpose of seclusion for serious, artistic work, thereby barring all visitors capable only of trivial, meaningless talk (Her immediate neighbour was a fashion designer; she had only seen him emerge from the apartment once, wearing a black T-shirt, black trousers, a black-and-white scarf, a gold earring) She thought, my little world is sealed against the great one outside, with a little door opening out as and when I want.

For her new world would not be a cloister; that was for those women who declared themselves dead to the world, and she was very much alive. She had never seen a cloister but as a girl had been impressed by pictures showing the seclusion and serenity of a Carmelite convent where it was said a woman walked in but was carried out. It meant that from the moment she stepped into a convent, its doors shut her out completely from the world to which she would return only as a corpse, carried out for burial. Since nuns usually lived to a very ripe old age, the time separating the live walking feet and the dead shrouded feet could be many decades.

Maria thought, I love the world too much to want to be so cruelly sequestered from it. She was rediscovering its pleasures, all the greater if savoured in the leisureliness and freedom of pure solitude – the shopping centres where shopping with the maid and Por Por had been rushed, anxious affairs, the cafés where she had enjoyed lunches with friends but experienced a special pleasure just sitting by herself having a sandwich and coffee, idly watching the world go by; the bookshops where she could spend hours browsing; and best of all the Botanic Gardens, scene of so much joy and pain, peace and tumult, which she could now visit in the capacity of a person renewed and recharged.

A call came from Maggie. How on earth had the girl managed to get her new number?

'Miss Seetoh, have to talk to you, there's nobody for me to talk, only you, my old teacher who I trust in the world,' she said in a tearful opening calculated to soften a heart much less steeled against her manoeuvres than Maria's.

'Alright,' Maria said wearily, 'what is it now.'

It was the same complaint about Angel not taking her studies seriously, taking that useless deejay guy too seriously, frustrating all Maggie's efforts to give her a good education.

For the first time the girl mentioned the name of the man in dark glasses. She called Sonny her close friend and supporter who also took care of Angel, but hinted there might be trouble involving all three of them. Talking rapidly and breathlessly, Maggie became incoherent in a sudden massive discharge of information about her life and problems. Maria listened desultorily, her mind occupied elsewhere with more pleasant thoughts. She heard only the rising inflections of Maggie's frustration and anger – 'so ungrateful, I want to kill her!', 'he all useless, adding to problem, not helping me solve, I want to kill him!' The girl's histrionics simply fell flat on her ears and she was jerked out of her inattention only when she heard Maggie ask urgently, 'So can you do this favour for me, please, Miss Seetoh?'

It turned out that Sonny had turned violent one evening and slapped her, pulled her hair and knocked her head against the wall.

'He all drunk and sexy, want, sex, sex, sex all the time. Miss Seetoh, how can woman always be there, give sex anytime? I said, 'You bastard, you idiot, go to hell!' '

She had warned him that the next time he abused her, she would go straight to the police and get a restraining order slapped on him.

'Then he cannot come near me or Angel, not even ten feet from us; I found out all about the restraining order.'

The favour she was asking of Maria was this: could her old teacher write a letter of support for her, a kind of testimonial, to take to the police to make sure she got that important order?

'You my old teacher. Also from Catholic school. Your testimonial very useful. Also, the police look at you and trust you, Miss Seetoh, because you very classy and educated.'

Maria said, 'Maggie, I really can't promise anything because I hardly know what's going on, and maybe don't want to,' adding, 'Maggie, I'm starting a new life in my new place, as you can see, and hope you understand if I ask you not to call again.'

There was a silence, and then Maggie said, in a changed tone of sly insinuation, 'Hey, Miss Seetoh, you ever wonder what happen to the Tiffany ring in the dark forest, whether anyone find it?'

Maria felt a rising tide of anger. The girl was being maliciously provocative all over again, trying to force a response from her, to extend the conversation and steer it towards her purpose.

Maria said coldly, 'I don't really care, Maggie. Now if you will excuse me, I'm rather busy.'

She heard Maggie say, in very aggrieved tones, 'Miss Seetoh, what happen to you? What happen to teacher I trust and love most in world?' before she put down the phone.

The phone rang again, and this time Maggie's voice came in a savage snarl. 'You know or not, Miss Seetoh, I could tell people you and Brother Philip had affair! Don't think I don't know!'

'How dare you!' screamed Maria. The girl had a huge bag of tricks, and now she had pulled out her trump card of blackmail. 'You're simply disgusting, Maggie. Don't you ever call me again!'

Maria banged down the phone. Maggie, in her messy world, had ruined an otherwise perfect day for her.

She had reckoned without the messiness of another world which she had almost forgotten. Rumours of V.K. Pandy were sweeping the society. He had returned to Singapore. The rumour about his death were just that, after all. The truth was that he had nearly died, in fact had died, according to some sources, but had been revived by a holy man from an ashram who, before passing away himself, had enjoined upon him the mission of doing good in the world by preaching kindness and forgiveness. The holy man, it was said, had been led to the corpse by the sobbing Mrs Pandy who said her husband had been dead twenty-four hours. She fell down at the holy one's feet when her husband began to stir, and he said to her, 'You too are restored,' at which point her cancer left her completely. She swore to spend the rest of her life helping the poor in the slums of the city.

Immediately after the miracle, V.K. Pandy entered into a trance-like state and went without food or water for seven days, his hair and beard now completely white. He entered the ashram and devoted himself to the preparation of his new role in the world. In a matter of a few years, he had become a holy man sworn to holy deeds, calling himself 'The Holy One', after the old saint who had brought him back to life, and made him promise to continue his good work. As proof of the legacy, he now bore the god-man's distinctive mark, a white scar, shaped like a small star, on the upper right of his forehead. To the astonishment of all around him, he could fast for weeks. It was said that a band of light encircled his head. He had come to Singapore, his beloved home for many years, to begin his mission of healing, preceded by the most astonishing reports of his powers. The lame walked, the blind saw, the deaf heard again. A twelve-year-old boy who was brought to him covered with horrible black growths was given back to his mother, his skin now smooth as an infant's. Singaporeans listened wide-eyed, then passed round the stories. There were stories about his astonishing powers to heal even those very ill and on the point of death.

It was said that he healed through some miraculous oil that oozed imperceptibly from his body, from a spot somewhere near his heart, a liquid that was the pure ichor of gods, giving the upper part of his body a wondrous sheen as if it were lit from within. A mere dab of the holy fluid was sufficient for the healing.

The question uppermost in Singaporeans' minds as they read newspaper reports of him and watched him on TV, with his luminescent skin, his snow-white hair and beard, his forehead daubed with red ash, was: would he forgive the great TPK enough to work a miracle for Mrs TPK, said to be beyond the power of modern medical science? Even more significantly, would the great TPK humble himself to ask?

'Oh my God,' gasped Maria as she watched The Holy One on TV, robed in white, sitting with crossed legs on a raised platform in some huge hall, a garland around his neck, his eyes closed, his hands pressed reverently together while around him

Singaporeans looked on, in awe and fascination. The national interest in him was too great for the media to block out news and images of him as they had done in the past. In any case he was no longer a political opponent but a holy Hindu man, as entitled to respect as any holy man or woman from any of the other religious faiths in the society.

Maria had vivid recollections of the shabby little man in Middleton Square with his pathetic pamphlets, crushed by the weight of his financial losses and the sickness of his wife, and also of the overwhelming floral tributes – symbol of a nation's guilt-charged conscience – filling the square after the news of his death in India. She recollected in every vivid detail his lunch with her when he spoke, with tears of bitter rage spurting from his eyes, about the great TPK's taunt of him, comparing him to crawling vermin.

Now he was a towering magisterial figure, as awe-inspiring as any visionary emerging from the wilderness with the fire of the sun in his eyes, for he had seen what was not granted to ordinary mortals. According to the rumours that swelled in fervour by the day, he had come to show forgiveness and to heal a whole nation, starting with the physical healing of poor Mrs TPK. Maria thought, no tale from my imagination, even at its runaway best, can match the amazing story of V.K. Pandy.

This was the great world outside that Maria had every desire to connect with.

Forty-One

From where she stood, among the huge crowd thronging the Singapore Exposition Hall which was being used by The Holy One to meet, touch and cure Singaporeans, Maria could not see him clearly. Despite the transformation in appearance and setting, she could recognise the V.K. Pandy of old, specially those close, deep-set eyes that had filled with angry, bitter tears that day when he had lunch with her. The recollection of the little donation of money in a brown envelope that she had shyly pushed towards him and which he had pushed back, made the transformation even more staggering. She had experienced some moments of surreality in her life, none exceeded by this one, as she continued to stare at the man she had never stopped thinking and speaking of as 'poor Pandy'. Now no commiseration was called for, only respect and reverence for the white-robed figure raised to sainthood; indeed, the image of the The Holy One, pure, transcendental, had already wiped out or rendered irrelevant whatever lowly image remained of the despised political opponent, just as a mighty prophet or seer would not be remembered for his earlier life as a goatherd or carpenter or water-carrier.

Maria thought, I wish I could believe all those rumours.

Already Singaporeans were saying, I saw with my own eyes, I was there when the crippled man stood up, somebody who saw it happened told me, the woman who had the evil spirit cast out of her was a relative of my mother's friend. Everybody talked about the wondrous method of healing: a tiny dab of the holy fluid that emanated from the holy skin, which some claimed had a fragrant smell that was not exactly like perfume but rather like the essence of some mysterious nocturnal flower.

Already, into the holy enterprise of healing the sick had crept the unholy element of competition. Some Christian churches had noticed a declining number in attendance, and a few had given subtle warnings from the pulpit about not being taken in by forces that were surely against the Holy Spirit. There was a tree in the compound of a Chinese temple that had been attracting worshippers because its bark bore the distinct face of the Monkey God, but since the arrival of The Holy One, there had been a drop in the number of devotees bringing joss-sticks, flowers and food offerings.

Through the excitement and wonder sweeping Singapore, the government of the great TPK must have been keeping an alert look-out for any signs of subversion that could result in disruption and disorder. But no, there were no political undertones in The Holy One's speeches, no evidence that his followers were spreading malicious rumours. Also, there was no evidence of potential religious conflict, for The Holy One's speeches were only about love, forgiveness and mercy. Indeed, the huge numbers flocking to see him included the entire range of faiths in the multiracial society, as well as the non-religious who came out of curiosity and wondered if there might be psychological and medical underpinnings to all those miracles after all.

It was whispered that the return of The Holy One had thrown the great TPK into a quandary that had little to do with the old politics. Mrs TPK had started having dreams in which The Holy One as well as the old mentor who had raised him from the dead, had appeared to her, promising to cure her. In his hand, he held a little phial of pure white fluid which gave out a heavenly scent. Mrs TPK woke up from each dream in tears, knowing that her husband scoffed at miraculous cures; moreover, his hatred of V.K. Pandy was probably too ingrained to allow him to face the once arch foe in the completely reversed role of a supplicant.

Maria felt a small tap on her shoulder. A man was standing next to her; from his white robe and daubed forehead, indeed his very demeanour, she could tell he was one of The Holy One's followers. He spoke in English and had a message for her: The Holy One had invited her for a special ceremony to witness the greatest miracle of all. The messenger gave the details of time and place and emphasised that attendance at the ceremony was by invitation only, and she was not to let anyone know.

Maria scribbled down the details quickly. Her thoughts went into a tumult of speculative wonder and fear. The fear was for the strangeness of it all; she was being invited into a world that she had little experience of and even less inclination for – the world of the supernatural, of faith and healing, of miracle cures that she had associated with simple-minded, unquestioning people like Por Por, or perfervid converts like her mother and her fellow churchgoers on their frequent pilgrimages to Europe, or those Singaporeans who went to pray to trees bearing images of temple deities. If the special event to which she was being invited was one more of the so-called miraculous healing sessions, she would not be at all keen to attend as a witness who was likely to be called upon later to testify at some public event, for holy men and women were not above the promotional stunts of business entrepeneurship. No, she thought, I don't think I'll go.

As she was about to leave the hall, elbowing her way though the crowds, she felt another tap on her shoulder. It was the same messenger.

He said, 'The Holy One requests to see you. Follow me.' It was bizarre, as if the god-man had read her thoughts and wanted to reassure her.

She was led to a small back room in the hall, where she waited a full twenty minutes before he appeared. He stood at the doorway, looking at her with the instantly recognisable deep-set, glittering eyes. She moved slowly towards him, as if impelled by an invisible force, aware of a strange sensation filling her entire body, causing it to tremble. He was aware of her moment of confusion when she wondered whether to offer her hand in greeting as an old acquaintance or to bow as a new devotee.

There was a slight smile on his face as he said, 'Miss Maria Seetoh, I have not forgotten you. You were the only one in Singapore to whom I opened my heart, a bitter and wounded heart. But it is wounded no more. It is full of love and compassion and forgiving.'

As her eyes filled with tears in the sensation of being in the presence of suprahuman greatness, her mind was alert with the need to ask questions of a purely worldly nature: 'Didn't Dr Benjamin Phang help you too? With money, influence? There were rumours regarding the Big Bird incident –' But one never asked rude questions of a holy man, only listened to what he had to say.

Through her tears she saw a smile on his face, and when she blinked them away, he was gone. The Holy One and his attendants had vanished. She was alone in the little back room. The whole experience had the bizarre feel of a dream.

On the eve of the big day of the ceremony, she was unable to sleep: what if her alarm clock failed to wake her up at the strange hour of four in the morning to allow her to be in time to reach the venue for the ceremony, a place she had never even heard of, tucked away in a corner of the island? The hours ticked away, as she tossed and turned, wondering about the mystery that would soon unfold. A strange place, a strange hour, a miracle to outdo all the miracles that The Holy One had performed in Singapore. A miracle that had to do with love and compassion and forgiving.

'Oh my god,' gasped Maria, in a moment of stupendous comprehension. Of course. The miraculous healing of Mrs TPK. The ultimate act of forgiveness.

She had heard rumours of TPK, out of sheer love of his wife, sending aides secretly to the holy man to ask for the magic phial she had repeatedly seen in her dreams, and offering any amount of money to build any temple or shrine he wanted. It was also said The Holy One had angrily rejected the offer of money, but promised to cure Mrs TPK.

Breathless with wonder and excitement, Maria was ushered into a small room which had only one other occupant who carried a camera. He was clearly a foreigner tasked with recording the ceremony; so The Holy One was not above the vanity of watching a replay of his miracle-working sessions.

'Do you know what's happening?' whispered Maria. 'Why are we here in this small room with only these slits and peepholes? Where is The Holy One?' but the cameraman simply put a finger to his lips and continued checking his equipment.

Maria could not take her eye off the peephole. It was as she had expected. She saw the great TPK, dressed in his habitual white shirt and white trousers, standing in what seemed like an open area, lit only by a large fire burning in the centre, surrounded by what appeared to be huge wooden or canvas panels to ensure utmost secrecy. He was accompanied by two aides, and he wore an expression of tense anxiety in place of the habitual stern bellicosity. He looked around nervously, as his aides, one on each side, stood by with stern impassivity. The Holy One was not in sight.

Then after about thirty minutes, by which time the nervousness had produced a pallor on TPK's face, The Holy One appeared accompanied by a small group of attendants, dressed in his usual snowy white robe opened at the chest to expose the holy sheen. He did not even look in TPK's direction. He walked to a simple wooden chair some distance from the fire, and sat down, his back upright, his eyes closed, his hands laid casually on his lap. All the while, TPK's eyes were following his every movement. The Holy One then signalled the aides to leave TPK's side. There was a little show of reluctance for they had come with the sole purpose of protecting the prime minister, but he said something to them, and they walked off to stand and watch from a distance. The Holy One then signalled something with a raised hand and a nod, and at once, two of his attendants went up to TPK and began removing his clothes. There was a slight scuffle as his watching aides made to rush over and were restrained.

'Oh my God,' gasped Maria who saw the great TPK now standing as naked as a newborn.

In a few seconds the attendants had put a white loincloth on him; Maria watched the prime minister grimace and wince at the indignity of having the long band of white cotton cloth strapped between his legs, then pulled up and wound tightly round his waist. She now understood the need for all the secrecy; it was gracious of The Holy One to agree to this condition for the conducting of the ceremony. She thought, as she continued to gaze fascinated at TPK through the peephole, 'How he must love his wife.'

The next stage of the ceremony was so bizarre that Maria whispered to the cameraman, 'Are you sure you should be recording this? Why don't you just skip it, out of deference to the Prime Minister of Singapore?'

For TPK, his face and naked body daubed with red and black ashes, was mimicking the movements of one of the attendants: he was prancing round the roaring fire, like a primitive warrior in a cheap movie, closely watching the attendant as if to make sure he had all the movements right. The comical stomping of feet, flailing of arms, thrusting of hips and jerking of head were completely at odds with the look of serious purpose on his face.

If Maria were not so shocked, if she were not convinced that religious rituals appeared comical only to profane outsiders, she would have let out a roar of laughter. She saw that the cameraman was smiling broadly and thought, 'Maybe they will edit out this part and concentrate on the real ceremony.' The real ceremony must be the handing over of the all-important phial, after which TPK would probably heave the greatest sigh of relief in his life, get dressed, go home to his wife, and put the unspeakably ludicrous incident behind him. Maria had no idea what the crux of the ceremony had been planned to be, and when she saw it, she understood its whole purpose, and broke into angry tears.

'Stop.' The Holy One waved an imperious hand after TPK had done a fourth idiotic dance round the fire. He stopped, panting and sweating, the red and black ash now brownish streaks running down his face, neck and chest. He stood expectantly facing The Holy One still sitting in his chair. One of his attendants went up to TPK and said something. There was a look of incredulousness, disgust, fear, loathing, all mixed together on TPK's face, and the attendant had to repeat himself.

'Oh my god, oh no,' cried Maria, for now she saw the great TPK get down on the ground and lie prostrated there, facing The Holy One who was holding up in his hand a phial of pure white fluid glistening in the light of the roaring flames.

It took three full prostrations to reach The Holy One who then handed over the phial. Maria thought she saw a smile on the holy face that said, 'At last.' The words that he uttered to her that day over lunch, his face all contorted with fury, came back to her: 'He told me, 'You will come crawling to me.' ' She had been invited to a ceremony, not of love and compassion and forgiving, but of revenge in the fullest manifestation of loathing and savage triumph.

Suddenly she turned to the photographer and said, 'Of course! You're from *The International Courier*!' So V.K. Pandy had included in his scheme of vengeance a fellow victim of the great TPK – the newspaper that together with him had been sued for huge sums of money. The man folded up his equipment, returned it to a large black bag, smiled and said, 'It will be in the papers tomorrow. Not of course *The Singapore Tribune*. But all the others. The Malaysian papers will be full of it.'

Forty-Two

'Dearest Brother Phil,' wrote Maria. 'I'm afraid this is going to be such a depressing letter, and so soon after the happy one I had sent off! It looks like happiness and peace of mind come only in small doses to me, to be savoured quickly before they disappear again. But no, I don't mean to wallow in self-pity. The one who deserves pity is the great TPK himself. Or The Holy One for being exposed as the exact opposite of what he had claimed to be. Or Mrs TPK who I understand is as ill as ever. Or Singaporeans taken in by the greatest act of fraudulence ever foisted on their society, the greatest fool being myself. So, yes, it's a kind of self-pity I'm wallowing in, only its true name is shame. Now I'm being incoherent and you will have to excuse this wildly rambling letter because right now I'm so angry, so confused, so humiliated that I don't know where to begin.

I had told you about my great excitement regarding the re-appearance of V.K. Pandy as The Holy One because of his message of love, compassion and forgiving: I should have listened to your advice about being cautious. When you wrote, 'A dose of scepticism is always healthy and a megadose here, which I know you are very capable of, my dear Maria, is in order,' you probably had no idea what this god-man was up to.

The most contemptible form of revenge which he must have been planning in his holy head right from the start. Perhaps the revenge was the sole purpose of the holy man persona. And I was party to it! He had made use of a little satirical poem I had written about the great TPK, comparing him to the almighty Tua Peh Kong, for he had the cheek to give it to *The Internationl Courier* to use as a caption for the pictures that appeared with the report. Do you remember that I had read the poem to you? They used the opening line *Even Tua Peh Kong must bow before a greater* to caption the picture of TPK lying prostrated at the feet of V.K. Pandy holding aloft the phial of holy liquid. And they deliberately published those pictures showing TPK at his most ridiculous, in that obscene loincloth, dancing like a drunken Red Indian round the fire. And of course The Holy One knows he can't be sued. It would draw attention to the whole fiasco that would make the poor Prime Minister of Singapore the laughing stock of the world. I understand that *The New York Mail* and *The London Times* have already carried the story – with those sickening pictures! (Did it reach any of your Irish newspapers? I hope not.) The Holy One is back in his ashram and must be laughing himself sick. I wish I could have gone up to him after that so-called ceremony and given him a piece of my mind. But this is mere bravado after the fact. I admit that when, upon his request, I had met him that day after he left his huge crowd of Singapore fans, I was overcome by a sense of his power. My God, what is happening in the world?

Dearest Brother Phil, I need you more than ever now to straighten me out, because, more than anything, I feel a deep sense of guilt with regard to our prime minister. I had detested him for his heartlessness, his utter ruthlessness, and you know what I have just found out? It may be a rumour, but

I believe it. It seems that while he had successfully sued V.K. Pandy for large sums of money (which, it was well known, he immediately donated to charity), he had been secretly paying for the expensive medical treatment of V.K. Pandy's wife! Today, if she is alive and well in India, it is not due to any holy man, but to TPK's generosity. V.K. Pandy did not have the decency to tell me the truth and even complained that his wife's cancer could have been caused by the stress of the bankruptcy suit and the loss of their printing business. The death in India, the restoration to life, the ashram, the commitment to a mission of love and compassion, the holy fluid, the miracles – all, all, a shameless fabric of lies! It will take me a long time to understand the scale and magnitude of this scam and the power of hatred once it is lodged deep in the human heart. In my most charitable moment, I had wished, for V.K. Pandy's sake, that the revenge he executed with so much skill and panache, would have expelled from his system whatever venom it carried from Singapore, and freed him, once and for all. Yes, even The Holy One needs healing, maybe more than anyone.

I had told you, dear Brother, about my new life, my new world, where I would do nothing but exactly what I liked, away from troublesome people, but now I am not so sure. I feel an urge to get out into that large, messy, ugly world out there because there is a huge falsehood that I had contributed to. (Who knows how much of my frank conversations about the great TPK, even my little satirical poem, had added to the man's anger and need for revenge?) I would like to see TPK to tell him the truth as I know it, go to his office and request an interview – I'm not even sure about the proper procedure. If that fails, I would like to write to the newspapers to give my account of the truth, and expose The Holy One (even in my present confusion, there's a little place for humour – I now think of him as The Wholly Unholy Holy One). In doing so, I'll be implicating myself and probably have to answer a whole lot of discomfiting questions. But that is more bearable than the present torment of guilt about TPK and rage against V.K. Pandy (also to a certain extent, his wife).

Wish you were here, dear Brother Phil, to help me clarify the thoughts in my head, the tumult in my heart. *Wish you were here.* How many times have I ended a letter to you, whether bearing good or bad news, with that longing.

Love
Maria.'

Forty-Three

'My dearest Phil,

As I had half expected, my request for an interview with the prime minister was turned down. I do not know whether it was because I had not stated my reason clearly or appropriately enough, or whether he simply wanted to forget what must have been the most horrible experience in his life. But I believe that my request has already created a secret dossier of Maria Seetoh Wei Cheng that is now part of their efficient surveillance machinery; my phone is probably being tapped this very minute! The latest I heard about Mrs TPK was that she is preparing to go the United States, to be a subject for the clinical testing of some new drug – that's the extent of the poor woman's desperation to stay alive because she is completely devoted to her husband and their two daughters and watches over their welfare even in her illness.

I had also written a letter to *The Straits Tribune*, and have not received any answer, which probably means that the paper doesn't want to be involved in anything that would displease or distress TPK. Poor TPK. I saw him on TV yesterday, doing his usual round of his constituency, shaking hands with hawkers and ordinary folk, but not looking his usual ebullient self. It is difficult for me, after that experience, not to superimpose upon the familiar image of strength and power that of the ridiculous pantomime figure, the slapstick buffoon, the clown in a schoolboy skit! The feeling is a most uncomfortable one, as if something exceptionally bad has happened to the whole society and things will never be the same again. I suspect it is the same with many Singaporeans. They do not seem keen to talk about The Holy One; perhaps the grapevine is already buzzing with rumours based on the report and pictures in *The International Courier*, but nobody is prepared to talk openly. It is probably an episode that Singaporeans would be happy to forget. It seems that many of those purportedly healed by him are complaining about fraudulence. A foreign journalist had written something about subjecting the holy fluid to a lab test. I don't care to know the results – I'm just so sick of it all!

I will try again to seek an interview, to interest the newspapers; perhaps the tabloids might be tempted to run my story, though I doubt it, everyone's so fearful. I don't know whether wanting to tell the truth, regardless of the consequences, is a good or bad thing, but right now, this turmoil in me, a mix of guilt and remorse and anger, is like a wound in the flesh that has to be cauterised away, an embolism in the blood that has to be cleared out! It bothers me even in my sleep.

Last night I had a dream in which TPK (the very first time he's appeared in my dreams!) was standing, in that awful loincloth, before a roaring fire and reading the satirical poem about Tua Peh Kong. His words did not come out clearly; at times, he seemed to be quoting from Shakespeare, Kahlil Gibran, Gandhi. Then he crushed the sheet of paper, threw it into the flames, and turned to face V.K. Pandy and myself who were among the large crowd watching him. He said in a loud voice, 'You know what? There is more real love in me than in all of you combined, you idiots, you hypocrites!'

His words are throbbing in my head as I am writing this letter. Dear, wise one, I usually ignore dreams, but what should I make of this one?

I will have to wait to see how things develop in the next few days. Weeks? Months? But I know what I should do meanwhile. I will continue to be happy. The deep peace in me since I moved into my new life has not really vanished, thank God (see how we disgusting atheists can't leave off the old pious invocations!); it is only temporarily perturbed, like the surface of a lake ruffled by a storm, that will appear calm again once the storm has passed. This storm will, must, pass, since it is not the first, nor will it be the last I will endure. Oh dear, who would have thought that a simple soul like me wanting only to be good and do good, to be happy in life, could be involved in so much mess?

Talking about mess, that dreadful girl Maggie called again. Or rather it was her sister Angel, who then passed the phone to her. She was in hospital, recovering from some injuries which she said had been caused by the abusive boyfriend Sonny. Of course I had no choice but to visit that wretched girl in hospital; I had a sneaking suspicion that some of the injuries were self-inflicted to provide convincing proof to the police of the boyfriend's violent behaviour, for she had her sister take photographs of every single one of them. But then again, they could be real injuries. Angel told me when we left the hospital that Sonny, when drunk, was capably of any brutality. Talk about misplaced scepticism! I simply had to ask this girl, who is certainly far more savvy than she looks, whether she appreciated at all her sister's love for her, the sacrifices she was making for her future. Her reply was a scornful, 'Love? She loves only herself, that's all. She's just making use of me.' Then she let me in on a scheme of Maggie's where I would play a part: help her get the police to restrain Sonny, and then the wily girl would be free to go with someone who is courting her, a rich businessman from Indonesia. She is the consummate survivor. I'll never understand her unruly world. I wouldn't be surprised, one of these days, to be dragged into it again, to testify in court in connection with some horrendous crime, like her attempting to kill the boyfriend, or his attempting to kill her, or that strange sister who makes me think of Lolita attempting to kill them both. It is said, You can be in the world, but you need not be of it. Oh no, one doesn't have that luxury. The truth is that as long as you are in the world, you have no choice but to be of it – taking on its savvy, cunning, wiles. I've come to the conclusion that Machiavelli is a far more honest – and effective – teacher than my Plato or Socrates. I'll have to learn something of Maggie's skills, whether to outwit her or to help her. It's a great burden when you are the only one in the world a young person can turn to.

I will wait for the appropriate moment to act, but meanwhile I can continue to go about the little things that make me happy. I am, will be, can be, must be, should be, happy – here's the old teacher of English grammar mobilising all its resources for her purpose! Two days ago I visited the Botanic Gardens again, for the sheer pleasure of watching little children feed the fish and ducks; yesterday Asma, the friendly security guard I told you about, promised to take me shopping, on her next day off, in her Malay market where I can get the best spices to try out the recipes in a new cookery book I bought, and this morning, after breakfast, I looked through some notes and found I had ideas for a collection of stories for children. Writing – that will be both passion and survival for me.

At the back of my mind is a little plan that you may laugh at, my dear Phil: I want eventually to write the biography of the great TPK! So far the books about him are all about his admirable achievements for Singapore, his fantastic leadership that has made Singapore the most successful economy in Asia. I have seen the human side, which makes him a much more likeable person. But I'm not sure how to tell his story fully and honestly because it is intertwined with the bizarre story of V.K. Pandy.

How I wish you were here, dearest, dearest Phil. I don't know how I can do without you! I am happy writing these letters to you and then receiving your replies. And dearest, do find time from your busy, busy schedule to write longer, more frequent letters to your old friend in Singapore! You know how happy you make me.

Much love
Maria.'

Epilogue

In 1998, Maria published a book for children called *Garden of Tales* and two years later, a collection of short stories called *The Godling and Other Stories of Singapore*.

She kept alive her desire to write a biography of Mr Tang Poon Kim, Prime Minister of Singapore, but her request for an interview was continually turned down. When Mr Tang retired from politics in 2002, after the death of his wife, and decided to write his autobiography, he at last agreed to see her. She brought along the notes she had made to give the truest account possible of all her dealings with V.K. Pandy, from the first time she spoke to him in Middleton Square, through his lunch with her and the final witnessing of that terrible act of vengeance. But the interview lasted a mere hour, with some polite questions from Mr Tang. It was the first and last time she had come face to face with the prime minister whom she never stopped thinking of as the 'great TPK'. When Mr Tang's autobiography finally appeared in 2003, a huge tome with several chapters devoted to his beloved wife, there was not a single reference to V.K. Pandy.

Brother Philip was posted to the Philippines where he continued to write to Maria. They never saw each other again.

He was killed in a motor accident in 2004. Maria learnt of his death only a week later, as she had been busy travelling to promote her books.

About the Author

A prolific writer, Catherine Lim has written more than 19 books across various genres – short stories, novels, reflective prose, poems and satirical pieces. Born in 1942 Malaya, Lim was a teacher, then project director with the Ministry of Education and a specialist lecturer with the Regional Language Centre (RELC) before dedicating herself fully to writing in 1992.

Lim has won several national and regional book prizes for her literary contributions, including the National Book Development Council (NBDCS) awards in 1982, 1988 and 1990; the Montblanc-NUS Centre For The Arts Literary Award in 1998; and the 1999 regional Southeast Asian Write Award. She was conferred an Honorary Doctorate of Literature by Murdoch University, Australia, in 2000, and a Knight of the Order of Arts and Letters by the French Ministry of Culture and Information in 2003. Lim was also Ambassador for the Hans Christian Andersen Foundation, Copenhagen, in 2005.

Many of Lim's works are studied in local and foreign schools and universities, and have been published in various languages in several countries. She was the first Singaporean author to pen an electronic-novella over the Internet, which has since been adapted into a movie.

Besides writing, Lim guest lectures at local and international seminars, conferences, arts/writing festivals and cruise ships worldwide. She has also appeared on radio and television programmes in Singapore, Europe and Australia.